NO

WAY

TO

KILL

A LADY

Other Books in the
Blackbird Sisters Mystery Series

NO
WAY
TO
KILL
A LADY

A BLACKBIRD SISTERS MYSTERY

Nancy Martin

AN OBSIDIAN MYSTERY

OBSIDIAN
Published by New American Library, a division of
Penguin Group (USA) Inc., 375 Hudson Street,
New York, New York 10014, USA
Penguin Group (Canada), 90 Eglinton Avenue East, Suite 700, Toronto,
Ontario M4P 2Y3, Canada (a division of Pearson Penguin Canada Inc.)
Penguin Books Ltd., 80 Strand, London WC2R 0RL, England
Penguin Ireland, 25 St. Stephen's Green, Dublin 2,
Ireland (a division of Penguin Books Ltd.)
Penguin Group (Australia), 250 Camberwell Road, Camberwell, Victoria 3124,
Australia (a division of Pearson Australia Group Pty. Ltd.)
Penguin Books India Pvt. Ltd., 11 Community Centre, Panchsheel Park,
New Delhi - 110 017, India
Penguin Group (NZ), 67 Apollo Drive, Rosedale, Auckland 0632,
New Zealand (a division of Pearson New Zealand Ltd.)
Penguin Books (South Africa) (Pty.) Ltd., 24 Sturdee Avenue,
Rosebank, Johannesburg 2196, South Africa

Penguin Books Ltd., Registered Offices:
80 Strand, London WC2R 0RL, England

First published by Obsidian, an imprint of New American Library,
a division of Penguin Group (USA) Inc.

First Printing, August 2012
10 9 8 7 6 5 4 3 2 1

LIBRARY OF CONGRESS CATALOGING-IN-PUBLICATION DATA:

Martin, Nancy, 1953–
  No way to kill a lady: a Blackbird Sisters mystery/Nancy Martin.
    p. cm.
  ISBN 978-0-451-23705-7
  1. Blackbird Sisters (Fictitious characters)—Fiction. 2. Socialites—Fiction. 3. Philadelphia (Pa.)—
Fiction. I. Title.
  PS3563.A7267N6 2012
  813'.54—dc23   2011053174

Set in Bembo
Designed by Ginger Legato

Printed in the United States of America

PUBLISHER'S NOTE
This is a work of fiction. Names, characters, places, and incidents either are the product of the author's
imagination or are used fictitiously, and any resemblance to actual persons, living or dead, business
establishments, events, or locales is entirely coincidental.
  The publisher does not have any control over and does not assume any responsibility for author or third-
party Web sites or their content.

For Nancy Curry

AUTHOR THANKS

I owe many thanks to people who have helped me create this book: Friends Lu and Molly Taleb always bring the best dishes to the block party. Scott Krofcheck from Pennwriters provided just the right information at the right time. Lisa Cataropa, a fellow pig enthusiast, had great suggestions. Ramona Long is my "great friend" and the best first reader any writer could ask for. My daughters, Cassie and Sarah, always provide research, common sense and lots of laughter. Ellen Edwards and Meg Ruley are the dream team behind the scenes. Everyone at NAL/Penguin is a pleasure to work with, including Kara Welsh, Claire Zion and the incomparable sales, publicity, marketing and production teams. My mother, Barbara Aikman, is still the smartest person I know, and I'm telling everybody right here. Not everyone gets to have two mothers, but I do. Nancy Curry has been an inspiration and a source of great fun all my life, even when she took my petticoat to clean up my little brother after the spaghetti dinner incident. My dear writer friends and backbloggers at the Lipstick Chronicles were the community I checked in with daily while writing this book. Oh, how I miss you! Just saying. And Jeff, of course, remains my hero.

NO
WAY
TO
KILL
A LADY

When a long-lost relative bequeathed us a fortune, I found myself locked in an epic battle with the most fearsome adversaries any woman can face.

Her sisters.

"It's not as if I'm going to buy breast implants with my share of the money," my sister Libby said over brunch at a sun-splashed table at the Rusty Sabre in early November. "I'm blessed in that department already, of course. But I need investment capital, Nora. I have a *plan*."

Our great-aunt Madeleine Blackbird had died at the age of seventy-five or eighty-two, depending upon whose story you believed, and not at her Bucks County mansion in the mahogany cannonball bed Ben Franklin had given to the family for reasons best swept under the rug of history. No, she died during an Indonesian volcanic eruption that blew her luxury tepee off the side of a mountain—according to the obituary page of the *Philadelphia Intelligencer.*

Libby said, "And I promise I won't run off to some exotic island with a cabana boy. Although nobody would blame me if I did. My children are driving me bonkers, and the best cure for motherly frustration is an exciting new relationship, right?"

My biggest fear for my sister Libby was that she was going to end up featured as the lead character in a tabloid sex scandal. I was pretty sure it was an item on her bucket list.

My sister Emma *had* been the lead character in a scandal, but the NFL hushed it up to save one of their players from looking very silly. Nowadays, though, she was looking less like a sex bomb than usual. She sat across from me at the table in grubby riding breeches, muddy boots and a large sweatshirt that strained over her pregnant belly, not caring if the other, more civilized restaurant patrons cast disapproving glances at her disheveled appearance. Her short auburn hair stuck out at all angles, as if she'd just rolled out of bed.

Deadpan, Emma said, "You'd probably kill a cabana boy, Lib."

"Well, yes, endurance is key." Libby had taken her compact out of her handbag and was checking her plump *décolletage* in the mirror. She wore a low-cut red paisley frock that gave her the look of a Playmate on her way to a royal wedding. "I need somebody strong, but sensitive, too. I have very complex needs. All my followers say so."

The sisterly bond may be the most trying one that a woman can have with another human being. There's love, of course—the kind that ties you together for eternity and certainly while washing mountains of dishes after Christmas dinner. But if there's a sister alive who has never suppressed the urge to bash a sibling over the head with a Barbie doll or the Rusty Sabre's fresh fruit plate—well, she's not related to me.

Emma looked up from her ricotta-stuffed French toast with sliced peaches and whipped cream. "Your followers? What, are you running a cult now?"

"My followers on PitterPat, that new social media thingie." Libby put her compact away and dug into the clutter of her enormous handbag to come up with her new cell phone. "My followers are all wonderfully supportive now, in my time of need."

I refolded the obituary page and put the newspaper on the table-cloth. "Your time of need?"

"Yes, of course. I'm devastated about Aunt Madeleine. She was an inspiration in my formative years."

"Only because she had a lot of affairs," Emma said. "Remember that Norwegian man who always had candy in his pockets?"

"Lemon drops, covered with lint," I recalled.

"Yeah, him. Gave me the creeps."

"He was Russian, not Norwegian," Libby said. "But he knew wonderful nuances of Scandinavian massage. Always rub in the direction of the heart. Did you know that? Preferably after a hot sauna. It's wonderfully sensual." When we stared at her, she blinked at us. "What? I was mature for my age! Aunt Madeleine's lovers always intrigued me. Which is why I'm devastated now. I identified with her."

"If anyone should be devastated by Aunt Madeleine's demise, it's Nora," said Emma.

"Me? I barely knew Aunt Madeleine," I said. The last thing I wanted that morning was to be dragged into another disjointed argument with my sisters. Those always ended with somebody getting offended and me getting stuck with the check.

"But Aunt Madeleine loved you."

"She had a funny way of showing it. Despite her Madcap Maddy reputation, she scared the bejesus out of me." The frustrations of the morning boiled over, and I said, "Really, Em, if you're going to eat like a lumberjack, the least you could do is share the coffee."

"Who lit your fuse this morning, Crankypants?"

If I had a fatal flaw, it was probably that I was too polite—too unwilling to rock the lifeboat of social harmony even as the waves of disaster crashed over my head. I longed to push Emma's face down into her peaches. But I refrained.

"She's missing That Man of Hers," Libby guessed. "Not to mention Lexie Paine. Have you heard from dear Lexie, Nora? Has she settled into the pokey, now that she's been sentenced?" Abruptly, Libby jumped, and she dropped her cell phone. "Ow! Emma, stop kicking!"

Emma gave her a meaningful stare. "We're not going to talk about Nora's situation, remember? We're just going to be supportive this morning."

I'd spent the past week embroiled in the hearing of my dearest friend. Lexie Paine had pleaded guilty to a horribly publicized charge of voluntary manslaughter. Despite a parade of character witnesses—including me—the judge had sentenced Lexie to four years in prison for pushing a man out a window. If he hadn't been threatening someone at the time, she'd have been accused of first-degree murder, so there was something to be thankful for. I was still reeling for her. And for our lost friendship. She might never forgive me for the role I played in her loss of freedom.

I looked down at the ring on my left hand. The diamond my sisters called the Rock of Gibraltar reminded me that although I was also physically separated from Michael at the moment, at least I knew he still loved me. And he wasn't going to spend the next several years in prison, as Lexie was. His sentence was considerably shorter.

Libby glared back at Emma. "I wasn't going to bring up anything upsetting. And you're not helping the least bit. We could die of starvation while you stuff yourself. Why aren't you as big as a house? I used to swell up like a hippo as soon as I conceived. Aren't you seven months along now?"

"Seven or eight, depending on which doctor I see at the clinic." Emma splashed coffee into my cup. "I don't get it, either. I eat like a horse, but never seem to gain any weight—except for Zygote here." She patted her distended belly, which stretched her faded sweatshirt to its limit.

No Way to Kill a Lady

I tried to suppress the twinge of jealousy that sprouted in the back of my mind at the mere mention of Emma's impending arrival. For ages, I'd been hoping for a family of my own. It was hard enough that Libby already had five children—despite their homicidal tendencies, they were a lovable lot—but Emma's accidental pregnancy made me feel even more like a failure in the motherhood department. Two miscarriages had shaken my firm belief that I'd soon have a brood of my own.

But I pushed those thoughts to the back of my mind to fester with all the other unpleasantness of late. There was no sense in wallowing in the swamp of my own maternal shortcomings.

Libby said to Emma, "At least now you'd be able to afford to keep that child in potato chips, if you decide to keep it. Don't you think it's terribly exciting we're the ones to inherit Quintain? I've hardly been able to sleep since we heard the news!"

Our great-aunt Madeleine Blackbird had been a great beauty who—like most of the Blackbird women—was widowed more than once. She had been luckier than most of us and inherited two fortunes along the way. Her great wealth enabled her to indulge in her pleasures and travel to exotic locales. Madcap Maddy sent lavish gifts and brought home colorful friends from St. Petersburg and various cities that had all but disappeared behind the Iron Curtain. She even rode camels along the dunes of the Sahara before finding her bliss on a faraway mountain. But after word came around the globe that an Indonesian mountain blew its top and took our aunt with it, we were even more stunned when her lawyers announced she had bequeathed her Pennsylvania estate . . . to us.

Specifically, her will read, "To Eleanor Blackbird and her sisters."

Nothing could have astonished us more.

Mind you, we were no strangers to luxury, my sisters and me. The Blackbird family had come to Philadelphia with William Penn and substantial wealth in their travel trunks. Once in the new world, our ancestors parlayed their small fortune into a large one with smart investments in railroads and safety pins. My sisters and I had grown up going to boarding schools and spending our holidays in places such as Paris and Bermuda. Along the way, I learned many gracious skills, including a ladylike calligraphy and the art of arranging a seating chart for a successful dinner party. After a spectacular family downfall, though, those skills enabled me to function in no other paying job but the one I had luckily landed—that of a newspaper society columnist. Libby had been a painter before she started marrying. Emma spent her youth riding horses—the kind that leaped Olympic-sized hurdles and flew first class to international competitions—and she continued to work in horsey circles as an adult. But I attended parties.

Good thing we'd found our respective callings, because our parents were known for throwing lavish galas with orchestras and cases of expensive champagne they couldn't pay for. Our mother loved jewelry and was famous for impulsively taking off her necklaces and clasping them around the throats of surprised friends—long before she'd paid the credit card bill from the jeweler. Our father adored luxury cars, but tended to borrow them from friends and then promptly drive them into ditches. Their share of the family money therefore evaporated in no time, but Mama and Daddy continued to live the high life on "loans" from unsuspecting acquaintances who might as well have thrown their money into the ocean.

Eventually, though, our partying parents were forced to pack up their evening clothes and run off with our trust funds. Now they happily spun around the dance floors of South American resorts.

My sisters and I had said reluctant good-byes to our comfortable years in the rarefied social world where we grew up. We'd all married, lost husbands and survived. These days, we struggled a bit to stay ahead of foreclosure, but we were afloat. I actually enjoyed working for the newspaper, which paid me a salary just big enough to keep the wolves from my door.

These days, I didn't mind the change in our circumstances. Not too much, anyway.

But inheriting Quintain might change everything again.

There were complications, though.

Emma speared a peach with her fork. "I'm just glad I can stop looking for a nice stable to deliver in. I was banking on three kings coming to my rescue. Anybody know what frankincense is? Would a pawnshop accept it for cash?"

Libby came out from under the table, where she'd found her cell phone. "This windfall comes at a perfect time!" she cried as she dropped the phone into her handbag again. "It's karma. And my latest brainstorm is going to put me in clover. I just need the seed money to plant the garden."

"Are you planning to spread the manure yourself?" I asked. "Or will you hire a handsome gardener to do your dirty work?"

"Yeah," said Emma. "You've kept us in suspense long enough. What exactly is your new scheme? You're not getting back into the sex toy business, are you, Libby?"

"Alas, no. As diverting as it was, that venture turned out to be nothing more than a Ponzi scheme. Don't you hate it when women prey on one another instead of being supportive? Now that the police have given back all my samples, I'm left with a garage full of boxes of sensual products that I can't even give away to my more adventurous friends. There's quite an odd smell coming from some of them—the expiration dates on lotions are coming due, I suppose. No, I've decided to devote myself to nurturing my son's gifts. He's going to make enough money to support me in high style."

I smiled. "Really? What's Rawlins up to?" Libby's eldest child was one of my favorite people in the world. Now that he'd given up most of the jewelry he wore in his face and discovered that not every adult was his enemy, he was very good company. "Has he decided which colleges to apply to?"

"It's not Rawlins who's going to make me rich. It's Maximus!"

After a puzzled silence, Emma said, "Max is one year old. What kind of gifts does he have already?"

Libby's eyes took on the mad gleam of misguided motherly verve. "Do you know how much money Tiger Woods made at the height of his career? And those sisters who play tennis in the skimpy outfits? They're gazillionaires! All because their parents started them young. So I'm doing the same for Maximus. He's going to be a football kicker! The kind who plays for only five minutes and makes tens of millions a year. I've been taking him to Mommy and Me gymnastics, and it turns out he's already an athletic superstar! The instructor says I should get him into professional training immediately. Do you know how much money a kicker gets if his team wins the Super Bowl?"

"Wait," I said. "Is Max walking yet?"

"That doesn't matter. It's the early steps of his development that are most crucially important."

"Let me get this straight." Emma pointed her fork at Libby. "You're going to exploit your baby son in the hope of cashing in on a Super Bowl decades away?"

"It's not exploitation if I'm making his dreams come true."

"He's old enough to dream?"

"He's old enough to train at the gym," Libby shot back. "And what little boy doesn't want to be a professional athlete? You should have seen him on the balance ball yesterday! He has extraordinary physical coordination. The trainer says if he trained five days a week, he could be kicking a football through goalposts before he's two."

"Who is this trainer?" I asked, suspicions aroused.

"His name is Randolph." Libby could not hold back her dimples. "And he's a total hottie."

"Ah," I said.

Emma nodded. "Now we understand."

"He's *far* too young for me. But he's wonderful with children."

Libby used her coffee spoon to snitch a smidgen of whipped cream from Emma's plate. "You won't believe how expensive private coaches are, though. Sessions with Randolph can be upwards of a hundred dollars a pop. That's why I need our inheritance money, Nora. Maximus should get started on his path to stardom right away."

"There's no way we can get Aunt Madeleine's money yet," I said. "It'll take months before the estate is settled. Maybe years."

"No, no, I've figured a way around all that." Libby dropped her spoon to fish her cell phone out again. Her thumbs madly typed a message on the phone's tiny keypad. "You know those places where you can cash your paycheck even before you have it in your hand?"

"You mean a loan shark?" Emma asked around another gargantuan mouthful of breakfast.

"Moneylending has been a misunderstood endeavor since biblical days," Libby retorted. "Anyway, there are companies that will give you an advance on your inheritance, too! See? Here's one." She passed her cell phone to me and pointed at the screen. "We could get half of our money right away. No waiting!"

I couldn't make sense of all the words blinking on the phone. To me, the screen looked like a miniature Vegas slot machine in the throes of a neon jackpot.

In an effort to be the voice of reason, I said as kindly as I could manage, "Just this once, Libby, could we try not to get carried away?"

"Oh, don't be a party pooper!" She snatched her phone back. "Soon you'll be able to put in gold-plated faucets at Blackbird Farm. Emma will have her baby with a real doctor, in a hospital. And Maximus will become famous and rich enough to support us all. We just have to sell Madeleine's little house and enjoy the proceeds. Simple!"

Simple? Hardly. And Quintain could never be described as "little." Not unless you were accustomed to living in Blenheim Palace.

But the possibility that we might finally regain our financial footing did seem tantalizingly close—even to me.

A tall shadow appeared over our table just then, and we gaped up at a broad-shouldered young police officer who pressed his hat one-handed to an impressively broad chest. He had a crew cut that looked as if it was buzzed every morning before reveille, and he filled out his khaki uniform to seam-straining perfection that turned heads throughout the restaurant. In fact, at table level, his trousers displayed what I can only delicately describe as the suggestion of a dauntingly prodigious manhood.

His voice was a deep baritone that surely rang the chimes of most women to their reverberating core. "Ladies? Are you the Blackbird sisters?"

Libby's eyes instantly bulged wide, and she touched her fingertips to her own throat as if to contain a cry of awe. At the astonishing specimen standing before her, however, she could only emit a startled squeak.

I saw Emma's mouth twist into a smirk, and I knew she was working on a blunt wisecrack of a greeting, so I said swiftly, "Yes, we are. And you must be Deputy Sheriff Foley."

I leaped to my feet and stuck my hand out to shake his. "It's a pleasure to meet you. Thank you very much for escorting us to Quintain this morning. I gather you're doing a special favor for us."

"For Mr. Groatley," he corrected politely, sketching a vaguely military bow. "Are you ready to go?"

Libby shot up from the table as if electrocuted. She grabbed her handbag, smiled brilliantly and said on a husky breath, "Lead the way, Sheriff Foley."

"I'm not finished!" Emma protested, her fork still poised over her breakfast.

"You can eat anytime," Libby snapped, seizing Emma by the arm. "Get your butt out of that chair and into the car this minute!"

"I gotta pee first," Emma grumbled, dropping her fork and heading for the loo.

Which gave Libby complete freedom to deploy all her feminine wiles. She sent a sideways, lip-quivering smile up at Foley and came close to spraining a hip socket as she sashayed out to the cruiser and claimed the front seat.

Twenty minutes later we were driven through Quintain's massive iron gates—as ordered by the court and the lawyers who represented Aunt Madeleine's estate—in the deputy's car.

Even two decades of neglect couldn't dispel the first impression of grandeur as the familiar turrets of the mansion rose over the early-morning mist. Quintain looked as if Hogwarts had been magically transported to bucolic Pennsylvania by an impulsive sorceress who waved a magic wand. The narrow lancet windows might have recently reflected cherubic magicians flying by on their broomsticks. The curving pond gave the impression of a moat, perfect for repelling marauding demons. The brick and stone walls looked as if they'd been overrun by enchanted ivy and rampant roses. Only ancient wizards in long, flowing robes would make the picture complete.

But upon closer inspection, Quintain looked sadly faded these days. After twenty years of abandonment, more than a few stones appeared to have tumbled from the walls. And the western wing of the building was obscured by untrimmed yews and dozens of oak trees—some of them splintered and rotting on the ground. A riot of weeds threatened to overtake everything. What was now thick underbrush had once been a lawn that rolled gracefully down to the tilting green.

"A what?" said the young deputy behind the wheel of the cruiser. His ears had been adorably pink ever since the moment Libby had remarked that she'd like to try painting their perfect shape and had asked whether Foley ever posed for artists.

"A tilting green is for jousting," Emma said. "For a while, our aunt was an Anglophile."

"Oh, is that the stone church down by the Burger King?"

Libby laughed trillingly. "You're such a wit, Sheriff Foley. I bet your wife is endlessly entertained."

"Oh, I'm not married," he said. "And I'm only the sheriff's deputy."

"Not married? Really?" Libby began to rearrange her hair. "How did a man as attractive as you avoid getting snatched up long ago?"

Emma and I exchanged a glance. Libby could find an eligible bachelor in a Vatican election.

"There's the drawbridge." Libby pointed out the window. "Doesn't it look romantic? Remember the year Madcap Maddy hired the bagpipers to stand up on the archway and play for the Grand Parade? The horses went crazy at the noise."

The young deputy said, "I applied for the equestrian detail a few years ago."

"How fascinating," Libby said. "I love horses, too."

Emma gave an equine snort.

"The whole place is real pretty," the deputy said.

"Wait until you see what's inside," Libby promised. "Treasures that will take your breath away."

The deputy prudently chose to park his cruiser a safe distance from the crumbling facade of Quintain, and we got out into the morning sunshine.

Libby clasped her hands in rapture. "Can't you imagine Prince Charming walking out of those doors, Sheriff Foley? Why—you look rather charming yourself in this light. I love how the sun glints on your badge."

"Uh—"

Before Foley could verbalize a suitable response, the black stretch limousine that had followed us onto the grounds came to a stop behind the deputy's car. Doors opened, and the lawyers climbed out. The young ones all adjusted their cashmere coats against the morning chill and checked their cell phones for messages.

Simon Groatley, though, emerged from the car and strode importantly across the cracked driveway toward us. He had been Aunt Madeleine's retainer for as long as I could remember, and this morning he was in all his masterful glory.

"Now then, ladies," he said briskly, "let me say once again how grateful I am that you could make the trip so early this morning. It's a busy day for all of us, so let's get started. Deputy, we'll have a quick look around, shall we? I want a cursory inspection by the family before we proceed to cataloging the most valuable items inside the house. You're here to make sure nobody tucks any knick-knacks in their pockets. Not that any of these charming ladies would do such a thing. But keep your eyes open."

Foley almost saluted. "Yes, sir."

Now in his late sixties, Simon Groatley still appeared to be as powerful as he had been back in the day when he helped my grandfather Blackbird command various family concerns. The two of them met weekly at Blackbird Farm, often clenching glasses of scotch in their fists as they discussed investment strategies, argued politics, and bemoaned current statesmanship. My grandfather had filled a war chest for Groatley's first run for office, and as the lawyer rose to higher and higher political positions, my grandfather benefited in many ways. Then rumors surfaced of Groatley's womanizing, and he lost an election to a younger man with a cleaner reputation. Now his name appeared on the bronze plate outside a prestigious firm that specialized in managing the estates of prominent Philadelphia families. From what I'd heard, Groatley continued to specialize in women, too.

With his Mount Rushmore brow, bulldog jaw, iron gray hair and barrel-chested frame, Simon Groatley looked better suited to declaiming from a bully pulpit than dallying with the fairer sex.

He buttoned his coat against the autumn air and gazed up at the tall walls of Quintain. "By thunder, the old place was grand in its day, wasn't it? Shame about the condition now."

"Why on earth has it been so neglected?" I asked. "Surely Aunt Madeleine made some provision for taking care of the house while she traveled?"

"Her staff ran off shortly after her departure, and she was too rich to care what happened to the place." Seeing my expression, Groatley turned defensive. "When I finally got wind of the situation, we hired a crew to board up the broken windows and fix the drains to keep them. But we couldn't make substantial repairs without Madeleine's direction. We held off the tax sale, you'll be glad to know."

"Nobody paid the taxes for twenty years?" I couldn't keep the disbelief from my voice.

"She sent checks now and then—nothing regular. We could have taken care of that easily, with her permission. But she ignored my letters."

"That sounds like Aunt Madeleine," Emma said. "Busy globe-trotting."

"She was larger than life," Libby said with a rapturous sigh. "And so beautiful. Men simply fell at her feet. I'd give anything to know her secret."

Still frowning, I said, "I wish we'd had the slightest idea there was a problem. We assumed our cousin had the situation in hand and never dreamed things had gotten this bad."

"Ah—your cousin," Groatley said. "Speak of the devil."

A silver Porsche spun through the gates and accelerated smoothly up the drive, dodging fallen tree limbs with the agility of an Indianapolis race car. With a jaunty toot of the horn, the car scattered the young lawyers like a flock of pigeons, then rocked to a halt in front of us. The driver's door popped open, and Sutherland Blackbird leaped out of the car with the panache of a star from silent movies who was greeting adoring fans. He drew off his driving gloves and tossed them onto the seat, then removed his sunglasses and smiled handsomely for the crowd—almost as if he expected camera flashes to bounce off the blinding whiteness of his perfect teeth.

"What a god-awful hour for doing business," he declared in a booming baritone. "Groatley, I hold you completely responsible for rousting my dear cousins out of bed this early in the morning."

Under his breath, Groatley muttered, "Looks as if you didn't skimp on your own beauty sleep, young man."

If Sutherland heard, he paid no attention. "Cuz!" he cried, launching himself toward me with enthusiastically outstretched arms. "How marvelous you look!"

Sutherland Blackbird was my second cousin, or maybe third. We shared a great-great-grandfather. But he hailed from the branch of the family that my own grandfather would have happily sawed off the family tree. Sutherland's ne'er-do-well father had made himself rich in an investment scheme that involved selling American surplus to Third World despots. After divorcing his wealthy but lackluster first wife, he married his glamorous cousin Madeleine, with whom he shared an affinity for travel. But she preferred chic European restaurants with sophisticated company, and he appreciated the heat of the tropics. Eventually, he met his end by drowning in a young lady's hot tub in Hawaii—circumstances my grandfather hushed up, of course. Blackbirds did not consort in hot tubs. .

When his father died, Sutherland sailed into the yachting world, too. Now he was sun-kissed and broad-shouldered—more youthful than his early fifties ought to have allowed. His hair was a little thin on top, though, and maybe the crinkles around his eyes no longer looked as if they'd been created by laughter alone. He still had the suave smile I remembered from when he showed up at family gatherings with the most beautiful girl on his arm and the most glamorous car waiting at the curb. The girl always had the look of a satisfied customer, too.

This morning, he wore a chestnut-colored leather jacket over a pink shirt, trendy jeans and tassel loafers, no socks. Very much exuding the manner of a yachtsman on dry land for as little time as he could manage.

Usually, men like Sutherland were drawn immediately to Emma, who radiated beauty and sexual availability. Or to Libby, who engaged men with the force of her personality and strategic deployment of her cleavage. But today Sutherland made a beeline for me and swept me into an exuberant hug.

He kissed my cheek. "Dear Nora, how long has it been?"

A little taken aback, I returned his hug and smiled. "Hello, Sutherland. Five years? Or six? I'm not sure."

"You look lovely. In fact, don't we look good together? I'm sorry I couldn't get back when your husband was killed. What a tragedy. But at the time I was literally caught in a typhoon off the coast of Hong Kong. Will you ever forgive me? My travels always seem to take me far afield when the family needs me most."

I could have pointed out that the extended family usually muddled through without him, but Libby closed in just then and distracted Sutherland with a voluptuous sort of snuggle that made him laugh. Emma shook his hand hard. Sutherland smiled with charm through all the pleasantries.

Then he turned to the phalanx of lawyers. "Gentlemen! Welcome to Quintain. Groatley, you old rascal. Are you still smoking cigars in all the Blackbird back rooms?"

"Not all," Groatley said. "But a few."

They clasped hands like two bulls locking horns. Sutherland barked, "Good man. Shall we have a look around? I don't like seeing my fair cousins standing out in the cold."

"We were just about to go inside," the old lawyer said peevishly, "when you made your grand entrance."

"Let's not delay another moment. Nora?"

He took my hand and pulled me across Quintain's drawbridge

and under the grand archway. The rest of the group followed. Our footsteps were muffled by piles of leaves decomposing on the stones. Overhead, the blank windows of the abandoned mansion reflected nothing.

The deputy had preceded us across the walkway and approached the imposing front entrance, fashioned, if I remembered correctly, out of a pair of wooden doors from a fourteenth-century Sussex abbey. He fumbled through a ring of keys and tried several before the lock gave a bang and the double doors swung wide with a creak of old wood and a screech of hinges that needed oil.

Then he stood back and raised his voice. "Step carefully, everyone."

"It's cold as a dungeon in here." Libby hesitated in the gloomy doorway. "Are the lights burned out?"

Beside me, Sutherland said, "The electricity's probably turned off. Shall I have a look at the generator? It's just behind this wall. The utilities were never terribly trustworthy. Let's see . . ."

Using a hidden spring, Sutherland opened a door in the paneling, and then he disappeared like a magician. We heard him thumping behind the wall as the musty smell of abandonment rose up around us.

Libby wound her hand around the deputy's arm and leaned in close. "Do you ever get nervous in old houses like this?"

"It's not the houses that make me nervous, ma'am."

A yank of a rip cord preceded the spluttering roar of a generator, and Sutherland gave a shout of victory. A moment later, he reappeared, rubbing his hands with triumph.

"Let's give the lights a try, shall we?"

He hit a switch, and the chandelier overhead sprang to life, illuminating the cavernous entry hall with a golden light that flickered unsteadily through a thousand dusty prisms.

"Wow." The deputy gazed upward with awe. "This is like a real haunted mansion."

Twenty feet over our heads, tattered flags hung from the rafters—each bearing a family crest or ancient order of something bloodthirsty. A collection of battered medieval weaponry was displayed on the walls and a dreary oil painting of a glowering Blackbird relative in a ruffled lace collar gave the impression that the Inquisition might get under way soon. A sudden flutter of wings made us all duck instinctively.

"A hard hat wouldn't be a bad idea in here," Emma said. "That ceiling could fall down any minute."

Despite the mess, I felt my heart lift with anticipation. Aladdin's cave might have held treasures, but none so marvelous as the beautiful things I remembered gracing Aunt Madeleine's salon.

With barely suppressed excitement, we crunched our way across the parquet floor—it was scattered with a fine rubble of fallen plaster and other debris I didn't want to think about—past a twin set of tarnished suits of armor that functioned as sentries. Beneath the carved oak staircase stood the elevator, doors closed.

I put my hand on the massive double doors to the salon and took a deep breath, prepared to be dazzled.

CHAPTER TWO

Disappointment stopped me cold.

For starters, the pair of magnificent tapestries that used to hang on opposite walls of the salon were gone. Both had depicted bucolic hunting scenes—gentlemen on horseback chasing stags through forests shot with gold threads of sunlight. But today, empty walls stared where the tapestries had once hung.

The rest of Madeleine's home once featured a decorative style my father called "early bordello." Time was, sumptuous furniture crowded art from every imaginable era and culture. On her travels, Madeleine had frenetically picked up enough treasures to fill her own museum. I remembered two Greek statues that stared loftily across the room at each other—one a man in a helmet and a fig leaf, the other a woman in a draped toga that bared one breast. But Madeleine often dressed them in funny costumes for holidays. Grand paintings hung on the walls, half-naked figurines stood on tabletops, shapely candlesticks and vases of every design littered level surfaces—along with piles of invitations to society parties. A great mirror used to reflect a grand piano big enough for a hefty chanteuse to spread out on. But today, none of it remained.

In a glass case in the center of the room, Madeleine had always displayed a jeweled Fabergé egg—not a large one, but an intricately designed confection of enamel and gold that opened to reveal a tiny baby chick inside. Today, the case was empty, its door half open, the glass shelf coated in dust.

All the treasures were gone.

My sisters and I looked around us in astonishment.

"Where is everything?" Libby cried.

"I'll be damned," Emma said. "Madcap Maddy was robbed."

All the paintings had disappeared. All the objets d'art. Aunt Madeleine's meticulously gathered collection of wonders had evaporated.

"What do you mean?" Groatley demanded hotly. "What's missing?"

"Everything!" Heartbroken, I spun in a circle to stare at the empty walls. "Where are the paintings? The Fabergé egg? The statuary?"

"This is the way we found the place," Groatley blustered. "You mean things have been removed?"

"Stolen," Emma corrected.

Yes, everything had disappeared. Everything except one very memorable painting.

Over the immense fireplace hung the same tall portrait I could remember from my childhood. Its colors were a little faded, and the canvas sagged damply in its frame. But Deputy Foley shone his flashlight on the picture, and Aunt Madeleine herself sprang to life. She leaned fetchingly against a marble pillar, dressed in a blue velvet gown that slipped off one shoulder. Her hand rested on her Fabergé egg. Tendrils of her Blackbird auburn hair teased her white skin. But her half smile and knowing gaze elevated the painting to something more than simply a picture of a very pretty young woman.

Everyone stopped, arrested by the vitality that smoldered on the canvas.

"She was so beautiful," Libby said on a sigh. "And how lucky was she to have her portrait done by Charles Maguirre?"

"Who?" Sutherland asked.

"Charles Maguirre, a French portraitist. His works are extremely valuable now. He squandered his youth with romantic carousing, but in his later years, he made a living traveling around painting portraits of society women, most of them in velvet dresses, just like this one. He must have been especially infatuated with Madeleine, don't you think? He really captured her personality."

"Infatuated is one word for it," Groatley harrumphed.

I admired the portrait. To me, Madeleine vibrated with intelligence—surely a trait very difficult to capture with mere paint and canvas.

Sutherland murmured, "I had no idea this painting could be worth anything. It was just another family picture."

"Painted by a very important artist," Libby added.

Emma was the first to turn away from Madeleine's likeness to cast her glance around the otherwise empty salon. "So where's all her other stuff?"

"This is very irregular," Groatley snapped. "How was I to know she abandoned things of value here? My operatives said this is exactly how they found the place when they set foot in it."

His underlings looked uneasy. Heads were going to roll.

Deputy Foley said, "Sir, we'll start an investigation right away. Even after all this time, there will be evidence."

Emma eyed him. "You get a new fingerprint kit for your birthday, kid?"

"Don't pick on him," Libby warned. "You'll stifle his youthful enthusiasm."

"Sutherland," I said, "perhaps you'll be the one to remember everything that used to be here?"

Sutherland frowned around the salon. "I'll do my best. But actually, I spent more time with my mother than here at Quintain."

I remembered it was his father who'd remained at Quintain with Aunt Madeleine while Sutherland went with his mother to live in Boston among her own family.

Loftily, he added, "This place was not my idea of fun."

"Heaven forbid you not have any fun," Groatley muttered.

We split up. The lawyers remained in the salon together—perhaps planning a defense for their shameful neglect of the estate. Libby announced she wanted to look for the paintings she remembered in the dining room. Emma headed for the stairs, saying she needed a bathroom and since she'd never been on the upper floors, she intended to have a look around. Aunt Madeleine always had guests staying up there—special guests that we children weren't to disturb.

I shared Emma's curiosity, but I had another exploration in mind.

It was the past that called to me. I slipped away from the others and headed for the study, where I remembered Madeleine spending most of her time. She liked a small, ladylike library off the breakfast room. Paneled with handsome shelves and featuring pink wallpaper, it also had an elaborate plaster ceiling depicting long-tailed griffons that menaced cherubs who peeped out from behind the protection of delicately rendered seashells.

I opened the door and paused.

Although the sun glowed rather meagerly through the streaked glass of the windows and motes of dust floated in the air like moths, I could almost see Madeleine sitting tall and elegant at the delicate curved desk. She might be writing letters in her perfectly slanted hand or studying glossy catalogs from the New York auction houses, holding a magnifying glass to examine details of the photographs. On one corner of her desk she kept the bust of some poet or other—a man with curly hair and his shirt open to his chest, although often he wore a paper hat she folded out of stationery. I remembered how she used to play her fingers idly on the statue as she spoke on her white telephone to arrange social engagements.

For all her reputation as Madcap Maddy, though, I remembered her more as a fearsome aunt who fixed me with a stern eye if I dared interrupt her. In my mind, she wore a dramatic black robe tied at the waist and loosened at the bust. She was vain about her figure—and rightly so. She had been slim, but shapely. And of course her hands always seemed weighted down by the gigantic jeweled rings she liked to wear. Surely at least one had come from a husband, but the others I assumed she had bought for herself. She hadn't been the kind of woman to wait for anyone to give her the things she wanted.

"To what do I owe this interruption?" she asked me one morning when I lurked timidly outside her study doorway while she finished speaking on the phone. She set the receiver down sharply.

I was about ten at the time, and I had been afraid to answer her. But finally I edged into the room and held out the broken pieces of a Meissen sugar bowl. "Miss Pippi said to bring this to you."

"Tea and crumpets?" Madeleine did not look up from the ledger book in which she was writing a notation.

"No. We were setting the table for lunch," I whispered. "I bumped the sugar bowl onto the floor. It—it broke. I'm very sorry."

"Sorry?" Madeleine glanced up from her work at last and fixed me with a midnight blue gaze. "Did you break it on purpose?"

"N–no, Aunt Madeleine."

"Then you should apologize for your clumsiness, but not be sorry. Sorry is a foolish sort of feeling, don't you think?"

At ten, I didn't know what to think.

"It's Pippi who should be sorry," Madeleine went on, "for conscripting children to do her work. She's supposed to be a socialist, after all. Here, drop those pieces into the trash." She tapped the toe of her mule against the leather bucket at her feet.

"Oh, we offered to help Pippi," I said in a rush, anxious to spare the housekeeper who shared cookies with us at her pantry table.

"We?" Madeleine repeated, sounding amused. "Who's we? You and your sisters?"

"Just Libby." I obeyed my aunt by letting the shell-like fragments of china fall through my fingers and into the bucket. Then I hid my hands behind my back lest they give away some other transgression she could criticize. "Libby was helping. Emma's too little."

"I imagine your sister Libby helps by lounging on my cushions, pretending she's the Sultana of Arabia. She's like her papa. He's already drinking my liquor this morning. At least he knows how to perk up a room with conversation, I'll give him that." She peeked into the bucket and raised her eyebrows. "What did you bring me those pieces for? Did you expect me to paste my sugar bowl back together?"

"N-no. I just—I needed to tell you it was my fault."

Did her face soften? "Be careful, young lady, or you'll turn into a dreary sort of child. Do you tattle on your friends? Whine for attention?"

A little flame of pride burned brighter inside me. The worst crime of all, it seemed to me, was whining. I said, "I believe in doing the right thing."

Aunt Madeleine laughed at that. "Well, you didn't learn that kind of behavior from your parents. Not a reliable synapse between them. I don't suppose they even keep their own checkbook, do they?"

I had seen my father frequently dashing off checks, so I said, "They do so."

Aunt Madeleine capped her pen and firmly closed the ledger on her desk. "They have no more sense than hummingbirds, either of them."

"They're very happy," I said in defense of my parents. And although I already sensed our place in the world was slipping, I loved that we laughed every day in our household.

Aunt Madeleine said, "As long as they're happy, you're happy, is that it?"

"Yes."

"You take everybody's happiness as your responsibility?"

"I—I don't know what that means."

Aunt Madeleine gave me a piercing look that made me want to step back from her desk and slip away. But she said, "It means you don't have to be a good little girl every minute of the day. You have choices, you know. You can break the rules once in a while without the world coming to an end." She eyed me. Perhaps with a shade less distaste than before. "Find yourself a talent, little miss. Make it your focus. Draw power from it. In the long run, that will make the tough decisions a little easier. Take it from me."

I couldn't quite muddle through all that, but it didn't matter. Suddenly she said, "If you want to make me happy, young lady— you can do the right thing after I'm gone."

"Okay."

"You'll destroy this book for me." She tapped her beautiful fin-gernails on the black ledger on her desk. "Burn it."

I thought she was testing me. I said, "It's wrong to burn books."

"Not this one." She reached and seized my wrist, hard. "A woman like me should keep her business to herself so nobody goes around blowing things out of proportion later. Will you do it? Burn this when I'm gone? Promise?"

"Where are you going?"

"When I die," she corrected sharply. "You're the one I can trust, aren't you?"

Her talk of dying frightened me. But I understood that she wanted me to stiffen my spine, to be strong. Draw power, she had said.

"Okay," I said, squaring my shoulders.

Now, years later, the encounter swept over me like an ocean wave and left me feeling beached. Like a bottle with a message in-side. Except I couldn't read the message clearly.

I caught my balance on the doorjamb. Maybe I still needed to hear her words. My own life had gone haywire lately. Lexie's legal troubles had ended with her turning away from me—from her whole life, perhaps. When she pleaded guilty and the bailiff escorted her out of the courtroom, I hadn't expected her to be whisked away so suddenly. Her stiff neck tore my heart. There were places I couldn't go with her. I'd written daily letters to her, but had received no reply.

Remembering Madeleine's words sharpened something inside me, though. It seemed there was still something I could do—if not for Lexie, then for Madeleine. I looked for her leather-bound book. Today the black ledger was not on top of the desk. Nor was it inside the top drawer, which I slid open for a peek.

Quietly, I looked around for other possible hiding places. Two filing cabinets disguised as Chinese chests stood against one wall. I tried the handles. Locked. That's when I noticed yet another treasure was missing. On top of the chests, Madeleine had once chosen to keep a set of Russian nesting dolls. The largest had been a woman in a kerchief that popped open to reveal another figure and another—each succeeding female a younger version of the last. The final, smallest doll—a smiling infant swaddled in yellow—had always fascinated me. Madeleine had allowed me to play with those dolls. But today they were gone.

I was tempted to try jimmying open the file cabinets in search of the black book, but I heard someone in the hallway behind me. Instinctively, I slipped out the door and down the corridor.

I poked my head into the kitchen and found it in deplorable condition—the floor tiles were heaved up from water damage, and someone had left the remains of a dinner tray on the white marble counter. The teacup was stained yellow at the bottom, and mouse droppings were unmistakable on the plate.

I stepped into the butler's pantry, where Aunt Madeleine's fine china and crystal were arranged behind dusty glass doors. The

Meissen plates—decorated with swooping birds, flirtatious shep-
herdesses and branches laden with springtime blossoms—looked
dusty, but otherwise perfect. The only missing piece was the sugar
bowl.

It was Sutherland who sauntered into the kitchen behind me and
poked his head into the pantry. He seemed to notice none of the
fine objects stored in the small room, but instead checked his own
reflection in the glass cabinet doors. I wondered if he was hanging
on to his heartbreaker looks with his fingertips.

He ran a finger along his hairline to adjust a fair lock and be-
stowed a smile on me. "How have you been, Nora? I hear you inherited Blackbird Farm."

I leaned against the pantry countertop. "Yes, Mama and Daddy
entrusted the property to me when they ran off to—well, when
they decided to go abroad."

"But they came back, right?"

"Only for a couple of months. They're happier in a warmer climate." I could have added that the climate in Philadelphia had gotten plenty hot for my mother and father before they absconded
again.

Finally desperate to be rid of them, I had deliberately left my
credit card on the kitchen table in the hope my parents would pilfer
one last thing and flee. My sanity was worth a few more dings on
my credit score. I didn't have the heart to cancel the card for a
couple of days. Once they safely reached Rio, though, I figured
they were on their own and I terminated my MasterCard. Now I
was relieved to have them out of my hair—and only felt slightly
guilty about using my credit card as a lure.

Sutherland smiled down at me. "So you're living out in farm
country by yourself? That doesn't sound like you."

"Emma's with me at the moment."

"Just the two of you rattling around in that big old house?"

"It's only the windows that rattle," I said with a smile.

"I heard a family rumor you'd gotten married again," Sutherland said. "To an ex-con, for heaven's sake. The aunts are in a tizzy."

A tizzy was better than a tornado, which is how I had felt when Michael first blew into my life. He'd swept me off my feet and into a love affair that was challenging and passionate and life-affirming, and certainly never dull.

But my aunts weren't the only ones who disapproved of our relationship. The universal disapproval of our match was sometimes daunting. I couldn't deny that Michael "the Mick" Abruzzo had served time in prison. For a fact, he was the son of a convicted New Jersey crime boss, and from time to time he had encounters with the law himself. Even now Michael was in jail again, after pleading guilty to a charge of conspiring with his family. I knew he'd done it for good reason, and his sentence was short, so I was clinging to the hope I'd feel his powerful force in my life again by summer.

Sutherland said, "Was I misinformed? You didn't marry him?" Then his gaze fell on the diamond ring Michael had given me. His eyes popped at the size of the sparkling rock. "Or you haven't yet, perhaps? Having second thoughts? Marriage is always a gamble with you Blackbird women, isn't it?"

"You're referring to the curse?"

"Well, there's no denying the female Blackbirds end up widows. Even Madeleine. My father took a chance, and look what happened to him. So, what's the story with your convict? Did you marry him or not?"

Was our marriage official? Well, perhaps the laws of Pennsylvania and most of its churches would say otherwise, but we had committed ourselves to each other, Michael and I, in an unorthodox ceremony conducted in the presence of my unorthodox family on a beach with weekend picnickers looking on. For better or worse, richer or poorer, in sickness and in health—the works. Except for the license. Frankly, I was afraid to make our union more legal than that for fear of Michael's life. I didn't believe in curses—not much, at least. But the Blackbird curse of widowhood gave me pause. So we had made our union a marriage in our hearts and in front of witnesses, if not on official paper.

Trouble was, Michael had gone to jail only a few weeks after we made our vows to each other. He'd pleaded guilty to conspiracy and obstruction of justice in a deal that sent other Abruzzos away for longer sentences. He refused to let me visit him in prison, and although I thought we might have outsmarted the Blackbird curse by making our vows in an unconventional non-ceremony, I couldn't help wondering if the curse had taken him away from me anyway.

When I didn't answer Sutherland's question right away, he said, "I hate the thought of you spending your evenings alone, Nora, that's all. Now that I'm in town, I wonder if I might visit. Or take you out for dinner? I've always been so fond of you. We should catch up—"

"Sutherland," I said, "cut the crap. What's on your mind?"

He feigned surprise. Not very convincingly. "Nora, I don't remember this side of you. You used to be so . . ."

"Gullible?"

"Sweet, I was going to say."

I turned and walked out of the pantry, through the breakfast room, across the loggia to the French doors. I unlocked one and gave it a shove with my shoulder to push the sticky door open. Sutherland followed me outside into the kitchen garden—now a tangle of fragrant weeds running rampant around the brick wall. A rabbit dashed from the gravel path and into some bushes to hide.

When I was sure we were alone, I turned to Sutherland and said, "Cuz, let's stop playing whatever game you started."

"Nora, I would never—"

"Don't insult me any more than you already have," I said. "Let's be honest. You're wondering why Aunt Madeleine gave this place to my sisters and me instead of to you—her stepson."

"Well, it's peculiar, I'll admit."

"To all of us," I said.

"I thought she had a few motherly feelings towards me, but perhaps not. It's not that I need the cash," he said quickly. "I'm hardly in beggar's rags. I have resources."

"Of course you do."

"It's just . . ."

"Yes?" I prompted.

"Well, I have fond memories of the old girl. As stepmothers go, Madcap Maddy was colorful. I liked her."

"So you want the estate?"

"Hell, yes, I want it." Sutherland smiled. "Half of Madeleine's wealth originated with my father, right? I'll fight you tooth and nail for this house and what's left of its contents. I'm not as young as I used to be. And I just learned a rock star's Caribbean vacation home has come on the market. Maybe it's time I settled down. In style, of course."

"And the lovey-dovey routine? You thought you might romance me a little first to see if you can avoid an ugly lawsuit?"

"Well," he said with another attractive twinkle, "we Blackbirds often marry our cousins. For the right reasons."

"Money, you mean?"

"Keeping money in the family," he replied, correcting me.

"So you're proposing an alliance?"

"Let's not use the word *propose* just yet." He flicked a lock of my hair with one fingertip. "I'm fond of you, Nora. You're not nuts like Libby, and you don't frighten me the way Emma does. Good Lord, now she's going to spawn! But you—you're delightful. And I'm not entirely revolting, am I? We could settle a family dispute before it gets started, you and I. Think of all the lawyer fees we'd be saving if we shook hands right now."

"How romantic."

"What do you say?"

Before I could say anything, we heard a bloodcurdling scream from inside the house.

CHAPTER THREE

We found Libby in hysterics in front of the open elevator. She had collapsed to her knees, shaking with terror and weeping.

I knelt, caught her around the shoulders and turned her away from the horror that lay on the elevator floor.

"My God," Sutherland said above us.

Emma skidded down the staircase and caught her balance on the open door of the elevator car. She cursed.

"It's a person," Libby cried, sobbing against my shoulder. "A dead person!"

It might have been a person once, but what remained on the floor of the old elevator was little more than a pile of graying bones and mummified skin dressed in gauzy tatters of fabric. If the sight wasn't already awful enough, the feeble light fixture at the top of the elevator flickered unsteadily, and the smell that wafted toward us was one I immediately thought must have greeted every archaeologist who ever set foot in an Egyptian tomb—a combination of dust and must and a spine-tingling horror.

Libby babbled, "I went looking for the paintings in the dining room. They were gone, so I decided to go upstairs, to Madeleine's room. I pushed the button. I heard the elevator come down to this floor. When the door opened—I—I—"

"It's okay, Lib," I soothed.

"Who is it?" She pointed a shaking finger at the bones on the floor of the elevator.

"We'll find out," I said.

I didn't feel so good myself just then. I was glad to be kneeling on the floor, but my head spun unsteadily. The bones lay in a neat line, but the skull had rolled sideways. The empty eye sockets stared at us, and the jaw hung open as if in a final shriek of agony.

Libby was hyperventilating. "I wasn't expecting—I never imagined—"

"Hush," I said. "You're okay."

She hiccoughed and tried to steady her heart with a hand pressed to her bosom.

"Well," Sutherland said, digging a handkerchief from his pocket. "This might explain why nobody was looking after the place."

"What d'you mean?" Emma asked.

He daubed the handkerchief to his forehead. "Isn't it obvious? This must be the caretaker. The housekeeper."

"Pippi," I gasped. "Oh, God, the poor thing."

"The electricity must have gone out. She was trapped in the elevator."

"And she died?" Emma sounded as appalled as I felt. "Of starvation?"

Libby burst into tears all over again.

The sheriff's deputy and some of the lawyers arrived then, all of them exclaiming in loud voices.

"Someone call 911," Sutherland finally barked, which made Emma laugh.

"It's a little late for an ambulance," she said.

Deputy Foley took charge. With the bluster of youth, he ordered us all to step away from the open elevator. Sutherland, he said, should stick around to provide information.

"The rest of you should go outside. We must preserve the crime scene."

His official manner was slightly spoiled by the way Libby clung to his arm. He finally seemed to notice how beautiful she looked when distraught, but he hastily handed her off to me. I helped Libby into the next room and eased her onto a dusty sofa. I patted her hands while she tried to pull herself together.

A moment later, Emma joined us in the salon. "I'm famished," she announced. "And any minute I'll have to pee again. What do you say we blow this joint?"

"We need to stay," I said. "The police will want to talk to us."

"What can we tell them that Foley can't? I'm hungry."

"Aren't you the least bit shocked?" Libby asked, still dabbing at her mascara with a hankie.

"I get hungry all the time. Nothing shocking about it anymore."

"That's not what I—oh, never mind."

I could see Libby was in no shape to make sensible observations for the police. Besides, I was a little worried how she might react to the arrival of even more testosterone when more cops showed up.

"Everyone else saw exactly what we saw," Emma said. "Let's clear out."

"Yes, let's go." Libby tucked her hankie into her cleavage, where it immediately disappeared as if down a bottomless crevasse. "I could use a restorative beverage. It's not too early for a margarita, is it?"

The three of us went outside. That's when we remembered we'd arrived in Deputy Foley's cruiser, so we were stuck for transportation.

"We'll have to walk," I said.

"In these shoes?" Libby protested. She teetered on a pair of heels probably bought from the back page of a Victoria's Secret catalog.

The three of us were staring at Libby's inappropriate footwear when we heard a rhythmic *clip-clop* and the merry jingle of harness. Then four perfectly matched black horses burst out of the woods, pulling Cinderella's coach into Quintain's storybook landscape.

"What in the world—?" I started.

Emma said, "I'll be damned. It's Shirley van Vincent."

"Who?"

"Vincente van Vincent's wife. The diplomat? The retired diplomat, that is. She's the horse fanatic. She used to be the world champion driver in coach-and-four competitions. She's hosting the big international preliminary next week, hoping to make a comeback. The van Vincent Classic." Emma waved her arm in the air as if flagging a taxicab. "I bet she's training right now. Maybe she'll give us a lift into town. Hey, Shirley!"

The magnificent coach glinted with polish. The wooden wheels, painted with yellow trim, flashed in the sunlight as they spun through the fallen leaves. The horses—all immaculately groomed and stepping in precise rhythm—bowed their heads as they approached. A pair of Dalmatians completed the picture by trotting in the wake of the coach.

On the driver's box, a spritely old lady in an emerald green Tyrolean hat commanded the reins and balanced a tall whip in her capable hands. "Whoa!" she called to her team as she caught sight of Emma. "Whoa, there!"

The horses and dogs came to an obedient halt, and Emma stepped out to catch the bridle of the lead horse. "Hey, Shirley," she said, easily controlling the huge animal. "How's it going?"

"Emma Blackbird," the woman replied, her accent still slightly tinged by her European roots. Her voice was a deep smoker's rasp, surprising coming from such a diminutive person. She plunked the whip into its holder and rearranged the reins in her gloved hands while eyeing Emma with disapproval. "You've brought shame on your family, I see. Or are you just getting fat?"

"No, it's a baby, all right." Emma gave her belly a lascivious rub.

"Your grandfather would have disowned you."

"Good thing he's not around to see me, then. How come you're still alive, you old crone?"

Shirley van Vincent didn't take offense, but rather warmed to Emma's taunting tone. She pulled a pack of cigarettes from one of the many pockets on the fisherman's vest she wore and drew a cigarette into her mouth directly from the pack before tucking it back into her pocket. She thumbed a plastic lighter and lit up—all without losing control of her team of horses.

Blowing smoke over her head, she said, "I'm too tough to die. Somebody's going to have to kill me if they want rid of me."

"Careful," Emma cautioned. "You might have people standing in line for that opportunity."

"Are you saying I'm not the most popular woman around?"

Emma patted the neck of the horse she held. "You've been known to cross a line now and then, Shirley."

"Only in the pursuit of excellence," the old woman retorted. "I have a competitive spirit. So do you. Speaking of which, will we see you at the Classic next week? I could use you."

"Maybe I'll be helping another team."

"Doubtful." Shirley van Vincent grinned. "You like to win as much as I do. And I always win. What are you doing out here today, may I ask?"

"Visiting Aunt Maddy's estate. You heard she died?"

"I read it in the newspaper." Gruff again, the old woman fiddled with the reins. "I expected that news a lot of years ago, to be honest. I never thought Madeleine would live to such a ripe old age."

"You knew Madeleine?"

"Of course I knew her. We were neighbors."

"Close?"

"That's none of your business," Shirley snapped. "But she could have been more generous with her tilting green. It would have made just the right spot for practicing tight turns."

"Fair enough," Emma said. She had a respect for horse training. "How about giving us a lift?"

"Where to?"

"Into New Hope? I'm starving."

"Animal appetites," Shirley said with more disapproval. "That's what got you into trouble in the first place. These are your sisters?"

"Yes, Nora and Libby."

"I can guess which one is which. Elizabeth was the one who pranced around pretending to be a princess all the time." She gave us a cold inspection. "You hardly look like royalty today, young lady. More like you've been run over by a milk wagon. What's the matter?"

"We've had a shock," Libby obediently piped up. "There's a dead body in the elevator."

The cigarette fell from Shirley's lips. "Good Lord, nobody's been in that house for years. Who is it?"

"It's not much of a body." I stepped on the cigarette before it could set dry leaves alight. "More of a skeleton, actually. It looks as though somebody was trapped in the elevator and died."

The elderly woman sent me a severe glance. "Trapped in the elevator, eh? That's what happens with modern conveniences. My father was an electrician—spent his whole life repairing things that had gone wrong. When something newfangled breaks down, you've got a tragedy on your hands. Give me a horse and carriage any day."

"You always had a big heart, Shirley," Emma said.

"It's a wonder worse didn't happen in that house, with all the crazy people Madeleine had moving in and out all the time."

"What people?" I asked. "Her houseguests?"

"If that's what you want to call them."

Emma had grown impatient. "How about that ride?"

"Climb up," the old woman said. "I'll take you into town."

It took Emma two tries to jump up onto the driver's box with Mrs. van Vincent. She wasn't as agile as usual, and I gave her a boost. Libby and I clambered inside the coach and made ourselves comfortable on the plush leather seats. A moment later we were off.

Libby collapsed against the cushions. "I'm in a state of shock," she said. "I'm partially claustrophobic, you know. Getting trapped in an elevator with no food, nothing to drink, no company—what a nightmare."

"It would be awful," I agreed.

"I'm sure I'd be one of those animals that chewed off its own foot in captivity. I'd probably suffocate in two minutes or less if I were stuck in an elevator. Now, if I had some company, why, that would be a completely different story."

Libby was on a rant, so I let her babble the whole way into New Hope.

We made quite a spectacle driving into the village in the coach-and-four. The horses' hooves clattered on the pavement. Their harness jingled as merrily as Christmas bells. People on the sidewalks turned to wave. A gaggle of small children—outdoors with their teacher from their day-care center—stopped and stared. But we also passed two police cars heading in the opposite direction. They were on their way to Quintain, I guessed, summoned by Deputy Foley to the elevator crime scene.

We arrived at the Rusty Sabre Inn in no time. Shirley van Vincent drew up the horses, and the carriage glided to a stop in front of a parking meter. I climbed out and helped Libby to solid ground. She headed for the sidewalk. Then I reached for Emma's hand to help her hop down from the box.

"Thank you, Mrs. van Vincent," I said to Shirley when Emma had landed heavily beside me and waddled after Libby.

Shirley effortlessly controlled her snorting team. "No trouble at all." She leaned down to me and said in a lower voice, "Make sure Emma takes care of herself. Keep her out of the liquor. I know she likes to tipple."

"Easier said than done."

"And you." She pointed her whip at me. "I hear you've been unlucky in love again. Your man is in jail now, is he?"

"He—"

"Just as well," she said. "Let him go, young lady. Find yourself a match in your own neighborhood. No sense slumming in the criminal element."

Without waiting for my retort, the old woman loosened the reins, cracked her whip and sent the team charging down the street.

People were always free with their opinions about my life, and I should probably have gotten used to it. But no, I still didn't like it.

Steaming, I followed my sisters into the Rusty Sabre. Emma made a pit stop, then ordered another breakfast while Libby and I contented ourselves with coffee. We hashed over the morning's events. We had received the news of Madeleine's demise when her lawyer called—announcing he'd heard from the Indonesian government. It had been a civilized way to learn of a death. But finding these remains in an elevator close to home hit us each differently.

Unaffected by the grisly discovery, Emma dug into her meal as soon as it arrived. "Shirley van Vincent agrees the body in the elevator is probably Pippi, the housekeeper. Do either of you remember her?"

"I do," I said, feeling the melancholy tug of sadness. "She was a friendly little thing. Always giving us shortbread cookies, remember?"

Emma shook her head. "It's not like me to forget cookies, but I don't. I was too young, I guess."

I said, "Aunt Madeleine brought Pippi home from one of her trips overseas. She worked in the household for years. She was always trying to teach Madeleine some Swedish words."

"Russian," Libby corrected. "She spoke Russian with Madeleine." She rooted around in her cleavage for her handkerchief. "Dear me, it's just too sad to think of Pippi dying all alone in an elevator. How horrible it must have been."

"Why didn't she climb out?" Emma cut a huge chunk of French toast. "Don't all elevators have some kind of escape hatch?"

"She was tiny," Libby said. "Probably too small to—to—oh, let's talk about something else, can we? It's just too upsetting."

I was feeling the burn of tears again, too. "It's very sad, isn't it? First Aunt Madeleine, and now Pippi."

I tried to remember some details of Pippi. Yes, she had been small and blond and not terribly proficient in English. Mostly, I recalled that she had been Aunt Madeleine's constant companion. More than a housekeeper, she had driven our demanding aunt everywhere in her white Bentley and carried Madeleine's handbag as they shopped Main Line boutiques or the prestigious floors of Philadelphia department stores. Pippi wore Madeleine's hand-me-down clothes—tailoring the expensive garments to fit her smaller figure. And when the hairdresser came to the house to fix Madeleine's hair, there was always an hour spent trimming and fluffing Pippi, too.

They ate breakfast and lunch together every day at a small table in the corner of the salon. In the evenings, I remembered Pippi bringing a tray of coffee cups into the television room so they could watch *Jeopardy!* together.

Madeleine relied on her industrious housekeeper, too. When something went wrong, I could still hear Aunt Madeleine's voice raised in a musical sort of cry. "Pippeeeeee!"

I cut across Libby and Emma discussing football kickers. "When did Aunt Madeleine hire Pippi?"

My sisters looked blankly at me. "What?"

"When did Pippi first appear? Where did she come from?"

"I don't remember," Libby said.

"Don't ask me." Emma warmed up her coffee by pouring more from the carafe.

"And why didn't she go with Madeleine to Indonesia?"

"Probably because Madeleine wanted to be alone with her lover," Libby replied. "Why would you want another woman tagging along on your romantic adventure?"

"But Pippi took care of Madeleine," I insisted. "She waited on her hand and foot. I can't imagine Madeleine moving anywhere without her."

Emma shrugged. "Who knows?"

"Maybe Shirley van Vincent knows," I said. "Could you ask her, Em?"

My little sister blinked at me. "Sure, what the hell. But what we really need to know is when Pippi died. Did she have anything to do with the stuff that disappeared from Madeleine's place?"

"Yes, when did all the art disappear?" I said, reminded of the many treasures missing from Quintain.

"It would be a terrible shame if kids broke into the house looking for a way to make some beer money," Libby said. "The statuary belonged in a museum, not in a roadside flea market. And the Fabergé egg! What if it's sitting in some child's Easter basket in a closet right now? It's possible the thief had no idea how valuable it was."

"Libby," I said, "could you do a little research? Make a list of the pieces you remember best? Surely the egg will have turned up somewhere. Things of that value don't just disappear."

"Well, I have to think of Maximus right now. And my PitterPat followers."

"Libby, this is important." I turned to Emma. "What did you see when you were upstairs? Before Libby screamed?"

She shrugged. "You mean before Groatley cornered me in one of the bedrooms?"

"He cornered you?"

She grinned. "He had his pants unbuttoned and everything, the old goat."

"But—but you're pregnant!" Libby sputtered.

"My stomach wasn't going to get in the way of what he had in mind. He almost had me bent over a dresser before I figured out what was—er—up. Don't look so shocked," she said to me. "I fought him off."

"Em, how awful."

Another shrug. "No big deal. He's a pig, that's all. He knew his way around the bedrooms, though."

"Men are such animals sometimes," Libby said indignantly. "They get themselves a little power and privilege and suddenly they're God's gift to women? They imagine every female within sniffing distance of their pheromones can't wait to rip off her panties and get jiggy. Well, no woman alive wants to be chased around the bedposts anymore."

"Really?" Emma grinned. "You don't want to be chased around the bedposts?"

"Certainly not!" Libby took out her compact and examined her reflection in the small mirror. "I want to choose for myself. I want atmosphere and consideration and respect for my adventurous nature, not some boar in rut. If Simon Groatley comes after me with his pants down, he'd better make sure I don't have a hatchet handy."

"You carry one in your purse, maybe?" Emma said.

"I bet Aunt Madeleine did." Libby powdered her nose. "Or the equivalent."

"You said Groatley knew his way around upstairs," I said to Emma. "I wonder how? Did he have a personal relationship with Madeleine?"

Emma set down the coffeepot. "Nora, you're acting like we should be investigating something. What are you up to?"

I sat up straight and stern. "Look, you two. Don't you see? Nobody's going to be on our side in this. You want your share of the inheritance, don't you? Well, we're not going to inherit a penny if it's already gone. Em, you'll deliver that baby in a stable. And Lib, you'll have to pay for Max's football training by cleaning toilets at the gym with your very own bucket of Lysol. We have to figure out what happened or we won't get one red cent of our inheritance!"

My lecture galvanized Libby. She dove into her handbag for a notepad and pen.

Elbow on the table, Emma cupped her chin in her palm and gave me an amused look. "Did you have time to discuss any of this with Sutherland?"

Alert to Emma's wry tone, Libby looked up from her notepad. "You had a discussion with Sutherland?"

"A short one," I admitted. "He put me on notice. He intends to fight us for Quintain. No surprise there, of course."

"The surprise was the way he looked at you," Emma said tartly. "I was watching from an upstairs window. That's how Groatley sneaked up on me."

"Sutherland looked at Nora?" Libby asked.

"He practically went down on one knee in front of her."

"Nora!" Libby dropped the notepad. "You and Sutherland?"

"Don't be silly. I have no interest in Sutherland. For one thing, he's our cousin."

"Second cousin. Or third," Emma said. "Aunt Madeleine married a cousin."

"And look how well that turned out."

"Sutherland's very attractive," Libby said slowly. "A little old for you, maybe, but that's not an insurmountable—"

"Isn't anyone listening?" I demanded. "I have no interest in Sutherland. I'm in a committed relationship."

Perhaps my tone was too sharp.

After a weighty pause, Emma said, "You've been there before, Sis."

"Thanks for reminding me."

Libby leaned forward. "What Emma means is you committed

yourself heart and soul to your first husband, Nora—even after he went crazy with drugs. You were in denial for a long time, and I'm not saying you enabled his addiction—"

"Thanks," I said.

"—but it took you a long time to admit he had a serious problem. Even after he was finally killed by his dealer—well, I'm your sister, so I can tell it to you straight. You were blind to the truth."

Emma translated. "Todd was a shit. You should have divorced him."

"And now," Libby continued, "That Man of Yours is in jail and may be away for a long time. I know you don't believe he's the least bit guilty of anything, my dear sister, but . . . maybe you should consider moving on with your life? Looking for some happiness for yourself? Your biological clock is ticking."

Sometimes I wished I could be as transparent as Libby—blurting out my desires to anyone who would listen. Or as good at controlling my feelings as Emma—with her blunt way of turning off her emotions when they got too difficult to manage. But I was somewhere in the middle. I'd put my heart in danger. And now, in their separate, annoying and yet deeply caring ways, my sisters were trying to protect me.

I said, "Don't worry about me. When Michael has served his sentence and comes home, we'll be perfectly happy."

"Well, good," Libby said, but her face was doubtful.

Her cell phone rang, and she checked the caller ID before answering. Over the past couple of years, her various children had caused plenty of uproars. When she answered the call, she kept her voice businesslike. "Yes, Rawlins?"

Emma and I glanced at each other. At least it wasn't Libby's daughter Lucy calling to announce getting kicked out of class for picking on the boys, or the thirteen-year-old twins lobbying to tour the city morgue. So far, Libby had fought off their requests, but we suspected she was weakening.

A call from seventeen-year-old Rawlins in the middle of a school day, though, signaled a different kind of emergency.

Libby's voice rose with annoyance. "You mean now? Why?"

Exasperated, she handed the phone to me. "Nora, my son says he needs to speak with you immediately."

I accepted Libby's phone. "Rawlins?"

My nephew's voice sounded breathless. "Aunt Nora, I think you'd better come home right away."

The mental image of various catastrophes that could befall Blackbird Farm tore through my mind like a wildfire through tinder. "What's wrong?"

"Nothing's wrong," he said. "Not exactly. I got a call at school to come over here. I figured—look, you better come see what's happening."

Libby was already repacking her handbag. Rarely did she want to be first on the scene of the crime if her children might be involved, so she decided she needed to recover from the morning's shock by having an immediate pedicure.

Emma volunteered to drive me home. She had left her pickup parked outside the inn, and after a detour to the bathroom for her, we piled into the front seat.

We made the trip up the winding road alongside the Delaware River in record time.

Pulling up the long driveway to Blackbird Farm, fence posts whizzing past, we saw police cars parked every which way at the back of the house under the oaks. I was glad not to see fire trucks—fire being my worst nightmare. But this couldn't be good.

In two hundred years, the Federal-style house had never enjoyed the full attention of well-paid carpenters who might have saved the porches from sagging, the roof from leaking or the shutters from hanging just a bit crookedly from the many windows. The chimneys had started to lean lately, a situation I fervently hoped might correct itself, since my meager salary from the newspaper could hardly pay the taxes, let alone cover repairs on the old place. The house was just one loose nail away from disaster.

Perhaps I should have sold the house when my parents dumped it into my lap along with a property tax bill that nearly stopped my heart. But the idea of selling off family history was beyond me. I couldn't allow the house to be bulldozed to make way for a discount store—not when George Washington's colleagues had camped on the front lawn before their fateful boat trip across the Delaware.

As Emma pulled around the trees, I saw with relief that the old house was still standing. But the police presence made my heart pound.

I bailed out of Emma's pickup and hightailed it to the back porch. I burst through the kitchen door, causing half a dozen officers to turn from their task.

The police might as well have been invisible.

Sitting at the table? Someone I hadn't expected to see for months.

"Michael?" I said, my voice strangled.

The notorious son of New Jersey's most celebrated crime boss gave me a lazy-eyed grin. "Hey, sweetheart. What's for lunch?"

CHAPTER FOUR

A second later, he said sharply, "Somebody catch her."

I didn't faint, but it was a close call. I saw stars against a dark, roiling backdrop of emotion. My nephew, Rawlins, obeyed Michael's command and came to put his hand under my elbow until my head cleared.

"You okay, Aunt Nora?"

Emma pushed through the door and stopped dead. "Hell, Mick, what did you do? Bust out of jail?"

My first impression was that the men in uniform were holding him down, trapping him in a chair and inflicting torture. Somebody had a screwdriver. Another man was leaning all his weight into Michael's leg with an electric drill.

I choked back a cry of horror.

"It's a monitor," Rawlins said in my ear. An undercurrent of excitement vibrated in his low voice. "An electronic ankle monitor. He's on house arrest now. Cool, right?"

I tottered over to a kitchen chair and slid into it.

From the other end of the table, Michael smiled at me, enduring the attentions of law enforcement with forced calm. The uniformed officers acted as if he were a wild animal capable of springing out of their control and going on a deadly rampage. They pinned him firmly, their jaws set.

One glowering young officer stood apart, holding a bag of frozen peas against his face. He must have found the bag in my freezer. On the floor at his feet lay the shattered pieces of a broken drinking glass.

Aside from the evidence of fisticuffs, I could also see that Michael had been allowed to take a shower before being subjected to this collaring ordeal. I knew he hated bringing home the smell of incarceration. He'd changed into a pair of jeans and a pullover that had been hanging in my closet upstairs since summer. His hair was wet—barely disguising a truly terrible short cut that must have been done with dull clippers.

When I could speak, I said, "How long have you known about this?"

Michael said, "Yesterday, they told me getting early release was a possibility. State budget cuts. The facility got overpopulated. This morning, my number came up, so here I am. I phoned, but you were out."

He was sorry to have shocked me. His steady gaze said as much.

Suddenly I felt sunlight dawn inside me. Michael was home. Out of jail. The relief and joy felt like daybreak in my chest. Michael's expression melted when he saw that, and if I'd had the strength, I'd have climbed over the table and kissed him on the mouth. He'd have met me halfway.

But he was trapped on his side of the table, and my head was still too light to make any sudden moves, so I sat very still with my knees squeezed tightly together and my hands in my lap.

Emma set a glass of water in front of me.

Another man, with a pair of reading glasses perched low on his nose, sat at the table, signing papers. "Okay, Mick," he said, when he dotted his last signature. "You heard the rules. You know the perimeter—only the house, the yard as far as the road out front, the barn in the back. You have my phone number. Stay in touch."

"My parole officer," Michael explained. "Nora, this is Jim Kuzik. Nora Blackbird."

Kuzik removed his glasses and tucked them inside his khaki jacket. He glanced around the large, rambling kitchen and up at the rafters, where a collection of antique cooking utensils hung alongside a scabbard reportedly left behind by Lafayette during a pre-Revolutionary visit. After studying the accumulated hardware, Kuzik gave me an offensive once-over, too. "You have quite a home, Miss Blackbird. Did Washington sleep here?"

"Yes," I said. "He carved his initials on a headboard. And the dollar he threw across a river? He borrowed it from a relative of mine."

Kuzik blinked. "No kidding?"

Plenty of historical figures had passed through the hallowed Blackbird halls. A few stayed long enough to make an impression on our family history, and the anecdotes had been passed down through the generations. But at that moment, I wasn't feeling hospitable enough to give the nickel tour. I didn't like the way they were manhandling Michael—as if to impress their will on him one last time.

"No kidding," I said.

"You've got a leak, though." He pointed at the shallow pond standing on the floor tiles around the kitchen sink.

Familiar with all the drafts, pests, and other expensive issues that required money and expertise I didn't possess, I said, "I'll get a sponge."

He eyed me a moment longer, trying to determine, perhaps, if I was holding back an angry outburst, but finally deciding I was as courteous as I pretended to be. "We need your permission, as the homeowner, to finish installing the separate phone line for the monitor. You see, we make sure of Mick's whereabouts by a wireless—"

"Where do I sign?"

He passed the papers across the table and skidded a pen to me, too. "Are there any guns in the house?"

"There's a blunderbuss hanging over the mantel in the library," I said as picked up the pen. "Last used by Aaron Burr, we believe. He took the gunpowder with him when he left, however."

"Interesting. But we'll have to ask you to remove it from the premises. Mick isn't supposed to have access—"

"I'll send it out immediately." I jotted my signature on the line at the bottom of the page and handed it back to him. "Are you gentlemen finished now? I wonder how soon you could move your vehicles off my lawn? There are heirloom varieties of flowers planted under the grass where you parked. I'll be disappointed if the bulbs are ruined."

My cool politeness had shamed them all into an uncomfortable silence. Finally, Kuzik said, "My apologies. And sorry about the broken glass, too. Bergamunder will clean it up. We'll be out of here in a jiffy."

The rest of the officers had finished their drilling and pulled the leg of Michael's blue jeans down over the blinking device they intended to leave behind. As they packed up their tools, they studied me with sidelong glances. Perhaps they'd assumed I'd be some kind of mob moll with a pistol in my garter.

I didn't speak as they gathered up their equipment, swept up the broken bits of glass and tromped out of the kitchen.

Another man materialized from the scullery, where he'd been muttering into a cell phone. I recognized him as one of the more recently hired minions who did Michael's bidding at any hour of the day or night. He must have been summoned by Michael. His name was Bruno Something, and unlike the usual suspects in Michael's employment, he wore a suit and tie. He had replaced Michael's last right-hand man, Delmar, who'd gone to jail for assault. Before that, it had been Aldo, who disappeared after being named the lead suspect in a gangland shooting. The turnover of Michael's personnel was usually six months or so. I didn't expect Bruno to last long.

Bruno must have also sensed his limited employment. Either that, or he didn't like the idea of his boss's activities being slowed down by the presence of a woman in his life. Since our first introduction, he had pretended I was invisible. He terminated his call, then pulled two more cell phones from his pockets and laid them on the kitchen table before Michael, who gathered them up without a thank-you.

"Five o'clock and ten p.m.," said the well-dressed thug. "Plus seven and eleven in the morning."

Michael got up from the table, tall and in command, checking the screens of both phones before tucking them into his pockets. He gave a nod of dismissal, and Bruno went out of the house. The kitchen door closed quietly behind him. We could hear the engines of various vehicles start up outside.

Emma said, "C'mon, Rawlins. I'm starving. I gotta pee again, and then you can take me out for an ice cream cone. I'm feeling low on calcium. Unless you want to go back to school?"

"No way. But—"

She grabbed the collar of his sweatshirt. "It's time to clear out, kid. Four's a crowd."

I said, "Before you go, grab the blunderbuss, will you?"

"Gotcha. We'll go out the front door."

Over his shoulder, Rawlins said, "I'm glad you're home, Mick."

"Thanks, kid."

"And I'm really glad you thought you could call me for the house key, too. Call anytime."

"Sure."

Emma dragged Rawlins out, and they disappeared.

Still seated at the table, I tried to say calmly, "What's at five o'clock?"

"Mass at Saint Dominic's."

"Who's going to mass?"

With a warm hand, Michael pulled me to my feet. He wasn't handsome—his battered face had a fallen angel roughness that sometimes frightened people, and he tended to keep his thoughts secret. But a smile played at the edges of his mouth and there was a teasing light flickering in his blue eyes. He said, "I'm allowed to leave the house for church services."

"Oh, Michael, you're not going to take any chances, are you? Surely house arrest means—"

"I can't be denied my religion." He wrapped both arms around me. "Or dentist appointments, come to think of it. I feel a cavity coming on."

"But—"

"Don't worry," he murmured. "Here with you is where I want to be."

He hugged me close and squeezed. His body felt delicious, but it was the sure beat of his heart against my breast that lit my fire. I put my arms around him, holding a deep breath but feeling on the brink of being swept away on a giddy surge of something I was almost afraid to call happiness. He was a man of dark depths I didn't always understand, but he was all the man I wanted—smart and witty and protective of me and so sexy I couldn't see straight sometimes. And he was home.

I whispered his name and released the breath of tension—one I realized I'd been holding for months. I probably wept, too, but soon we were laughing as he spun me around—as giddy as teenagers cutting school together. Looking up into his vivid blue eyes, holding him close, I felt as if my heart might burst out of me.

Spin over, he backed me gently against the refrigerator and kissed me until my knees went weak.

As kisses went, it was pretty great. Then we smiled at each other and said a few things that hadn't been said in a while.

Later, we sat side by side on the back porch steps, breathing fresh air and sharing a peanut butter sandwich. Michael stretched his long legs into the sunshine and tipped his face up to the sun. Overhead, the oak trees whispered with drying leaves. It was a lush November day—no nip of frost in the air yet, just warm sunlight and crisp wind. Emma's speckled spaniel, Toby, rolled contentedly in the grass in front of us. Out in the pasture, Emma's latest herd of ponies bit and kicked at one another.

I hugged my knees, and couldn't keep my eyes off Michael. He looked pale and a little thin through his face, but his shoulders were laced with new muscle, as if he'd spent his time in jail burning off his frustrations with exercise.

He said, "Sorry about the broken glass."

"What happened?"

He shrugged, playing casual. "I lost my temper. I came down from the shower and one of Kuzik's guys was acting like he owned the place. Using your telephone, hanging around, filling a drink from your faucet."

"You hit him."

"No big deal."

"They could have carted you back to prison for that."

"Kuzik saw it my way. He's not a bad guy. So tell me what happened this morning. You came in the house white as a ghost."

I licked peanut butter from my fingers. "I was happy to see you."

He smiled. "I'm glad. But that wasn't all of it. Something's up."

"All right," I agreed. "My aunt Madeleine died last week."

"Rawlins told me that much. I'm sorry." His brow twitched into a frown. "Were you close to her? I don't remember you saying much about a Madeleine."

"I wasn't close, no. In fact, I hadn't seen her since I was a child. But a funny thing has happened. She left her estate to me and my sisters."

Michael looked surprised. "That's good news, right?"

"It would be good news indeed," I agreed, "except other family members object."

"She had kids of her own?"

"A stepson," I said. "Her husband's child. Her husband was a distant cousin of mine, also a Blackbird." I saw Michael's expression and laughed. "Yes, it's very complicated. They were not exactly related to each other, but kind of."

"I've got a few cousins like that myself."

"Then you know what I mean. Anyway, the stepson—my cousin—has already fired a warning shot. And there are other cousins who may come out of the woodwork, too."

"So maybe you won't inherit after all?"

"My guess is the pie will be cut into very small pieces."

"Damn. The money would have solved a lot of problems around here," he said. "Listen, I didn't want to come through your door with this news, but as long as we're talking finances, this seems like the right moment to tell you. I'm broke again."

When I first met Michael, he was building a scattershot business empire that included a limousine service, a fly-fishing outfitting store, a garage that supposedly fixed cars but seemed to be more a source of hard-to-find secondhand parts, and a used-car dealership that he plunked on a portion of Blackbird Farm that I'd sold to him in a moment of financial desperation. That's how we'd first met— with me trying to dig myself out of my tax troubles by selling just a couple of acres of the farm. The endeavors were all passions of his, and he was trying out things that suited his nature. None of them had been particularly successful at first, but they got him interested in business. And once Michael's interest was engaged, he became tenacious.

At the time of our meeting, Michael had also still operated in a peripheral part of his father's business. How the Abruzzo family made their money was a tightly knotted web of crime often covered in the newspapers along with pictures of his father and half brothers in handcuffs and covering their faces with magazines. To his credit, Michael had quietly begun to untangle himself from his family. As for whether he had entirely separated from Abruzzo affairs—well, his recent guilty plea told the tale.

All along, Michael had been expanding his legitimate ventures to include a couple of gas station–convenience stores with the unsavory name of Gas N Grub. As the price of gasoline soared, so had his profits. He built a couple more Gas N Grubs, and a few more after that. Wheeling and dealing in gasoline required not just a ruthless streak but the kind of immunity to intimidation that he'd earned in spades while working for his father. He'd made his first million about a year ago.

"How broke?" I asked. "As broke as me?"

"Sweetheart, nobody is as broke as you." Fondly, he ruffled my hair. "One of my employees seized the moment when I went to jail. He embezzled just about everything I had, including the petty cash at the garage. Then he took off."

"Where did he go?"

Michael smiled. "I'll work on that, don't worry. Trouble is, the money could be gone for good—up his nose, or maybe he blew it at a dog track."

"You've called the police, right?"

He shook his head. "The cops aren't going to be sympathetic to me. I'll take care of this myself."

"Oh, Michael. I can't stand it if you—"

"Take it easy. No knee breaking."

"Promise?"

He didn't promise. Instead, he said, "There's more. Family stuff. I— We can talk about it later. Thing is, until I figure out what I can get back from the moron, I could start selling off assets to put some cash in my wallet. But that may take a while. Right now, I don't have enough dough to buy us another jar of peanut butter."

But he had enough money to buy a couple of cell phones, I

thought to myself. Or perhaps those phones had come from his father? And what "family stuff" was there to talk about that he couldn't say to me now, in the light of day?

But so far, our relationship had two unspoken truths.

First: He would do his best to extricate himself from the Abruzzo family.

Second: I wouldn't ask questions concerning how he managed the extricating.

But sometimes I ached with the uncertainty.

Today, I said, "I can afford plenty of peanut butter."

We got up from the porch steps and strolled out to the pony pasture, hand in hand. Toby scrambled up and followed. Emma's herd of Shetland ponies rushed over to investigate us, biting one another to get close. They shoved their shaggy heads through the split rails. One particularly nasty black beast tried to muscle his way through the fence.

"That's one funny-looking pony," Michael said.

"It's not a pony. That's your Christmas dinner."

"A pig?" Michael looked more closely. "Emma's into pigs now?"

"No, someone dropped him off. It happens all the time—people abandon unwanted pets here, thinking we're a working farm and won't mind. Don't get attached to this character. He's going to the butcher in a few days."

Michael tossed the last crust of his peanut butter sandwich to the pig, and the scrap disappeared in one gulp. The pig was big and bristling with black hair. The ponies tried to bully him, but he stood fast. Michael leaned down and scratched the animal behind his ears. The pig cast a lively, curious eye upward, and Michael said, "What's his name?"

"We don't name animals we're going to eat."

"He's kinda lovable, though. And his nose makes him look a little like my uncle Ralphie."

"Michael, do you like pork chops?"

"Okay, okay. See you at Christmas, Ralphie." He gave the pig one last pat and turned around to look at the house. "Wow. Is the roof looking weird to you? Over by that set of chimneys?"

"I'm not looking."

"That's one strategy, I suppose. Maybe you better fight hard for Aunt Madeleine's money."

"I'd like to. Trouble is, she mostly invested in beautiful things—art and antiques. And they've disappeared."

Michael's interest sharpened. "Poof?"

"Like Houdini pulled his best trick. The house used to be filled with a priceless collection. But we took a look around today, and most of it's gone. Including a Fabergé egg." I glanced up at him. "Do you know what that is?"

He didn't take offense at my question. "Russian, right?"

"Yes. Beautifully enameled and decorated with gold and jewels. It's gone. All that's left in the house is either falling apart or ruined."

"Where'd the good stuff go?"

"We don't know."

"You gonna call the cops?" Michael asked. "Looking for pretty stuff makes them happy—no danger involved."

Michael's opinion of police work was biased, and I didn't take him seriously. Instead, I put my hand on his arm and squeezed. "We'll talk to the police once we get a list of missing items worked up. Any other tips?"

"You'll need good lawyers where the will is concerned. Not the polite kind who play golf."

"I can only imagine your kind of lawyer up against the ones Sutherland can surely hire."

"Sutherland?"

"That's Aunt Madeleine's stepson."

Indulgently, he said, "How come nobody you know is ever named Joe Smith?"

We smiled at each other.

"Aunt Madeleine's dying isn't the big headline today," I went on. "We went over to her house this morning. Quintain is amazing—"

"Who?"

"Quintain is the house, not a who. It's a castle, really. But tumbling into ruin. It's worse than Blackbird Farm."

"Hard to imagine."

I poked him with my elbow. "Maybe with all the time you'll be spending around here, you could learn a few carpentry skills."

"You have a hammer I can borrow?"

"There are tools in the cellar. Surely some of them were made in this century. Thing is, when we were looking around Madeleine's estate, we discovered a dead body. It was in the elevator of the house, nothing left but bones."

Michael touched his hand to my cheek. No longer teasing, he said, "You okay?"

"It was a shock," I admitted.

"Aunt Madeleine?"

"We think it must have been Madeleine's housekeeper, Pippi."

"How'd she die?"

"Sutherland suggested the electricity might have gone off while she was in the elevator. She must have been trapped and . . ."

When my voice trailed off and I struggled with my emotions, he said gently, "It happened a long time ago, Nora."

"Still, it's awful to imagine how she suffered. The estate's been vacant for twenty years. Aunt Madeleine left, locked the door and went on a world tour, and nobody ever guessed there might be someone trapped in the elevator."

"So nobody missed the dead lady? What about her family?"

"Pippi was her name. I don't know if she had family. She was very close to Madeleine. She baked cookies a lot. That's about all I can remember."

I told Michael about our trip to Quintain—the lawyers, the tour of the house, the fantastic treasures that had once been inside. And about the sheriff deputy's taking charge of the crime scene.

"So you'll have some answers," Michael said. "Maybe not soon, but eventually."

"I hope so."

The pig poked Michael's ankle monitor inquisitively with his snout. Michael crouched down and scratched Ralphie's head again. I thought I heard the pig give a little sigh. Michael said, "I bet your sisters are excited as hell about inheriting big bucks."

I couldn't prevent a smile. "Libby's already thinking up ways to blow her share. You'll be delighted. It involves the Super Bowl."

"I can't wait to hear the whole story. And Emma?"

"Emma's being . . . cautious."

"That doesn't sound like her." He slanted a look up at me. "How's she feeling?"

"Fine. She quit smoking. That was an ordeal. Hasn't had a drink in a while, either, as far as I can tell."

"That's great. And her baby?"

"It's a boy."

Michael waited.

Here, at last, was the elephant on the table—the subject the two of us had endlessly discussed before he went to jail. The issue that was never far from our thoughts.

I said, "She hasn't decided what she's going to do after the baby's born. I mean, she hasn't decided whether she's going to keep the child or not. She knows she's not a candidate for Mother of the Year. She even jokes about it. She and I talked seriously about—well, we discussed whether you and I should take him, raise him. Adopt him. And she was thinking it over. At first, it seemed like a logical choice to her—best for her. Best for the baby."

Michael nodded. Before he'd gone to jail, we'd decided we'd like to adopt Emma's child. It had been Michael's suggestion, and

I'd jumped—perhaps too eagerly—at the possibility. Michael said, "But now?"

"Well, Emma has had second thoughts."

He stood up again. "With me in jail, you mean."

"She didn't say that—"

"But it had to figure into her thinking. Why give her kid to us if I'm not around to do my part?" Michael looked up at the sky. "I'm sorry, Nora."

I took his hand and laced my fingers with his, trying to ease his regret at spoiling our chance. "She's still thinking."

"What about the kid's father? Has he resurfaced?"

"Hart? No. He's going to marry someone else. For a while, he broke off his engagement, but it's back on again. He's marrying a very wealthy young woman from a wonderful family. She can do a lot of good for his career. It's like a royal alliance. Emma's not talking, but I think she's crushed. She really cared about Hart, and now—well, if he's chosen someone else, you know Emma. She's going to reject him even harder."

"What's his opinion on custody of his child, though?"

"If he has one, Emma hasn't heard it. Look, if she decides she's ready to be a mother—that's great. Really. She'll learn on the job. She'll be fine."

Michael shook his head doubtfully. "That's hard to imagine."

I squeezed his hand again and tried to smile. "We have time to have our own children."

"With me trapped here in the house, it seems as if we have a lot of time on our hands." He laughed a little. "You busy right now? I've been locked up with six hundred men for months."

"Is that your way of saying I look pretty?"

He pulled me into his arms again. His voice was husky in my ear. "You look beautiful."

His embrace was tight, but different. He wasn't quite himself.

Not yet. I knew from before that he needed a day or two to recover from a stint behind bars. Maybe this time it would take a little longer.

I wanted to wrap myself up in him for as long as it took.

But at that moment we heard the steady sound of an engine—a rhythmic concussion that soon developed into the *whup-whup* of a helicopter. It appeared over the treetops, and at first I thought it was passing by—perhaps a medevac headed to one of the big hospitals in the city.

But the helicopter swooped low, blowing its downdraft onto us as it hovered directly over Blackbird Farm. The autumn leaves that had already come off the trees whirled up in a cyclone of noise. The ponies snorted and dashed away in a tight herd. Ralphie the pig hunched his shoulders and stood his ground, squealing his outrage.

Michael put a protective arm across my shoulders. "What the hell?"

I tried to peer up through the choking dust kicked up by the helicopter's rotors. That's when I saw a photographer leaning out of the open door, his camera pointed down at us.

"It's the press," I said. "Taking your picture."

Michael cursed, and we headed for the house. We dashed across the lawn together. Once safely inside, we heard the helicopter bank and fly off.

"So much for keeping a low profile," Michael muttered, shaking dust from his hair.

"They won't be back," I promised. "Surely they've taken one picture, and that's enough." But I had an awful feeling our lives were going to be fodder for the media for a while.

"Let's hope," Michael said, but he didn't sound convinced.

"Listen, I'm sorry about this, but I have to change my clothes and go to work. I'll be home by ten, I promise. We'll have a nice dinner, open a bottle of wine—"

"The hell with that. I'll order a pizza. We'll eat it in bed."

No Way to Kill a Lady

As wonderful as it felt to be in his arms again, I laughingly pushed out of his embrace. "Okay, but right now I have to change my clothes."

"I'll come up and watch."

"I know where that leads, and I don't have time. I'm serious, Michael. I have to get to the office, then to a couple of parties."

After my husband was killed and my parents absconded with the trust funds, I took the low-paying position as a social reporter for one of the city's less-than-prestigious newspapers. At first, I'd been someone's assistant, but I'd built my own place at the paper by covering philanthropic events. As newspaper circulation steadily declined, many of my better-qualified colleagues had been let go. But the society page still attracted lucrative advertising, and my salary was one of the lowest on the staff. So I wasn't a big investment. Not long ago, the managing editor had gruffly told me I might be the last reporter to leave the building.

"Be sure to turn out the lights," he'd said sourly.

Fortunately I was good at the work of reporting social events, and I had contacts that were hard to beat. I also knew how to promote the kind of charitable giving that kept so many nonprofit organizations alive and thriving. And my improvements to the lifestyle pages had brought in more advertising that appealed to the readers who followed my column. That advertising kept the newspaper alive. The online editor started saving plenty of space for my party reports, too. My school prom coverage set records for the paper's Web site.

I went to the office twice weekly to gather my mail and respond to invitations. The rest of the week, I was free to attend whatever functions I felt were important. Usually, I dropped in on social and philanthropic events four or five nights a week, and then wrote my column and short pieces at home. Today, I had a full dance card.

Michael let me go and I dashed upstairs, splashed water on my face and redid my makeup.

While at the mirror, I noticed one of the many notes and cards I'd stuck into the frame last Christmas. A postcard from Aunt Madeleine. The photo on the card showed a picturesque beach in Indonesia. I slipped the card out of the frame and flipped it over.

Happy holidays, Madeleine.

Nothing more. No personal note detailing one of her madcap escapades. I peered at the signature and tried to divine something—anything—from it, but it was a generic sort of handwriting from an era when everyone was encouraged to use the same penmanship. I sighed at the lack of information and put the postcard back into the mirror's frame. It had been Madeleine's responsibility to maintain the relationship, hadn't it? I'd been a child when she left. Was it my fault for not keeping in better touch with her? Surely now my only job was to remember her fondly.

I was running late. I stripped off my jeans and sweater and dove into my closet for something appropriate to wear to the office and the engagements later in the day.

When I first accepted my job, the biggest quandary had been what clothes I could wear if I attended black tie events every week. My own wardrobe included a few elegant pieces—during the first flush years of my marriage to Todd, I'd taken weekend trips to Paris to scour the vintage boutiques—but I'd found the best solution in my grandmother's stash of priceless couture. She'd had a keen eye for fashion and often traveled to shows and the best couturiers, and she had maintained her collection well, so that most of it remained in pristine condition. Later, two of her friends had bequeathed me even more vintage pieces, so my wardrobe was now perhaps quirky, but enviable.

For tonight's events—a difficult mix of casual and very formal—I chose a black lace Ann Pakradooni pants suit that included a froth of lace down the front. The matching bell-bottomed pants hugged my hips almost too tightly and flared gracefully wide at the knee. Grandmama Blackbird had worn it to dinner with a young Elton John. In the attic, I'd found a faded photo clipped from *Hello!* magazine to prove it.

I swept my hair up to better show off the cut of the jacket, then slipped on a pair of relatively sensible stilettos.

The whole outfit made me look as if I were wearing lingerie, which would not do at all for my third stop of the evening, so I pulled a black Dior afternoon-suitable swing coat down from a padded hanger, and selected an extra-long black pashmina for later.

When I hurried downstairs, I found Reed Shakespeare on the back porch with Michael and the dog. Reed had been hired by the newspaper's owner—a longtime Blackbird family friend—to drive me to and from my social engagements. The limousine company for which he worked was one of Michael's side businesses.

Reed had a glass of iced tea from my fridge in one hand and stood with one foot on the bottom step, his hand braced on the railing while Michael lounged on the top step, still enjoying the sunshine. For a young man who rarely cracked a smile, Reed seemed genuinely happy to see Michael.

He sobered up when I pushed out through the back door.

I greeted him. "Hello, Reed. Thanks for coming on time."

"I'm always on time," he said defensively. As usual, he avoided looking at me below the neck. Reed rarely approved of my clothes. Vintage couture was not his taste.

"Yes," I assured Michael, "he is always on time. You should give him a raise."

"I wish I could."

Michael cast his gaze appreciatively down my body. He always liked what I wore, but the black lace put an expression on his face that promised a long night when I returned.

Just as I'd intended.

I pulled Michael to his feet, and the three of us strolled down the flagstone walk to the gravel parking area between the house and the barn. The intrusive helicopter was long gone, and Emma's ponies galloped to the fence again. The shaggy beasts snapped and kicked at one another to get the best positions to watch the humans. Ralphie worked his way to the front of the mob and squealed at Michael.

"Damn," Reed said respectfully. "Those are some ugly animals."

"Speaking of ugly," I said.

Parked on the gravel was not the austere black town car that Reed usually drove me around in. Instead, I was confronted by a formidably huge black SUV with darkened windows and tires big enough to negotiate both sand dunes and alligator-infested swamps.

"What's this?" I stared at the behemoth. "The army doesn't need all its tanks anymore?"

"It's not a tank," Michael soothed. "But it's safer than the town car."

"Safer for whom? You could squash a tractor trailer with this thing. Michael, I'm just going to a few parties, not trying to survive a roadside bomb."

"Humor us," he said. "It's safer, and Reed won't feel like all those stuffy chauffeurs he has to wait with during your evenings out."

I stole a glance at Reed and saw his jaw was set. I knew he resented appearing foolish when he drove me around. Perhaps the SUV made him feel more like a man of his own generation. "Okay," I said reluctantly. "But how do I climb up into the seat?"

Michael boosted me up into the backseat of the SUV with a steady, familiar hand on my butt. When I regained my balance on that perch, I looked down at them. "Is Reed going to perform that service from now on?"

Reed looked uncomfortable. The two of them consulted briefly, then went off to the barn. The pig shouldered his way out from among the ponies and ambled along the fence in Michael's wake.

They returned with an old milking stool that dated back a couple of centuries and could probably send the curators on *Antiques*

Roadshow into swoons of delight. While Reed climbed behind the wheel, Michael set the stool on the front passenger seat and closed the door. He came around to my door to kiss me good-bye.

"See you tonight." He took my face in his hands. "I love you."

His smile made my heart turn over. "I love you, too. I'm so glad you're home."

CHAPTER FIVE

As Reed pulled down the long drive, he carefully avoided looking at me in the rearview mirror.

Finally, I said, "Reed, there's no way I'm going to learn to drive this monster."

"I couldn't come in the town car today, could I?" His voice went up half an octave. "It'll take Mick ten seconds to figure I wasn't the one who messed up the front fender. This was the only way I could keep the secret."

"Are his guys at the garage going to fix the car? Without telling him?" My little accident could have been easily covered up if not for Michael's early homecoming. I felt guilty about dragging Reed into a collusion.

"Yeah, they're repairing it now," Reed said. "You and me are just gonna have to put your driving lessons on hold for a while."

I sighed. "I was doing so well, too."

Reed said nothing.

"Wasn't I?" I demanded. "I thought I was making real progress."

"I've never known anybody more dangerous behind the wheel than you. And that includes my grandma."

"But I'm learning! Cut me a little slack!"

"Just don't go on any public roads yet, okay? You're gonna smash up something worse than a fender."

Because I'd gone to boarding school, then attended college in New York City, where a car was a liability, I'd never learned to drive. And for a while I'd developed an annoying habit of fainting when things got stressful, which meant getting behind the wheel was forbidden by the Commonwealth of Pennsylvania. But with my husband's murder slowly fading from my consciousness, I was getting better at not fainting, so I had applied for a learner's permit. I had wanted to become a proficient driver while Michael was away. Surprising him with my skills behind the wheel seemed like a great plan. Surely at thirty-three, I wasn't too old to learn.

But I wasn't very good yet. I had trouble figuring distances and speeds and turning radiuses and—well, just about everything that came after buckling the seat belt. I had crashed the town car into the side of the barn—which was a very large target, I admit. For once, Reed had lost his cool with me.

But I was determined to learn. "I just need more practice."

In the rearview mirror, I thought I saw Reed roll his eyes.

At the end of the driveway, two cars pulled up and parked. Three scary-looking men got out and stretched as if they planned to stick around for a while. One waved at Reed.

"What's this?" I asked.

"Some of Mick's guys. They're just going to set up a little road-block. A checkpoint."

"Why?"

"To make sure nobody gets to the house unannounced."

Standard operating procedure in the mob. When things got hot in Michael's world, we sometimes had extra protection at Blackbird Farm.

I didn't like the way the tide was turning.

Reed pulled onto the highway and headed south. Most of my neighbors still had pumpkins and scarecrows on their properties. The weather was dry and cool, and colorful leaves blew attractively along the asphalt. In another month, they'd be a sodden, slippery mess on the roads, but for now it was autumn, my favorite season.

I composed myself by opening my bag and spreading my papers on the backseat. The best way to cope with Philadelphia traffic was to work while Reed drove me into the city.

I didn't feel much like working today. Too many distractions. Often when I needed diversion, I used the time to telephone friends while Reed drove. In the late afternoons, I could sometimes catch my best pal, Lexie, just as the stock market closed for the day. She'd put her feet up on her desk and regale me with her financial triumphs. Or I could amuse her with the latest misadventures of my sisters. Today I really wanted to talk to her about Aunt Madeleine. And tell her about Michael's sudden homecoming. But I couldn't call her in jail.

I knew what Lexie's advice would be if I could reach her. Get to work. Immersing herself in work had always been her game plan. I was sure she'd advise me to do the same.

I needed to focus.

So I used my cell phone to RSVP to a couple of parties and to interview the caterer of the van Vincent Carriage Classic next week. The event promised to be very glamorous, but the caterer was worried about the November weather. If snow blew down the refreshment tents, the Classic would be a bust.

Reed was driving opposite the city traffic, so we made it into Center City in less than an hour. I asked him to stop outside a liquor store so I could buy a bottle of wine to share with Michael later. I slid awkwardly out of the SUV and although Reed was there to catch me, he bobbled my hand and I ended up running slap into a parking meter. I shot him a look, and the one he shot back at me was just as annoyed.

When I came out of the liquor store, he was ready with the milk stool. I climbed carefully into the SUV and buckled up. A few minutes later, Reed dropped me in front of the newspaper building. With the milk stool and his steadier hand this time, I managed to get out of the SUV without embarrassing myself. We made a plan to rendezvous after my last event of the day, and I assumed he intended to drive over to the library to do some studying while I was busy. I never asked what he did during his downtime, and he rarely volunteered.

I dropped a letter to Lexie into the mailbox outside my office.

At the Pendergast Building, I passed through lobby security and noticed the staff was putting away Halloween decor and unpacking Christmas decorations. I smiled at the thought of having Michael home for the holidays. I took the elevator up to the floors of the *Philadelphia Intelligencer*, where my colleagues all had their eyes on their computer screens, concentrating on finishing their work for the day.

Skip Malone whistled at me from the sports desk and gave me a thumbs-up on my outfit. I saw he still sported a black eye from the story he'd done on the Eagles football team. A player hadn't taken kindly to one of Skip's sophomoric jokes.

My desk overflowed with paper invitations. I was one of the few social page writers left in the city, so my name appeared on guest lists for everything from donkey basketball games for good causes to elegant charity balls and even birthday parties for small children whose prominent or social-climbing families thought their kiddies needed face time in the newspaper. The coming holidays meant that triple the usual number of invitations came my way. Quickly, I sorted through the mail, wrote a couple of return notes and e-mailed a lot more. Thank heaven for e-mail. It saved me a fortune in notepaper and stamps, not to mention the time it took to compose and write a gracious paper note.

I made careful notations on my calendar and tossed the bulk of the invitations into the trash.

When my cell phone rang, it took me a few moments to dig it out of my handbag. I answered on the third ring.

Emma's voice said, "The cops are here."

"Where?"

"At the farm. You were right. We shouldn't have left the crime scene this morning. They asked me a bunch of questions. They want to talk to you."

"Now?"

"Soon. Mostly, they're peeved we left Quintain without permission. And I think the other reason they're here is to see if the Godfather is behaving himself."

I sighed. It was subtle harassment, but harassment just the same. "I'll be home tonight. You okay?"

"Sure. Mick's making dinner for me and Rawlins. He says I need more vegetables."

"Good for him."

A shadow fell across my desk, and I looked up. "Gotta go," I said to Em, and hung up.

"Nora? Can I ask you some questions about what happened at your aunt's house today?"

Joe Hogarth—a reporter who claimed he'd never retire from newspaper work, but die facedown on his keyboard—pulled a notebook from the hip pocket of his shabby corduroys. He made an effort to smile, but since he did so infrequently, it came across as halfhearted.

He said, "I hear you're related to Madcap Maddy Blackbird. She owned the fancy house in Bucks County, right? Where they found a body in an elevator this morning? Mind if I sit down?" He was already pulling a swivel chair over from another desk. "I thought you could tell me what happened."

Instantly wary, I said, "Joe, I don't want to be quoted in the paper, okay? The family is already in an uproar without me blabbing to the media."

"I get that. So let's just talk. Off the record."

Joe might play the doddering sad sack, but he hadn't won four Pulitzers for nothing. Now, of course, he no longer worked for the city's respected newspaper—they'd replaced him with a younger, cheaper model—but he still had the same nose for news. His faded tweed jacket and brown knit tie looked shapeless and colorless and as if they hadn't been cleaned in decades. And when he pulled a pencil from his breast pocket, he licked the tip. But I knew the good-ol'-boy act was just that—an act.

He said, "Who's the body in the elevator?"

I gave him the basic information—that we didn't know who had died in Quintain's elevator, that the house had been abandoned for years. The local police would investigate. I didn't speculate that the body might have been Pippi. He didn't jot down any notes, but drew circles on his notebook while I talked.

"Yeah," he said, nodding. "The local TV affiliates sent their trucks out to the house. I saw all the pictures on the noon news. We had a photographer taking some aerial photos for tomorrow's edition, too. That estate is quite a place. A real old-money mansion. You spend much time there?"

"Not since I was a child."

"But you've been inside? When your aunt still lived there?"

I hesitated. "Aunt Madeleine left the country when I was in my early teens."

"So you knew her?"

I wasn't sure what Joe was up to, but I had a feeling I should be very careful. I folded my hands on the desk. "Is your story about Madeleine? Or what happened at Quintain this morning?"

Joe shrugged and closed his notebook. He poked his pencil into his ear and wiggled it around. "I'm just getting the facts straight. A dead body in a big mansion—that kind of story always interests people. Rich folks misbehaving. Your aunt Madeleine, though. I remember her."

I perked up. "You were acquainted with her?"

"No, but she was always around the edges of big stories when I got started."

"Around the edges," I repeated. "What does that mean? What kinds of stories?"

"Just stuff about people, I guess. She knew a lot of bigwigs."

"Hmm."

"Like a lotta rich ladies, she gave money to museums and good causes. And campaigns. That's the fast track to rubbing the right elbows." Joe removed the pencil from his ear and studied the tip with a frown. "She went to a lot of big parties."

"That's all possible, I suppose."

"She had her fingers in a lot of pies."

I smiled. "I wouldn't know anything about her pies."

Joe put his pencil back into his pocket and looked me square in the eye at last. "I remember one old reporter saying he wouldn't be surprised if Madcap Maddy Blackbird got herself killed someday. Funny how a line like that sticks in your head. Now here she is, dead under suspicious circumstances."

I said, "What suspicious circumstances?"

Another shrug. "I thought maybe you'd know."

"There's nothing suspicious about it. She died in a volcano. A natural disaster. The Madeleine I knew was a respected lady— emphasis on *lady*. She enjoyed herself. Enjoyed her friends. And, last I heard, there's nothing wrong with giving money to causes you believe in. I can't imagine why anyone would spread something insulting about my aunt, who was a lovely, generous person."

"Well, thanks for the information, Nora." My testy outburst did the trick. He climbed arthritically to his feet and paused. "Just one more thing."

"Yes?"

He dropped a tear sheet on my desk. I flipped it over and looked down at a picture of myself in the arms of—as the headline so tastefully put it—THE GANGSTER OF LOVE. Michael and I were photographed running across my lawn and taking cover in the house. The accompanying article breathlessly announced Michael's release from prison and speculated about how he planned on taking over most of the illegal activities from Philadelphia all the way to Sicily. Once again, the *Intelligencer* demonstrated it was a journalistic class act.

I glanced up at Joe and saw his smirk. "I guess I should be thankful you didn't show his mug shot," I said.

"You have a statement about your boyfriend? Something we can print?"

I handed him the photo. "No thanks."

With a glare, I watched Joe shamble away. I thought about the kind of retorts I could make if I weren't a lady.

When he disappeared, I considered my delicate position. What was my obligation to my employer when my personal life crossed into the news? I wasn't sure. And there wasn't anyone in the newsroom I could ask. Once again, I longed for Lexie's opinion. She could help me with my dilemma.

Joe's insinuations about Aunt Madeleine really irritated me.

What suspicious circumstances?

On impulse, I picked up my phone and called the obituary department.

Annette Downey picked up, and we chatted for a moment about her cat, Cleo, who needed insulin shots, last I'd heard. Annette sounded a lot less stressed about her pet now that she'd learned how to inject the medication.

Then I cut to the chase. "Annette, can you tell me who wrote Madeleine Blackbird's obituary for the *Intelligencer*?"

"Sure," she said. "It was Mark. Except he didn't really write it, because all the information came in pretty much the way we used it."

"Where did it come from?" I asked. "Who sent it?"

"Let me check." I could hear her clicking her computer keys for a moment before her voice came back on the line. "Here it is. Yeah, it came by e-mail. From one of your relatives, I guess. Sutherland Blackbird."

"That's my cousin," I said, keeping my voice steady. "You mean the news of her death didn't come from Indonesia?"

"What do you mean? Sometimes we get bulletins from the wire services if a famous person died, but we don't get information from countries. A person has to send it to us."

"Hmm," I said. "I wonder if the other newspapers received the information from anyone else?"

"Says right here," Annette said. "I can see the same e-mail went to a bunch of papers, not just ours. From the same guy. Why do you ask?"

My thoughts had strayed in various directions, but I pulled myself together. "No special reason. Just curious. Thanks, Annette. And good luck with Cleo. Don't get scratched."

"Too late!" She laughed, and we hung up.

Sutherland had sent the obituary to the newspaper.

But how had he learned of Madeleine's death?

I would ask him as soon as I saw him again.

Out of habit, I checked my watch. Nearly five o'clock. No time to stew about Aunt Madeleine or crime lords. I had other problems. Fleetingly, I wondered if Michael was on his way to mass. Or using it for a ruse to go somewhere else.

The real reporters were putting on their coats to go home, so I rode the elevator down with them and thought about what it would be like to be stuck in one alone. On the street, I walked briskly a couple of blocks south to start my workday.

I shared the sidewalk with a bustle of pedestrians. Not long ago, I had lived just a short distance away, in a luxury condominium in Rittenhouse Square with my husband, Todd. A doctor who never practiced medicine, Todd had done research in organ transplants, while I tended mainly to our social life. That was before he became hooked on coke, and our hellish journey began. Those dark days seemed like a lifetime ago. Today I could almost enjoy a stroll through my old neighborhood. It finally felt as if the most painful memories of the past were easing. But Rittenhouse Square didn't feel like home anymore. Now I felt the tug of Blackbird Farm.

Within a few minutes, I pushed through the door of a new shop on Walnut Street.

A crowd of mostly young women dressed in autumn colors and expensive high-heeled boots fluttered around lovely displays of very pretty lingerie. Brassieres, panties, corsets, stockings of every color and description. The ceiling was crowded with pink Chinese umbrellas—an attractive decorative touch. For the grand opening, a caterer served tea in small china cups. Nobody took note of the array of scones beautifully arranged on a platter, however—too many calories, considering the scanty merchandise on display. And nobody talked to anybody else. Everybody had her nose pointed down at a cell phone screen. Most of them seemed to be reading text messages, but a few snapped photos of the merchandise with their phones.

I could have chatted with a few acquaintances—I had once socialized with many of the young married women who lived in the nearby posh condos—but everyone was focused on communicating with people by telephone instead. So I picked out a pair of panties made of delicate pink lace—just the thing to tempt someone later.

I met Lynnette Dankenbaugh, the shop's owner, at the register, where she was playing both clerk and hostess for the opening.

"Oh, Nora, thanks for coming! And you're so sweet to buy something. Maybe you'll start the trend. If everyone would stop using their cell phones, that is." Lynnette gave me two kisses before accepting my debit card. Her forehead looked suspiciously wrinkle-free for a woman just starting her own business. She wore her blond hair in a smooth ponytail, too, and—always a meticulous dresser— she sported a trim black pinafore over a polka-dotted blouse, leggings and a pair of pink Mary Jane shoes. She was going for the youthful *couturier* look.

Sometimes when I found myself with a couple of hours between social events, I slipped into the symphony's rehearsal hall to listen to the music or hiked over to the museum to take a docent tour. I had noticed Lynnette on a couple of the tours, and after a look at ancient Greek pottery she invited me to have coffee with her in the museum's café. I had learned that she'd found herself at loose ends when her wealthy husband encouraged her to quit working and focus on making their home beautiful. Home decorating had gotten old fast, and she started roaming the cultural scene in the afternoons, too. She had jumped at the chance to talk to someone about what we saw in the museum together, so we met every few weeks for coffee.

Her dissatisfaction with her home life had eventually led to a divorce. She spent a few months searching for a way to earn a decent living for herself and ended up choosing to open a lingerie shop. I had listened to her planning process for several months and hoped she could make a go of her new enterprise.

I signed the debit slip. "Everybody thinks the shop is gorgeous, Lynnette."

"I just hope they buy, buy, buy."

"Holiday season," I said as she handed me a decorative bag with my purchase tucked inside. "Husbands will soon be breaking down your door for gifts. And wait until Valentine's Day. You'll be swamped."

"I hope so." Lynnette managed a bright smile.

"Mind if I snap a few pictures? Just in case we have room on the *Intelligencer*'s Web site?"

Lynnette had been hoping for a little free advertising in the newspaper, I knew, but I couldn't justify making print space for a store opening. The online version of the newspaper always needed fresh content, though. Lynnette broadened her smile. "By all means! Everybody else is."

The newspaper rarely budgeted money for a photographer for me anymore, so I had to muddle through with photos I took myself. I posed Lynnette with some of her would-be customers and tried to crowd some of her wares into the pictures, too. Nothing too racy, though. I snapped a few shots with my phone camera and said good-bye.

After the shop opening, the weather was fair enough to keep walking, so I stowed my new lingerie in my handbag, buttoned up my Dior coat and hiked across town to a gallery on the Delaware, a stone's throw from some glamorous lofts where young hipsters lived.

Outside the gallery I spotted a familiar electric scooter—a sort of low-powered skateboard with a long handle. It had been fastened to a bike rack with a bicycle lock. With a smile, I pushed through the gallery door with the expectation of meeting an old friend.

"Nora!" Jamison Beech called to me from across the gallery and made his way through the crowd. Around his neck, he carried the camera that was never more than a few inches from his hand. "Don't you look charming this evening. Open up that coat and let me see."

I flashed open the Dior to show him my lace suit. "Well?"

"What a minx! You must be planning to get laid later."

"You're wicked."

"I really am, aren't I?"

He kissed my forehead. When he retired from PR work, Jamison had reinvented himself as a guerrilla photographer who snapped photos depicting street life in Philadelphia. Eventually one local paper made him a deal—a small fee for a city-themed photo collage that would appear weekly in the Sunday edition. The fee hadn't made a difference to him, but the weekly space had given him a forum at last. From that point, he branched out into taking pictures of just about anything that spoke to his creative aesthetic— from professional models and street kids with quirky clothes sense to shop windows with a point of view and graffiti scrawled on bridges. Now he was a local character—a well-known man-about-town with influence. People often recognized him on the street and asked him to take their pictures.

He made fashion statements himself, too. Tonight, Jamison wore a velvet smoking jacket over a black T-shirt and black jeans— very hip, very rock-and-roll, despite his age, and a long way from the business suits he wore for many years as a public relations agent. His white hair had been expertly fluffed, his gaunt frame honed to meet *Rolling Stone* magazine's expectations. On his feet he sported a pair of velvet slippers with a gold embroidered monogram on the toes. Those slippers gave him away as a Philadelphia aristocrat playing at the fashion game.

"Jamie, it's always good to see you." I gave him a hug. "What on earth are we doing here?"

"What do you think?" He threw his arms wide. "We're in a meat market!"

The visiting artist had created a whole installation of objects made from raw meat. Slabs of beef had been fashioned into lamps, vases of flowers, a desk arranged with a stapler, an electronic calculator and a sheaf of papers. Around his displays, he had thrown various knives and cleavers. I suppose it was intended to be avant-garde.

Jamison said, "You don't even need to look around. The smell will make you sick, and besides, I can give you the lowdown in a printable sentence or two. Instead, we must talk. I heard about your aunt Madeleine. Good God, do you think she murdered her house-keeper before she bolted?"

CHAPTER SIX

"News travels faster than ever, doesn't it?" I said grimly. "The smoke signals have been floating all over town. That, and Twitter. Oh, how the blue bloods love their tweets. Is it true? A dead body in Madeleine's elevator?"

"Yes, in the elevator at Quintain. We don't know who yet."

"What a delightful scandal! You must tell all."

It hadn't felt delightful when we discovered the body. The memory of it made me accept a restorative plastic cup of generic Chardonnay. I allowed Jamison to tuck me into a folding chair near the back of the gallery where we could have some privacy to chat.

"What an appalling art installation," I said when he sat down.

He said, "Meat is an important new medium, darling. Many up-and-coming artists are using it. If you ask me, they're all imitating Lady Gaga, but years too late. How dull is that? But don't say I told you so in the newspaper. I'm supposed to be hip enough to appreciate it."

He clinked plastic glassware with me and leaned close. "I knew Madeleine back in the day, you know."

"When was that?"

"Her heyday, you could say. She was the belle of the ball. Mad-cap Maddy always knew the most interesting people—gathered them together for wild parties. Plenty of beautiful women and powerful men. She was never one of those girls who needed to be the only good-looking woman in the room, either. She surrounded herself with beautiful people. Like me, she always thought having children would be a bore, so she had parties all the time. I remember a 'happening' at a club not far from here when she was just a slip of a thing. She took off all her clothes except for her go-go boots and let Andy Warhol paint on her tushie, and that was the beginning. I have the photo to prove it." He sighed for the bygone era.

"I remember her as beautiful, but not a party girl."

"Well, the tushie painting was just a one-time thing. Madeleine connected with everybody. And, like all you Blackbird girls, she took up with the wrong sort of man, which always makes for delicious scandal du jour."

Unable to disguise the chill in my voice, I said, "What man did she take up with?"

"Men, darling." If Jamison noticed my reaction to his opinion, he chose to ignore it. "She went around with one man after another—no drips, let me tell you. Social types, artists. You name it. I hear tell she even had a long-running affair with a very famous Cold War spy. Of course, nobody knew he was a spy until later. We should have guessed she'd wind up in a volcano. That's Maddy—going out with a bang."

Jamison suddenly got interested in a pair of passing art lovers who sipped wine and frowned contemplatively at the meat. The woman wore a street-smart combo of ragged chiffon under a leather jacket. Jamison studied her feet for a long moment—she teetered on sky-high ankle boots—then he lifted his camera and snapped a surreptitious photo.

"For your collage?" I asked. "What's your theme this week?"

"Boots," he said. "See the cut of her heel? Very fashion-forward. Biker-meets-Balanchine."

"And waterproof," I added. Jamison might have been the observant type when it came to fashion, but sometimes he missed the practical. To regain his attention, I said, "Jamie, did you know Pippi, too?"

"Pippi, the housekeeper?"

"Yes. Where did she fit into this story? Where did she come from?"

"Russia, I think. The Soviet Union then. Just after Reagan knocked on the Berlin Wall and supposedly started detente single-handed." He let go of his camera again and turned to me. "Pippi was the daughter of one of Madeleine's men friends—very hush-hush. I don't remember him. But after his wife died, he wanted his daughter here in the U.S., so Madeleine went and got her. She sailed over and back in her husband's yacht, the story went, and orchestrated some kind of dramatic rescue. Action-movie stuff."

I couldn't contain my surprise and set my wine down on a nearby chair. "Madeleine rescued Pippi?"

"Well, not like a puppy from the pound, but something like that. Madeleine always had mysterious people around. I never knew the whole story, but they each probably had a tall tale attached." Jamison picked up my glass and finished off the remaining wine. He crossed one leg over the other. "Who's going to inherit that crazy trip of a house?"

I caught a glimpse of knowingness in the back of his eyes. "My sisters and me. But you knew that. More gossip?"

"Yes," he admitted without a blush. "Why not her own stepson? The yacht gigolo?"

"I have no idea why Madeleine skipped Sutherland. The will came as a complete surprise to us."

"Madeleine was mercurial." He shook his head with admiration. "The Cold War spy? She ditched him when he took ill with cancer. Suddenly she had no time for him at all. She was easily capable of disowning her stepson for being useless."

"Or maybe," I said lightly, "she simply loved us more."

Jamison's gaze twinkled again. "What's not to love? I hope you enjoy the spoils, darling."

We chatted just a little longer after that, but I circled back to something he'd said about Madeleine. About her not having children. I said, "Did you make a conscious decision not to have a family, Jamison, or did it just happen that way?"

"Conscious decision, darling. And I never looked back. It's not like I don't have family, of course. I have two sisters and loads of pals, so I'm the fun uncle to their children. I've had my share of taking kiddies to the zoo, and it's not to be missed. But I have a very fulfilling life." He patted my hand. "You will, too. I have an instinct about these things."

I don't know whether his suggestion that I might be childless forever offended me most, or whether the hand pat felt patronizing, but I knew it was time to get back to my job.

For my column, I quickly asked Jamison for the facts and figures about the gallery show. He told me more about the meat-loving artist, then took me over and introduced me to a rather grubby, inarticulate young man who looked at my breasts, not my face. If he intended to make a meaningful statement with his meat, the concept hadn't quite reached his own brain. He invited me for a beer later. I declined.

When the artist wandered off, I noted to Jamison that the guests were mainly people I didn't know.

"Sad, isn't it? Our crowd," Jamison said, "comes around only when they want to learn something or to buy something. But you can't really hang meat over your pre-Revolutionary mantel, can you? Let's face it, Nora, families like yours and mine are a vanishing breed. It's the fast cash that counts now. Buy low, sell high—that's the prevailing attitude. Those of us who really love art and fashion and the good things in life, we're getting to be dinosaurs."

I checked my watch and realized I had allowed our talk to distract me from my schedule. I made my apologies, kissed Jamie good-bye and dashed outside. Running late, and with Reed dismissed until I was ready to go home, I had no choice but to grab a cab.

As the driver whisked me across town, I thought about Aunt Madeleine. To me, she had seemed a mysterious but prickly woman, but clearly I hadn't understood her at all. I found myself wondering why she had chosen to reward my sisters and me—relatives who barely knew her. She might have left her fortune to a ballet company or to another good cause. But no, she had excluded all philanthropic possibilities as well as her stepson . . . in favor of three nieces whose names she could hardly remember.

Puzzled, I stared at the passing scenery without really seeing it. What had caused her to make such a choice?

Upon arriving at a large city hotel, I ducked into the ladies' room to check my face. I touched up my lipstick and powdered my nose. Then I took off my Dior coat and unwound the black pashmina. I draped it over one shoulder and let it swing sari-like down one side of me. Suddenly my lace pants suit looked almost sedate— but a little exotic, too. Perfect. I left my large bag at the coat check and took out an evening clutch to hold my pen, notebook and camera phone.

Ready for action, I headed for the welcome table.

I showed my invitation to the cheerfully inept girls who were checking the guest list, and then I proceeded to the security station, where a woman in uniform wanded me for weapons. As I joined the line to get into the ballroom, I bumped into a familiar couple— Anahita and George Fareez. Anahita and I exchanged hugs while George looked on, smiling. He rarely spoke—whether out of shyness or a still-rudimentary grasp of English I couldn't tell—but his smile was always broad.

"Ana, those are killer shoes!"

"Nordstrom Rack," she confessed, displaying one silver-clad foot for my admiration. "Great, right? You look smashing, as always. Your granny's duds?"

"Yes, of course. Without her, I'd be dressed by H&M. Now, tell me quick before someone drags you off to take a glamour shot. Are you still on the board of the Mid-East Women's Association?"

She rolled her beautiful dark eyes at the mention of the organization that was throwing tonight's bash. "I used to be. But what a headache! I gladly gave up my MEWA seat to someone who has more time to put up with all the phone calls."

"What kind of phone calls?"

"Every time something awful happens to a Muslim woman, I'd get a call asking for a statement for the press. Sorry, Nora. I know you work for a newspaper and you're friends with reporters, and I mean no disrespect. But I just want to live my own life for a while, not feel like the spokesperson for every woman in a hijab."

"I understand. I was so pleased to be invited tonight," I said as we finally slipped into the ballroom. "I assumed I had you to thank for including me."

She shook her head. "Oh, heavens, it wasn't me. You're getting to be so well known, Nora. Of course you'd be invited to an event like this."

In the last year, I'd come to recognize my own rising star. Unlike regular reporters, who were often held at arm's length, I had a strange sort of insider access to the movers and shakers. I was welcomed into ballrooms and living rooms—perhaps because of my family name, but also because of the job I'd created for myself. All kinds of people and organizations wanted access to my column.

Still, this evening's event was a very big deal, and I had been a little surprised to be included. Honored, too.

Walking into the ballroom with the beautiful Anahita didn't hurt, either. Many heads turned our way. Anahita's husband, who had taken the Western name of George years ago when he first began teaching at a local university, looked very proud to be seen with his beautiful wife.

From circling waiters, we accepted glasses of fruit juice and nibbled on the vegetarian hors d'oeuvres. Anahita introduced me to several board members, all of whom spoke to me about the organization, which raised awareness for causes affecting women in Middle Eastern countries. Everyone was beautifully dressed. A few women wore headscarves, but not many. Most wore exotic jewelry and very high-end fashion. A string quartet provided Western music. No belly dancing, I noticed. It was a sophisticated, cross-cultural crowd.

After the reception hour, we split up to find our assigned tables and sat down to a sumptuous meal that featured savory lamb with fresh mint, rice pilaf with almonds and raisins—all delicious and beautifully styled on our plates. Conversation at my table ranged over many topics—none of them frivolous.

After dinner, a former secretary of state stood up, and she made a surprisingly detailed speech concerning current issues in the Middle East. After-dinner remarks were rarely so lofty, in my experience. My table companions nodded vigorously during her talk and afterward stood up to applaud.

The speaker waved from the podium, then took her place at the center of the receiving line.

Fortunately, the *Intelligencer* had sent a real photographer to take pictures at this event, so I made sure all the key players were snapped together. I was pleased to be introduced and shake the former secretary's hand.

"Oh, I knew your aunt!" She lit up when she heard my name. "Madeleine Blackbird, right? She was quite a character. And a great patriot. I'm very sorry for your loss."

"Thank you," I managed to say despite being in awe. I didn't usually get tongue-tied, but she had caught me by surprise. "So many people are affected by the volcano. I hear the relief funds are growing steadily."

"Yes, yes. Is someone in the family going to write a book about Madeleine? I know I'd read a page-turner like that. We should talk."

I had not a second to ask a follow-up question because someone from her staff eased me along to keep the line moving. But I was astonished.

Madeleine had known the secretary of state? Maybe the State Department was more of a party crowd than I had realized.

I reclaimed my coat and bag and slipped out a few minutes ahead of the rest of the still-animated crowd, who had remained behind for strong coffee and more talk. But I was anxious to get home.

Outside, I maneuvered through a group of Secret Service agents posted at the front of the hotel. The Philadelphia police were out in full force, too. I smiled at the officers and wended my way around the temporary barriers.

The night was chilly, but clear. The bustle of police and pedestrians made me feel safe, even on a block that sometimes was a little iffy late at night. At the next corner, though, a young woman stepped out from an empty doorway.

"Miss?" she said.

I paused, assuming I should know her.

But she wasn't familiar to me. Petite, with a dark face and black eyes that looked frightened from beneath a headscarf, she wore a heavy coat over long, loose trousers and cheap flat shoes.

"Miss, are you a reporter? Can you help me?"

I realized I still had my press credentials around my neck. "Do you need a cab?" I assumed she hadn't seen the line of vehicles parked alongside the hotel rather than in plain sight. I turned to point. "They're over—"

"No," she said. "It's my sister." She handed me a printed card with a woman's face on it. Half the text appeared to be in Arabic, the other half in English. Hastily, she said, "My sister is in Syria. Her husband won't let her come back to the United States to see our mother, who is ill. My sister was born here. So was I. But our parents encouraged us to marry men in our homeland. The Syrian government, though, won't help her come home. Can you help us?"

"I'm sorry," I said. "This isn't something I know anything about."

The disappointment on her face was painful to see.

"Look," I said, "maybe this isn't the right place for you to be tonight. The police are surely checking everyone for blocks, and if—"

"Yes, they have chased me away already. They threatened to arrest me. But I must try, you see. My sister—"

"Yes, of course," I said. "I have sisters, too."

Hope bloomed on her round features. "Then you understand what I must do! That I must make a great effort."

I felt a tug in my heart. "I wish I could help. But I have no idea what I could possibly accomplish."

"The power of the press," she said. "Maybe you could write something for us?"

"I'm not that kind of reporter." I was beginning to feel helpless. "I'm just the social page. But here. Take my card—"

From behind me, a male voice gave a shout, and the two of us turned to see a uniformed police officer marching toward us. He waved at the young woman and used an authoritative but almost fatherly voice. "Hey, didn't I say you should get out of here, young lady? Run along now. Stop making trouble and go home!"

I stood my ground. "I don't think she's making trouble."

He wasn't belligerent, and he pulled an exasperated face, not an angry one. "Don't you start with me, too, honey. We've got our hands full here tonight. Just go home, will you? Scat!"

"It's all right," my new friend said quietly. "Go. I don't want to get anyone else into a predicament."

"Here," I said, pressing my card into her hand. "Let's stay in touch."

She accepted it eagerly.

The cop chivvied me down the block, and I reluctantly obeyed. I turned to look over my shoulder and saw her walking in the opposite direction. As I tucked the young woman's printed card into my bag and went looking for Reed, I acknowledged that there were women who had worse problems than inheriting big houses from their eccentric relatives.

I spotted Reed, and before he could get out from behind the driver's seat, I opened the rear door of the SUV myself. I frowned at the backseat. It might as well have been Mount Kilimanjaro—insurmountable in my snug lace pants suit.

Reed abandoned the book he'd been reading and clambered out of the vehicle. He brought the milking stool to the rear passenger door. With a flourish, he plunked it onto the pavement. "There. Step up."

"This is ridiculous," I muttered, accepting his helping hand. "You couldn't have found another town car? What's the use of a vehicle if it takes a stepladder to get inside?"

"It's no ladder, it's just one little step."

I put my foot on the wobbly wooden stool and endeavored to get myself up onto the seat. But suddenly we heard the rip of fabric. I felt a cool breeze and blushed at the thought of what Reed must have seen as I struggled the rest of the way onto the slippery leather seat.

"Dammit, Reed! This suit is worth a fortune!" I felt like wailing at the damage done to such a nice outfit.

"You just ate too much dinner," he said, slamming the door on my further outrage.

By the time he got behind the wheel, I had gathered my dignity. "Drive around the block, will you, please? There's someone I'd like to find."

He obeyed, and we trolled several blocks without any luck. By streetlight, I checked the card to look for her name and found it. Zareen Aboudi. An e-mail address was listed below her name. At least I had a way of reaching her.

"Where to?" Reed asked when we gave up the search.

Lately, I'd been finishing off my work nights by stopping at a bar for drinks with friends—anything to avoid going back to my house alone. But tonight I fastened my seat belt and decided to forget about my ripped seam. I could have it repaired by a seamstress, after all. I had something good waiting for me back at Blackbird Farm.

With my spirits rising, I said, "Home, please."

I turned on my laptop in the backseat and wrote up a quick summary of my stop at Lynnette's lingerie store and the art gallery. The dinner took a longer time to write about, and I took care to do a good job. I could e-mail my column from home.

When we arrived at the farm, Reed lowered his window and spoke to the men who were still camped out at the entrance to my driveway. I could smell their coffee, but they didn't lean into the vehicle to speak to me. Reed rolled up his window and drove to the house.

At the end of the driveway by the barn, I tucked my laptop into my bag and shouldered it, then pulled the bottle of wine out from under the backseat and slid to the ground as if on a sliding board. I wrapped my pashmina around my waist to hide the damage to my pants and bade Reed good night.

The ponies had gone off to sleep in the barn, I noticed, but the pig remained vigilant at the fence.

"Go to bed, Ralphie," I told him.

He gave a forlorn grunt and stayed where he was, looking lonesome.

Letting myself in the back door, I found Emma eating a bowl of cereal in the kitchen while a gawky, very young man I didn't know knelt on the floor in front of her. I stopped short at the sight of him.

I was used to discovering Emma alone with attractive men, but this one had a thicket of brown hair and puppy eyes that made him look as if he was barely out of school.

Emma waved to me with her spoon. "Hey, Sis. How was your night?"

I stared at the young man, who blinked placidly back at me, unimpressed by my Pakradooni suit. I said, "Fine, thanks. What's going on?"

My little sister took another mouthful of cereal and spoke around it. "Mick's working in the library. Some of his guys brought a computer and a bunch of stuff, so he's got a regular office going on in there. He looks like a captain of industry, sitting in Granddad's chair."

"That's not what I mean. Who's this?"

"Oh. This is Duncan O'Keefe. He works at Thomasina Silk's barn. You know—she specializes in Hanover jumpers, but she's got a pair of ponies ready for the international show at the van Vincent place next week. I think she's going to do really well."

Duncan O'Keefe didn't look like a Hanover jumper to me. I shook his hand. "I'm Emma's sister Nora. How do you do?"

"Hello," he said without getting up.

"Wouldn't you be more comfortable in a chair?"

"I'm proposing," he said. "But Emma's not listening."

"I'm not," she agreed, and used her spoon to mash up her cereal.

Earnestly, Duncan explained, "She's having my baby. I want to marry her."

"Wait—you're pregnant with Duncan's baby? I thought—"

"He thinks it's his," she reported. "It's not."

"Just in case," Duncan said hastily, "I want to marry her."

I gave Duncan O'Keefe a more careful examination. He wore a respectable flannel shirt and heavy khaki pants—the kind suitable for horse work—and an expensive pair of boots in good condition. He had shaved recently. His dark eyes had long fluffy lashes. He looked about eighteen.

In other words, he wasn't the usual kind of low-down character I assumed Emma hung around with.

I said, "I don't suppose it would do any good for me to venture an opinion."

"It wouldn't," Emma said, crunching cereal.

"All righty, then. Good luck to you, Duncan." I grabbed two glasses and a corkscrew from the pantry and headed for the hallway.

"Hey, uh," Em said after me. "Take it easy on Mick, okay? He's having a rough night."

I paused in the doorway, my arms full. "Trouble in the underworld?"

"If I had to guess, I'd say he's having a little trouble adjusting to the real world."

We exchanged a glance, and I said, "Thanks."

Outside my grandfather's library I found the shattered pieces of a cell phone scattered on the floor. I put the wine and glassware on the stairs and picked up the bits of the phone. Someone had thrown the phone against the wall, and I could guess who.

I knew the signs. Todd had thrown things, smashed things. Many a night I had quietly swept up shattered china, afraid the noise might trigger another rage—or worse, a drug-fueled tantrum that ended with him slamming out of the house to score more coke. The memory cut me like a knife. Todd had evolved into a violent man. But Michael . . . he'd had a violent past. He'd told me as much, although I'd seen very few manifestations of it. Until now.

Steeling myself, I dropped the pieces into a cut-glass ashtray on the table. Then I eased into the oak-paneled room.

It hadn't changed much since my grandfather's day—bookshelves crowded with dusty volumes and leather chairs gathered close to a fireplace that often crackled warmly. But tonight the embers were dying, and Michael sat behind the desk, staring at a cell phone in his hand. Hardly the picture of frustrated fury. He looked more stunned than angry.

No Way to Kill a Lady

I leaned against the doorway for a long time, taking in the picture he made here and letting my heart steady at the sight of him engaged in his work. He had a stack of papers at his elbow, and his computer screen glowed. A bottle of beer had been forgotten on the desk. My painful memory of Todd's ugly behavior faded.

Lightly, I said, "Does the Department of Corrections have rules about what you do with your time while you're under house arrest?"

Michael snapped the phone shut and collected himself. "Hey, hi. Sorry. No, they don't. How was your night?"

"I met a secretary of state." I went over to the desk and gave him a nuzzle. "How was yours?"

"Okay."

"Emma said . . . Never mind. How about closing for business? Just for a few hours?"

"Sounds good," he said, but he didn't get up.

I leaned down to give him a kiss, but felt distraction in his half-hearted response. I drew back and met his eye. "What's going on?"

"Nothing." His gaze wandered back to his cell phone. A crease had appeared between his brows. "Sorry. I'm— I just— It's been a busy evening."

I wondered what he'd been doing in my absence. His laptop computer was spinning a screen saver. He'd been on the phone for a long time, I guessed. "Are you searching for your embezzler?"

Michael mustered a half smile. "I know where he is now—that's progress. And I'm buying and selling gasoline, trying to get the gas stations back on track."

"And the men in my driveway? What's that all about?"

"Yeah, sorry." Reluctantly, he admitted, "With my father and brother in jail for the time being, it seems like a good time for me to dismantle a few family rackets. Numbers, video gambling, that kind of thing. Nobody in the organization is happy about that."

Dismantling sounded like good news to me. But the presence of guards stationed outside our door was unsettling.

A year ago, I had seen a newspaper story that included a family tree—a chart of the hierarchy of the Abruzzo family with Michael's father—Big Frankie—at the top and perhaps thirty men arrayed at various levels beneath him. They had names like Petey Pop Pop and Road Kill, and instead of educational degrees listed after their names, the newspaper had included their indictments. Michael's name had floated out in the margin of the article. Now, I realized with an awful pang, with his father in jail, it would be Michael's name at the top of the chart.

Anxiety throbbed in my chest again. My voice came out softly. "Are we in danger?"

He put his hand on the small of my back to reassure me. "Not with the crew out there. They're my father's guys—old school, taking it seriously, going to the mattresses. More than we need, but I don't like discouraging enthusiasm. Don't worry."

"What will happen when you're finished . . . dismantling?"

"Everything will be great."

Chances were, he was already thinking far ahead, and I had to trust that he was being smarter than everyone else. But, still, I worried. Gently, I touched a stubborn cowlick of his hair that needed to be trimmed by a more expert barber. "Are you ready to take a break?"

"Yeah, in a minute. How was your night?"

He hadn't been listening the first time he asked, so I said again, "I met a former secretary of state. She gave a wonderful speech. I learned a lot, in fact. The people I sat with talked about the situation in Iran, and then I met a woman whose sister can't get out of Syria. I got to thinking on the way home, I wish there was a way to help her. Do you think that's a crazy thing to do?"

He blinked. "What?"

I felt another twinge of concern. I'd thought he'd be eager to carry me upstairs for a hot night together. But clearly his mind was far, far away. "Michael . . ."

He snapped back to the present again and apologized sincerely. "I'm sorry, sweetheart. Look, maybe we better have a talk."

My heart gave a real jerk of fear. There was definitely more to the family problems than he'd first let on. "What is it?"

He stood up and pulled me over to the leather sofa. "Let's sit down a minute."

"I don't want to sit down. Sitting down means bad news."

"Okay, so we'll stand. That phone call just now—she—" He stopped.

"Oh, God." My imagination was suddenly jammed with awful possibilities, and the room didn't have enough oxygen. "It's something terrible, isn't it?"

"There's this girl," Michael said. "She wrote me a letter a week ago, and when I got out today, she decided she wanted to see me. I'm still getting used to the whole idea, but—"

"Slow down," I said. "What are you talking about? A woman contacted you while you were in jail? You mean, a prison correspondence thing?"

"I—"

"Now there's a crazy person who's decided to be in love with you?"

"No, no, no. She's completely normal."

"Who is she?" I asked, panic rising. "A friend? An old lover?"

"She's my daughter," Michael said.

For a second, I couldn't comprehend. My whole brain froze while I absorbed the bombshell. I sat down hard on the sofa.

Michael stayed on his feet before me, but he ran one hand over his hair in bewilderment. "I didn't know she existed until last week. Yeah, that sounds lame and stupid, but she's the daughter of a girl I knew back in, like, high school. We went out a few times before I went to jail for stealing motorcycles. Then I got locked up, and I just—hell, I forgot about her. I never thought about what might have happened to her or if—"

"You have a daughter," I said.

"I know, it's crazy, right?" He looked as dazed as I felt.

"How old is she?"

"Nineteen. Get this. She's in the army."

"The army?" I knew I was sounding stupid, but the core of the matter was hard to accept.

"Yeah, serving her country, be all you can be, you know?" Michael began to pace aimlessly. "Her mom died a month ago, so she's home on leave for a while. Back from Afghanistan. Can you believe it?"

"Afghanistan."

"She drives convoy trucks. While she was home, she decided to figure out what happened to me. So she tracked me down. We talked on the phone earlier today, then again just now. She's a little emotional. Hell, I guess I am, too."

"Her mother is dead? Your old girlfriend?"

"She wasn't a girlfriend. Just somebody I knew."

"You must have cared about her."

"I was sixteen. What do sixteen-year-olds care about?"

"You slept with her!"

"We had sex in a car a couple of times, Nora. I hardly remember her." He stopped pacing and squinted into the murky distance of memory. "I think she used to wear an old fur coat to school. Drove the nuns crazy. Or maybe that was somebody else."

"Michael," I said, gathering my wits at last, "whatever you say to this girl on the phone, do not say her mother was meaningless to you."

"Right," he said. "Good thinking. Anything else?"

"Give me a minute," I said. "I'm trying to get my brain around the idea of you having a daughter."

"That makes two of us," he said, and we both contemplated for a moment.

"The other thing is," he went on, his voice heavy, "she's just figuring out who I am."

"You mean—?"

"Yeah. Not just some guy her mother knew."

"You're Big Frankie's son," I said.

Locating her father wasn't the big headline, I realized. Michael's daughter had also discovered her daddy belonged to a family of notorious mobsters. I could only imagine her reaction. A girl's fantasy probably ran to waking up and finding herself with a doting handsome prince for a dad or maybe a dashing tycoon who could grant her every wish. Instead of a dream come true, she'd found a crime family with a sordid history. No wonder Michael was doubly shaken.

His phone rang, and I jumped.

He pulled me to my feet. "It's probably her again. She hung up on me a few minutes ago," he said. "I better talk to her. Run some hot water into that bathtub of yours. I'll be up in a few minutes."

But he didn't come. I stripped off my black lace suit and hung it carefully in the closet. I took my bath and tried to read in the tub. But Michael didn't come upstairs. Alone in bed, I stared at the ceiling for a long time, thinking about Michael's idea of family and how a teenage daughter might fit into the picture.

CHAPTER SEVEN

I didn't know when he came upstairs, but I was aware that Michael tossed and turned most of the night—on his side of the bed. He finally fell deeply asleep about the time I woke for the day. To the sound of early-morning rain pattering against my leaky roof, I slipped out of bed and pulled on jeans and a warm sweater. As I dressed quietly, I tried not to look at the electronic monitor around Michael's ankle.

But I couldn't help watching him sleep for a moment. In the days before he went to jail, I had felt him withdrawing. He pulled everything inside himself—not just his emotions, but his opinions, his sense of humor, as many outward signs of his personality as he could tamp down. I could only guess what he'd been through while imprisoned—the people he associated with, the lack of privacy and free will.

Now he was home . . . and he'd been hit with a whammy. A daughter.

What was he feeling? The smashed cell phone, the man he'd punched in my kitchen—surely these were signs that there was much more turmoil going on in his head than he wanted me to know.

How was I to help him through this?

I slipped out of the bedroom and carefully closed the door behind me. I leaned my head against the door and let myself have a maudlin moment of self-pity. I'd always hoped Michael and I could start a family together. As a couple, we could have experienced all the miraculous steps along the way. But now that he already had a child with someone else—no matter who or how long ago—had another door been shut for me?

Downstairs, I found Emma in the same place as the night before—eating cereal in the kitchen. She was watching *Sesame Street* with the sound off. Judging by the condition of her boots, I guessed she'd already been out in the barn feeding ponies. Toby lay attentively at her feet.

"Whoa," she said, taking a look at my face. "Why aren't you upstairs taking advantage of the just-released prisoner?"

"Let's go to the grocery store," I snapped. "I need chocolate."

She heard my tone and dumped her bowl in the sink. "I gotta pee first."

As we blasted past Checkpoint Charlie at the end of the driveway, two of Michael's minions tipped their invisible hats. The other one spat on the gravel. Across the road sat a state trooper in an unmarked car. Keeping an eye out for escaping prisoners, I supposed. Nobody was going to get in or out of Blackbird Farm without being noticed.

In Emma's ancient pickup truck, speeding along the road to New Hope, I ate an apple for breakfast. Toby sat between us, panting happily, while I took out my frustration on the fruit.

Emma glanced uneasily at me a couple of times and finally started talking. "I've got nine kids coming for pony class on Saturday. It's a four-week introductory class for beginners."

"Um."

"The kids will be around for a couple of hours. I'll teach 'em how to saddle and mount and maybe trot around the paddock a few times. Nothing too strenuous. Mostly, I thought it would be a good way to get my name spread around among the parents, you know? So I can build up to more classes with more students in the spring."

"That's nice." I slumped in my seat, my mind far away.

"I mean, it could be a good living for me. Some of the other barns have quit teaching preteens because the kids are a pain in the butt, but that's where the real money is. So I thought I'd give it a shot. That is, if you don't mind me using the farm."

"Right," I said.

"And I talked to Shirley van Vincent, like you asked. She said Madeleine helped bring Pippi here from Moscow back in the day when that kinda stuff didn't happen much. I got to thinking, maybe Madeleine did the same thing for Shirley, too—before Shirley married up. I mean, Shirley's German accent? She's not the Main Line heiress you'd expect van Vincent would want on his arm, right? Shirley's a dirt-under-her-fingernails girl, if you ask me. So how'd she end up in this neck of the woods? It's a little puzzling."

"Okay."

"You know she's hosting the big coach-and-driving show next week. You've been invited to the opening shindig, right? It's going to be a big deal. Competitors from all over the world. Maybe there will be somebody we can ask."

"Uh-huh."

"Have you heard one word I've said?" Emma finally exploded. "What the hell's going on? You should be bouncing off the walls with joy to have the Love Machine home again, but you're acting like—like—I don't know what, but it's weird. What's happening?"

"A lot of stuff." I threw my apple core out the window. I told her about Michael's newfound daughter. To her credit, Emma didn't drive into a tree when she heard the news.

"Holy shit! I knew something big was going down. I assumed it was a big disturbance in the Abruzzo force. Does the kid know what kind of family she just walked into?"

"I think she figured it out fast. Thing is, Michael didn't come up to bed until I was asleep."

Emma nodded sympathetically. "Yeah, it would take something this big to put his light saber on the fritz. Too bad you missed out on the great first-night sex."

"It certainly wasn't the night I expected to spend with him." I took a deep breath and tried to calm down. "Don't get me wrong. Sure, there's nothing I want more than making love for hours after he's been gone so long. But I'm truly concerned about Michael. About his state of mind. He was a little off when he first got home, but now this complication has made things worse. And he's not talking. At least, not to me. Did he say anything to you last night?"

"Sorry. I was busy."

I shot her a look. "Oh, right. With your young gentleman caller. Should we be making wedding plans?"

"Nope." Emma rolled down her window as if she suddenly needed some air. Her short hair blew around her head in a *whoosh*. "Duncan's a nice kid. But I don't want to be tying his shoes and opening his juice boxes all my life, you know?"

I almost brought up Hart Jones at that moment. The father of Emma's baby had been a verboten subject these last few weeks.

But Emma said, "Forget about me. I'm feeling sorry for Mick."

"Me, too," I admitted, my spirits sinking lower. "I shouldn't expect him to be his normal self right away. He needs time to decompress, I guess."

"Yeah, the surprise daughter must be a kick in the gut. And jail can't be a picnic, even for him. He looks like he spent the whole time lifting weights. I mean—hubba hubba. But do you think he had to fight his way through a bunch of crazy convicts to be the top dog? Or is that haircut the worst of his punishment?"

"I don't know," I said. I searched for the right word to describe how Michael had acted last night, and I came up with one that surprised me. He had been . . . troubled. Which was so far out of character he might as well have been orbiting Mars.

"Give him some time to get over the prison stay," Emma said. "He's bound to be a little spooked for a while. He'll snap out of it."

I doubted he was going to snap out of sudden fatherhood, however. All at once, Michael had a lot of issues to handle.

We arrived at the New Hope Super Fresh market. Emma whipped her pickup into a parking space, and we left Toby in the truck with the windows rolled down a few inches.

Just inside the store entrance, there was a line of people waiting to buy lottery tickets, so we skirted around them through the newsstand department. I saw a stack of newspapers with Aunt Madeleine's photo on the front page. I grabbed a copy. The photo was forty years old and showed her at her most glamorous. An obituary—longer than the previously published terse announcement of her death—took up a long column.

"Slow news day." Emma peered over my shoulder.

Below Madeleine's picture was another photo—this one of Quintain's battlements looking pitiful. The accompanying article included a braying headline: BODY IN THE BELFRY!

"There's no belfry in that house," Emma said with scorn. "Don't newspapers have copy editors anymore?"

The caption under the photo said: "House of ill repute."

A photo of Michael and me—the one taken from the helicopter—appeared under the fold. The picture made it look as if he was abducting me. I tossed the newspaper into my shopping cart. We could read the articles at home.

Emma headed for the bathroom, and I set off rolling the cart down the first aisle to choose an assortment of healthy fruits and vegetables, then proceeded to the fish counter. Emma caught up with me as we passed the bakery, where I noticed a gawky young man loading a white box with doughnuts. He caught sight of Emma, and his head nearly swiveled off his shoulders as he watched her stride past. Another young admirer, I supposed.

After deciding to pass on fish, I headed for the olive oil section and spent several minutes choosing the varieties Michael preferred. He enjoyed cooking, so I made another circuit around the store to buy all his favorite ingredients. Now that he was home again, we'd have home-cooked meals instead of all the salads and prepared dinners I tended to consume if left to my own choices. Win-win for everyone.

I managed to steer Emma away from the sugared-cereal aisle, but we lingered in the chocolate department to make our selections with care. Eventually we headed for the checkout. There, I scanned our purchases and prayed my bank account could withstand such a hit.

The young man from the bakery had been waiting for us beside the self-checkout line. He had a freckled face and adorably prominent ears. In one hand he balanced the box of doughnuts. In the other, he held a single red rose, clearly purchased from the refrigerated cooler by the registers. He was even younger than Emma's visitor last night. His sweatshirt featured a local community college.

"Emma?" he said hesitantly.

My sister paused in the act of piling broccoli on the conveyor belt and finally noticed him. "Oh. Brian. How you doing?"

He blushed to the tips of his very large ears. "Emma, you're—I mean, I didn't know you were—I— You look beautiful."

"Yeah, well, I've been thinner," she cracked.

"No, I mean it. There's nothing more beautiful than a woman in your condition."

"Thanks, kid, but there are days when I'd be a hell of a lot happier if I could see my feet."

"I want you to know that I'll make things right. I'll marry you." He extended the rose to her. "We can be a family."

Emma eyed the rose as if it might have poisoned thorns. "That's a real nice offer, Brian. I appreciate it. But I can handle this on my own."

"I—I want to do the right thing," he insisted. "I'll give you anything you want—a home for you and—and our child. Everything."

Emma ignored the rose. Instead, she lifted the lid on the bakery box and picked out a doughnut with orange sprinkles. "This'll do just fine, Brian."

"But—"

"It's not your kid." She chomped into the doughnut. "But thanks just the same."

Disappointed, Brian took his rose and his doughnuts and disappeared.

"That was a very sweet offer," I said.

"Sure," agreed my little sister. "I never turn down a doughnut."

"Em—"

"Don't start," she said, her voice suddenly shaky.

She grabbed the bags and pushed past me, striding out to the truck so quickly I couldn't see her face. I followed, biting my tongue. She also needed time, I knew.

But for a woman in Emma's situation, time was running short.

In the front seat of the truck, Toby was barking and dashing from one window to the other. Normally, he was content to wait for us, but today he was frantic.

"Take it easy," Emma said to the dog through the glass, but he didn't heed her.

As we loaded the bags into the truck's bed, a white Crown Victoria suddenly pulled into an adjacent space. A roly-poly man with a balding head got out of the vehicle.

He marched over and said, "Nora Blackbird?"

I was surprised, but polite. "Yes?"

He stood several inches shorter than me. A cute fringe of white hair curled around the equator of his round head, but a not-so-cute bristle rambled down the back of his wrinkled neck. I guessed his age at eighty-plus. He flashed a badge at me, then dropped it quickly back into his pocket. "You're under arrest."

The next thing I knew, he snapped a handcuff down on my wrist and pushed me toward his car. Toby's barking went up an octave, and the dog threw himself against the passenger window.

"Hey!" Emma turned, her arms still full of grocery bags. "What the hell are you doing, Grandpa?"

"Hold on a second," I objected.

"Get in the car," he commanded, holding both my hands behind my back and fastening the handcuffs tight.

For as small as he was, he had all the right moves. I couldn't wriggle out of his control. I was also a little afraid to fight too hard. He was so old I feared I might hurt him.

In a heartbeat, he'd bent my head and shoved me into the backseat of his car. I sprawled across the seat, unable to catch my balance.

"Just a damn minute!" Emma came after us. "What the hell's going on?"

The old man slammed the door. I struggled to sit up, hearing the two of them yell at each other outside the car. In another moment, though, he got behind the wheel, started the engine and pulled out of the parking lot so fast I tumbled back against the seat. I caught a glimpse of my sister dashing around to the driver's side of her truck. She scrambled behind the wheel and tried to start her engine. But I could hear it grinding. Her truck wouldn't start. Then I lost sight of her.

My arresting officer spun his car onto the street and accelerated fast, putting a city block between us and the grocery store before I could manage to sit up. I looked around and suddenly wondered if maybe he wasn't a police officer at all. His car had an air freshener dangling from the rearview mirror—Yankee Candle, coconut bay fragrance. His keys were clipped to a key chain that featured a smiley shamrock over the Notre Dame logo.

A bumper sticker had been stuck to the dashboard. It read: MODEL TRAINS ARE AMERICA'S HOBBY!

"Just what is happening?" I asked. "I have a right to know what I'm being charged with."

"Button your lip, missy."

"I will not," I snapped. "Stop the car this instant."

"Pipe down," he ordered. "Or I'll charge you with resisting arrest."

"I haven't resisted in the slightest! It's you who's resisting telling me what this is all about."

"I'm an officer of the law. I don't have to tell you a thing."

If the whole situation hadn't been so annoying, I might have been amused. I felt as if I'd been kidnapped by one of Santa's elves. "See here. I know a thing or two. You have to read me my rights."

"What rights?"

He paused at a stop sign, which gave me a second to look around. I happened to see a real police cruiser across the intersection.

I screamed. "Help! I'm being kidnapped!"

Behind the wheel of the cruiser, I recognized Deputy Foley, the handsome officer who'd driven my sisters and me to Quintain. His crew cut and adorable pink ears made him unmistakable. When my abductor drove through the intersection, the deputy pulled out behind us. He hit the siren, which *whoop-whooped* twice.

"Goshdarnit," my kidnapper muttered. He pulled over to the curb and parked.

Deputy Foley appeared at the window a moment later. He leaned down. "Aw, Pee Wee, what the hell are you doing?"

The old man slumped down in the driver's seat. "I haven't done her any harm."

Foley peered into the backseat and blinked. "I know you. You're one of those crazy Blackbird sisters."

"I'm not crazy," I said. "I'm being kidnapped."

"Your sister is crazy," he replied. "She telephoned me last night. I could hardly get rid of her. Pee Wee, you can't go around grabbing women off the street. You know that."

"I didn't grab her."

"You did, too!" I cried. "He handcuffed me." I tried to twist around to show the deputy my situation.

Foley groaned. "Aw, for crying out loud."

He opened the door and helped me out. "Hand over the key, Pee Wee."

Reluctantly, the old man produced a small key, and Foley unlocked my handcuffs. "There," he said. "No harm done."

"No harm done?" I spun around, almost sputtering with rage. "You're going to let him go?"

"He's harmless," Foley assured me. "He retired from the force a long time ago. Look, miss, driving around his old patrol route is good for him. And he keeps an eye on things for us. With all our budget cuts lately, we can use his kind of help."

"He wasn't helping anybody today." I rubbed my wrists. "He grabbed me out of the Super Fresh parking lot!"

The radio on the deputy's shoulder crackled. He reached to touch a button on the device and listened to a squawky voice for a second. When the squawking ceased, he said to me, "Look, Miss Blackbird, I've got things to do. Pee Wee probably thought you were up to something, so he put you in his car to calm you down—"

"I was completely calm! Until he arrested me!"

"He'll take you right back to the Super Fresh, I promise. Won't you, Pee Wee?" Foley leaned down to glare into the car again. Pee Wee looked down at his lap, lower lip protruding in a pout.

Firmly, I said, "I'm not getting back into that man's car."

"He'll let you ride in the front seat," Foley promised. "C'mon,

I've got another call. You'll be fine, Miss Blackbird. If you can handle being around that sister of yours, this guy is a piece of cake. I gotta go. Pee Wee, you apologize to this nice lady, okay?"

Foley jogged back to his cruiser and waved good-bye.

If it hadn't started to rain, I'd have walked back to the grocery store. But a few cold drops hit the pavement around me, blown on a gust of wind. In a minute my hair was going to get wet. So I stormed around the front of the old man's car and got into the passenger seat. I slammed the door.

"Are you going to apologize?" I demanded.

"Sorry," he mumbled, head down.

"What do you want with me in the first place? Or do you just go around grabbing whoever strikes your perverted fancy?"

"I'm no pervert!" He flushed. "I had personal business with you."

"What kind of personal business? Just who are you, anyway? Surely your name isn't really Pee Wee."

"Peter McBean," he said. "Retired New Hope PD."

I had a soft spot for retirees, and I felt my anger start to deflate. "How long have you been retired?"

"Twenty-two years," he reluctantly replied.

I gave Pee Wee McBean a more careful perusal. If he was telling the truth, he'd been a police officer back in the day when departments didn't have height requirements.

"What's your personal business with me?"

He sulked for a while longer. Then, still glaring out the rain-spattered windshield, he finally sighed. "It's about Madeleine Blackbird."

That caught me off guard, and I couldn't hide my surprise. "Aunt Madeleine? What about her?"

"She died, didn't she?" he asked gruffly.

"Yes, in Indonesia."

"The newspaper said she died in a volcano."

"That's what we understand, yes."

"Is that for real?"

"I have no reason to doubt it. The volcano erupted last week, but we only learned about Madeleine recently. May I ask how you knew her?"

"My wife," Pee Wee said suddenly. "My wife worked for Madeleine Blackbird. She traveled with her."

Suddenly I realized Pee Wee McBean was struggling with his composure. His belligerent tone had turned hoarse, and his face was dark. His bushy eyebrows were drawn into a glower, but there was a distinct quiver in his chin.

I almost reached out to touch him. "I'm so sorry," I said. "You haven't heard from your wife since the catastrophe?"

"My wife was Madeleine's maid, her driver, her companion—her everything! I have a right to know if—"

"Hold on a minute. Your wife is Pippi?" I was astounded. "She was married to . . . you?"

"Dang right. Why should that be such a big surprise?"

"I can't . . . I never realized—good heavens." I was flabbergasted by this development. "I had no idea Pippi was married."

"We got married when she first came to town," he said gruffly. "We met right there at the supermarket. She told me there was some mix-up, and she needed a green card, and I—well, I thought she was real nice. We didn't get to spend much time together, though. She mostly lived up at that castle with the Blackbird lady. I don't care what anybody has to say, she was a respectable woman. We planned on spending our retirement years riding around in my RV. But then she ran off, and I never heard from her again."

I was amazed to learn Pippi had been married.

"What do you mean, respectable?" I asked.

"Just what I said. There was never any funny business with her."

I tried to process that information. I didn't want to be the one to tell the poor man it was likely his wife hadn't run off to Fiji, but had died in Madeleine's elevator.

My concerns about being kind didn't matter much, though.

The next words out of his mouth were: "What I want to know is, did the Blackbird lady leave anything to my wife?"

"I beg your pardon?"

"In her will. Am I going to inherit something from the Blackbird lady now that she's gone? I mean, my wife put in a lot of years for that family. They owed her something, right?"

At last, I realized his morning mission to grab me hadn't been generated out of grief for a beloved wife, but rather greed.

"I don't know. We haven't seen the entire will yet. It only just . . . Look," I said as gently as I could manage, "how about if I contact you as soon as we learn the specifics?"

He squinted at me. "How can I trust you?"

"You have my word." I cleared my throat. "See here, you can't go around impersonating a police officer whenever you feel like it. You could have telephoned me like a civilized person, and I'd have told you anything you want to know."

"I doubt it," he snarled. "What's in it for you?"

Making such a repulsive person understand that I wasn't in the habit of cheating people was starting to feel like an impossible mission. So I ended up saying very firmly, "You'll just have to trust me, Mr. McBean. In the meantime, I think it's best if you take me back to my sister. Immediately, if you please."

For a moment, I thought Pee Wee had more to say. He worked his jaw, then suddenly started the car, flipped on the windshield wipers and drove back to the grocery store. With the panache of a former officer of the law, he whipped into the parking space beside Emma's truck.

She was outside, oblivious to the rain, pacing the asphalt and yelling into her cell phone. When she saw me in the passenger seat of the old car, she terminated the call and shoved her phone into her jeans. Then she yanked open the driver's-side door and grabbed Pee Wee by his lapels.

"Get out of the car, you little weasel. I've already called the cops. They're going to arrest your ass any minute."

"Calm down, Em." I bailed out of the cruiser. "We've already spoken with Deputy Foley."

Her fists remained knotted in McBean's jacket. She seemed happy to have a target for her pent-up anger. "Oh, yeah? What did he have to say?"

"Well, I don't think he's going to be phoning Libby for a date anytime soon. And he asked me to take pity on Mr. McBean."

Pee Wee snarled, "I don't need your pity!"

"McBean?" Emma repeated with a taunt in her voice.

"Pee Wee McBean."

"Hell." She released his lapels. "I can't be mad at a guy with a name like that. He's suffered enough already."

I got out of the car. "Let's just go," I said to my sister.

"I can't. My damn truck won't start. Wait—Pee Wee, do you have something to do with my truck not starting?"

He reached into his pocket and pulled out a distributor cap. Silently, he handed it over to Emma.

"I should have known," she muttered. She opened the hood and replaced the vital part.

I leaned down to look at Pee Wee. "Look, I think the police are going to come to talk to you soon. To—well, as they investigate Madeleine's death, they're going to learn more about Pippi. If you'd like to talk with me after you've seen them, you should come to my house. Ring the doorbell like a civilized person. I live at Blackbird Farm. Do you know where that is?"

"Wasn't that place condemned a few years back?"

With that nasty parting shot, he put his car in gear and pulled out of the parking lot, leaving me fuming in the drizzle.

Emma said, "What the hell was that all about?"

"Let's just say that more than ever, I need the chocolate we just bought. You okay?"

"Of course I'm okay." She had her gruff face back in place. "Let's go back to the farm before somebody else proposes to me. Mick's probably awake by now. Maybe he'll make breakfast."

CHAPTER EIGHT

On the way home, I read the newspaper aloud to Emma, and we learned another bombshell. Libby must have read the same story, because her minivan was turning into Blackbird Farm just ahead of us. She blew past Michael's security checkpoint, and we did, too.

Michael was out in the backyard, dressed and drinking coffee while his posse of criminal misfits stood around him in a semicircle—perhaps receiving their orders for the day. I recognized most of them—a couple of hulking biker types with tattoos and shaved heads, a squirrelly little guy in grease-stained overalls, and another burly man in a tracksuit and parka big enough to conceal any number of weapons, perhaps even a bazooka. Bruno stood aside, arms folded over his chest. Today, he wore a pin-striped suit with a pink tie. Very natty. He ignored my sisters and me.

Ralphie the pig, I noticed, had escaped the pasture fence and stood at Michael's heel, keenly observing the action. He blended right in with the rest of the motley crew.

In the middle of the semicircle hunched a skinny man I didn't recognize. He was shivering, with his hands shoved into the pockets of his khaki pants. In a button-down shirt and Hush Puppies, he appeared to be wearing the uniform of salesmen and casual-Friday office workers—hardly the sort of person Michael usually hung out with. Except that his shirt had come untucked and was ripped down the front, and he appeared to have fallen face-first in mud. Plus his face was streaked with tears. He wiped his nose with the back of his hand.

Michael seemed unperturbed by this newcomer's emotional state. He lifted his coffee cup to me in a cheerful greeting. He didn't look as if he'd just shoved a man's face into a puddle to extract mob secrets, so I calmed down.

Libby bailed out of her minivan. "Oh, my God," she said. "Nora, why is That Man of Yours here? Did he escape from prison? Should you call the police?"

"The jail was overcrowded," I said, "so they sent him home with an ankle monitor. He's under house arrest."

"You mean he can't leave the house? Then why is he outside?"

"He can't leave the property," I explained. "Where's Maximus?" Although Libby was a good mother and her children adored her with admirable devotion and loyalty in spite of her weaknesses as a sensible adult, I sometimes feared she might get carried away and leave her son in her wake. Today she looked flushed—in high gear.

"Max is with my sitter. She's doing calisthenics with him." Libby gave Michael a long examination. "That Man of Yours looks very . . . physically fit."

Emma said, "Is that drool on your chin?"

"What are they doing?" Libby frowned at the meeting of the minds being conducted in my driveway.

"My bet is," Emma said, "they're discussing possible penalties for embezzlement."

I made a good effort to seem spritely. "Let's go inside, shall we?"

This morning Libby was wearing a seasonal orange velour

tracksuit with the jacket unzipped just enough to reveal a low-cut T-shirt underneath. In sequins, the shirt read CARPE DAME. She carried a newspaper in her hand, but she continued to gawk at Michael and his crew of thugs.

"Come on." I took Libby by the arm. "We'll watch Emma eat."

Casting curious glances over her shoulder, Libby hustled down the flagstones to the back porch. "I have an appointment later, and I want to get there early for the free erotic aromatherapy session. But I wanted to show you the newspaper. Have you seen this appalling story?"

"I was just reading it aloud to Emma in the truck."

On the drive home from the grocery store, I had started the newspaper article about the discovery of the body at Quintain. The lurid prose made the whole family sound like escapees from a P. G. Wodehouse novel, but the insinuations about Madeleine made me see red.

The back doorknob came off in Emma's hand. She passed it to me and shoved the door open with her shoulder. "Nora saw your Deputy Foley this morning."

Libby forgot about appalling newspaper stories and brightened. "You did? Did he mention my name?"

Emma said, "He didn't have a chance during the five minutes he spent rescuing Nora from being kidnapped."

Outraged, Libby cried, "Why can't I ever get kidnapped?"

"Next time it happens to me," I said, "I'll call you."

Without missing a beat, I handed the groceries to Libby and grabbed the screwdriver off the windowsill. I reattached the doorknob. I'd gotten pretty good at it lately.

"I didn't mean to sound insensitive." Libby wilted under my steely glare. "Tell me what happened."

To the sounds of his posse departing in their vehicles, Michael came inside—he pushed Ralphie back out the door when the pig tried to follow—just as I began my story about being snatched off the street by Pee Wee McBean. Libby lost interest as soon as she figured out Deputy Foley hadn't played a vital role in the morning's events, but Michael's face grew increasingly stony as I told the tale.

"Who the hell is this maniac?" he demanded.

I gave him a kiss on the cheek. "Good morning. He's not a maniac. He's a retired police officer. Really retired—as in he looks ninety years old. His name is Pee Wee McBean."

Emma added, "He's the size of a hobbit."

"McBean?" Michael pulled out his phone again. "Let me do some checking."

He went back outside, and Libby sighed. "Nothing exciting ever happens to me. You get kidnapped. And Aunt Madeleine turns out to have had a secret life nobody knew about. Is there any pastry? I could go for a cheese Danish."

"Nora's turning into the vitamin Nazi," Emma said. "She only bought healthy stuff."

"Have a banana," I suggested, and began putting away the groceries. "Aunt Madeleine didn't have a secret life. The reporter I talked to yesterday was trying to dig up some dirt on her. When he didn't find any, he obviously fabricated this whole awful story."

"Awful, indeed!" Libby poured herself a cup of coffee and went searching in my refrigerator for cream. She launched into exclamations about the morning's revelation in the newspaper. "I can't believe it. Who knew all those houseguests of hers were sex workers she smuggled into the country?"

"Oh, for heaven's sake, Libby, you can't believe everything you read in the paper! There was one sex worker!" I cried. "Just one woman came forward with that story. It doesn't mean Aunt Madeleine was some kind of . . . of . . . trafficker."

I should have guessed something was in the wind when Joe, the *Intelligencer* reporter, questioned me. But I never guessed he was building a story that portrayed Madeleine as a criminal who brought women into the country to hook them up with powerful men.

"All those women upstairs at Quintain," Emma said.

"They were her *friends*," I insisted. "Not prostitutes."

"Just wait," Libby predicted. "By the evening news, there will be dozens more hookers crawling out of the woodwork with their stories. Our name is mud. We'll never be able to hold our heads up in polite society."

"We haven't been able to do that since Mama and Daddy stole money from their friends," Emma said.

"This is different! It's sordid!" Libby sat down at the table with her coffee cup and pointed at the newspaper. "This woman says Madeleine helped her get into the United States from Cuba, and she went to work as a hooker in Baltimore. She even names the streets where she worked!"

"It does sound pretty bad." Emma put her finger on the list of acquaintances quoted in the story. "Everybody who ever attended a party with her suddenly thinks she was setting up assignations the whole time."

"Well, she wasn't," I said.

"Still," Emma said, edging toward the powder room, "it's a wonder nobody's called us about the story. Why aren't reporters beating at the door?"

"They probably can't get past Michael's checkpoint."

At that moment my phone rang. I groaned.

Emma crossed her legs and grabbed the receiver off the wall. "Hello? No, she can't come to the phone right now." After a pause, she said, "No, Miss Blackbird doesn't want to make any statement for your viewers. And if you bring a big-ass TV truck onto her property, she'll call the police."

Emma hung up with a grin. "That wasn't too hard."

Then her cell phone rang as she headed for the powder room.

"You see?" Libby said to me while we heard Emma curtly discouraging another reporter. "This is going to be a terrible ordeal. Sometimes I'm glad my children don't carry the Blackbird name. Can you imagine the school taunting? Nora, did you have any idea about this?"

"I spoke with Jamison Beech last night, and he hinted that Madeleine had a more colorful past than we thought."

"Jamison Beech! Did he take your picture for his collage? It's the first thing I flip to in the Sunday newspaper." Libby's eyes got round with horror. "What did he say about Madeleine? Was she doing something worse than trafficking? Heavens, she didn't peddle drugs, did she? Oh, my God, what if she was selling weapons to some horrible international cartel?"

Michael came inside again with the doorknob in his hand. He gave it to me. "What international cartel?"

"A figment of Libby's imagination," I said, reaching for my trusty screwdriver. I made short work of the repair while Michael restrained Ralphie from pushing past me. I said, "What did you learn?"

"Word is, McBean was a dirty cop."

"How did you find that out so fast?" I sat back on my heels, feeling increasingly as if I was losing control of my household. "Do you have a source in the police department? Or have you planted a listening device in city hall?"

"I Googled him," he reported, holding up his phone. "Jeez, Nora. Sounds like McBean was the usual kind of corrupt cop—blow jobs in the cruiser from underage teenage girls who'd do anything to keep their parents from finding out they'd been caught drinking. He busted country club poker games and took bribes to forget about what he saw. And he beat up frat boys on a regular basis—that kind of thing. We need to make sure he stays away from you."

Emma returned, adjusting her jeans. "Being harassed by Pee Wee now is sorta like being chased by a Chihuahua. He can make a lot of noise, but he's not gonna do much damage."

"Still," Michael said, "I don't like Nora getting grabbed out of a supermarket parking lot."

"It was a little embarrassing," I admitted as I closed the door and tested the knob. "I've taken self-defense classes. I should have had him flat on the pavement in ten seconds. But I was afraid to hurt him."

"You're too polite to use your skills," Emma said, pouring cereal into a bowl and reaching for a banana. "That's a handicap."

Libby sighed. "I took a self-defense class once. The instructor wore a musky sort of cologne that drove me wild."

To avoid hearing more about the effects of musky colognes, Michael said to me, "I saw the morning news on TV. Looks like your aunt had an interesting past."

I filled him in with details from the newspaper story while I replaced the screwdriver. "I hate hearing this kind of thing about her. She wasn't a madam. I'm sure of it. But I suppose we'll have to prove it or everyone will believe the newspapers."

"What does that mean?" Michael asked. "You want to restore her reputation?"

"Anything wrong with that?"

"There is if you put yourself in danger."

"Pee Wee McBean is not dangerous. Mercenary, maybe, but not dangerous."

"Mercenary?"

I said, "Here's the other big thing I learned today. Turns out Pippi the housekeeper was married. To Pee Wee McBean."

Michael whistled low. "Did you tell him she's probably dead in an elevator?"

"I didn't have the heart. But right away, he asked me if there was something in Madeleine's will that he could claim. Which, I must admit, made me dislike him. But I felt sorry for him, too."

"You feel sorry for the asshole who kidnapped you?"

"A little, yes."

"Well, start feeling sorry for yourself. The state police were here earlier. They want to question you about what you saw at the crime scene."

My heart took a dive. "Should I call them?"

He shook his head. "They're delighted to have an excuse to pay a return visit."

"I'm sorry, Michael. This just makes your situation more complicated."

He reached for the coffeepot and said cheerfully, "Complicated is better than incarcerated."

The house phone rang again, but Emma had just shoveled half a banana into her mouth, so I picked up the telephone, prepared to fend off an attack by another reporter. "Hello, dammit."

"Nora? It's Sutherland."

My cousin's voice sounded smooth and seductive in my ear.

With everybody watching me, I decided to carry the phone into the dining room. I didn't speak until I was alone and my rapid heartbeat had steadied.

"Hello," I said, keeping my tone friendly but cool. "How long were you stuck at Quintain yesterday?"

"Hours and hours. I thought I'd go mad with boredom. It's too bad you left so suddenly. I could have used some good company. The police in other countries work at a much more efficient pace. Honestly, I almost asked if I could take a nap while they went over that damn elevator with their toothbrushes."

"How much contact do you have with police in other countries?"

He laughed lightly. "That was just a figure of speech. Groatley turned into a bear, growling at everybody, so he was hardly good company. Did you know he parks in a handicapped space every day he goes to the office? One of his assistants told me that. And he keeps two mistresses in separate condos. One of them is practically a teenager. Which is good, because she doesn't demand expensive jewelry—only fancy cell phones, which are much less expensive."

Thinking of Emma's interlude with Groatley at Quintain, I said, "He's certainly a prince."

More gravely, Sutherland said, "I see Madeleine hit the newspapers today."

"It's a very ugly story," I said.

"It does make her look rather tawdry. I thought we might knock heads about this business before all our names are dragged into the sewer. Are you free for dinner tonight, Nora? We could talk about how to present a united family front during this crisis."

"As a matter of fact, there are a few things I'd like to discuss with you, too, Sutherland."

"First," he said, "I should tell you the latest development. Are you sitting down?"

I didn't want to hear any more bombshells, but I braced myself.

He said, "There's no way to say this gently, so I'll just put it on the table. I think the body in the elevator was Madeleine."

"Madeleine! What?"

"Remember her rings? After you left, the police found them with the bones."

"But . . . that's impossible. She must have given the rings to someone else." Even as I said the words, I doubted them. Madeleine would never have parted with her diamond rings. I felt my legs crumple beneath me, and I sank onto a chair. I put a shaking hand to my forehead, as if I could stop my brain from imploding. "How on earth—?"

"I can't explain it. Not now on the phone." His voice took on some urgency. "I think we should have dinner together. We can talk about Madeleine." In a different tone he added, "And maybe we should discuss what's to become of Quintain."

I was shocked, but not so much that my bullshit detector was completely destroyed. "Sutherland, I can't help noticing that all our trouble began when you arrived in this country."

"I can explain everything, I promise. Dinner? Shall I pick you up?"

"I have to work this evening," I said. "But I can squeeze in a drink around seven if you can meet me in the city."

"Come to my boat instead. I'm in the harbor, under a very large bridge."

"You're staying on a boat?" Of all the sinful extravagances in the world, I did love a yacht above everything else. Before I could check myself, I asked, "A nice one?"

"Magnificent. Come at seven. I'll chill a bottle of wine."

Sutherland gave me directions, and I told him I'd be prompt. We said good-bye.

I turned off the phone and sat alone in the dining room for a moment, reeling.

For one thing, why had Sutherland sent Madeleine's obituary to the newspapers if he hadn't learned she was dead in Fiji? I began to think Madeleine had a very good reason for cutting Sutherland out of her will. Because she didn't like him? Or didn't trust him?

And if Pippi wasn't dead in the elevator, where was she now?

From behind me Michael said, "More bad news?"

I spun around. "Is it that obvious?"

"You look half sick."

I took his hand and pulled him into the entry hall. We sat on the staircase, out of earshot of my sisters. There, I told him that Sutherland thought Madeleine was the dead body in the elevator, but that he'd been the one who earlier told the newspapers she'd died in the volcano.

"What's his scam?" Michael asked.

"To be honest, I never thought Sutherland had enough brains to concoct a scam. He always seemed more interested in how he looked than anything else."

"He's got some explaining to do. You're determined to see him tonight, aren't you? Take Bruno with you. You'll get your answers faster."

I gave him a shaky smile. "Sutherland might die of fright if he saw Bruno coming at him."

"Would that be a bad thing?"

I closed my eyes and leaned back against the staircase. One of the spindles in the hand railing fell out and landed in my lap. I shoved it back where it belonged. Michael straightened it, and we both steadied it in place, holding our breath that it would stay put. Then his hand turned gentle on mine.

I looked up at him and knew it was time for a serious talk. "I'm getting uncomfortable, Michael. Who was that gentleman weeping in my driveway?"

He pulled his hand from mine. "My embezzler. The guys found him for me and brought him here without asking. Sorry."

"Where are the . . . um . . . guys taking him now? He's not going to sleep with the fishes, is he?"

I was almost joking, and Michael knew it. He smiled wryly. "It didn't hurt that he thought he might get wet."

"Michael . . ."

"I know I shouldn't bring this stuff into your house, especially now with everything else you're coping with. I'm sorry. But I'm between a rock and a hard place. I have to settle business personally, at least at first. And I can't let somebody steal from me and just roll over, either. If I let that happen, everybody's going to try to bull-doze me, and that's just . . . embarrassing."

"So what are you doing to your embezzler?"

"He's going to disappear for a while. No, don't panic. We asked him some questions, and he spilled a little, but then he clammed up. Sometimes interrogation goes better if you just let his imagination run wild for a while. I'll send him off to a safe house to sweat more information out of him."

"And to allow your enemies to think he's dead? Oh, Michael—"

"Take it easy. Can I help it if my enemies—that's your word, not mine—can I help it if they think the worst? He'll be fine. In a few hours, he'll be up to his ears in pizza and all the ESPN he can take."

"Meanwhile, the rest of the underworld is supposed to think you've killed him."

"Can I help it if they have good imaginations?"

I didn't like the situation, but I couldn't offer any alternatives. It all made me uneasy—as if we were starting down a slippery slope. But I had to trust that Michael knew what he was doing.

"And your other problem? Your daughter?"

He sighed, and I could see embezzlement hadn't been on the front burner of his mind. We were all trying to cope with too many things. He said, "That's a different animal altogether."

"You talked to her again? What's her name, by the way?"

"Carrie. Yeah, we talked again last night. For a long time. I think she was hoping I'd be a TV dad who smokes a pipe and would give her an allowance. I was honest with her—as much as I could be on a telephone that might be tapped. She's disappointed I'm not what she expected. A little mad, too, I guess. There was a lot of silence on the phone. We're both—I dunno. This is going to take some time."

I slipped my arms around him. "I wish I could help."

"I wish you could, too." He rested his chin on top of my head. "But you've got your own troubles."

"Yes. I'm going to see Sutherland tonight. I have to find out what really happened to Madeleine, and he obviously knows. I can't stand the idea of her reputation being ruined."

"You going alone?" Michael asked dangerously.

"I don't need one of your wise guys tagging along." Perhaps my voice was cooler than I intended. I pulled out of his embrace. "Sorry," I said. "I must be more shaken up than I thought. What a mess. I'm sorry I've been so distracted just when you've come home."

"You're not the only one who's distracted." He ran his thumb under the neckline of my sweater and touched bare skin. "I'm sorry about last night, Nora. Believe me, it wasn't the way I wanted our first night to go."

I smiled a little, feeling my skin turn warm beneath his gentle caress. "Me neither. I bought new underwear."

His gaze sharpened. "Oh, yeah? Can I see it now?"

I touched his face. "Later. When we have enough time for you to appreciate it properly."

He eased closer for a kiss. "I don't think there's going to be anything proper going on."

CHAPTER NINE

Before the kiss got good and steamy, we heard raised voices from the kitchen.

"He's not even walking yet!" Emma said. "He couldn't kick a football now if you put it in his lap! As usual, you're being an idiot!"

Michael and I reached the kitchen in time to see Libby spread a colorful brochure on the table. It pictured young children playing various sports and looking as cheerful as the Hitler Youth.

"If you plan to keep your baby, Emma, you could share your child-rearing opinions as much as you like. But we all know you're not the motherly type, so kindly keep your rude suggestions to yourself."

Emma made the rudest of suggestions.

Libby swelled with offense. "You don't know a single thing about children! Have you even started taking Lamaze classes yet?"

"I'll wing it," Emma said tartly. "If you can do it, I should be able to muddle through."

"Hey," I said, trying to restore peace. "There's no need to start insulting each—"

"Who's going to be your partner?" Libby inquired. "A stranger off the street, like all of your other paramours? Or the baby's actual father?"

"Leave him out of it," Emma snapped.

Michael and I exchanged uneasy glances.

Libby said, "Surely you've been in touch with him lately. Shared the usual milestones with him? Has he seen the sonogram films?"

Emma's face settled into sullen lines. "No."

"Did he go with you to hear the baby's heartbeat?"

"Is this any of your business?"

"I'm just wondering, Emma, what you're thinking. Having a baby is not like buying a few wild ponies and keeping them in Nora's pasture for her to look after. Have you decided to keep this child? You, of all people? The one who thinks cereal is a food group? I've known cats who are more responsible than you are!"

"Libby," I began. But Michael squeezed my hand.

Emma said, "I can do my own damn thinking without any help from you. Either one of you." She jabbed her finger in my direction.

As luck would have it, Michael's cell phone rang in his pocket. Reluctantly, he pulled it out and checked the screen. He sent me an apologetic look and headed for the door. Whether he was off to talk to his newfound daughter or negotiate the end of illegal gambling in the tristate area, I couldn't guess. When he had closed the door quietly behind himself, Libby launched the rest of her ammunition.

"Emma, you've been around during all my pregnancies, my ups and downs, my highs and lows. You've seen how difficult child-rearing can be, how draining it is for a single woman—even one as unsinkable as I am. I can't believe you haven't reached a few conclusions about your own situation by now. What are you going to do? Wait until you're in labor before you make your decision? Leave a basket on a stranger's doorstep?"

"Take it easy," I said.

"No, Nora, it's time Emma made a choice. Where, exactly, is Hart in this equation?"

Emma glared at her in silence.

"Are you prepared to raise this child alone? Because, to be honest, dear sister, I don't see you managing everything. Not while continuing to conduct your life the way you have been. Forget a Grand Prix career. You can't jump in a truck and go to a horse show in Florida when you feel like it. And you certainly can't go running off to meet your randy young men at all hours of the night."

"Okay, maybe having a kid isn't exactly my kind of gig," Emma said, pointing at her stomach. "What am I supposed to do about it now?"

"Have you thought about adoption?"

"Of course I have."

"What about Nora and That Man of Hers? Have you considered asking them to raise this child?"

Emma shoved her plate away and got up from the table with surprising speed. "I may not be the best decision maker in this family, but even I can see what kind of risk that would be."

"Risk?" I said carefully, determined not to lose my cool.

"What risk?" Libby demanded.

"Listen." Emma planted a forefinger on the table. "I like Mick as much as the next person. He's a good guy under the whole Corleone thing. One of the best. But do I want my kid sleeping in a bed that might end up with a horse's head in it?"

"What nonsense," Libby said.

"Is it?" Emma transferred her glare to me. "You've got armed guards at your front door, Nora. And Mick has an official bodyguard now. The guy running numbers down at the ice cream parlor is ready to start a gang war because he's being driven out of business. So how come you aren't the pregnant one here, Sis? Don't tell me it's because you haven't been lucky. It's at least partly because you're afraid to bring a kid into his world."

I said, "Michael would protect a child with his life."

"That's what I'm afraid of," Emma said. "I don't want him dead any more than you do. There aren't any easy decisions around here, see? All I'm saying is—oh, hell."

Libby stood up to give her a hug, but Emma shoved out of her embrace and slammed out of the house. I rushed to the door in time to see her brush past Michael, Bruno and Ralphie. With a stormy look on her face, she climbed into her truck and fired up the engine.

Beside me, Libby said, "Well, that didn't go very well." She sat down again at the table to fold up her brochure. "I started some research about Aunt Madeleine's art collection. Would you like to hear?"

Shaken, I managed to say, "I'm not sure I could absorb any information right now, Lib."

"No?" She checked the clock on the wall. "Just as well. I missed aromatherapy, but I can just make my Zumba class if I take off right now, so we'll have to talk about this later. Bye-bye."

I opened my mouth but decided trying to be reasonable with Libby was a lost cause.

I went upstairs to change my clothes. I tried to forget what Emma had said in the heat of the moment. Maybe she was right. But I didn't want to think about it. Not now, while Aunt Madeleine was on my mind.

Upstairs, I reached for my trusty black Calvin Klein pencil skirt. Wearing that skirt, I could show up with confidence to anything from a Little League game to a formal gala—depending on accessories, of course. Likewise, my black Chanel boots. I pulled a cotton camisole from Target over my head and finished off the look with an Alexander McQueen jacket from a few seasons back. The fabric was a swirl of different colors, but mostly blue, with tiny feathers woven into the warp. It had come from Penny Devine, a Hollywood star who decided to chuck fame and fortune for a life on the beach with a rotation of handsome young men. I put on her jacket and felt as if I could conquer Louis B. Mayer and anyone else who got in my way.

When I came back downstairs, Libby had gone and Michael was busy in the library. He had the television turned on to the futures market, the sound off.

With the phone pinned to his shoulder, Michael spread his hands apologetically at me, but his voice was cold. "No," he said to his caller. "The price per gallon should be based on the cost per barrel in the futures. So don't try to finesse me, Dave. I can see the numbers right here on my screen. I can go to your competitor, you know. He's a phone call away."

Bruno lounged on the windowsill, chewing on a toothpick and staring out the window with an expression that communicated how hard he wasn't listening to Michael's phone conversation about the price of gasoline. I wondered if he had a gun under his pinstripes. Or was Michael adhering to the letter of the law and making sure no weapons were in the house? I fervently hoped so.

I gave Michael a kiss on the cheek and didn't interrupt. I could wait to discuss Emma's outburst when we were alone this evening. Surely we'd also talk then about the latest development with—what was her name? Carrie? My head spun just thinking of all the new wrinkles in our lives.

I went outside, where the pig had taken up a position on the porch. He looked up alertly as I came through the door, but disappointment quickly clouded his piggy gaze.

"Sorry, Ralphie," I said. "Michael's busy."

Ralphie settled down to wait.

"He loves barbecue," I warned.

Ralphie's expression said he doubted me.

Beside Bruno's parked car, the SUV and Reed waited for me. He already had the milk stool in place at the rear passenger door.

Reed glanced at my face. "You don't look happy."

"If I have to ride in this behemoth again, at least let me drive it as far as the end of the driveway."

Reed's eyes popped wide with consternation. "Now? You want to try driving now? With Mick watching?"

"He's on the phone."

"But—"

"Just to the end of the driveway."

Reed set his jaw, but he couldn't resist for long. He helped me up behind the wheel, then climbed into the passenger seat, buckled his seat belt and pulled it extra tight. "Take it slow," he said. "Really, really, really slow."

I tried a K-turn first, but to turn the big vehicle around took me several laborious maneuvers, and Reed let out one strangled yelp when I got a tiny bit too close to the pasture fence.

"Take a chill pill, Reed. I'm doing fine."

I could have sworn he gave a little whimper.

I finally got the SUV headed in the right direction and put my foot on the accelerator. The vehicle jumped, and gravel flew, so I hit the brakes, and Reed's head snapped forward. I tried inching my way around the side of the house and finally straightened out and headed for the road.

"Slow," Reed said, gripping the door handle as if his life depended on it. "Slower. Please, slower!"

I smiled to see Michael's men all scattering in mock terror. I didn't expect any of them to have a sense of humor. When I finally got the SUV stopped, they crept out from behind the safety of their vehicles.

As I climbed down from the driver's seat, I realized I had put the front tire of the SUV halfway into the drainage ditch.

"Funny how it's so hard to judge distances when you're sitting up so high," I said.

"It's okay," Reed said, sounding calmer.

"You see? I'm getting much better, Reed. I just need to practice."

Without a word, he helped me up into the backseat and drove me into the city.

In the backseat, I wrote my daily letter to Lexie. Usually I filled my notes with silly news, but today I took the time to describe the arrival of Michael's daughter. That news would surely break up the monotony of prison life. I decided not to write about the latest development in Aunt Madeleine's story. By tomorrow, I'd have answers from Sutherland and everything would make sense. At least, I hoped so.

After finishing the letter, I got to work. In recent weeks, I had begun reviving the custom of including society weddings in the lifestyle section of the paper. A while back, the editors had cut weddings entirely, and they refused to believe that the subsequent drop in newspaper subscriptions was a related phenomenon. But I'd started doing a cute Q&A with newly married couples—asking how they'd met, where the proposal happened, details about their wedding and honeymoon. I printed the interviews with photos. My gut feeling? Everybody loves a love story. Especially with pictures of dresses and shy little boys carrying pillows. Interest in the page had shot through the roof, so I'd been given the go-ahead to do more.

Choosing which wedding to feature had become a tough job, though. Families flooded me with e-mails and letters. Sorting through it all had become a time-consuming chore. But a fun one.

As I pulled all the papers from my bag, I came across the card I'd received from the young woman who had accosted me outside the hotel after the MEWA dinner. I sat back and read her name again. Zareen Aboudi.

I stewed for a while. Zareen had a problem, all right, but I was the wrong person to help her with it.

Except . . .

I'd been helpless to do anything for Lexie during her courtroom drama. And I wasn't doing much good for Emma at the moment, so I really wanted to do something useful for at least one person in the world.

Perhaps I could call Anahita about Zareen's plight. Even though Anahita had complained about getting phone calls about every woman wearing a hijab, she was my only option. She might have a suggestion about how to help someone slip out of Syria long enough to visit a sick relative.

I pulled out my phone and took a chance on reaching Anahita at her office. But she was busy with a client, so I ended up leaving a message. I explained the situation and asked her for advice. Before the beep, I said I'd call her back sometime soon.

That done, I tucked Zareen's card into the front pocket of my bag for later.

My first stop of the day was a children's party at the museum. I dashed up the steps where part of the *Rocky* movie had been filmed and worked my way through the crowd of museum-goers who were leaving for the day.

In a distant room, I found the party. Perhaps it was the wrong event for me to attend after Emma's hurtful remarks, but I had already responded that I'd show up. I tried to adjust my attitude as I walked through the door. The event was intended to raise money for a new program to expose underserved children to making and appreciating many forms of art. Some organizer had the brilliant idea of mixing kids from a homeless shelter with the brightly dressed four-year-olds from families who donated money to such causes. I took one look at the room full of kids wearing smocks and flinging paint at big rolls of paper and wondered if perhaps the cultural mix had been too ambitious. The intrusive suburban mothers were all talking to the homeless children in loud, patronizing voices. And all the kids just looked as if they wanted to splash their paint.

I snapped a couple of pictures and spoke to one of the moms I recognized.

"Oh, Nora!" She shook my hand. "I'm Reggie Markelson. We met at the party for the animal shelter. I wore a red dress by Tory Burch, remember? You took my picture for a Web site."

"It's nice to see you," I replied, careful not to pretend I recalled the specifics of our previous meeting. I had learned not to lie. It was too easy to make an embarrassing faux pas.

"Yeah, I check out your social tidbits almost every day. My twins, Dante and Donora, are here this afternoon. You want to take their picture?"

"Sure."

She led me to two adorable cherubs who were fighting like rabid hyenas over possession of the same square of paper. They rubbed paint on each other's drawings, and the result was blobs of angry-looking purple. I tried snapping a photo with my camera phone.

Reggie said, "I saw the article in the paper about Madeleine Blackbird. She was your aunt?"

"Great-aunt, actually."

"My dad knew her. He says she introduced him to his first wife."

I looked away from my camera lens. "Really? His first wife?"

"Yes, their marriage didn't last long. She had worked in an embassy office in Stockholm. I guess that's how she met Madeleine—from some parties. She didn't like living here and so she went back to her family in Sweden. After their divorce, they kept in touch and were friendly, but my dad met my mom, and they've been married ever since. Look, it's just—I can't imagine my dad consorting with—well, with any woman who was—you know, what the newspaper said. He's very straitlaced."

"I firmly believe the newspapers are all wrong about Madeleine."

She looked relieved. "It's good to hear you say that. Because if he thought anybody imagined his first wife was a—a—well, he'd have a stroke or something."

I wanted to ask more questions—I wasn't sure I'd ever met Reggie's father—but little Dante chose that moment to splat a fat dollop of purple paint squarely across his sister's face. She burst into wails of outrage.

Reggie told her son he was getting a "time-out" as soon as they got home, a threat that didn't daunt him in the least. He went back to painting while his mother took his sister off to wash her face.

I snapped Dante's photo just to be on the safe side. It didn't hurt to make a reader happy—especially one who visited the newspaper's Web site every day.

The woman in charge noticed me and rushed over to demand that I put my camera phone away.

I produced my card. "I'm Nora Blackbird from the *Philadelphia Intelligencer.* You invited me."

"Oh, I didn't recognize you. Sorry. We have to be very careful," she told me after she had relaxed. "You just never know who might turn out to be a creep taking pictures of innocent kids and turning them into Internet porn. At my daughter's gymnastics class, the instructor had to ban cameras completely from the gym."

I murmured my dismay. There were even more treacherous threats against children than the ones Emma had considered.

"Yes," said the woman in charge, "being a parent nowadays requires extra vigilance. Have you met Sandra? She's our chief fundraiser."

I shook Sandra's hand, and she gave me the lowdown on the organization. They were making an honest effort to provide a quality program for kids who didn't get much exposure to the arts, and although today's event wasn't going to overflow the bank account, she told me about future events that sounded as if they'd be more successful.

I didn't have time to stick around to ask Reggie Markelson more questions. Over the wails of furious children, I took a few final notes for my column and thanked Sandra before slipping out of the museum.

A sharp wind blew up from the Schuylkill River, so I tucked my nose down into my scarf and hiked back toward city hall. I passed a mailbox and dropped in my latest letter to Lexie.

On the stroke of six, I ducked into my next event, at a revered men's club that was at least a hundred and fifty years old. I hoped to encounter a little more civility under its venerable roof.

The building was a beautiful example of Romanesque architecture, with a wide marble staircase and winged-footed runners poised on the newel posts, holding bronze lanterns aloft. On the paneled walls, heavy-framed oil paintings of early Philadelphia landmarks hung next to portraits of stern gentlemen—some of them wearing the blue uniform of the Army of the Potomac. In an upstairs smoking room, I knew, there was a painting of a splendid horse carrying a rather dyspeptic-looking General Ambrose Burnside. The painting had been donated by one of his club member friends—my great-great-grandfather Blackbird.

Inside the club, the mood was everything the children's party had not been—hushed and staid. I might have chosen the word *lifeless* if I hadn't bumped into a friend of my mother's in the gilt-mirrored ladies' room.

"Nora, you look radiant," said Mrs. Banks as she kissed my cold cheeks.

"I just walked from the museum," I told her with a laugh.

"How intrepid! Vigorous exercise must be how you keep your good looks. Myself, I can barely make it through my yoga class every morning. I must be getting old."

"You look younger than ever," I said promptly.

"Do you think so?" She checked her reflection in the mirror and adjusted a lock of platinum hair. She wore a heavy silver dress that was perhaps jumping the holiday season by a few weeks, but it suited her figure. "My husband insisted we come out for this party tonight, but of course I'd rather spend a quiet evening at home."

Judging by the fur coat over her arm, the diamonds on her hands and the towering heels she wore, I had the feeling she was lying through her teeth.

"Are you on the committee?" I asked.

Tonight's event honored an environmental group that championed the cleanup of local waterways. I knew that Mrs. Banks and her husband—despite their fine clothes and good manners—had inherited a rough-and-tumble river salvage business. They earned their income from big companies that were forced to clean up old industrial sites.

"No, no," she said. "I'm past committee work. Let the young people have their day. No, we're just very committed to this cause. If we don't take care of our rivers, what will the future be for our children and grandchildren?"

"It's a wonderful mission," I said, aware that without government regulations that required clean water, her husband's company might have gone out of business years ago for lack of customers. "I have a friend who used to get out on the river every morning for exercise. She told me there's been a huge improvement in the quality of the water in recent years. So you're obviously doing something right."

Margo Banks gave me a sideways look. "You're talking about Lexie Paine, aren't you? How tragic that she went to jail."

"Yes." Mentally I kicked myself for bringing up Lexie. I had vowed not to gossip about my friend, and here I'd opened the subject myself.

"It's a shame about her," Mrs. Banks said. "I knew her father, of course. He'd be horrified to learn she killed someone."

"It was a terrible tragedy," I said faintly.

"Some people say it wasn't her fault. But, of course, she admitted to pushing that man out the window. She pleaded guilty, right? So whatever made her do it doesn't matter much, does it? She committed a horrific crime. So she must pay the appropriate price."

The moral complexities of Lexie's case had consumed me for months. I didn't want to try breaking it down for the likes of Mrs. Banks.

I pulled a pen from my bag and changed the subject. "Can you introduce me to anyone on the committee? I should try to get an interview before I move on to my next event."

"I'm so impressed that you have a job now, Nora. Your mother must be proud. Have you heard from her lately?"

"Not this week," I said brightly, fully aware that Mrs. Banks was itching to hear the latest gossip about my parents, too. "Have you?"

"Unfortunately, no." Mrs. Banks tucked her lipstick into her evening bag. "I gather they're having a wonderful time. Of course, your parents certainly know how to do that."

I avoided responding to her remark by opening the door and standing aside so she could precede me out of the ladies' room. She sailed out into the carpeted hallway and was immediately hailed by friends, so I sidestepped her and continued into the party alone.

I had expected the evening's crowd to be younger and more vital than the usual club membership, but I should have guessed by the early hour of the cocktail portion of the evening that the guests would be mostly senior citizens. Around Philadelphia, there were many "rescue the rivers" organizations, and this one was more old-money than most. The guests were mainly retired folk—a trend I had begun to notice among many philanthropic causes. Younger working people didn't have time to attend weeknight events anymore. They devoted long daylight hours to their jobs and were anxious to get home to their families at night. I wondered if all charitable organizations might suffer from the lack of young people to energize them.

Once again I reminded myself it was up to the likes of me to find ways to coax my own age group back to good works.

No Way to Kill a Lady

The club might have been a forbidding old place, but it was kept in beautiful condition because it was a popular wedding venue. Income from large society weddings kept the chandeliers polished and the marble in good repair. A beautiful inlaid mosaic marble floor had been added since my last visit. It was a good complement to the already magnificent first impression the decor elicited.

Tonight's cocktail nibbles were mostly frozen quiches that had been feebly reheated, but I assumed the menu had been chosen to please older palates and so I gave the kitchen a pass. Although my stomach rumbled, I decided not to waste the calories.

I made a few notes, but chose not to take any photos. My column wouldn't be brightened by a report from this event, and I doubted the guests were likely to check online for pictures of themselves.

As I headed for the door, I encountered Mrs. Banks again. This time her husband stood with her, holding a drink. He'd inherited his fortune from his blue-collar father—a rough man with a boat and name that had more syllables and consonants than "Banks" did. But once his father left this earth, Frederick Banks had changed his name and turned to golf, leaving his office every day at noon to play eighteen holes with cronies. I'd heard he passed on the leadership of his business to a nephew who worked hard and skipped the country club scene.

Mr. Banks proffered his hand. On his square, still suntanned face he had pasted that mild, pleasant look elderly men sometimes assumed at cocktail parties when they couldn't hear a thing.

I shook his hand. "Hello, Mr. Banks. How nice to see you."

He had good manners—smiling as he shook my hand, although he obviously had no clue who I was.

Mrs. Banks raised her voice. "This is Nora Blackbird, Freddie. You remember."

"Hello, hello," he said vaguely. "How's your dad?"

"Traveling again. Having a ball."

"Give him my best."

On a whim, I said, "You've been friends a long time, haven't you?"

"He sponsored my membership at the country club," Frederick Banks said. "He could have been a helluva golfer, your dad, if he had concentrated. But he'd rather learn a new joke than put in extra practice time, wouldn't he?"

"He loves to laugh." Then I decided to seize the moment. I said, "Mr. Banks, did you know my great-aunt Madeleine?"

Mr. Banks looked thunderstruck.

I didn't know what I said wrong, but it must have been my day to endure the behavior of people who lost their civility.

Mrs. Banks made a choking noise in her throat, and her face turned very red. "How dare you bring up that woman to my husband!"

Then she stepped forward, raised her hand and slapped me across the face.

CHAPTER TEN

Tasting blood, I grabbed a cocktail napkin and scooted down the club's steps as quickly as I could. I was lucky to catch a cab outside the hotel next door. Breathless, I gave the driver directions, then subsided in the backseat to regain my composure. I opened the mirror on my compact. The force of the slap had cut the inner side of my cheek against my teeth.

No marks on the outside, thank heavens. I'd have plenty of explaining to do if I developed a fat lip.

I sat back against the seat, stunned. At the mere mention of my aunt, Frederick Banks had looked as if he'd swallowed a frog. I tucked my compact back into my bag and tried to think. What was his relationship to Aunt Madeleine? I knew the newspaper story about her was wrong, but obviously Mrs. Banks knew something I hadn't learned yet.

"Miss?"

The cab had arrived at my destination without my realizing it.

I paid the driver and got out into the darkness. A cold, damp wind whipped across the water and hit me hard. The first hint of coming winter. A few lights illuminated the deserted marina. I glanced down across the boats that were tied side by side along one dock. Some already wore their winter covers. Others bobbed, waiting to be pulled from the water and trailered away to storage. Or perhaps waiting for one more day of good sailing.

My husband, Todd, and I had enjoyed sailing before his addiction took over, so marinas like this one were familiar territory.

At the end of the main dock there was a spectacular yacht, and it didn't take a genius to know this was the one Sutherland had brought up from southern waters.

It was the biggest, most modern yacht in the marina—a sleek black vessel with beautiful curves, strong steel masts and graceful canopies arching over her decks. A small dingy was lashed upside down to an upper deck and two Jet Skis hung on the stern. By the light of a lantern, I could see someone had painted a Picasso-like sketch of a bare-breasted woman on the bow. Her hair streamed back from bare shoulders. Her right arm pointed forward, as if aiming for the high seas. The boat's name and luxurious port of origin danced on her stern:

ARIADNE

MYKONOS

Just to be sure, I stopped at the marina manager's office. I knocked and poked my head into the small shanty—a building with big windows on three sides, heated by a small space heater that blasted warm air up from the floor. Still, the manager was wrapped in a parka. A football game muttered on a portable television near his foot.

"Hi," I said. "I'm looking for Sutherland Blackbird's boat?"

The manager didn't get up from his stool. He was an older gentleman, wearing a Flyers cap over a thatch of gray hair. He hadn't shaved in a while, and his eyeglasses were smudgy. He looked up from a crossword puzzle on the table in front of him. "Yeah, sure. Slip number twelve."

"Thanks."

Before I could close the door, he added, "It's been a long time since we had a Blackbird around here."

I stepped in and closed the door to keep the warmth inside. "Oh, yes?"

"Sure," he said. "When I first started working here, another couple kept a boat in this marina. Nice people. She was a beauty. And he always brought us a nice bottle for the holidays."

He meant Madeleine, I realized, and her husband—Sutherland's father.

I said, "You worked here when they sailed?"

"Yep. Helped them out a couple of times, too. They were the real deal, weren't they?"

"Yes, they were."

A radio crackled on his desk, and he flipped a switch to answer the call.

While he was occupied, I took a quick glance at the clipboard on his wall. I read down the information on the boats until he finished talking to someone on the radio.

When he hung up his microphone, he turned to me. "Yeah, I remember they used to bring us bottles of Russian vodka. That's strong stuff, lemme tell you."

His radio squawked again, and he waved me on my way. I went outside and hurried along the dock toward the yacht, stepping carefully to avoid catching my heels between the boards.

I spotted Sutherland waiting for me in an open door above the gangway. A glittering light shone behind him, beckoning me into the warmth. He held a thick glass in one hand. His shirt was unbuttoned to the middle of his sternum. The picture of romantic welcome. Except his neck looked a little saggy to carry off the picture perfectly.

He caught my arm and helped me up the gently bobbing gangway. His voice was smooth. "Hello, Cuz. Nice of you to join me."

Only a quick turn of my head prevented him from planting a kiss on my mouth. He grazed my cheek instead.

"Hello, Sutherland. It's a cold night for sailing."

"But a perfect night for a cozy drink together," he countered playfully. "I gave the crew the night off, so I'll do the honors myself. Can I pour you something?"

I slipped past him into the yacht's luxurious salon. But I walked only a few steps across the marble tiles before I stopped, awestruck by the interior design. Sutherland pulled the door closed behind himself then strolled into the cabin and over to me, waiting for my response to the surrounding grandeur.

"Well?" he said, as I glanced appreciatively around the salon. "Did you bring your luggage? We could sail around the world together, you and me."

"She's gorgeous," I said when I could speak. "I love the furniture. And that painting—! Is it a de Kooning?" I recognized the slashing strokes and vivid colors of the artist's abstract expressionism.

"Yes, indeed. The other one's a Motherwell, worth a small fortune. Let me take your coat. Shall we put your bag down here?"

I let him play host and took a more careful look around.

Four tufted sofas upholstered in white sharkskin were gathered around a beveled-glass table that had been etched with a seascape design of roiling waves, leaping dolphins and the same half-naked woman depicted on the bow of the yacht. This time, though, she wielded a trident and a come-hither smile. Around the salon stood deep, comfortable chairs, gilt-legged tables and cabinets winking with porcelain figures and fine glassware. Lead-crystal lamps stood under silk shades. Sutherland lived in fabulous luxury.

I said, "It must be easy living this way."

"I'd be lying if I said it wasn't very easy," Sutherland agreed.

On the marble floor tile lay an Oriental rug swirling with subtle ocean colors—unique and probably custom-woven. I guessed the rug alone was worth more than most luxury cars.

Through a darkened doorway, I could see the lacquered dining table and chairs. "This looks like the boat of a Saudi prince."

Indulging himself, Sutherland said, "Check this out, Scheherazade."

He used a handheld remote control to dim the lights, lower the window shades and cue up music from hidden speakers.

"Electronics," I said, shaking my head with amusement. "That's a man's fantasy, I'm afraid. All you need is a Bond girl to make the picture complete."

He thumbed the remote again, and an enormous television rose from inside a cabinet. A football game blazed onto the screen.

"You just spoiled the mood, Sutherland."

"Give me a break," he begged, unapologetically insincere. "I've been out of the States for years. I need my football fix."

"Just turn down the sound, will you?" I plugged my ears. The crowd noise was loud enough to make me believe I was standing in the middle of the stadium alongside the players.

"Oh, have it your way." He turned off the television and tossed the remote aside. "You act like a woman who knows what a man enjoys, though. Does your current flame watch football?"

I thought of Michael and his various sports obsessions—all of which only reminded me that his family ran a vast illegal betting operation. But I said, "He's more than a current flame, you know. We're in a committed relationship."

"A committed relationship," Sutherland repeated, amused. "Why do I think you're not telling the whole truth?"

"I am, though. You're barking up the wrong tree, Cousin. If you brought me here to talk romance, it's time to change the subject. We have much more serious matters to discuss."

Sutherland smiled. "How about that drink first?"

"Ice water?"

"I can do better than that," he said playfully. "Let me show you the wine collection."

I put my hand on his arm to stop him. "No, just water, please. I hurt my lip earlier."

His brow clouded. "I'm sorry to hear that. An accident?"

"I hope so," I said more lightly than I felt.

"That sounds mysterious. What's up?" He went behind a bar that looked as if it had been cut from a block of jade. He prepared a glass of ice water.

"It was something I said. I mentioned Aunt Madeleine's name, and suddenly a lady clobbered me." I described what had happened at the club.

"She hit you! Good God, who was it?"

"A friend of my parents."

"Why would she slap you?"

"Clearly she had some kind of beef with Madeleine."

Sutherland handed me a cut-crystal glass. "Madeleine's been gone a long while. Time to forgive and forget."

I accepted the drink. I wanted to talk about how long she'd been gone, but I asked, "Did you see today's newspapers?"

He pulled a face. "Yes. What a pack of lies."

"So you don't believe the story?"

"That Madeleine was some sort of Mayflower Madam? Of course not."

I sipped the water gingerly. The cold felt good on the sore spot in my mouth.

Sutherland continued. "Not that she was a prude, of course. Both she and my father had affairs. None of that tiresome American *bourgeois* morality for either of them. They met someone interesting and—off to bed! In Madeleine's case, to read poetry, I'm sure." He winked. "Maybe that's what your slapper was annoyed about. Maybe her husband slept with Madeleine? I remember her getting on a private jet with a randy billionaire from Texas. They flew to Norway for dinner. Who knew there was a decent restaurant in Norway?"

"Sutherland," I said.

He continued to blather.

I sat on the sofa and crossed one leg over the other, but the longer I sat there with his nonsense sailing over my head, the more my mouth hurt and the more I couldn't control the angry sensation that had started boiling in my chest. I felt offended on Madeleine's behalf. I was sick of my cousin's sneaky ways. I was tired of being a good girl. I wished I'd accepted Michael's offer to bring along one of his goons to beat Sutherland senseless. Sometimes it must feel good, I thought, to shove somebody's face in a puddle—especially somebody who'd done you wrong or hidden the truth or otherwise committed a self-serving act at the expense of others. My head hurt.

I set my glass down and got up from the sofa. Sutherland stopped babbling. The next thing I knew, I was plucking the electronic remote from the table and heading for the door. On my way, I grabbed the Motherwell painting off the wall.

Sutherland yelped.

With the painting under my arm, I stalked out onto the deck of the yacht. I threw the remote overboard.

Sutherland skidded to a stop at the railing just as the remote control hit the cold water with a splash. "Nora! What's gotten into you? Wait—no!"

"Stand back," I snapped. "Or the painting goes, too."

"Have you gone crazy?"

"Just what the hell have you been up to, Sutherland?"

"Up to?"

I dangled the painting over the water.

"No! Please! It's worth millions!"

"So start talking. Today you told me Madeleine has been dead in an elevator for twenty years. But a week ago, you sent her obituary to the newspapers."

"I did no such thing!"

I let the painting slip just an inch. He screamed and clapped both hands over his mouth.

"Do I have your attention now, Cuz? I *work* for a newspaper. It took me one phone call to figure out it was you who told the newspapers Madeleine was dead in Indonesia. You made that up! In five minutes, my teenage nephew could have found a way to send an obituary without your name right on it, but you bungled it, you—you master criminal!"

Sutherland dithered, his eyes as wide as saucers.

"Why on earth did you send an obituary before you knew she was dead?" I demanded. "Because you must have already *known* she'd been in that elevator for years! So talk! Before I lose my grip on your expensive artwork."

"All right, all right! But, please—the Motherwell!"

I kept the painting right where it was—hanging over the water and twisting in the wind.

"Okay, okay, I knew Madeleine died a long time ago. I went to Quintain—to see the place. I was really very fond of it— No!" When I leaned over the railing, he stopped embellishing his story and went on hastily, "After Madeleine announced she was going to Indonesia, I went to the damn house to see if I could—if there was anything of value she might have left behind that might—well, that I could take. She'd never have noticed if a few of her silly baubles went missing, would she? And I was broke. So I went to the house. But I—well, the electricity was off, so I turned it on, and then the elevator opened, and there she was—dead as a doornail. Let me tell you, it was a horror. It took me years to recover from the sight of her—"

"So you stole her things. You stole everything out of the house instead of calling the police?"

"No, of course I didn't steal everything," Sutherland said. "I took one or two little items, but— Oh! Nora, please! That painting isn't mine. If something happens to the damn thing—"

"Keep talking! You stole her belongings? Without telling anyone she had died? And then?"

"And then nothing. Do you think I'd willingly go back to that house, knowing she was rotting there?"

A powerful wave of regret—or was it nausea?—swept up from inside me, but I fought it down. "Was it you who pretended she was still alive? You sent the postcards?"

"Me? No, I don't know anything about that."

I had already thought ahead to Pippi. If Pee Wee was telling the truth—that she had disappeared about the same time Madeleine planned to leave the country for Indonesia—perhaps she had been the one sending postcards, pretending Madeleine was alive and well. Which meant Pippi knew Madeleine was dead. Had she killed her? And stolen the treasures of Quintain to finance a new life for herself far away?

"I should phone the police right now," I said to Sutherland. "I don't know why I haven't done that already. I'm giving you a chance to come clean this minute, Sutherland, and then we'll discuss what you can be prosecuted for. How did Madeleine die?"

"I presume it happened just the way you saw for yourself. The electricity must have gone off, and she was trapped. Look, she was beyond help. Why shouldn't I have helped myself just a little?"

"You're appalling," I said. "She died of thirst and starvation, alone, trapped in an elevator. And all you thought of was yourself." I threw the painting at him.

He caught it, bobbled it, then hugged the frame against himself as if it were a kitten he'd saved from drowning.

I had more questions, of course. But I was so angry with Sutherland just then that all the possibilities were jumbled up in my head. And what had Michael said? That eventually the rough interrogation tactics stopped working? It was time to let Sutherland stew. I asked, "When you told the police it was Madeleine in the elevator, what did Foley have to say?"

Sutherland hugged the painting, silent.

"You didn't tell Deputy Foley," I guessed. "You knew it was Madeleine, but you didn't mention it?"

"I didn't say anything. Not then. Not with all the lawyers gathered around."

"What do the lawyers have to do with anything? They've been deceived, too, if they were led to believe Madeleine had moved to Indonesia."

"I'm not worried about all the lawyers," he said. "Just Groatley."

"What does that mean?"

"I've been a fool, Nora. I know that now. But I—I caught Groatley. After Libby found the body in the elevator, before the police came and—well, everybody wandered around the mansion for a while. Groatley was in Madeleine's little study. I caught him rummaging in her desk. Clearly, he was searching for something. Something important. He was sweating and breathing heavily—he acted like a guilty man. He turned three shades of red when I came in the door. He pushed past me to get out, blustering something about client privilege."

"Did he have anything in his hands?"

"No, nothing. I suppose he could have tucked something small into one of his pockets, but my impression was that he didn't find what he was looking for."

"Well, he was Madeleine's lawyer," I said. "Unlike you, maybe he really did have her best interests at heart."

"Or maybe he was covering up something."

"There's a lot of that going around."

Sutherland flushed. "I caught him ransacking her desk. He's up to something."

"What do you think he's doing?"

"Who knows?"

"I'm calling the police," I said, turning away from him. "Let them sort everything out."

"Wait, Nora. Please. Another day or two won't hurt the police investigation—not if the crime happened two decades ago. You and I should think things through."

I didn't know what to think. Except I could hear Aunt Madeleine's voice in my head. She had said, "You're the one I can trust, aren't you?"

Glaring at my cousin, I could understand why she didn't trust him, why she had cut her own stepson out of her will. Even now, Sutherland was working an angle. I had spent enough time in Michael's company to spot the signs. Sutherland didn't have a plan yet, but he was working on something profitable.

But I'd lost my stomach for torturing the truth out of him. I felt sick—sick of myself as much as anything else.

I checked my watch. "We're definitely going to talk more about this, Sutherland, but not now. I'm going to be late."

He tried to look disappointed. "Why don't you stop by again later? We can talk a little longer. And," he said in a different tone, "we can explore the rest of the boat."

"Shut up," I said. "I'm not going to be your accomplice. I want you to come to Blackbird Farm tomorrow. By then I'll be able to think straight. Come for lunch. We'll figure out what happens next."

"Sounds good." Sutherland smiled. "I can meet your committed relationship."

I smiled, too. I figured Sutherland was still lying to me. But tomorrow I just might turn Michael and his thugs loose on him and watch the fun.

CHAPTER ELEVEN

wanted to rush home and spill the new developments in the Madeleine story to Michael. He would have a theory about her death. Not to mention insight into the ruse somebody had perpetrated to keep us convinced that Madeleine was living in Indonesia.

But I had another event to attend. In better weather, I'd have walked the distance to the convention center. I could have phoned Reed to pick me up, but I knew he'd gone to visit his mother in Philadelphia and it would take him the better part of half an hour to reach me. So Sutherland called me a cab.

He actually tried to kiss me good-bye, but I dodged him.

I was a few minutes late arriving at the convention center, where many players from the Flyers hockey team were making good use of their night off the ice by helping a local charity to kick off a big holiday toy drive.

On my way inside, I was air-kissed by several women I knew. I was also bussed hard on the cheek by three men I did not know in the slightest, and one inebriated man who mistook me for someone else and kissed me full on the mouth. In fact, if I hadn't ducked in time, I was pretty sure I would have gotten some tongue. I grabbed a glass of wine to wash off the taste of him.

Fortunately, the photographer from the *Intelligencer* was already on the job, snapping photos of the hockey players as they posed with some local cherubs.

"Hey, Nora," Lee Song said, barely looking away from his camera's lens. "Still working the rubber chicken circuit, I see. How've you been?"

"Eating a lot of chicken, Lee. You?"

"Busy. The paper laid off all the photographers except me and Josie. So we're doubling our hours to get everything covered. I'll be lucky to see my kids at all between now and Christmas."

"I'm sorry to hear that."

"Yeah, well, the extra dough'll help pay for their presents. You want me to shoot some pictures of the hockey wives? They're all babes. A nice change from your usual old broads in pearl necklaces."

I liked Lee, but I decided not to beat around the bush. "Was it you who took pictures of Quintain? And me at my house? From a helicopter?"

Lee stopped shooting and had the grace to look embarrassed. "If it's any consolation, I got airsick. I snapped a few of the castle. And, yeah, I plead guilty to photographing you with your boyfriend. I tried to hide your face. I hope you noticed that."

"Thanks for small favors."

"Sorry, Nora. I do what I'm told. That's why I still have a job."

"I get it. Do a good job for me tonight, and all is forgiven. I need some great shots for the Web site."

"Thanks, Nora. And really—I'm sorry."

He got busy snapping photos of the players' wives, most of whom looked adorably young and normal compared to the wives of pro football players and basketball superstars, who paid big bucks for hair extensions, lip-plumping and breast augmentation. The hockey wives, though, were athletic, Canadian girls-next-door—some of whom spoke only French and giggled a lot.

I chatted up one, Chanterelle, who told me she was expecting twins in the spring. She patted her tummy, encased in a big knitted angora sweater. "So we want to give a good Christmas to less-fortunate children now, see?"

"Yes, I see." I jotted down her quote, expecting to lead my story with it.

I strolled around, making conversation with a few people I knew and accepting a spicy canapé from the circulating waiters. With a glass of club soda in my hand, I looked like any other guest at the party, but I kept my ears open for good quotes to use in my column.

Several more people kissed me exuberant hellos. I was starting to think I'd wandered into a kissing frenzy.

The charity in charge of the event had arranged for a silent auction of sports memorabilia, so many ticket holders were cruising the display tables and putting in bids on items signed by local sports heroes, past and present. In the crowd, I bumped into an elderly retired baseball player and his Cuban American wife whom I knew from American Heart Association events—their favorite cause. They were very sweet people, and we chatted for the better part of fifteen minutes. No kissing.

While talking to them, though, I suddenly spotted Simon Groatley across the room. He was glad-handing some other men, and they all guffawed together as one of the young hockey wives walked past.

Groatley looked over the head of the man in front of him and met my gaze across the room. He winked.

The retired baseball player noticed and reacted with surprise. "Do you know Simon Groatley, Nora?"

"Only very slightly," I said. "Family business."

"Hmph. I hope you keep your distance. Nice girl like you shouldn't have to put up with a man like that."

I smiled. "Are you protecting my honor?"

He frowned. "If I thought it was in danger, I'd go knock his teeth down his throat right this minute. Has that man been hassling you?"

"No," I said with perfect honesty. "But he gave my sister Emma a hard time."

The baseball player's wife laughed. "I imagine Emma took care of him double quick."

Her husband did not see anything humorous. "Seriously," he growled. "The way he brags about women, it's indecent. And he spends money faster than a river. The man's no good, I can tell."

"Josh," his wife reprimanded. "Hush."

"No need to hush if it's true," he said. "You stay away from him, you hear, Nora?"

"Thank you, I will."

The sight of Groatley suddenly sickened me. Whatever he'd been doing in Madeleine's study hadn't been in her best interests. But I wasn't ready to confront him. Not yet. And tonight I sure didn't want any social kisses from him or any of his cronies.

I couldn't get out of the convention center fast enough.

Although I should have stayed a little longer at the party, a different plan took shape in my head as I rode the elevator down to the street level. I had plenty of material for my column, and Lee's photos would take up most of the space anyway. But since I knew where Simon Groatley was tonight, I could do a little poking around myself. I phoned Reed and asked him to pick me up early.

"I'm parked around the corner," he said.

The wind had died down, but the night air was still chilly. Behind the hotel, Reed was already out of the SUV, setting the milk stool out on the pavement.

"Thanks, Reed," I said as I climbed up into the warm backseat.

On the way out of the city, I pulled out my phone and dialed Emma's cell number.

She picked up after the first ring. "Yeah?"

"It's me," I said. "Are you at home?"

"Actually, I'm sitting at a drive-up window, waiting for a cheese-burger."

I could have lectured her about all the healthy food I'd bought that morning, but mindful of her earlier outburst, I held my tongue. Instead I said, "Are you okay?"

"Never better," she replied, clearly intending to put her emotional meltdown behind us.

So I said, "Which drive-up window, exactly?"

Emma told me she was at Bertie's Burgers, a hamburger joint just a few miles outside New Hope. A place renowned for milk shakes and teen romance.

"Wait there," I said. "I'll meet you."

"Hungry, too?"

"No, but I need you to drive me somewhere."

"Tonight?" She sounded surprised. "Don't you have a romantic rendezvous at home?"

"I'll meet you in half an hour."

It was more like forty minutes by the time Reed maneuvered out of the city traffic. Eventually, he pulled the SUV into the park-ing lot of a fast-food restaurant full of teenagers hanging out on a Friday night. Reed gave the teenagers a long look, reminding me that he was only recently out of high school himself.

"Thanks, Reed." I reached for the door handle.

He eyed my reflection in the rearview mirror. "The boss doesn't like it when I don't follow the plan."

"You and I managed just fine while your boss was out of the picture," I reminded him. "There's no sense getting him involved again, is there?"

Reed sighed. "You be careful."

"Yes, sir. Good night."

I clicked across the parking lot in my high heels—perhaps looking a little incongruous in my McQueen feather jacket. But the hamburger crowd was more interested in Reed's enormous vehicle and respectfully watched him depart.

When I climbed into the truck, Emma was listening to an oldies radio station, leafing through a comic book and wiping her mouth with a paper napkin. She had her window cracked open a couple of inches, and the truck felt like a refrigerator.

I leaned over the dashboard, turned down the radio and cranked up the heat. "Had any proposals lately?"

"Not unless you count the kid who mistook me for a blimp and asked me for a ride. Do you have to blast that thing? I'm roasting."

"It's your hormones. I just saw Simon Groatley at a party."

"Oh, yeah? Did he keep his dick in his pants?"

"Yes, but he was definitely ogling anything in a skirt. I saw Sutherland Blackbird tonight, too."

Emma wadded up her napkin and paused in the act of reaching for the cold drink in the cup holder. "Oh, yeah? What did Cousin Slick have to say? Or did he spend the evening practicing nonverbal communication?"

I told her everything Sutherland had admitted to me while I threatened to destroy his painting.

"He knew all along she was dead?" Emma gave Sutherland a few crude names. "Who the hell sent us postcards?"

"Somebody," I said, "who wanted to cover up Madeleine's death."

"Whoa." Emma had already made the same mental leaps I had. "If somebody pretended she was alive by sending us Christmas cards, that person knew she was dead, too. And maybe killed her?"

"Maybe. I think we need to learn more about the people around Madeleine at the time of her death. But Sutherland seems to think it's a bad idea to ask Simon Groatley."

Emma feigned astonishment. "He's not suggesting Groatley might be a shady lawyer?"

I told her how our cousin had caught Madeleine's attorney rummaging in her desk while the police were busy examining her remains in the elevator. And then I told her about Madeleine's black book.

When I finished, Emma's straw made a noisy gurgle at the bottom of her plastic cup. She said, "So what do you want to do? Bust into Quintain under dark of night? Search for Madeleine's black book yourself?"

"As a matter of fact," I said, "that's exactly what I had in mind. At the very least, I need to know if Simon Groatley stole it from her desk."

"And I get to be your partner in crime?"

"Consider yourself my getaway driver. I'm breaking into Quintain alone."

"How come you get all the action?"

"Because you're a pregnant lady," I retorted. "In a delicate condition. I'm the one doing the dirty work this time."

"Delicate, my ass. Things have been too damn quiet for me lately." Emma pulled the truck around the side of the fast-food restaurant, rolled down her window, and dumped her trash into a receptacle. Then she cut the truck sharply around to the drive-up menu. The loudspeaker crackled with a voice too garbled for me to understand, but Emma leaned out the window. "I want a chocolate milk shake."

Suddenly ravenous, I said, "Order one for me, too."

Emma did so, and in a couple of minutes we were driving down the street, guzzling milk shakes and heading north toward Aunt Madeleine's estate.

"About Mick," Emma said as she drove.

"Yes?"

"I'm sorry about what I said earlier."

"It's okay. You're under a lot of stress."

"Yeah, but—well, I'm sorry. He's a good guy."

"Yes, he is. Em—"

"Don't," she said. "I heard enough from Libby today."

"Okay."

"Drink your milk shake."

"Right."

After a short silence, she said, "I'll figure out what to do about this baby when the time comes."

I wanted to scream. But Libby had already done enough damage for one day, so I kept my silence. I'd already made myself clear to Emma—that Michael and I were happy to take the baby; even eager, if I was willing to be honest with myself, to raise it as our own. Emma was going to have to make her own decision. I just hoped she could do so before her baby's first tooth arrived.

A few spatters of rain hit the windshield, and Emma flipped on the wipers. "How are you going to break into Aunt Madeleine's house?"

"Smash a window? Or is that too loud?"

Emma laughed. "There's not another house within half a mile of Quintain."

"Except Shirley van Vincent's place. Let's hope she watches television with the sound turned up high."

CHAPTER TWELVE

We passed a few ramshackle houses that faced the Delaware River, then took a right turn at the overgrown pillars and headed up into the woods. Wet branches swiped the sides of the truck as we jounced up the narrow road. Emma's high beams blazed against the glistening dark trees. Abruptly, her lights hit the locked gate, and she braked. A long swath of yellow crime scene tape had been wound around the gate, clearly warning against trespassing.

I unfastened my seat belt. "You'll have to wait here. I'll walk up to the house alone."

"In those clothes? Don't be ridiculous. Hang on. I've got some wire cutters in the back of the truck. I'll cut the lock while you change. I've got some breeches under the seat. And there's probably an extra pair of boots in the back. They'll fit you."

My capable little sister shut off the headlights and swung out of the truck. I wriggled out of my skirt and into a less than pristine pair of riding breeches. As I exchanged my Chanel boots for her rubber Wellingtons that smelled dubious but were certainly warm and dry, Emma took it upon herself to ignore the yellow police tape and cut the lock on the gate.

She looked at me. "Does that coat have feathers on it?"

"Yes."

"Trade me, Tweety Bird." She started to pull her sweatshirt over her head. "You can't go up there wearing that."

I stopped her hands. "Yes, I can."

We squabbled, and I won for once, keeping my fancy jacket. In a few more minutes, we were heading up the narrow lane toward the house.

"Don't drive off the edge," I warned, "or we'll end up in the moat."

Emma cursed and swerved as a small animal scuttled out of the overgrowth. "What was that?"

"Raccoon, maybe?"

As we rattled over the decorative bridge, I saw Quintain differently than before. It was a fantasy castle—maybe one woman's idea of a princess's dream come true. But tonight it looked forbidding and very dark.

"Here's a flashlight. I hope the battery lasts. And take your cell phone," Emma said. "If I see trouble coming, I'll call you."

"If you see any sign of trouble whatsoever, you should run," I told her. "Don't worry about me."

I let myself out of the truck and headed across the matted weeds toward the house.

Perhaps a swarm of intrepid warriors might have stormed just such a castle. Crossing the moat, dodging boiling oil. Me, I slogged through the mud in the dark, skirted the front entrance—plastered with more yellow police tape—and pushed through the overgrowth around the side of the house. I prayed no creepy crawlies made their home where Emma's boots sank into the cold muck beneath my feet.

Around back, I climbed over the low stone wall of the kitchen garden and made my way to the terrace. From there, I could see the many dark windows that faced the rear of the property. Some of the second-floor bedrooms had balconies. But Michael always said the most obvious choice is the easiest route, so I felt my way along the downstairs windows. With the flashlight and my bare hands, I checked each one for an unlocked sash—the kitchen, the pantry and on down the line.

The glass of one of the breakfast room windows was cracked. I wiggled it gingerly, and a shard slipped out of the frame with ease. I reached my arm inside and groped around until I found the window lock. It was stiff, and I panted, my face pressed against the cold, dirty glass, while trying to jiggle it open.

The mechanism cracked off in my hand. I said a word I normally didn't.

I tossed the broken metal down onto the terrace, and it clanged at my feet. I held my breath, half expecting to be caught red-handed.

But only the wind in the trees sounded around me.

I reached back inside the broken window and shoved at the sash. It moved! Then got stuck again. I shoved and muttered and shoved some more until the window slowly budged open far enough for me to get a good grip on it from the outside. I pushed it upward.

A moment later, I climbed into the breakfast room.

The inside of the house was deathly quiet. Underfoot, dust and debris crackled—sounding loud in the empty building. I tried to steady my heart, but the more I flashed the light around the weird shapes of the furniture, the more panicky I felt. I rushed across the breakfast room, bumped into a chair and knocked it over. The crash sent me skittering into the hallway.

Suddenly, my cell phone vibrated in my pocket. I gave an involuntary squeak of fright. Emma calling to warn me? I grabbed the phone and answered.

In my ear, Michael said, "What the hell are you doing?"

"It's you! Oh, uh, nothing out of the ordinary." I hoped my voice sounded convincing.

"Cut the act," he said. "Reed called. He tells me you and Emma went off together, looking anything but innocent. What are you doing?"

"Getting a milk shake."

"Nora."

"Okay, okay. I'm just—I let myself into Aunt Madeleine's house."

A short silence, and then he said, "Isn't that place a crime scene?"

"Well, technically . . . yes."

He said, "I hate it when you do your Jessica Fletcher routine."

"How do you know who Jessica Fletcher is?"

"Cabot Cove, Angela Lansbury. You'd be amazed what people watch in prison. You okay?"

"I'm fine. Better than fine. Exhilarated, in fact. I'm starting to understand what you see in the underworld."

He laughed. "Don't get arrested. I'll have to find a new girl-friend, and that's a hassle."

I told him I loved him and signed off. As we talked, I'd been edging my way through the house with more confidence. It had been encouraging to hear his voice.

I remembered my way around pretty well. Only once did I make a wrong turn in the dark. In a few minutes, I found Aunt Madeleine's study. Her writing table looked just as it had when I was in the house before. Groatley hadn't ransacked the room as badly as Sutherland had claimed.

But the filing cabinets were unlocked and open—a sign that somebody had been in the room since I left it. Holding the flash-light clumsily in one hand, I searched the drawers for the black book. No luck.

I cast the light around the room, trying to imagine a good hiding place and hoping someone else hadn't beaten me to finding it. I shut off the flashlight to save the battery.

As my eyes became accustomed to the dark, I stewed. Where might Madeleine keep her ledger book? Or had Groatley whisked it out of Quintain after all? And what had he hoped to accomplish? To conceal evidence of her murder? Or protect himself somehow?

With a sigh of frustration, I sank down in Madeleine's tufted chair to look at the desk.

My phone buzzed again, triggering another moment of panic. I answered, expecting to hear Emma warning me of imminent discovery.

But it was Libby who said, "I feel a little guilty about being so pushy with Emma earlier. Do you think she went on a bender?"

"She's on an eating binge, not a drinking binge."

"You never know what might set her off, though." Libby sighed with dismay. "Oh, Nora! What a mess! You do realize Emma needs help making a decision. Otherwise, you're going to have to make it for her."

"Me!"

In the background, I could hear the buzz of Libby's kitchen blender. I pictured my sister whipping up a frothy drink for herself. She said, "You're the only one of us who can make the tough decisions, Nora. I want you to sit down with Rawlins, too, about his college choices. But first help me decide what to do about Em. I should make a gesture of apology, I think. Do you have time to talk?"

"Right this minute?"

"I was thinking of sending her to a spa for a day—you know, get her a gift certificate—but then I wondered if maybe she might insult those nice girls down at the Pink Windowbox. That's my favorite spa, and I don't want to spoil my relationship with them. They help me take photos for my PitterPat followers." She shut off the blender, and I could hear pouring. "And don't you think they do wonders with candles? So peaceful, and yet seductive."

"Your followers?"

"No, the girls at the Pink Windowbox!" She sipped her drink and hummed with pleasure.

I said, "Libby, this isn't a good time."

"Why? Are you seducing That Man of Yours?" She blew another gusty sigh. "I'm so desperate for sex I'm thinking of—"

"Don't tell me," I said. "I don't want to hear the lengths you'd go to."

"Oh, all right. What are you doing? If not slipping into your best lingerie?"

"Actually," I said, "I'm sitting in Aunt Madeleine's desk chair."

"You're *what*?"

"I broke into Quintain."

"Why didn't you *call me*? I'd love to break into something!"

"Sorry. It was spur of the moment."

"I can be there in twenty minutes!"

"No, wait—I'll be gone by then. Look, Libby, I'm a little busy."

"What are you looking for?"

"A kind of notebook. She kept it in her study. It was a black—"

"Yes, yes. I used to think it was her diary, so I peeked, but it was mostly numbers—nothing very interesting."

"Well, I'd like to find it, so if you'll excuse me—"

"Check under her chair."

"What?"

"I bet it's under the seat cushion of her desk chair. At least, that's where she used to keep it."

I stood up and lifted the chair cushion. Sure enough, there lay the black ledger.

"Libby," I said, "you're a genius."

"Just snoopy," she said. "And I have a good memory. Call me later. *Dancing with the Stars* just came on. I love the men when they have all that lotion on their muscles."

She hung up on me.

The leather-bound book in my hand looked exactly as I remembered it. Automatically, I flipped it open to look inside, but all I could see was columns of names and numbers. I took a chance on the flashlight's battery long enough to take a closer look. The handwriting was neat and ladylike. But all the numbers meant I needed more time to study the meaning of Madeleine's notations. I'd have to take it home.

I sat down in the chair again and paused a moment to absorb the details of Madeleine's study, her private sanctum, trying to understand the woman who'd selected everything in the room. I felt as if I was teetering on the brink of a big discovery about her. Maybe about myself.

But instead, I said aloud to Libby, "What do you mean, I'm the one who has to make the tough decisions?"

My phone suddenly vibrated in my pocket again.

I answered, prepared to demand that Libby explain herself, but this time it was Emma, low-voiced and urgent. "Hurry up. Somebody's coming."

Her words acted like an electric cattle prod on my heart. Adrenaline zinged through my bloodstream until my fingertips tingled.

"Go," I commanded. "Leave now, Em. Call me back when you can—"

"Too late," Emma said. "It's the cops. I'm screwed."

She hung up.

I switched off the flashlight, tucked Madeleine's book under my arm and ran. I groped my way to a window. From that vantage point, I could see down the long driveway. Sure enough, a police cruiser had arrived, red light flashing as it pulled close behind Emma's truck.

I had only a few minutes to get out of the house.

I found my way back to the breakfast room and scrabbled out the window with Madeleine's book. Once outside again, I blundered across the kitchen garden, vaulted over the stone wall and struggled through the overgrowth to the woods. Mud sucked at the boots on my feet. Branches swatted my face. In the open field that had been the tilting green, I started to run.

Emma? Normally, she could bluff her way out of just about any situation. Or she'd seduce her arresting officer and get off scot-free. But those options worked better when she wasn't hugely pregnant.

Somewhere to my left lay the van Vincent house—and probably a safer route to the main road than Quintain's drive, where the police might be looking for me. I caught another glimpse of the red flashing light—no doubt the police with Emma—and my decision was made. I hugged the book tight and struck out across the dark landscape to the sound of my wet footsteps and the chattering of my teeth.

I saw the lights of the van Vincent house over the next rolling hill. I edged closer, climbed through a split rail fence and found myself leaning a hand against the side of the horse barn to catch my breath. I could hear Shirley's horses inside, stamping and snorting in their stalls. They could sense me, and I made them restless.

I waited until my heart stopped pounding. The low, modern lines of the house cut smoothly into the landscape. By moonlight I could see that preparations for the international horse show had begun on the lower part of the property. Two large tents stood on the sides of a wide, mowed field. Stacks of orange cones sat next to piles of lumber that would eventually be arranged into obstacles on the driving course. Someone had already begun to string colored flags in the trees, too.

A dog barked in the house. A second later, another dog took up the alarm. Probably Shirley's Dalmatians.

I pushed off from the barn and started to run. If Shirley turned her dogs loose, they'd find me in minutes. I hurtled down the slope of the lawn, heading for the woods again.

Eventually I found myself stumbling over the old furrows of a cultivated field. Emma's boots were soon heavy with caked mud. I slogged onward and finally reached a ridge piled with stones—perhaps the work of the first farmer who had cleared the property for cultivation. I clambered over the heap and headed for the trees.

But as I stepped over a tangle of brush, something snagged my foot and I fell into a washed-out gully.

I landed on a rock, and the force blew all the air from my lungs. I lay stunned for a second, my chest locked, the breath driven out of me so hard that a constellation of stars burst in front of my eyes. Seconds or hours ticked by, and I couldn't breathe, couldn't cry out for help. I felt my consciousness start to fade. A loamy blackness whispered up around me like fallen leaves as I sank into the earth.

Convulsively, I stretched out my hand as if to grab a lifeline from the grave.

My fingers found something smooth and hard, and I fumbled for an instant, then seized it with the last iota of strength I could manage. Long, like a stick. I gripped the shaft in my palm and looked. It was slender and gray in the moonlight.

A bone.

The shock made me suck in a cold gulp of air and I stared at the thing in my hand.

Slowly, my brain began to clear, and the details of a magical kind of glade swam into perspective around me. The trees leaned down around an open space of dirt with tufts of grass and a rubble of white stones that looked as if they'd been washed by years of sporadic floods. Now it was a peaceful place, quiet and still and cool.

But with my cheek still flat on the ground, my body still spread-eagled in the dirt, I blinked calmly at the bone in my hand, as if in a dream. Not just a bone, but a human one. Whose bone? Here for how long?

Madeleine's voice, sharp in my ear, said, "Did you break it on purpose?"

A slender shaft. So delicate, yet strong. A human bone.

An ulna. I knew it from having helped Todd memorize the skeleton back in his medical school days. We ate salty popcorn as we leafed through his textbooks with their drawings. We had laughed together as I quizzed him. I could almost taste the salt as I recalled how gracefully the ulna and the radius bowed together, like two graceful figures dancing. They joined at the wrist by—what was it called? Oh, yes, the styloid process.

I sat up slowly. The rubble of stones around me turned out to be more bones that lay scattered—not in any order, but in a jumble, as if dug up, gnawed and abandoned long ago by animals, perhaps. Why I didn't shriek and leap to my feet, I'm not sure, but instead of panic or horror, I felt a strange peace. Salty popcorn on my tongue. Or maybe it was my own blood in my mouth again. Without thinking, I began to identify the other bones—a scapula, vertebrae cast like dice on the earth, and small bits that might have been— what? Metacarpals?

Finally, I set the bone down. Returned it gently to its companions.

Unsteadily, I got to my feet and dusted myself off. I bent down to pick up Madeleine's book, then took two steps back. And two more. Staring down at the circle of bones on the ground, unwilling to leave them. It. Her. Him. Whoever it had been once. But I felt Todd in that moment. Not Madeleine or anyone else who was now gone from this earth, but Todd. As I stepped backward, almost as if dreaming, I left him. Or he left me—perhaps that was it.

I turned away and pulled out my cell phone. 911. I should call for help. But . . . surely the time for emergency assistance had passed? And how was I going to explain my presence here at this time of night? With my sister arrested just a short distance away? With a rush of guilt, I put my phone back in my pocket.

The dogs were barking again.

Clutching the book, I turned my back on the bones and hurried into the trees.

Finally, I reached the embankment above the main road. By then I could think straight. I found a thick tree and crouched behind it. With shaking hands I tried phoning Emma first.

She didn't answer.

Just then, a car slowed down on the road. I could hear its throaty engine as it came to a stop below me. I realized my phone's blue screen had probably given me away, and I snapped it shut. I held my breath and prayed it wasn't the police looking for trespassers. I'd have to explain myself. The stammering of a woman who'd had the wind knocked out of her—and with it went her wits, too—wasn't going to make a good impression on the police. Because I still thought I'd left Todd back there. Intellectually, I knew the bones weren't his, and yet . . . I'd experienced something strange in that cool clearing.

A moment later, a male voice carried up to my hiding place, startling me. "Come out, come out wherever you are."

"Michael?"

I edged out from behind the tree. On the road, one of Michael's jacked-up muscle cars idled noisily. I slithered down the bank to the road. When Emma's rubber boots hit the wet asphalt of the road, my feet went out from under me and I landed on my butt with a splash.

I scrambled up and squinted across the road at the car. "What are you doing here?"

Michael leaned out the car's window to get a good look at me. What he saw made him barely hold back laughter. "I'm on my way to church. Want a ride?"

"I'm filthy dirty."

"No kidding," he said. "You smell funny, too. What did you do? Wrestle a bear?" Then, sharper, "You okay?"

"Y-yes," I said. "Something strange just—I found—I left—"

He got out of the car. "What's wrong? You look— Nora? There's blood on your lip."

His hands on my arms felt wonderfully strong. I said, "I fell. It's nothing."

He swiped gently at the edge of my mouth with his thumb, but he saw that I was safe. Teasing gone, he said kindly, "Get in the car."

He pulled me around the hood and helped me into the passenger seat. When he got back behind the wheel and closed the door, the bang jump-started my brain again. I forgot about Todd.

I said, "How did you know where to find me?"

"Emma called. As she was being arrested for trespassing, as a matter of fact." He put his hand through my hair and turned my face to his. He looked at my mouth again, double-checking for serious injury, before his gaze probed mine to look for hysteria. "She said I could find you out roaming in the woods. Driving past, I saw the light from your cell phone screen, so I stopped."

"You shouldn't be out of the house."

"It's okay. I called in, told my keepers I was headed to mass." He scanned my face once more before his brows relaxed and he released me. "Where I'd better go now, since they're tracking me with some kind of GPS magic. So buckle up."

He was all brisk business again, so I obeyed, first twisting around and dropping Aunt Madeleine's book on the floor of the backseat, then reaching for my seat belt. My hands were still shaking, but oddly, I'd forgotten why. "Is Emma okay?"

"She's not happy. I called Cannoli and Sons. They're going to take care of her. They think they can have her processed in an hour or two. There will probably be a fine to pay."

I groaned. Every time I got a few dollars ahead, something happened. "Well, I can get Libby to take me to a cash machine, then we'll pick up Emma. Maybe I need a shower first. But after that—"

"A long shower," he said with good humor. He put the car in gear and started to drive. "But first, church."

Something in his tone made me forget my own situation and

turn toward him. In the light of the dashboard, I could see an urgency in him. He had thought I was lost in the woods, and now that I was safe, he was back to focusing on something else. His jaw was tight, his foot firm on the accelerator.

With the car's momentum pressing me back into the seat, I said, "What's going on?"

"The long story will have to come later. I'm seeing her at Saint Dominic's—Carrie, that is. She wants to meet face-to-face."

I forgot about communing with bones in the woods. "What are you going to say to her?"

"I was hoping you'd think of something."

"Me?"

"Come on," he begged, clearly unnerved. "I'm desperate. What do you say to the kid you've never met?"

CHAPTER THIRTEEN

Over the last couple of years, I had decided that if you find yourself in a dysfunctional family, the most sensible course of action is to create a new family of your own. That was the mutual thinking that drew Michael and me together in the first place, and it kept us going toward the horizon together—both believing we had a chance at happiness if we started our own family unit. Until now, I was the one who had to get past my hormonal sisters, and he was the one with the felons in his homicidal family tree. We hadn't quite accepted each other's family yet, but we had found ways to cope.

Now this.

As he got out of the car five minutes later and headed across the parking lot toward a tall young woman in a pair of desert cammo cargo pants, I realized our family dynamic was about to get turned on its ear.

I stayed in the passenger seat and watched the father-daughter meeting unfold.

Under a streetlight outside Saint Dominic's church, she stuck out her hand to shake his, and he took it. No hug. No weeping with delight. No joyous exchange of emotion. In fact, they both took a cautious step back and gave each other a once-over that stretched into an awkward silence.

I couldn't see her very well in the shadowy lamplight. She was very tall—nearly six feet, I guessed—with a dark topknot of hair that made her seem taller yet. She shoved her hands into the front pockets of a hoodie sweatshirt and stood with her weight evenly distributed on both feet. Parade rest, perhaps. Or maybe she was preparing to make a quick departure if she decided she didn't want to stick around.

Michael was the first to speak. I couldn't hear what he had to say, but it didn't go over well. She didn't smile. She said something short back to him, and he laughed. Which offended her, I could see. Her whole posture stiffened, but she didn't look away. She glared up into Michael's face.

I tried willing him to say something pleasant. Something kind. But he didn't warm up to strangers quickly. There was a natural wariness in him.

It looked to me as if Carrie had the same nature.

Michael glanced my way over his shoulder. Telling me to stay put? I couldn't guess.

The girl looked at the car, too, and I scrunched down in the passenger seat.

They had a short conversation thereafter, her snapping, him responding more gently, thank heaven.

Abruptly, they turned toward the car and came my way.

"Oh, boy," I whispered.

I climbed out of the car and hoped the streetlamp didn't illuminate my filthy clothes.

"Nora," Michael said, "Carrie wanted to meet you."

"Hello," I said, feeling like an idiot and hoping I didn't smell as bad as I thought I did.

"Hey." Towering over me, she put her hand out. "I'm Carrie Hardaway."

"Hi, Carrie." I accepted her hand. "How nice to meet you. I'm Nora Blackbird."

My first realization was that her mother had been African-American. Carrie had skin the color of café au lait, and her hair was braided into a topknot that complemented the curve of her cheekbones and a wide, smooth forehead and arching brows. She had Michael's nose, though—at least, the nose I assumed he'd had before it had been broken. And, remarkably, she possessed the same athletic ease he had. Except in her it was feminine.

I said the first thing that hit me. "Michael's mother used to be a showgirl in Atlantic City, you know. I've never met her, but I've seen pictures. You're just as beautiful as she is."

Surprise bloomed on her face. "I didn't know that."

Michael said, "Carrie's read about me in the newspapers. Nobody mentions my mother."

"Well, don't be fooled by the newspapers, Carrie," I said lightly. "He's not nearly as awful as they say he is. He cooks. And he likes to go fishing."

"I'm allergic to fish," she said, voice flat.

"Oh."

"Okay, not really." She wrinkled her nose. "I just don't like the taste. Too . . ."

"Fishy?" I guessed with an encouraging smile.

She nodded, but her gaze slipped down my ruined feathered jacket to Emma's crusty riding breeches and splattered rubber boots. "What happened to you?"

"It's a long story," I said. "And very embarrassing."

"I bet."

Michael took out his handkerchief and tenderly wiped a hunk of something sticky off my eyelid.

"Thank you," I said. "But I wish you'd done that ten minutes ago."

"Sorry. Listen." Michael gave me the handkerchief and hooked his thumb toward the church. "I gotta go inside and say hello to Father Tom. Okay if I leave you two . . . ?"

"Sure," I said.

"Don't tell her all of my bad habits," he said and left us alone together.

To Carrie, I said, "He's nervous about meeting you."

Watching him go up the stairs and into the church, Carrie said, "I'm nervous, too."

"You were very brave to contact him. That took a lot of courage." More gently, I added, "I'm very sorry to hear about your mother."

Carrie's jaw hardened, and she nodded. "Yeah, she was sick for a few years. Breast cancer. We thought she had it beat, but . . ."

"I'm sorry," I said again.

She turned and looked at me more carefully. "I don't know what I expected. I mean, I saw his pictures in the paper and stuff. My mom never really talked about him. I guess she never told him about me, either."

"She must have had her reasons."

"She was really young. I mean, she was sixteen when I was born. So I guess I—I grew up with this idea I had a perfect dad somewhere. A fantasy dad, you know. When I found out it was him, I—well, maybe my mom was right to keep me away."

I thought maybe everybody kept the fantasy of perfect parents alive for as long as possible. I wondered if there really was such a thing. For her, Michael must have seemed a kind of light at the end of a long, dark tunnel—a parent who appeared just as she lost her loving mother. But like the old joke, he turned out to be a speeding train. I didn't know how to make her feel better about learning who her real father was, so I said, "Do you have other siblings?"

Carrie shook her head. "Just me and my mom. My grandmother was alive for a while when I was little, but she died, too."

"So you're alone now."

A proud gleam shone in her eyes. "I'm not alone. I got friends."

"And Michael says you're in the army."

She gave me a curious stare, her dark gaze scanning my face in an effort to read my personality. Her brows twitched. "Why you call him that? I thought his name was Mick. That's what I read in the news. That's what my mom called him."

"That's what he calls himself, too, but I—I just never used that name. It always seemed like the name of a man I didn't really want to know. I know him as Michael."

"Not as The Mick? Not as the mob guy?"

"He's not in organized crime."

"He went to jail."

"Yes, but—that's behind him now."

Carrie made a disgusted noise in her throat. "You brainwashed, or something?"

"Maybe I am," I admitted. "But I accept him as the man he wants to be. He's done some things he's not proud of, but now he's trying to do the right thing."

"Huh," she said.

"Maybe you've been sent for a reason," I said. "To be a part of his new life, too."

She stuck her hands into her pockets again. "I'm not asking to be a part of anything. I just wanted to meet him. Tell him a few things."

My heart ached for this solitary young woman who was disappointed to discover that her dream dad wasn't the man she'd hoped for. I said, "I know he'll want to hear what you have to say. He's a good listener."

She shrugged, unwilling to confide in me.

We stood quietly for a moment as the night sounds whispered

around us. The river murmured a few hundred yards to the east in the darkness. From inside the church, we could hear the baritone cadence of a solitary voice—Father Tom speaking to his late-night flock. Only three other cars were parked in the lot. On the nearby road, a pickup truck with a whining engine drove past and kept going. The truck's radio played a thumping rock song.

"My mom raised me right," Carrie said when the music faded into the distance. She sounded argumentative. "She worked hard, helped me with school. I'm going to college as soon as I get done with my hitch."

"That's wonderful. She was very proud of you, I'm sure." I heard the stupid guidance counselor tone of my words and felt foolish for being patronizing to this capable young woman.

Carrie rolled her eyes, but they were suddenly glassy with tears. "Listen, my mom was great. She wasn't some welfare crack whore. She was a teacher, and plenty of kids loved her. She made a big difference. She wouldn't like me being here, meeting him. She didn't ever want me to know him, and she probably had her reasons—good reasons. I should have honored her wishes. I shouldn't have come."

She turned away from me, full of remorse, but I reached out to seize her hand. "Don't go, Carrie."

She pulled free of my touch. "I shouldn't have done this."

"Come home with us," I urged. "We can make omelets and talk."

Carrie didn't stick around to listen to more. She put her back to me and walked away. I wanted to run after her, but it wasn't my place to chase her. She hadn't come to meet me. I was an added complication, that's all. A moment later, Carrie climbed into a low, dark car and drove away.

Michael came out of the church a little while later. "What happened?"

"I'm sorry." I stopped pacing the parking lot. "I'm really sorry. She left."

"What did you say to her?" There was a note of accusation in his voice.

"I said at least twelve more sentences than you did," I shot back. "You ran like a frightened rabbit, Michael!"

He blanched and ran one hand through his hair. "Sorry. You're right. I was scared to death. Which way did she go?"

"We're not following her," I said firmly. "She's already prepared to be afraid of Don Corleone. Let's not push that button, all right?"

"She wasn't afraid. Did you see the way she looked at me? Like I was a worm or something."

Softening, I touched his shoulder. "You're not a worm. Her mother had a lot of years to tell her side of the story. You'll have your chance soon. She'll call again."

"You think so?"

"Give her time."

Michael swore under his breath, perplexed as I'd ever seen him.

We had been standing in the middle of the parking lot, but suddenly a set of headlights raked over us. It was a police cruiser.

The car pulled close and the driver's side window went down. "Mick," said the cop. "You headed home now?"

Michael didn't answer.

"Come on." I took his arm and felt the tension in his body. He was on the edge of an outburst, but I steadied him. "Let's get you home before you turn into a pumpkin."

While the state trooper watched, we got into Michael's car.

When he'd started the engine and pulled out onto the highway, he said, "What about Emma? Should we swing by the police station? See if she's been turned loose?"

"No, I don't want both of you spending the night in jail. Let's get you home before some kind of ankle alarm goes off. Anyway, I have to regroup before I can cope with Emma's situation."

The cop followed us the whole way home. At Blackbird Farm, Michael paused at the end of the driveway and exchanged monosyllables with his crew, who were gathered in a tight knot and blowing agitated puffs of cigar smoke into the air. One had a base-ball bat in hand. I could see something had them worked up.

"Now what?" I asked when Michael rolled up his window with an exasperated sigh.

He drove around the back of the house in the dark. "Something's making a weird noise out in your pasture."

"One of the ponies?"

"Nope. Whatever it is, it's making scary yowling noises. They decided it's Bigfoot."

"Bigfoot! Oh, for the love of—! It was probably a cat, that's all."

"Bruno went to check it out, but he hasn't come back. So they're spooked."

I had observed that most of Michael's posse were the inner-city kind of mob enforcers. They didn't like getting their shoeshines muddied up. Country life alarmed them more than the hint of gangland war. I knew one of them had quit when he was handed his Green Acres assignment.

As the headlights swept the paddock fence near the barn, we could see eight inquisitive pony faces poking through the rails. Their ears were pitched toward the pasture, listening alertly.

Toby dashed partway out into the pasture and back, barking. Ralphie ran back and forth after him, squealing with anxiety.

"Now what?" Michael asked, exasperated.

We climbed out of his car, and I saw immediately what had Toby and Ralphie going crazy.

Emma marched out of the darkness, hitching up her pants. Be-hind her, Bruno followed, daintily hopping over piles of manure and cursing. He held one hand to his swollen eye socket.

I ran across the grass. "Em! What are you doing here?"

She was cussing a blue streak. "What the hell does it look like I'm doing? I had to pee, but the house is locked. So I went out behind the trees. Next thing I know, this asshole is whacking the bushes like I'm an alien intruder. Who locked the damn door?"

Michael was right behind me, trying to smother his laughter. "Sorry, Emma. That was me. I gotta say, you have the smallest bladder of anyone I've ever known."

"The size of my bladder is not the problem, you smart-ass bastard." She punched him in the chest and blew past us.

Michael planted his hand on his chest and turned to me. "What'd I say?"

"You're a man," I explained rationally. "She's taking out her frustrations on the nearest representative of your sex."

"*I* didn't get her pregnant."

"I hate all men!" she bellowed over her shoulder.

Michael called after her, "Wasn't it me who called my lawyer to get you out of jail?"

She spun around, enraged. "I'm sick of men, all men, every man on the planet." She pointed a shaking finger at Bruno. "That one had to come scampering into the woods! Scared the hell out of me."

Bruno kept his hand clamped over his eye. "We heard a noise. I went to check. She jumped out of some bushes and hit me."

"I had my pants down around my ankles and he sneaked up on me! With a baseball bat!"

He said, "It was a tree branch."

"He tried to clobber me with it!"

"It was mistaken identity. I thought—that is—when she . . . er . . ."

"It's okay, Bruno," Michael said. "Go get some ice."

Emma whirled around and marched for the house. As she walked, she ripped the neon orange POLICE CUSTODY wristband from her arm.

I soothed the dog and the pig and Emma, too, as I used my key to let us into the kitchen. Toby ran past me, and Emma shoved through right behind him, taking time to deposit her wristband around Ralphie's ear. I barely prevented Ralphie from shouldering his way inside, too. As fetching as he looked with his ear ribbon, I didn't want a pig in my house. Once inside, I flipped on the light. Emma's face was red. She turned the faucet on to wash her hands.

"Take a deep breath and calm down," I said. "Getting this worked up can't be good for the baby."

"Cut the mother hen routine."

I tossed Aunt Madeleine's book on the kitchen table. "Are you hungry?"

"Starving. The cops gave me a candy bar an hour ago. You owe me big, Sis. I haven't been arrested since I was picked up for shoplifting a six-pack back in school. It's your fault I got nabbed tonight."

"I'm sincerely sorry."

"I hope it's worth it. Did you find anything in Quintain?"

"That can wait. How on earth did you get home? Where's your truck? It's not parked outside."

"The police towed it." She dried her hands on the kitchen towel. "I have to go back tomorrow. I hitchhiked here, then sneaked through the woods so Mick's goons wouldn't see me. The last thing I wanted to do was explain myself to a bunch of grinning wiseguys."

I decided against telling her she'd been mistaken for Bigfoot. She had punched Bruno for less of an insult.

She threw the towel onto the counter. "Do you know how hard it is for a pregnant hitchhiker to get picked up? I spent twenty minutes with my thumb hanging out before Floreen Donaldson stopped for me."

"Floreen, who used to clean for Mama?"

"Yes. She took one look at me and started on the story of Bathsheba. Why is it Bathsheba's fault if King David grabbed her off a rooftop, anyway? She got the bad rap, but he was the one who coveted his neighbor's wife in the first place. It's always the woman's fault."

While she talked, I grabbed a loaf of whole wheat bread and the jar of peanut butter. Sugar and carbs—always an antidote for female rage. With luck, I had a few chocolate chips in the pantry. I could add them to her sandwich.

Michael poked his head through the back door, using his knee to keep Ralphie from barging inside. "Is it safe to come in?"

"Sure. I could use a punching bag." She was rubbing her belly as if to soothe the child within. Or maybe herself.

"Just so you know, there's somebody coming up the driveway," Michael said.

"Who? Libby?"

"Nope. A guy in a BMW."

Emma exploded with more swearing.

Michael ducked back outside. I made Emma a peanut butter sandwich and let her fume. When Michael returned, he was followed by a man I couldn't have been more surprised to see on Blackbird Farm.

"Hart," I said, hardly able to conceal my astonishment. "What a pleasure to see you."

He stepped into the kitchen, looking bewildered. "There's a pig on your porch. I think it's wearing a hair ribbon."

"Really?" I asked with false cheer. "I wonder how that happened."

Hart Jones, a successful stockbroker and Emma's summer paramour, wore a two-thousand-dollar suit and a pale silk tie, as if he'd just been called away from the symphony. He gave me a head-to-toe glance that absorbed the mud-spattered condition of my clothes. If his first impulse was to recoil in horror, he mastered it with the kind of social skill men of his socioeconomic class probably learned from the cradle. "Hello, Nora. Did you have some kind of accident?"

"Heavens, no," I said breezily. "Just doing a little late-night gardening." The stress of the evening was finally starting to get to me, I realized, and it took an effort to fight down the bubble of hysteria that threatened to burst out. "Hart, this is my—this is Michael Abruzzo. Michael, this is Emma's—this is Hart Jones."

They shook hands politely, but I could see both men already knew plenty about the other's background. Last summer, Michael had listened to all of our sisterly discussions about Hart, and Hart had no doubt read all the newspaper coverage of the infamous heir to New Jersey's mob rackets. I wasn't sure which of them was more influenced by the other's advance publicity. Impressed or filled with instant loathing, I couldn't tell.

"What are you doing here?" Emma demanded, still flushed with embarrassment. But she was clearly determined to bluster through. She kept the table between herself and Hart.

"You called me." Hart sounded just as testy. "From jail. Remember?"

"That was before my lawyer showed up," she snapped. "I told you, you didn't have to come."

"You said you'd been arrested," he replied. "You think I could stay away after a call like that? I left Penny in her family's box at the opera. You think that was easy to explain?"

Hart Jones was a Philadelphia financial wunderkind who'd hooked up with Emma a few months back when he was trying to decide whether to settle down for better or for worse with Penny Haffenpepper, a Main Line heiress. I'm sure he intended his fling with my hot-blooded sister to be a one-night stand in a hotel suite, but it turned into a monthlong, torrid affair that resulted in Emma's current predicament. At the end of summer, though, Hart had disappeared from her life. I assumed Emma had broken things off with him and he'd gone back to his well-behaved fiancée.

From the way the two of them glared at each other now, it didn't look as if the embers of romance were going to rekindle anytime soon. And yet . . . a dangerous static crackled in the air.

Emma said, "Well, you shouldn't have made the trip. Go home. You've probably got wedding details to plan."

"They're already planned. The wedding's Christmas Eve."

"Very romantic. Not to mention it'll be easy to remember your anniversary."

"I'm not a forgetful person," Hart said.

The electricity in the room was starting to feel like the buildup of lightning before a thunderstorm. Hastily, I gathered my jacket and Aunt Madeleine's ledger and began to edge toward the doorway. "Michael, why don't you and I . . . ?"

He deliberately ignored my suggestion, continuing to glower at Hart. "Maybe Em needs some help here."

"I can fight my own battles, big guy."

"Michael," I said again.

Unwillingly, he headed across the kitchen. "Okay. G'night, Em. Glad to see you out of jail."

She made another anatomically impossible suggestion without taking her glare from Hart's equally stormy face. Together, Michael and I fled the kitchen before the thunderclaps started.

CHAPTER FOURTEEN

Upstairs, I stripped off my sodden clothes and ran a hot bath in the claw-foot tub. I hung the McQueen feather jacket on a hanger and gave it a long look. Only a miracle worker was going to save it. My hands must have trembled on the hanger, though, because the next moment Michael was taking them into his own, his palms warming my suddenly freezing fingers.

"You okay?" he asked.

"It's been a long night. I— There wasn't time to tell you earlier, but I found another body."

He cursed. "What the hell?"

"Not a body, exactly, but a skeleton. While I was blundering around in the woods, I slipped and fell and—well, suddenly I was holding a bone. I landed in the middle of—of—"

"Nora." He took me in his arms and held me tightly. "Why didn't you say something earlier?"

I wrapped my arms around him and held on, pressing my cheek to his chest, very glad to be home at last. "I don't know. You came along, and there was Carrie to worry about, and I just—I forgot, I guess." Letting my weariness slip, I said, "I should call the police."

"Not this minute." He held me away and looked into my face. "You're shaken up."

"I was afraid to call 911," I admitted. "Because I'd have to explain what I was doing out in the woods. With Emma getting arrested—I have to get my story straight, don't I? That sounds awful, but . . ."

"You're right. You have to think it through," he said, sounding just as sorry about the situation as I felt.

I told him about falling and knocking the wind out of myself and how I'd ended up with a human bone in my hand. I hadn't been thinking straight.

"You were in shock," he said gently. "I should have realized it before. C'mon. Take a bath and relax. Those bones aren't going anywhere. We'll figure out what to say to the police, and you can call in the morning."

He ran the hot water while I stripped off my underwear. When his cell phone rang, I sprinkled bath beads into the water and swirled it with my hand. Suddenly I couldn't wait to soak my cares away.

In the adjacent bedroom, Michael sat on our bed and spoke briefly to his caller. Then he checked his cell phone messages.

"Anything from Carrie?" I called as I sank into the blessedly warm depths of the tub. I shook a few more bath beads into the water and breathed the fragrance.

"Not yet." His voice carried easily from the bedroom. A moment later, he asked, "What's this book?"

"I stole it out of Aunt Madeleine's house." I lathered up a loofah and set about scrubbing Quintain mud from my skin. "Take a look, if you like."

As I shampooed my hair, I wondered what might be transpiring in the kitchen below.

Emma and Hart weren't exactly an odd couple. Hart, for all his sedate bankerly ways during the workweek, had a reputation for partying hard on the weekends. He rode a fast horse with one of the suburban fox hunts, and he had been known for knocking back a lot of liquor without showing many side effects. Like Emma, he enjoyed a good laugh. I imagined they partied hard when together.

I thought Hart had ended his roguish bachelor ways when he proposed to Penny Haffenpepper, who had the kind of pedigree as well as social and business contacts that could launch Hart into the top tier of the banking hierarchy. Penny's clan had a few quirks, of course, but they were very family-oriented. Strict values, emphasis on education and quality time spent with each other. I thought her influence might have tamed Hart a little.

But Emma had phoned him tonight when she needed help. And he'd come running.

I wondered how soon they'd get around to discussing their baby.

After a while, Michael came into the bathroom with Madeleine's black ledger. He sat on the edge of the tub, unbuttoning his shirt one-handed and skimming the pages with a puzzled frown on his face. "What is this, exactly?"

"I don't know. It was important to Aunt Madeleine, that's all I'm certain of. A long time ago she asked me to destroy it when she died."

"Oh, yeah?" He went back into the bedroom and came back a minute later with his shirt off and wearing his reading glasses. "Have you read any of this stuff?"

My first glimpse of Michael's naked, post-prison shoulders took my breath away. His jeans rode low on his hips, too, showing a tantalizing expanse of touchable muscle. It took all my self-control not to pull him down into the water that instant. Although my mouth had gone dry, I managed to say in an almost normal voice, "I haven't had a chance yet. Why?"

"It's . . . I dunno. It's definitely a list of transactions."

"What kind of transactions? Household expenses, you mean?"

"No," he said.

At that moment, his cell phone rang again, and he went back into the bedroom to answer it.

I finished my bath as he spoke to someone on the phone, then made another call. I could tell from his tone it was business. Part of me hoped he'd shut off his phone for the night and join me in the tub. We'd begun many passionate nights just that way—soaking and talking and exploring. I felt myself tremble at the memory of fierce love we'd made together. But now, he was distracted. Big-time.

I pulled the plug from the drain and climbed out of the water, maybe not exactly fully in possession of my wits, but smelling wonderful, if I do say so. While Michael murmured in the bedroom, I wrapped myself in a plush towel. I shook my hair out, buffed it almost dry and left it tousled. I brushed my teeth and looked at my reflection in the mirror while holding the towel against my glowing body. I looked good. Maybe not like the vixenish courtesan Libby probably became when she was in the mood, or the dangerous sexpot Emma undoubtedly was in the bedroom.

But I could hold my own.

On the shelf over the tub I kept a collection of candles. Some of them had been gifts from Libby—probably from her peace-and-seduction-loving friends at the Pink Windowbox. With my sister's words of wisdom ringing in my ears, I lit two of the candles and carried them into the bedroom, still wrapped in my towel. I put the candles on the bedside table and snapped off the lamp. Instant ambiance. With a bottle of lotion, I sat on the edge of the bed.

I handed the bottle to Michael, and he pinned the phone to his shoulder while listening to his caller. He lathered up his hands and smoothed the fragrant cream onto my bare back.

"Okay," he finally said to his caller. "If you take any more bets, you cover them yourself, got it? We're out."

When he terminated the call, then shut off the phone and dropped it onto the bed, I said, "How's your gambling situation?"

"It'd be easier if there weren't so many big football games this weekend."

"Exactly how much money does the Abruzzo family make in the gambling business?"

"About a million two a day."

I must have been out of my wits for asking the question in the first place. But when I heard the answer, I utterly forgot about seduction. I clutched my towel tight, turned around and blinked at him. "A million dollars? Every day?"

He seemed equally surprised at having blurted out the information to me. "About that, yeah. Depends on what sports are in season. It's divided up, of course."

"Divided among your employees, you mean."

"The employees aren't mine." He turned me around again and applied the lotion. "And some are more like partners. At various levels, there are street guys and management guys. And in-between guys. It's complicated."

"And lucrative."

"Well, that's why nobody really wants to stop doing it."

"I wonder," I said tentatively, "if there's a way to keep doing it a little bit? Just enough to fix the roof, maybe?"

He laughed. "That's how it starts. First it's fixing the roof, and then you'll want a condo in Fort Lauderdale, and next thing you know you're negotiating the price of a compound in Switzerland."

"I can see how it could be very tempting."

"I'm pretty sure you have no idea how tempting." Michael feathered lotion onto my skin.

"And the stolen cars? What about that?"

For the first time in our relationship, Michael didn't decline to discuss an Abruzzo family business. "It's more adventure, less pay-off. Guy in Serbia wants a new Mercedes, one of my idiot cousins goes shopping at the mall parking lot."

"You ship to Serbia?"

"And Libya and Turkey. A few places in between. Lots of South America. Venezuela. Haiti, too, maybe, but I'm not sure yet. Basically, the more unstable the country, the better for business. You don't want to know more."

No, I didn't really want to know more. Carrie had been right about me—I was a little brainwashed. All I truly knew was that tonight I wanted to forget it all except that Michael was here with me in the candlelight. Totally with me. His hands felt wonderful, and I could feel his attention slowly leave whatever business he was conducting and transfer to the job at hand. His touch grew more gentle, more languid. And when he finally brushed his lips to the back of my neck, I closed my eyes and released an unsteady sigh of desire.

"I've missed you," I whispered.

"I'm here now," he said against my skin.

I put my hand up to his cheek.

In my ear, he said, "I wanted to be here for you during Lexie's hearing. Was it bad?"

"Terrible. But I— For some reason, it was important for me to get through it alone. I owed Lexie my full attention."

"You would," he said with wry affection.

"It was difficult for me, but horrible for her. I'm not sure she'll ever forgive me, Michael. She'd have run away rather than face the judge, say what she did, if I hadn't insisted that she stay. So I wanted to stand with her. Take the punches, if that makes any sense."

He kissed my bare shoulder. "It does."

"But I worry she's lost to me forever."

"You made the right choice."

"I don't know . . ."

"Lexie had to face the consequences. It's part of the process."

"Don't do the crime if you can't do the time?"

Michael didn't respond to that banality. In a moment, he said, "She's got to think things over for a while. It'll be good for her."

"Will she think about—what? Redeeming herself?"

"Whatever you want to call it. Changing her life. She was getting to be a powerful person. I know what that does to a soul. She'll see that, if it isn't too late. I don't think she's gone forever."

"Michael," I said after a while, "Libby said something today."

"Uh-oh."

I smiled at his pretended trepidation. "No, it made me think. She said I'm the one who has to make the tough decisions. She wants me to talk to Rawlins about college. And to Emma about her baby. But I—why does it have to be me?"

"It takes a lot of strength to make a hard choice."

"I'm not strong."

"Yeah, you are."

"Todd, though." I thought of the worst failure of my life—the thing that still pained my heart. "I couldn't keep Todd away from the drugs. I should have had him arrested, maybe, or sent to rehab—something, anything. But I—I couldn't do that."

"Now you could," Michael said. "Because he died. You'd make the hard choice now. You've already done it. For Lexie. With me."

"I haven't made any choices for you."

"You've given me the choices, and I had to pick. Either you or the life." He pulled me back against him and was silent for a while, holding me snug. When he spoke again, his voice was rough in my ear. "I love you."

He had stopped caressing me, so I said, "Are you okay?"

"I'm getting there." He let out a sigh, and his breath was warm along the nape of my neck. "Look, I'm not sure I can explain it. But there's . . . You have to keep up a lot of shields in prison. Hold yourself inside."

"You don't have to do that with me."

"No, but—I haven't been able to turn the switch, you know?"

He'd always been able to burn off excess energy by going to work—immersing himself in the day-to-day management of whatever marginally criminal activities captured his creative mind at the time. He enjoyed outsmarting adversaries, took pleasure in staying just on the edge of the system.

My sisters laughingly called him the Mafia Prince, and part of me knew that's exactly what he was—a prince of darkness, albeit one struggling to fight off his natural tendencies and find his way into the light. I worried that trapped at home, he had no release valve.

I had a feeling it was easier for him to tell me what was in his heart without looking into my face, so I leaned back into him. "You can't hurt me."

"Yes," he said. "I can."

I pushed the towel away and took his hands in mine. I guided them up to touch my body, to explore all the places that ached for his attention. He let out a shaky sigh in my ear. When I drew his hand into my warmest, most tender spot, he gave up trying to hold back. We peeled off the rest of his clothes and pushed the bedclothes out of the way for a long, slow, luxurious reacquaintance. There was a stormy interlude in the middle, but I let him take what he needed. Maybe I needed it, too.

A couple of hours after we started, we went downstairs and made an enormous meal.

Emma and Hart were gone. Emma had left a note. She'd call tomorrow. While the food cooked, Michael pulled me into the scullery and stripped off my bathrobe again just to kiss me all over. We ate as if famished for more sustenance than mere pasta and went back up to bed to sleep wrapped tightly together, as if to prevent ever being apart again. For a few hours, it felt good to forget about our complicated lives.

CHAPTER FIFTEEN

n the morning, I took care not to wake Michael when I slipped out of the bedroom.

I carried Madeleine's book downstairs and found the drafty old kitchen as cold as a cave and cluttered with the dishes we'd abandoned during the night. I reread Emma's note. She had gone off with Hart, she wrote. She'd call later. Emma's absence had given us the privacy of the house, but I wondered where she had spent the night. And how.

I lit the oven and left its door open to heat the room while I brewed coffee. Since the oven was already warming, I decided to bake muffins. As I worked, I thought about my little sister and what a disaster she could make of her life if she didn't think things through.

My thoughts traveled back to last night's encounter with the bones in the woods. I washed the dishes while the muffins baked, considering my options.

As I dried my wooden mixing spoon, I gathered my courage. After tucking the spoon into its slot in the drawer, I phoned the police.

The state police arrived around nine: a plainclothes detective and a stern state trooper in uniform. The uniformed trooper was the same one who'd followed us home from the church, so I assumed he had tagged along with the detective to check up on Michael. I let them in and poured coffee.

Setting a plate of muffins on the table, I told them I'd found a skeleton in the woods near Shirley van Vincent's house.

They stared at each other, clearly unprepared for this bit of news.

I didn't bother to explain why I was wandering around at night, and maybe they were too surprised to ask. I told them in detail what I'd found and where.

The trooper jotted notes and stepped outside to make a call.

While he spoke on his cell phone, the detective finally noticed my trembling hands and made the effort to assure me that bodies were frequently found in the woods. "It was probably a homeless person or a hunter or maybe someone with dementia who wandered away from home. Sometimes people just disappear. It happens all the time."

"But," I said, "surely somebody reported this person missing?"

He shrugged. "Yeah, but the body wasn't found until now. Who knows how long it's been there? Don't let it bug you. We'll check it out."

When the trooper returned, we sat at the kitchen table. The detective questioned me for nearly an hour about the case on their front burner—relentlessly going over the details of what I'd seen at Madeleine's house when the body in the elevator was found. Feeling guilty for having left the scene of the crime—even one that had been committed twenty years ago—I patiently answered all his questions.

"Have you identified the body in the elevator?" I asked at last.

The detective told me the process would take weeks.

Finally, I said, "Madeleine Blackbird had some very distinctive jewelry. Three diamond rings she always wore."

The two of them sat still and absorbed what I had said. They glanced at each other again.

I had decided it was ridiculous to pretend we hadn't guessed it was Madeleine herself in the elevator. Sutherland may have had his reasons for keeping the truth from the police, but I did not. In fact, I was pretty peeved with Sutherland.

I told the detective about Madeleine's postcards, and when he realized what I already knew—that someone had pretended to be Madeleine after her death—he was suddenly on my side. I handed over one of the postcards and suggested there might be a way to compare the handwriting. If Pippi had been pretending to be Madeleine, maybe somewhere there existed a sample of her handwriting? We brainstormed together quite companionably. They finally accepted muffins, and the two of them even laughed when I made a joke about Sutherland.

I did not tell them that the black leather-bound book that lay on the table right in front of them was the one I'd had stolen out of Madeleine's home.

Only when they prepared to leave did the uniformed trooper ask after Michael.

"He's sleeping," I said, although I'd already heard the shower turn on upstairs. "He had a long night. Can you come back later?"

They assured me they didn't need to, and we parted on pleasant terms.

I was sitting at the table, sipping hot coffee and reading Aunt Madeleine's ledger, when Libby drove up and pounded on the back door. Against my better judgment, I let her in.

She blew in like a storm, carrying her year-old son, Max, into the kitchen. "Do you know there's a pig on your porch?"

"His name is Ralphie."

"Never mind. You won't believe this. I spent last night being *interrogated* by the police—and they were all business, not even a *spark* of concern for a private citizen's emotional well-being. The whole ordeal was agonizing and exhausting, so I desperately need a break this morning. But my usual babysitter has cramps, which is terribly inconsiderate, so I'm throwing myself on your mercy." She pushed Max into my arms and stopped her tirade long enough to take a long, speculative look at me. "Good heavens, Nora, you look positively ten years younger today. What have you done to yourself? A facial? Grapefruit? I hear grapefruit does wonders for your skin, but they give me heartburn. Or—oh, for the love of—! You've been up all night with That Man of Yours, haven't you?"

Since I had already baked the ultimate Libby distraction, I said, "I made muffins. Help yourself."

"Ooh, they smell heavenly! Here, take a quick snapshot of me holding one for my PitterPat followers."

I took a photo with her cell phone. While she dispatched the picture to her cyber friends and pulled butter from the fridge, I cuddled Max close and gave him kisses. The baby squirmed with delight and grabbed handfuls of my hair. I wiggled my nose into his tummy to make him giggle.

"My followers love it when I post food pictures! And last night after those dreadful police finally left, I posted a photo of my new pedicure, and my hits went through the roof! It's wonderful having so many people paying attention to me. It's like having a fan club."

Libby fluttered around the kitchen—selecting a mug and plate from a cupboard, pouring coffee and choosing a large muffin for herself—before settling at the table like a broody hen getting comfy on her nest. For the morning's outing, she wore another stretchy tracksuit—ruby red this time—over a T-shirt emblazoned with the word SPECIAL.

Libby planted her elbows on the table and blew across her coffee, eyes alight. "Now. Tell me everything about the sex. Is he taking out all his pent-up frustrations on you after the forced abstinence? Keeping you awake till all hours? Tying you up, maybe?"

"Libby, you appall me sometimes." I fed Max a hunk of my muffin.

"I don't mean tying up for real, just for play. You know—captured-slave sex."

"No," I said firmly. "There's no slave sex whatsoever."

"Well, that's disappointing. I have a theory about tying up. I think some women enjoy that fantasy because it means they don't have to be in charge for once. We're saddled with every other responsibility—I mean, after I've raised the children, paid the bills, kept the house, fed the dog and made myself desirable by dieting and exercising and exfoliating until my skin literally peels off, shouldn't I get a pass when it comes to making whoopie? Why shouldn't somebody tie me down and bear the burden of making the sex great?"

"That's actually rather profound, Libby," I said. "Almost a feminist doctrine."

"Thank you. Is he very demanding, though?" Her entire face sparkled. "Insisting you do everything in the book?"

"I don't think you and I read the same book, Lib." Desperate to change the subject, I asked, "How about you? Making any headway with the deputy?"

She preened, clearly happy to switch to talking about herself. "As a matter of fact, he telephoned yesterday. He asked if I'd accidentally left a spritz bottle of perfume in his car, and could he return it?"

"Did you? Leave perfume in his car?"

"Well, not on purpose." She turned pink. "He might drop by this afternoon. Do you like my hair?"

"It's lovely."

Libby helped herself to a second muffin. "So tell me everything about last night when you broke the law."

"No laws were broken."

"I mean about breaking into Quintain! Do you have sex on your mind all the time? What happened? And where's Emma?"

Reluctantly, I told Libby about my escapade at Quintain, Emma's arrest and my discovery of another dead person. But Emma's departure with Hart Jones elicited a cry of delight from Libby.

"Hart's back in the picture?" she exclaimed when I had related the whole tale. "Oh, Nora, do you think he might sweep her off her feet this time? Where do you think they went together?"

"Probably not home to meet his mother."

"Do you think they've run off for some kind of romantic tryst? Only Emma could seduce a man when she's seven months pregnant!"

"Eight," I said. "And let's remember he's engaged to be married."

"Into the Haffenpepper family," Libby replied. "And they hang on to their in-laws with talons. Once he's married, he might as well be cemented to Penny. They'll never divorce. Family values—that phrase might have originated with the Haffenpeppers."

I had been thinking about Emma's choices lately. I said, "Hart's a good man, Lib. If we could choose someone for Emma to be with, it would be him, wouldn't it? Somebody stable, but fun. Employed, but not wedded to his career. He'd be a wonderful father, too."

Libby nodded. "He coaches a baseball team, doesn't he? Of handicapped kids? Just the kind of selfless work the Haffenpeppers love."

"Last night, Emma whistled, though, and Hart came running."

Libby sighed. "Why can't I engender that kind of passion in a man?"

"You do." I pointed at her phone. "On an hourly basis. How many PitterPat followers do you have at the moment?"

"Eighteen thousand."

"Eighteen—!" I was astounded. "Libby, I had no idea! Surely one of them wants to meet you in the flesh?"

"I'm not so sure," she said, suddenly uncertain.

"Well, you should ask them. Invite one of them to meet you for a drink somewhere."

"What if they all turn out to be . . ."

"Nerds?" I asked.

"Perverts," she said, her eyes shifting sideways.

"Is that a bad thing?"

"Maybe not." She smiled warmly again and broke off a bit of muffin. "I'm glad we can have these sisterly chats now and then, Nora. What's that you're reading?"

"Aunt Madeleine's ledger. It's a record book of some kind."

Munching on her muffin, Libby pulled the ledger across the table and flipped through the pages. "This made no sense to me back when I was a child, and it still doesn't. What was she keeping a record of?"

I took a deep breath for courage. "Actually, I'm starting to worry about that."

Libby put down the book and gave me a solemn stare. "Does this have something to do with the sex trafficking?"

"I never believed that story," I said. "Even the morning news says there was only one woman who turned to prostitution, so we can hardly conclude that's what Madeleine was up to. But it certainly looks as if she was accepting money from men for something."

"What are you—? Wait a minute! You mean she was—? Money for sex? Nora, that's a perfectly preposterous conclusion."

I told Libby first about my long-ago encounter with Aunt Madeleine and her request that I destroy her book in the event of her death. Then about the slap I'd been given when I mentioned Aunt Madeline's name to Mr. and Mrs. Banks. At last I flipped through the ledger book and found a name on one of the pages. I pointed it out to Libby.

"See? Mr. Banks. Listed three times. Each time with a sum of money in the opposite column. Clearly, he paid her. His wife must have assumed he paid Madeleine for . . . some other reason."

"Maybe he was buying something. A painting. Or—or a statue. Or—some service."

"I'm trying to guess what kind of service Aunt Madeleine performed."

"Nora! She wasn't prostituting herself!"

Michael arrived in time to hear that declaration. "Prostitution? At breakfast? Hey, it's Max! Hiya, little buddy!"

Maximus splurted his muffin out of his mouth and reached his arms to Michael. "Da!"

"Hello, Libby."

"Good morning," she said coolly, as Michael leaned down and kissed me.

Then he snatched Max from my possession and swung him high. The baby gurgled with delight. His favorite playmate was back.

Libby said, "It's good to see you out of jail."

"Yeah, thanks. It feels good to me, too. Max, I missed your birthday! Look how big you are! How much do you weigh now?"

"He's twenty-three pounds," Libby supplied.

"A linebacker," Michael said, carrying the baby to the kitchen counter. "Let's see what we've got here. Muffins? What kind of breakfast is that for guys like us? Personally, I don't want to look at scrambled eggs ever again, so let's see what kind of leftovers we have to work with."

Max was happy to find himself snugly tucked into the crook of Michael's arm. He sucked on his thumb, gaze full of anticipation while Michael checked the fridge and gathered up the fixings for a substantial hash.

Watching, Libby said to me, "It's good for Max to have a man in his life. Even if it's—"

"Max always has Rawlins," I interrupted before Libby could put her foot in her mouth. "He's practically a man these days."

"Yes, I know. But he'll soon go off to college. Me with a child in college! I haven't broken the news to my followers yet."

"Most of 'em already know," Michael said from the stove.

Libby sat up, prettily alert. "How would you know anything about my followers?"

"On that whatchamacallit, PitterPat thing, right? Half the guys in the joint are following you."

Libby's mouth opened in a thunderstruck O before she began to sputter. "What? Are you—are you saying my followers are—are *prisoners*?"

"Sure," Michael said over his shoulder. "Who else has all the time in the world to spend on the Internet?"

"But—but—"

"In minimum security, everybody gets an hour a day in the computer lab. They take turns reporting on you. Sometimes they print out your pictures. The really—uh, you know—attractive pictures. You're the pinup girl of cell block A."

"Oh, my God!" Libby buried her face in her hands.

"Michael," I said gently, "why don't you take Max outside? I'll make your breakfast."

"No, no," Libby said from behind her hands. "Don't try to shield me, Nora. I need to know the ugly truth."

I patted her arm. "Don't be upset, Lib."

"I'm not. I'm really not." She lifted her trembling chin. "I should have known, I suppose. Who else would say such nice things to me? Be so encouraging of my creative spirit? So appreciative of the passion and joie de vivre I pour into my PitterPat profile? Only men behind bars!" She burst into sobs.

"I'm so sorry, Lib."

"Hey," Michael said, "you're doing a public service. Instead of researching how to make bombs out of fertilizer or new ways to commit credit card fraud, they're surfing the Web for more pictures of your feet."

"Michael," I said.

"What? It's the truth."

Libby snuffled. "I don't know what I was thinking. Maybe I've been seduced by the belief that everyone can be a celebrity now. All it takes is deciding to make yourself into somebody. Somebody big and exciting and worthy of attention. It really doesn't matter if underneath it all you're just a nobody. It's seductive—having people watch you and listen to what you say and do. Very seductive. It makes me think I'm better than average. It's not exciting, being average."

"You're never average, Libby. And clearly, your followers enjoy you."

Libby gathered her composure. "I suppose if—if imprisoned followers are involved, I could look at my efforts in the context of public service. Distracting them from detrimental influences. That—that's a noble cause, right?"

"Damn straight," Michael said.

Hopefully, she asked, "So there's no need for me to . . . stop?"

"If you did, you might trigger another Attica prison riot."

She dried her eyes on my napkin. "Well, I certainly wouldn't want that on my conscience."

Michael brought Max back to me to hold while he cooked. First butter went into the cast-iron skillet, then some diced onion. While the fragrance wafted up from the stove, he said, "Now, what did I hear about prostitution?"

I sighed. "It's Aunt Madeleine. I finally got a chance to read a few pages of her black book."

"And?"

"I think she was accepting large sums of money from her friends."

Libby said, "We're afraid Madeleine took money in exchange for . . . Oh, dear. For sex."

Michael looked at me. "What makes you think that?"

"I don't think that. But she annotated all her deposits with a man's name. And usually the names of hotels. See?" I held up the book.

I had looked through all of the names. All of them important men like Mr. Banks. Many of them were dead now, contemporaries of Madeleine. A few names I didn't recognize, but the ones I did know were all men of property—men who could have handed over large sums of money without feeling the sting.

Michael was busy adding some chunks of red pepper to the skillet and didn't bother to look. "Yeah, I noticed that last night when I skimmed a few pages. I didn't think of sex right off. I guess she could have been pretty great in the sack."

"And why not?" Libby got ruffled. "She was a beautiful woman."

"Yeah, but ten thousand bucks?" Michael flipped the contents of the skillet before strolling back to the table and pointing to one of the notations in the ledger with his favorite kitchen knife. "And some guys didn't just pay her once or twice, but several times. That's a lot of money for a roll in the hay. Not that I have any firsthand experience paying for sex, of course."

"Of course," I said.

"And, anyway, my family never got into the sex trade, but we all know the first rule of doing any kind of crooked business is not to put anything on paper. She was smart, right? Too smart to create evidence that could be used against her."

"Maybe she didn't know that rule," I said.

Libby asked, "What else do you think she could have been paid for, if not sex?"

Michael had a good mind for crime, it could not be denied. And the same way Libby threw herself into the practice of erotic yoga, he enjoyed exercising his criminal creativity. He said, "It doesn't look like gambling to me. Could be blackmail, though. Extortion. Or bribery, maybe. Insider trading, or some kind of real estate scam, or maybe illegal campaign donations—"

"Wait, wait." Already I reeled with the possibilities.

"Receiving stolen property," he continued. "Or drugs—"

"Drugs!"

Libby snapped her fingers. "What about the Mayflower Madam? Maybe Madeleine wasn't accepting money for sex, but arranging assignations between men of her social circle and high-class call girls."

"Yeah," Michael agreed. "Maybe that. But it doesn't feel right to me."

I put my forehead down on the kitchen table. "I don't want to hear any more."

Libby said, "It might explain all the special guests she had upstairs at Quintain."

"Special guests, huh?" Michael sounded amused.

"Stop." I sat up. "When I spoke with the secretary of state, she said something very sweet about Madeleine. That she was a great patriot. And she wanted to know if one of us might write a book about her. Surely, a respected international diplomat wouldn't encourage us to write about a Mayflower Madam. It really bothers me that Madeleine is being seen in such an ugly light. I want to protect her."

"I know one way to find out what she was doing," Michael said over his shoulder. "You could go see a lady I know."

Libby practically leaped from her chair. "A madam?"

"Retired," Michael said. "A friend of an uncle of mine knew the whole prostitution scene from top to—uh—bottom. I bet she'd remember if your aunt was mixed up in call girls."

Which was how I found myself speeding down the highway in the passenger seat of Libby's minivan while little Max spent the rest of the morning in Michael's care. I wanted to clear Madeleine's name, and at the moment our errand felt like a crazy way to accomplish that.

"I can't wait!" Libby cried. "We're going to meet a real madam!

Do you think I should go home and change? I want to look my very best!"

"Libby—"

"You never know what kind of tips we might pick up from a professional."

"I can't believe you're behaving as though this person is some kind of role model."

"Just wait," Libby predicted. "You're going to like her. I'm sure of it! You need extensive social skills to be a success in her business."

We arrived at the address Michael had provided and found ourselves staring at the sign on the front of the large white building that had been constructed to look like a grand Victorian-style hotel. White rocking chairs lined the porches, and someone had lavishly decorated for the season with hay bales and pumpkins.

"Shady Rest Home?" Libby's excitement deflated like a balloon popped at the end of a party. "How old is this madam, anyway?"

"Michael did say she was retired."

Libby parked in the visitors' lot. We trooped through the front door of the Shady Rest Home personal care facility and into a pleasant lobby with a front desk surrounded by elderly men and women in wheelchairs.

"Can I help you, girls?" piped a voice from the middle of the pack.

Libby and I waded through the sea of perky faces to the front desk, which was occupied by a stout middle-aged woman with a wide smile. She wore a smock covered with little animals kicking soccer balls. On the desk in front of her lay several bingo cards and a basket full of letters and numbers. The name tag on a lanyard around her neck read: SHARYN, SOCIAL DIRECTOR.

"Hi," I said. "We're here to visit one of your residents, please."

"We love visitors! First-timers? I can tell just by looking. I've been here twelve years, so I know everybody's relatives." She pulled a clipboard off a hook and handed it to me. "Sign your name, sweetie, and leave your driver's license with me."

"Actually, I don't have a driver's license."

"Me neither!" A cranky voice spoke up at my elbow.

As Libby dove into her handbag in search of her driver's license, I turned to an elderly gentleman who looked like either he had shrunk considerably since his shirt was purchased or somebody had made a very big Christmas blunder. He wore it buttoned up tight around his scrawny neck. In his lap, he held a bingo card and a large orange marker. From the look of things, he was close to shouting, "Bingo!"

He peered up at me accusingly. "My son took away my driver's license two years ago. Do you think that's fair?"

"Now, now, Mr. Jackson, don't go taking out your frustrations on our guests. Your son was only thinking of your own safety."

"Safety? The only thing that wasn't safe was my own garage door! I kept bumping into it, but I never hit anything else, did I?"

"A few dozen mailboxes and one skunk," Sharyn said. "But who's counting? Don't mind him, sweetie. Who are you here to see?"

"I'm sorry to interrupt your game. Um, actually, we're here to see"—I lowered my voice and leaned closer to Sharyn—"Miss Foxy Galore."

"Foxy Galore!" boomed Sharyn. "Miss Foxy, where are you?"

Everyone in the wheelchairs craned around to look for their missing comrade until one wavery voice finally said, "She sneaked off to the bathroom again."

"Tch, tch." Sharyn shook her head. "That lady just can't give up the smokes. You want to try talking some sense into her?"

"Well, this is more of a social call."

Mr. Jackson burst into guffaws. "You're not the kind who usually pays social calls on Foxy!"

"Please, Mr. Jackson." Sharyn gave him a disapproving frown. "Let's be sensitive to our fellow residents, shall we? Here, girls, pin these passes to your coats. We don't allow anyone to just stroll in here anytime they want, so you might get stopped by security. If you want to find Miss Galore, go through those doors and turn right at the beauty parlor. Then turn left at the dining room and right again when you see the swimming pool and one more left at the fish tank. Got that?"

"Beauty parlor, dining room, swimming pool, fish tank. Got it."

Glumly, Mr. Jackson said, "They're always making us do those brain puzzles. Remember this, remember that. Just sometimes, I'd like to forget a few things. The only thing worse is that danged exercise class."

Libby said, "You should start doing yoga."

He transferred his glare to her. "Yoga! That's ridiculous!"

"On the contrary, it will keep you young and supple. It's great for the endorphins, too."

He gave Libby an up-and-down perusal and perked up. "You look pretty supple yourself, young lady. Where can I get some of those dolphin things?"

"Why don't I bring my mat some afternoon, and we could all try a few poses? There's nothing I like more than sharing my spiritual quest with the unenlightened."

"Who you calling unlighted?"

I grabbed my sister's arm. "C'mon, Libby. Let's go see Miss Galore."

Mr. Jackson shouted after us, "Beauty parlor, dining room, swimming pool and fish tank! See? I'm as lighted as the next guy."

Libby and I headed for the beauty parlor, got turned the wrong way and ended up at the wrong fish tank and found a shortcut through the dining room—we saw lobster mac and cheese on the menu—before finally locating the powder room nearest another fish tank. If I hadn't known better, I would've said the building was a day-care center, judging from all the cute photos and cardboard decorations festooning the walls and doorways. A nurse's station had been decked out with a barnyard theme that featured a dozen construction-paper turkeys cut in the shapes of handprints. One of the nurses waved gaily at us.

The powder room turned out to be more of a ladies' lounge with a couple of plush sofas and a trickling waterfall on one wall and the toilet stalls discreetly tucked around a corner. To me, it felt like a place where an introspective resident could hide out for a few minutes of peace without being harassed by cheerful staff members.

Sitting on one of the sofas was a skinny woman in a turban and a pink satin robe belted over purple velour pants and a pair of puffy slippers. She heard us coming and was hastily tamping out a cigarette with one hand and fanning the air with the other as we pushed through the door.

"Damn!" she said with relief when she saw us. "I figured I was caught in the act again. I get any more smoking demerits around this place, and they're going to kick me out on the street!"

I had seen the fond look on Sharyn's face when she'd spoken of Foxy's smoking habit, so I doubted there was any real danger of her getting kicked out of Shady Rest. "Miss Galore? Would you mind if we sat down to talk with you for a few minutes?"

"Yes," Libby said eagerly. "We're big fans."

"Fans?" Foxy looked from Libby to me and back again. "What kind of fans?"

"Actually," I said, "we're here because Michael Abruzzo suggested we pay a visit. He called you earlier this morning, didn't he?"

Foxy Galore had skin like an alligator—suntanned and scaly—and the wrinkles on her face sagged as if she'd been left hanging on a line to dry and forgotten. From underneath the turban pink scalp showed not a single lock of hair. Her eyebrows had been drawn on her face, too. She had graceful hands, though, and an imperiously nearsighted manner of looking down the length of her nose at whoever was speaking to her. Her lipstick was pink and perfect.

"Ooh, Mickey!" Foxy relaxed into the sofa and smiled dreamily. "Now, there's a fellow I wouldn't mind seeing again. What's he doing these days? He in jail again?"

"Not at the moment." I eased down onto the sofa beside her and tried to decide how best to open a discussion with a retired hooker.

Foxy Galore rearranged her turban. "I suppose he's raising hell somewhere, riding that motorcycle, chasing girls, stealing cars—no, wait, he's all grown up now, isn't he?"

"He is," I said. "All grown up and settling down."

"That's darn disappointing. He could put a gleam in a girl's eye, let me tell you. Take my advice, okay? Don't pussy-whip that one. Give him a little space to do what comes natural. He'll always need an outlet, you know what I mean?"

"I think I do," I said.

She pointed a bony finger at me and grinned. "That's part of what you like about him anyway, am I right?"

"Well—"

"I also knew his uncle, come to think of it. Now, that's a man who ought to be in jail." Her expression darkened. "Not a kind bone in his body, that one. Mind if I light up?"

"Go right ahead. Actually, we're here to ask you about someone else. Michael thought you might know something about Madeleine Blackbird."

"Madeleine who?"

"Blackbird."

Libby had plunked herself down on the opposite sofa and now she cut to the chase. "She was our aunt, and we think maybe she became a Mayflower Madam. You know—with call girls, expensive hotels, exclusive clientele? Did you ever hear of her? Professionally, I mean?"

Foxy Galore snapped a lighter and sucked on her cigarette, then blew a plume of blue smoke over her head. "Nope. Never heard of a Madeleine Bluebird."

"That's Black—"

"I knew all the madams, clear back to Eisenhower's day. There was a real firecracker of a girl named Greenbaum who worked a corner in South Philly for a month before she could afford a decent dress and started sitting at the bar in the Stern Hotel. Eventually she had a string of eight girls working for her. Now, she could tell a joke, lemme tell you. And then there was—oh, never mind. Who did you ask about again?"

"Madeleine Blackbird," Libby supplied. "Red-haired. She went to Vassar. Lived in Bucks County."

"Vassar? I don't know that corner. Nope, never heard of her."

"Are you sure?" Libby pressed.

Foxy narrowed her eyes against the cigarette smoke and looked hard at Libby. "Why do you think she was tricking?"

"We don't really think she was—er—tricking," I said. "But maybe she was a madam? We have a book she kept—with names and amounts of money."

"How much money?"

"Tens of thousands in each transaction."

"And when did you say this took place?"

"Twenty or thirty years ago."

Foxy shook her head. "No, no, honey, back in those days nobody made that kind of money. Not in Philadelphia, that is. Maybe in New York or Paris with Hollywood actresses, but not in our territory. No, I'd say you were barking up the wrong willow tree. And I should know. I had the phone numbers of more men than any other pro in Philly."

"I have a few phone numbers myself." Libby dimpled and brought out her cell phone. "Have you ever heard of PitterPat?"

Foxy sat up alertly. "You're on PitterPat? Can you show me how to do that? I was thinking it might be a way for an enterprising woman to make a few bucks."

"Well, you can certainly make a lot of friends. I'd love to show you! You'd be a big hit, I just know it! Do you have a cell phone?"

"Back in my room." Foxy was already purposefully stubbing out her cigarette.

"Let's go." Libby helped the woman to her feet and dragged her walker closer. "We should talk about erotic yoga, too. This place could use a leader—someone to get a group going."

"Could I charge money for that?"

Foxy led the way back past the fish tank and along the sunny hallways, pushing her walker and chatting with Libby the whole way. Once again, my warmhearted sister had made a fast friend. I trailed behind them, however, thinking we might have struck out in the search for information.

We passed the hallway marked MEMORY SUPPORT NEIGHBOR-HOOD, and behind a locked gate I caught a glimpse of a patient walking on the arm of a sweet-faced young man who chatted amiably as they strolled. Since Shady Rest was a well-known local personal care home with a good reputation in the community, I had a sudden idea. As Libby disappeared with her new friend, I stopped at the nursing station and asked to visit Vincente van Vincent.

"Oh, are you a friend of the van Vincent family?" The no-nonsense nurse gave me a direct look. Her name tag read, JANET. NURSING SUPERVISOR.

"A little," I said, instantly feeling guilty for having used a ruse to discover Vincente van Vincent's whereabouts. "I know his wife, Shirley. I haven't see Mr. van Vincent in years."

"Well, I'm afraid he's not very receptive to visitors these days. But we could try. His wife called to say she's busy today—something about police searching for a body on her property!—so he's probably lonesome, poor dear. Would you like me to escort you to his apartment? He's accustomed to me. I'm a familiar face."

"If I'm not interrupting your work."

She got to her feet and pulled a set of keys off a hook. "My best work is with the residents," she said. "It's the paperwork I don't mind interrupting."

She took me down the hall and unlocked the gate that opened onto a common area where patients were allowed to roam around. I saw the sweet-faced young man and his walking partner make another lap around the room. The elderly man had a slack face and frightened eyes that pierced my heart like an arrow.

Janet took me through a set of locked French doors and down a painfully merry hallway that was lined with hospital rooms. The floor had lines of symbols laid out in patterns—stars led from one room the whole way around the perimeter of the hall and back again. A cat pawprint marked the path from another room around the hall and back. Each door had a bright photograph or cartoon on it—no doubt so confused residents could find their way back to their own quarters. Janet stopped at a room marked with a large photo of a Percheron horse pulling a farm wagon. Shirley van Vincent sat on the wagon, her hands expertly holding the reins. I wondered if her husband still recognized her.

Janet knocked on the door and called, "Mr. van Vincent? May we come in?"

No answer, but she knocked again, then pushed the door open just a couple of inches before asking again, "May we come in?"

A faint voice responded, and we entered the small apartment.

Vincente van Vincent had been a dapper gentleman in his prime—not very tall, but elegant and courtly in his manner. He had been a respected college professor before inheriting enough money to travel and donate to political campaigns. I remembered him on the edges of my grandfather Blackbird's coterie before he was sent to various embassies for his financial contributions to a grateful president. In that president's eight years of office, van Vincent moved a couple of times and eventually ended as an ambassador to Germany. He'd had an admirable career as a diplomat.

Now he was a sorry sight—a bony shell of a man slumped in front of a television set playing a recorded travelogue program. Scenes of green pastures and flowing rivers had been filmed from a helicopter while a soothing voice narrated the landscape. His gaze had strayed from the television, though, and he appeared to be staring anxiously at pictures arranged on the wall.

"This is his favorite show," Janet told me as she put her hands around van Vincent's shoulders. She leaned into his face. "Hello, dear. How are you?"

If Vincente van Vincent responded, it was not anything I could hear. He might have looked into Janet's face, but no flicker of recognition shone in his gaze. His palsied hands remained in his lap. I recognized the last stages of his illness.

I sat on the small coffee table in front of him and smiled, but he barely looked at me. "Hello, Mr. van Vincent. I'm Charlie Blackbird's granddaughter."

He avoided my gaze.

Janet spoke as if nothing was amiss. "Shirley's busy with her horse show today. This young lady stopped by to say hello. How are you feeling? Did you enjoy your morning cookie?"

She talked gently with him, and I respected her easy manner. Obviously, there was little I could contribute except to be pleasant and nonthreatening.

On van Vincent's windowsill a lineup of framed photos fought for space with a few sentimental knickknacks—small ceramic horses that pranced around a carved wooden bird. In the photos, van Vincent posed with various dignitaries—including presidents and senators. Also several with his wife. And one with Aunt

Madeleine—a group shot with other people I didn't recognize. In the background of the photo was the flag of the Soviet Union.

Looking at the collection of pictures, I reflected on van Vincent's career. He'd moved in powerful circles and enjoyed many accolades as well as relationships with international movers and shakers. And yet here he sat—alone in a room. Where were all his friends now?

Shirley's picture stood at the front of all the other photographs, but I assumed she had put it there herself. It showed her much younger and very pretty, holding the head of a handsome pony. Judging by the background scenery, I guessed the photo had been taken in her homeland. A mountain chalet with geraniums cascading from a window box showed behind the horse. Maybe it was the way Vincente best remembered his wife—from their early days in Germany.

"Does Shirley come often?" I asked Janet.

"Almost every day. Except lately, she's been busy with her horse show."

Vincente suddenly said, "Shirley."

His voice was clear, but an instant later, he sank back into himself.

Within a few minutes, Janet indicated we'd spent enough time with Vincente van Vincent, so I smiled and said good-bye.

On her way out, Janet snatched a pack of cigarettes off a shelf. "I've asked Shirley not to leave these in her husband's room. I'm afraid he might be confused and try to eat them."

She tucked the cigarettes into her pocket, and I followed her out.

Back at the nursing station, she shook my hand. "Thanks for coming. I thought you were just being nosy, but you were real nice to him. It may not seem as if he appreciated you, but it can't hurt."

I thanked her and said, "You're making a lovely home for these people here."

She said, "We do what we can. Come back. It helps to have visitors around."

Libby found me in the lobby a while later. She chattered about Foxy Galore as we went outside to the parking lot. I hardly listened. The good news was that we'd established that Aunt Madeleine hadn't been involved in prostitution. The bad news was that we still didn't seem any closer to figuring out what she *had* been up to.

We were back in the minivan and heading home when my cell phone rang.

"Good morning." Emma's voice was a little raspy in my ear. Clearly, she hadn't consulted a clock yet, because it was going on one in the afternoon. She said, "Did you get my note?"

"I did."

"Damn, that means you got out of the bedroom. From the sounds of things last night, I thought the two of you were going to spend the whole weekend pounding the mattress into sawdust."

I decided not to take offense. "Where are you? What's going on?"

"Get this," she said. "I've been kidnapped."

CHAPTER SIXTEEN

Five minutes later, Libby cried, "Why can't I *ever* get kidnapped?"

I stashed my phone in my handbag. "I don't think she was being serious. She's with Hart."

"Have they run off together? Is he leaving Penny? Did they talk about the baby? Oh, heavens, I hope they eloped!"

"They did not elope. But it doesn't sound as if she's coming home anytime soon."

"Is that good?"

I wasn't sure. Emma didn't sound happy, that's all I knew.

To Libby, I said, "She says Hart got plastered last night and told her some stuff about Simon Groatley."

"Hart just volunteered information?"

"Emma fed him martinis until he broke. Hart says everybody in the city knows Groatley is a crook. He stole money from one client and called it a campaign contribution. Except the client had been comatose for a year. His firm hushed it up, but fired him. Now he's at a new firm, and he's living an expensive lifestyle. New cars, fancy penthouse, mistresses. But Hart thinks he's living off cash he keeps in a safe-deposit box."

"Where'd the cash come from? The comatose client?"

"Hart doesn't know. He thinks it's only a matter of time before Groatley is caught."

"That's typical!" Libby burst out. "A man who thinks he's so wonderful, he's above the law. It's the same reason he feels he has the right to bully women into having sex with him. He's entitled! Nora, I'll bet you a pound of chocolate he's been stealing money from Aunt Madeleine, too."

"The question is," I said, "did he have to kill her to do it?"

Libby exploded into a tirade of outrage. "That's our inheritance!"

When she calmed down, she said, "How did Emma sound? Sober?"

Sober, yes. But devastated.

We had arrived at the driveway to Blackbird Farm, and there Michael's crew had stopped a series of minivans and expensive SUVs. Half the vehicles were decorated with stickers proclaiming the names of their daughters and their respective sports.

"Oh, God." I clapped my hands to my cheeks. "It's Saturday!"

"Of course it's Saturday," Libby said.

"It's Emma's day to teach her pony classes!"

Suddenly the purpose of Emma's phone call became clear. She wasn't coming home, and I was left with a fresh disaster. All her students needed attention or she'd lose her opportunity to earn a living. The line of vehicles bearing Emma's students was making slow progress through Michael's checkpoint. I jumped out of Libby's minivan and ran to the head of the line that the goodfellas had roadblocked.

The cause of the clog was my cousin Sutherland, who stood outside the open door of his Porsche. He braced his hands on the roof of his car, and his legs were spread wide as he was frisked by one of Michael's more enormous hoodlums. Today Sutherland had come decked out in a starched white shirt with a pastel lavender cashmere sweater thrown around his shoulders and tied in front. His trousers were neatly pressed, and his tassel loafers were shined. He looked ready for a stroll around Monaco. But he'd been mugged along the way by one of the Sopranos.

He caught sight of me as he was being roughed up by the burly thug. "See here, Cuz—isn't this a bit extreme? I've been treated with more dignity in airports!"

"Shut up, Poindexter," the thug growled, grabbing Sutherland's arm.

"That watch is worth more than your car!" Sutherland wrenched his arm free.

"Looks like a fake to me. And I oughta know."

"Oh, heavens, let him through," I said as I raced up to them. "Let everyone through!"

"Hang on a minute," said another thug. He held a large white pastry box in one hand. "We haven't checked this out yet. Could be a bomb."

"It's not a bomb," Sutherland cried with exasperation. "It's a cheesecake!"

All the crew perked up. "A cheesecake?"

"A gentleman always brings something when invited to lunch."

I'd completely forgotten I'd invited Sutherland for lunch.

I said, "Let us through, please. Can't you see there's no need to stop these people?"

"We don't do no racial profiling," said the wise guy in the tracksuit. He handed the white box back to Sutherland. "Here you go, buddy. You could use a little more meat on those scrawny bones."

The ragtag security team stepped back and let us get into the Porsche without further bodily inspection. Sutherland drove up the drive with the cheesecake in his lap.

"What on earth is going on here today?" he asked in wonderment. "First I'm manhandled by the teamsters union. Now I see you've got a dozen hysterical little girls running all over the lawn. Their parents look like fashion models."

"It's Emma's pony class. Except today Emma is—well, she's been detained, so we may have to vamp for a little while."

"Vamp?"

"Can you saddle a pony?"

"Me? Nora, remember who you're talking to!"

"Well, go schmooze with the parents."

"I can do that."

At the back of the house, it was mayhem. More of Emma's students were climbing on the fence, shrieking with excitement and sending the ponies into a stampede around the pasture. Their surly parents stood nearby looking as furious as only entitled rich parents can do when their children have not been properly attended to.

I figured if I needed to catch ponies in the pasture, I'd better go find my boots, so I dashed for the house. Near the back porch I found the young man from the grocery store bakery—the one who had proposed to Emma in the checkout line. He stood nervously at the foot of the steps. From the back porch, Ralphie glowered threateningly at Brian and pawed the porch floor with his hoof. His message was clear. *Stay off my turf, Bub.*

Brian took off his hat to me. In his other shaking hand, he carried a small shopping bag with a jewelry store's logo on the side. He looked even younger than he had yesterday. His face was pink—as if he'd scrubbed it extra hard this morning to make a good impression.

"Uh, hi," he said. "Is Emma home?"

"Not at the moment. It's Brian, isn't it? We're a little chaotic here right now. Would you like to come back later?"

Brian blushed and stammered, and generally looked to be deeply in love.

Poor, misguided boy. I couldn't stop myself from giving him a hug.

Sutherland strolled up the sidewalk and gave Brian a knowing look as the boy climbed into his battered little car to leave.

Still holding the pastry box, Sutherland gestured at the house. "The old place looks a little worse for wear, Nora. Has a tornado blown through?"

"There's no place like home," I said, shooing Ralphie off the porch.

"Is that young man your boyfriend?"

"This isn't exactly the time for— Look, I'll get my boots and be right back. Here, give me that box. I'll put it in the kitchen. Meanwhile, make yourself useful, please!"

The doorknob came off in my hand again. Barely containing a shriek of frustration, I gave it to Sutherland and shoved the door open with my shoulder. In the kitchen, I plunked the box on the table, exchanged my shoes for my rubber gardening boots and my jacket for the mackintosh I kept on a peg by the door.

Michael stuck his head around the pantry door, Max in one arm and a cell phone in the other hand. "Everything okay? It sounds like a riot out there."

"A riot would be easier to subdue."

"You're all pink. What can I do? I'll be off the phone in a couple of minutes."

"You've got Max to look after, so stay inside. I don't want either one of you getting trampled."

Back outside, I nearly collided with Libby.

"Half the ponies are loose!" she cried. "And that pig of yours chased that poor boy's car all the way down the driveway. He barely escaped!"

At that moment, Ralphie charged past us toward the annoyed parents. They had gathered beneath the oak trees as if planning to storm the house to demand their money back. As soon as they saw Ralphie heading their way, they scattered like bowling pins.

Their screams seemed to inflame Ralphie's tantrum. He cut one father out of the herd and chased him all the way to the pasture fence, where the father leaped over the rails to safety, but landed in an unfortunately fresh pile of pony droppings. His outraged cry was drowned out only by the high-pitched shriek of another father who had become Ralphie's next target. As Ralphie bore down on him, snorting like a maddened bull, the man sprinted past us, heading for the springhouse.

"Be careful!" I shouted. "That's not a safe—"

Before I could warn him, the father leaped for the springhouse roof. He scrabbled for an instant, then grabbed the gutter and hung on for dear life, with his knobby knees pulled up to his chest to avoid getting head-butted by Ralphie. But the weakened gutter immediately began to sag under his weight, and inexorably, he started to droop lower and lower—perilously closer to Ralphie's waiting tusks.

"Help! Help me!"

Sutherland said, "I know a suicide mission when I see one."

"Ralphie!" I shouted.

The pig turned toward me. He had a maniacal gleam in his little piggy eyes. I could have sworn he was laughing.

But the laughter was actually coming from Michael's security detail, who had all come up the driveway and were watching the action as if they were spectators at a sporting event. They were definitely cheering for the pig.

I ran toward Ralphie. "Stop that!" I shouted at him. "Get back in the pasture!"

"Somebody open the gate!" Libby bellowed. "We'll herd him back inside!"

But Ralphie dashed the opposite way. And as soon as the most intrepid of the little girls swung the pasture gate open, four more ponies galloped out and took off in four different directions. A herd of preteen girls chased them, shrieking at decibels that nearly punctured my eardrums.

Ralphie took off in hot pursuit, making a horrible noise that almost everyone understood to be growls of menace, but I was absolutely sure were grunts of glee. Michael's men cheered as Ralphie barely missed goring Sutherland, who leaped for the safety of the tire swing in the knick of time. Sutherland grabbed the rope, jammed one tasseled loafer into the tire and was immediately flipped upside down with one leg hopelessly tangled.

"Help! Cuz!"

"Need a push, Poindexter?" shouted one of the wiseguys, and they all doubled over with laughter.

I abandoned Sutherland to his fate and ran into the barn. I came out with the lure I had seen Emma use—a pan full of oats. I rattled the oats around in the pan, and the ponies immediately came running. While they bullied one another to get a mouthful of oats, Libby waded through them and started snapping leads on halters. My toes were stepped on, but within a few more minutes we had the ponies under control.

By then, Ralphie had all the parents cornered around the springhouse. I decided he was doing me a favor and left them there.

We were tying ponies to a fence and starting to put saddles on them when the police cruiser arrived in the back driveway. Michael's hoodlums magically disappeared.

Deputy Foley stepped out of the police car. "Miss Blackbird? We got a 911 call. Something about disturbing the peace?"

I made an effort to look innocent. "Really? I can't imagine who might have called."

Foley took a look at Sutherland, still hanging desperately from the tire swing, and the pony-lesson parents cowering by the springhouse. Ralphie appeared to be taking a nap nearby, although I could see his beady eye keeping watch on his captives. He looked like a kid who'd had too much Christmas. None of these sights caused Foley to pull his sidearm, which I took as a good sign.

He squinted in Sutherland's direction. "Does that guy need some help?"

"My cousin? Well, maybe. If you wouldn't mind . . . ?"

Foley ambled over to assist Sutherland, and I could hear Sutherland squawking about some minor injury. Foley very kindly helped him down from the tire swing and bent to examine Sutherland's ankle. Within a few minutes they disappeared into the house together.

Libby took over the pony lessons, for which I could have kissed her. With her natural motherly authority, she soon had the little girls trotting around the paddock in an orderly fashion, and they took turns jumping the ponies over fence rails laid on the ground. Even Ralphie lumbered over to watch at the fence, and soon the parents ventured over to observe, too. Everyone seemed happy, if a little flushed from the earlier excitement.

Two hours later, happy parents had packed their children into vehicles and departed. Libby, exhausted but pleased, took possession of her son, then climbed into her minivan and left. The ponies rolled in their pasture.

In all the pandemonium, I hadn't noticed when Deputy Foley pulled away. Or when Sutherland took his leave—before I had a chance to question him further about Aunt Madeleine.

But when I went into the house, I discovered Ralphie in the kitchen with his snout buried in cheesecake. When I screamed, he lifted his head from the pastry box. He had a cherry stuck in one nostril.

I chased him out of the house and slammed the door. Then I sat at the table and tried to decide whether to laugh or cry.

That's when I noticed that Aunt Madeleine's ledger was missing. Someone had stolen it from the kitchen table.

CHAPTER SEVENTEEN

I went upstairs and took a long, restorative shower.

When I emerged from the bathroom, Michael had come upstairs. He'd been unaware of all the action that took place while he was handling some kind of gasoline crisis on the telephone. He relaxed on the bed while I dressed to go out for the night and told him what had happened that afternoon.

He said, "I missed my chance to meet your slippery cousin, huh?"

"You didn't miss much," I said. "He spent most of his time cowering in terror of your pig. If you plan on keeping that animal as some kind of team mascot, by the way, I wonder if there's such a thing as a pig obedience class?"

"Ralphie behaves himself for me."

"Why is that?" I demanded. "With everyone else, he's a perfect—"

"Pig?" Michael suggested. "You can't expect a pig to be anything but a pig, Nora. Obedience class is just going to give you indigestion. Him, too."

"Speaking of pigs," I said, sitting down at the vanity mirror, "Emma learned some interesting things about Simon Groatley last night." I told Michael about Hart's information that Groatley had fleeced a comatose client and was likely living on cash he'd stashed in a safe-deposit box.

"So the list of charges against Groatley gets longer and longer," Michael said as I applied my makeup. "You think maybe he killed your aunt to get easy access to her dough? Or was it your cousin who did that? It would have been pretty simple to close an elevator door and walk away. No muss, no fuss. You don't have to be a violent person to commit that kind of crime."

"Thing is, Groatley is probably capable of violence," I said, tapping my mascara tube thoughtfully on my thigh. "If you tangle with Emma, you have to be sure of yourself. But you're right. Turning off the electricity is a way to kill somebody without getting blood on your hands. Nonviolent is more Sutherland's style."

"You think he's capable of leaving his stepmother to die?"

"Twenty years ago he might have been."

Michael had been admiring my bare thigh, but he said, "What did you learn from Foxy Galore? Did she think Madeleine was a madam? Maybe with dissatisfied clients who wanted her dead?"

"No, Foxy had never heard of Madeleine. I'm back to thinking the ledger wasn't a record of prostitution. I shouldn't have doubted Madeleine. It must mean something else. I don't know what, though. And now somebody has stolen the book, so I'll have to come up with another way to figure it out." I sighed and touched up my eyelashes with care.

"I must have been upstairs changing Max's diaper when it was stolen," Michael said. He'd already listened to me rant about the missing ledger. "I didn't hear anybody in the house. Sorry."

"Only two people could have stolen the ledger. Sutherland and Libby's Deputy Foley. And my money's on Sutherland. He's been quite the sneaky customer since he arrived."

"Want me to send somebody to get the ledger back from him?" Michael grinned. "I've been looking for something to occupy my crew."

"Although I agree they need a constructive distraction, he'd probably die of fright," I said. "I don't want that on my conscience."

Michael shrugged. "Have it your way. Too bad Foxy turned out to be a wild-goose chase. I figured she might be able to help."

"Actually, I found someone else at Shady Rest, so it was hardly a wasted trip. Vincente van Vincent lives there now."

I told Michael about Shirley's husband, ill with Alzheimer's and fading fast.

"He was a respected diplomat back in his prime," I said. "A friend of Madeleine's. Or a kind of colleague. I saw some old photos that included her, but he wasn't able to tell me anything." I sat still for a moment, picturing Vincente in his solitary room. "Michael, when we get old, we'll live together no matter what, okay? I can't stand the thought of you as alone as he was."

He smiled. "Neither one of us is going to be alone."

I set aside my mascara and put a finishing touch of powder on my nose before brushing out my hair. Michael was amused, but I'd meant every word.

"Where are you going tonight?" He reclined on the bedclothes, long legs crossed comfortably and arms folded behind his head. Only the steady gleam in his otherwise lazy eyes gave away his real mood. I had been sitting at the mirror in my new panties with a towel lightly wrapped around my body, and although he hadn't said a word, I knew he'd been eyeing my new pink underwear. If we'd had enough time, I knew we wouldn't be talking. He said, "Are you headed to a charity ball to save the whales or something?"

"We're saving a hospital this evening." I gave my hair a little spritz of spray and checked my reflection in the angled mirror of my dressing table. Not bad.

I wanted to forget it all and climb into bed, though, and let him slip off my pink panties. Another night under the covers with Michael was very appealing. But I had work to do.

Reluctantly, I left my towel on the chair and went into the closet. I had thought long and hard about which item to wear this evening, and I'd spent a few hard-earned dollars to have it altered to fit me just right. I pulled Grandmama's favorite David Roth off the hanger and stepped into it. Wriggling, I drew it up and went out into the bedroom. "Will you zip me, please?"

The dress started with a golden beaded bodice deeply cut into a sweetheart neckline that made a feature of my white shoulders and naked throat. The gracefully curved bodice displayed a coy hint of cleavage—no bra tonight—and cinched my waist tight. At the hip, Roth had designed a clever detail of teardrop prisms hanging every two inches on gold threads. The skirt was yards and yards of peach-hued chiffon, with a tea-length hem that fell slimly from my hips to curl coquettishly upward at the bottom. Layers of successively paler blond chiffon flashed beneath the upturned hem. I did a pirouette, sending the skirt into a swirl.

"Are you testing my self-control?" Michael sat up and pulled me onto his lap, careful not to crush the dress. Despite being a tough guy whose closet contained little more than jeans and T-shirts and black leather, Michael was turned on fast by a touch of lace and lipstick. Add ladylike underwear, and he was like a teenager with his first naughty magazine.

Somehow he managed to slowly zip up my dress while nibbling my neck.

I slipped my arms around his shoulders and began to think seriously about skipping the hospital fund-raiser. In his ear, I whispered what I wanted most to do just then, and he slid one hand underneath my skirt to trace a long, seductive trail up my thigh.

The doorbell gonged downstairs, and we looked at each other with dismay.

"Now what?" Michael asked, barely holding back his frustration.

"Maybe it's Sutherland," I said. "Maybe he brought back Aunt Madeleine's book. Maybe he's willing to start telling the truth."

Michael helped me gently off his lap. "I'll take care of the door. I want to get a look at this guy, anyway."

"Don't scare him," I called as Michael went out into the hallway. "At least, don't scare him too much."

He laughed and went down the staircase.

At the bottom of my meager jewelry box, I found a pair of diamond earrings—a Valentine's Day gift from Todd back in the good days. I hadn't been emotionally able to wear any of the gifts he'd given me before he started spending money on drugs—not that many pieces were left that he hadn't stolen out of my jewelry box and sold for coke. Or that I had sold to pay the taxes on Blackbird Farm. Looking at myself in the mirror, I decided the moment in the woods with the bones felt cathartic. Maybe I was finally putting the past behind me. I slipped the earrings on and smiled at my reflection. I thought Todd would have been happy to see me wear them again.

I went back into the closet to find a wrap warm enough to see me through the evening. I pulled out a cashmere stole designed with interlocking loops of tiny glass beads.

I stepped into my tan satin Jimmy Choos and went down the stairs with the wrap over my arm.

In the entry hall, I discovered our visitor wasn't Sutherland at all. It was Carrie.

She had a sullen set to her jaw, but she couldn't help glancing around the house with open curiosity.

"This place is a wreck," she was saying as I came down the staircase. "I thought you guys were rich."

"Not for generations," I replied. "Hello. It's nice to see you again."

She gave my outfit a long stare, taking in the flirty skirt and the diamonds in my ears, too, and clearly concluding I was lying to her. She said, "Where are you going? To some kind of prom?"

"Actually, it's my job. I write for the *Philadelphia Intelligencer*. I report on charitable events, so I have to dress up sometimes. To you, I probably look a little silly. Again."

She had come wearing a hooded gray sweatshirt and jeans with a pair of boots that had probably been all over Afghanistan. Grudgingly, she said, "You look okay."

Michael had gathered his courage, I could see. He'd been astonished to find Carrie at the door, but now he appeared capable of intelligent thought. He said, "Carrie remembered your name. Found you in the phone book and tracked down the address. Pretty smart, right?"

"Very smart," I said warmly. "But, after all, she's a grown-up. Why don't you come inside? I'll get you something to drink. Michael?"

"Sure. Anything. Let's go in here," he said to Carrie, standing back so she could precede him into my grandfather's library. "This is one room where you won't get frostbite."

"He's warm-blooded," I said lightly. "Me, I've lived here long enough to know to wear extra sweaters. What would you like? A beer? Coffee? I think I have some diet soft drinks."

Carrie wasn't sure what to make of our banter, so she scooted into the library. Over her shoulder, she said, "I'm not old enough to drink beer yet. And anyway, this isn't really a social visit."

Michael and I exchanged raised eyebrows and shared the same thought. By law, she was old enough to carry a weapon in defense of her country, but not old enough to drink alcohol. He took a deep breath and followed her into the library. I went off to the kitchen. I took my time making up a tray with a crystal pitcher of water, two glasses with ice and lemon slices. I found a few crackers, too, and sliced up some cheese. They needed a chance to be alone together, so I took my time.

When I got back to the library, Carrie had clearly blurted out her mission.

Michael was sitting in one of the deep leather chairs, looking grave. To me, he said, "Carrie needs me to sign some papers."

I set the tray on the big coffee table.

Carrie sat opposite Michael in the matching chair, but she perched uncomfortably at attention on the edge of the seat and had wrapped her arms around herself. Between them on the table lay a sheaf of official-looking documents.

To me, she said, "I have a shot at a promotion. But now that my mom is gone, I need somebody who can sign papers. For the promotion."

"And somebody to notify if you get hurt," Michael said.

"Yeah, that, too."

He reached for the papers and gave them a cursory skim. "What kind of promotion is it?"

"Just a new job. It requires a higher security clearance than I have at the moment. I should warn you, there will probably be some people coming around to ask questions, too."

He glanced up. "What kind of questions?"

"Just stuff. It's not a big deal."

"They want to be sure you're not mixed up with Al Qaeda, I guess?"

"That kind of thing, yeah."

Michael reached for his reading glasses and put them on. While he read the first sheet, Carrie shot another peek at me. There was mistrust in her eyes. I saw I'd made a mistake, bringing the crystal on a tray. That detail combined with my frilly dress and fancy shoes made me alien to her. I began to wish she'd come a few hours earlier when I'd been wearing my jeans and chasing ponies around the property. Tonight, I probably looked like some kind of debutante. No help with a military promotion.

Michael continued to read, and he wasn't making a good impression, either. I knew he was dismayed to imagine this young girl risking her life in the military. But to her, he seemed standoffish.

A door banged far away in the house, and I realized Reed had let himself in the back door. He was early. I went to the library's doorway and called to him. A minute later, he showed up, but he stopped short at the sight of a pretty young woman sitting in the room with Michael.

"Hey, boss," Reed said.

"Hey, Reed." Michael didn't look up from his reading.

"Reed, this is Carrie Hardaway. Carrie, Reed Shakespeare."

"Hey," he said to her.

"Hey," she replied.

Once again, I read her mind. Reed had come in his standard outfit—blue pants, white shirt and a Windbreaker. He dangled the car keys from one hand. All he needed was a chauffeur's cap to look like a chump in her eyes.

The best thing I could do was leave quickly. I gathered up my wrap and said, "Well, good night, you two. Michael, I'll be home before midnight."

"See you then." He stopped reading long enough to accept a kiss from me. His gaze darkened when he met mine. "Be careful."

"Of course. Good-bye, Carrie. It was nice to see you again." I shook her hand.

"Yeah," she said. "Bye."

Two minutes later, I was outside with Reed and heading for the car.

Reed's usual stone-cold demeanor thawed considerably. "Who was that?"

"Prepare to be amazed," I said. "She's Michael's daughter."

"Get out!" Reed stopped dead on the sidewalk. "You gotta be kidding."

"I'm not," I said. "She showed up yesterday. She was . . . a bit of a surprise to all of us."

Reed wanted to know the whole story, so I told him what I knew as we stood outside the big SUV under the trees in the half-light.

"She's good-looking," he said when I had finished. He glanced over his shoulder as if hoping Carrie might come running out the back door after us.

"Michael hasn't discovered his protective inner father yet," I warned. "But that's going to happen. So watch your step, Reed."

"Good point." He managed to get his aloof facade back into place.

"Since we're early, I'd like to make another stop before we go into the city," I said.

He groaned. "You're not going to drive again, are you?"

"Not tonight. But I need your expertise."

With the help of Reed and his magic cell phone, we figured out an address in New Hope.

Pee Wee McBean lived in a modest ranch house outside of town, on a low ridge alongside a group of identical little homes. Each house had a side carport, aluminum siding, bay windows, and front doors located under a porch roof too small to shelter a single trick-or-treater on a rainy Halloween night. The houses were not ostentatious in any way, but tidy—although maybe a little shabby around the edges. The siding was faded, the shrubbery too large. I spotted Pee Wee's white Crown Victoria parked in his driveway. He had a worn Fraternal Order of Police sticker on the back bumper.

"What're you doing here?" Reed asked when he pulled into the driveway.

"I need to speak with the owner. Reed, if I don't come out in fifteen minutes, will you knock on the door?"

He turned around and looked at me over the seat. "That doesn't sound good."

"I'm sure I'll be fine. The homeowner gets overly excited sometimes, that's all. Will you do it?"

He grimaced and got out of the SUV. He came around to open my door and help me down. As I went up the sidewalk to the front door, Reed waited in the light of a gas lamp to show Pee Wee I hadn't come alone.

Pee Wee answered the door wearing gray boxer shorts, a faded Notre Dame sweatshirt and green socks with a gaping hole in one toe where a long yellow toenail showed through. He carried a can of beer and blinked at me with astonishment.

"Hello," I said calmly. "May I come in?"

"I was expecting a pizza," he replied, but he automatically stepped back to allow me to enter his home.

Pee Wee's house was decorated entirely in green plaid. Someone had painstakingly wallpapered the living room with a green tartan design, then added a plaid sofa and two plaid recliners before topping off the decor with assorted accessories bearing shamrocks and the Notre Dame logo. The television was the size of a car, and it blasted a college football game.

From one recliner, an elderly dachshund snarled at me. I'd have snarled, too, if forced to live in that kaleidoscope of the Emerald Isle.

Displayed in a large glassed-in case were various guns—a couple of rifles, an old shotgun and some handguns in many shapes and sizes. The case, I noticed, was not locked.

The air smelled of burned meat, and a smoky haze hung in the room. From the kitchen, I could hear the frantic beep of a smoke alarm.

Pee Wee stood holding the front door open and gaping at me as if I were a fairy princess who'd walked into the lair of Rumpelstiltskin.

"I was on my way to a party," I said, "but I have a few extra minutes, and I thought we could talk."

Pee Wee had used intimidation and false pretenses on me on the previous day, but I had other weapons at my disposal. I fully intended to intimidate him right back with my good manners and my graceful long skirt that looked as if it cost as much as a year's worth of his mortgage payments.

It worked.

Belatedly, Pee Wee closed the door and realized he was underdressed. He snatched a plaid blanket off one of the recliners and wrapped it around himself like an overgrown kilt. With a remote control, he thumbed the volume down on the television.

"I wasn't expecting no company," he said with as much dignity as he could muster while wearing green socks with holes in the toes. "Except the pizza man. I burned my dinner."

"I'm sorry to hear that. I won't stay long. I'd like to ask you a few questions."

"About what?"

"About Pippi."

He glowered at me. "I got nothing more to say about her than I already told you."

"Why don't we go shut off that smoke alarm?"

"But—"

Following my nose, I led the way to the kitchen, where a frying pan sat smoking in the sink. Two charred hot dogs smoldered in a puddle of greasy water.

The rest of the kitchen wasn't going to win any prizes, either. Dishes sat stacked in a drainer beside the sink, and the counters were cluttered with boxes. Dozens of cereal boxes were lined up beside boxes of Hamburger Helper and instant mashed potatoes. Several plastic jugs of pre-mixed iced tea stood on the floor. I didn't see a single fresh vegetable or piece of fruit.

I opened a window and flipped on the fan over the stove. Almost immediately, the smoke alarm ceased shrieking. Over the fan's rattling roar, I said, "Let's clear the air, shall we?"

"I got nothing to say to you, lady. Unless you tell me I got something coming from your relative."

"We're a long way from learning the details of Aunt Madeleine's will. Shall we scrub out this pan while it's still warm?"

He elbowed me out of his way and reached for the frying pan. "Don't touch that stuff. You'll get all covered in grease."

I stood back and let him fill the sink with soapy water. "Can we talk about Pippi now?"

"What do you want to know about her?"

"How did she come to this country?"

"I told you that. Your aunt brought her here. On a boat."

"On a boat? A yacht, you mean?"

"I don't know nothing about what kind of boat. It was just a boat, that's all."

"But Pippi didn't have a green card?"

"Right. She wasn't no ballerina or famous scientist like all the others who got special treatment."

"Like all the others?" I repeated.

"Yeah, the Blackbird lady always had foreigners staying at her house—big-deal people, I guess. Not like the newspapers said. No prostitution. But Pippi was a nobody, see? And a Russian to boot, so it was hard for her."

I began to arrange the cereal boxes in a neat line at the back of the counter, tidying up. "And Madeleine introduced the two of you?"

"Naw, I saw Pippi shopping at the store a couple of times, so I asked her if she wanted to get a cup of coffee. That first time, she said she had to get back to work, but the next time she said her boss lady told her it was a good idea to meet some people from the community. So we had coffee, and one thing led to another."

I guessed Madeleine had brought Pippi into the country illegally and had seen Pee Wee as a way for Pippi to acquire citizen status. But I didn't say so. Instead, I asked, "When Madeleine announced she was leaving for Indonesia, did Pippi plan to go with her?"

"She didn't tell me so, no. Not until the last minute when she came to say good-bye. They were leaving the next day, she said. Getting on an airplane. First I heard of it."

"Madeleine and Pippi went together?"

"Yeah, right."

"Do you remember the exact date?"

"Yeah, sure, I got it written down someplace."

I thought that information might be helpful to the police, but I asked, "Do you remember anything that happened that day? Anything specific? About who Pippi or Madeleine might have seen besides you? Or if anyone else planned to travel with them?"

"I don't remember anything like that, no. Just that Pippi stopped by in the afternoon. To say good-bye."

I realized Pee Wee was scrubbing the pan so hard that water splashed in all directions. He clenched his jaw, too. Maybe I'd misjudged him. I thought he'd been solely looking for a piece of Madeleine's estate, but now I realized he was probably worried that Pippi had never loved him. That she'd used him to get a green card.

I touched his shoulder. "I'm sure she was sorry to leave."

He shook off my touch. "She seemed damn happy to me. They were going around saying good-bye to everybody that afternoon. Your aunt waited in the car while Pippi was here."

"They were paying other calls?"

"To people in the neighborhood, yeah. Bragging about their trip."

I had already calculated that I'd been away at school the year Madeleine left Bucks County. Now I wondered if she'd stopped at Blackbird Farm to see my parents one last time. I'd have to ask my mother when she phoned me from whatever resort she had landed in recently. Maybe Mama remembered something about that afternoon. Knowing Madeleine's state of mind would be helpful. And maybe Mama could guess what Pippi's role in their travel to Indonesia might have been.

I didn't have the heart to ask Pee Wee if he thought his wife was capable of locking Madeleine in an elevator and running off to Indonesia to impersonate her. But it was a theory that was starting to sound possible to me.

I took a dish towel from its hook on the wall. Pee Wee handed me the frying pan, and I dried it while he pretended to wipe perspiration from his brow.

The doorbell rang. In his blanket-wrapped glory, Pee Wee pushed past me and headed for the door. I replaced the dish towel and followed.

It was the pizza man making his delivery. Behind him, Reed waited anxiously on the sidewalk. When I bade Pee Wee good-bye and went outside, Reed took my arm protectively. "You okay? That guy looks like a nut."

"I'm fine, thank you." I wasn't so sure about Pee Wee. As we walked away, he stood in the doorway of his house, alone and holding his pizza.

In the car on our way into the city, I phoned the state police. I reached the detective who'd come to my house and told him Pee Wee probably knew the exact date of Madeleine's supposed departure for Indonesia. Then I asked about the bones in the woods.

"Yeah, we found 'em just where you said to look."

"Any idea who it is?" I asked nervously.

"It was a woman," he told me. "With a hole in her skull, so she didn't die of natural causes."

I felt sick. "No identification?"

"Nope. Just a funny clue. She had some special metal in her teeth. Nothing like dentists use to fill cavities here in the United States. She was from some other country."

"What country?" I asked.

"No idea yet. Got any suggestions?"

With a dreadful feeling inside, I said, "Think about Russia."

CHAPTER EIGHTEEN

After I spoke with the detective, I thought about Pippi and Madeleine until my head was spinning. If Pippi was dead, who had been sending postcards pretending to be Madeleine?

Between my visit to Pee Wee and a traffic backup, I missed my first event—cocktails to raise funds for a rare blood disorder that was found mostly in the African-American community. I would owe someone a note of apology for skipping.

By the time I arrived at the ritziest of downtown hotels, I had shoved murder out of my mind and bailed out of the SUV, determined to focus on work. Outside, I met my friend Delilah Fairweather, the best professional party planner in the biz. She stood on a red carpet that had been rolled out in front of the hotel. She was working her cell phone like the commander of a battleship in the midst of a storm at sea. But she spotted me emerging from the backseat of Reed's SUV and snapped her phone shut in midsentence. With a big grin on her face, she charged my way.

"Nora! Babycakes, it's been weeks since I've seen you! Give me some sugar." She enveloped me in strong arms and a cloud of intoxicating perfume. Dressed in the perfect little black dress with a matching coat and a shredded sort of scarf in an African textile via Seventh Avenue, Delilah teetered expertly on a pair of spike-heeled platform shoes that marked her as the Amazon in charge.

"I should have known you were running this show," I said. "The advance press has been terrific."

"I've worked my tail off," she said happily. "They should name a whole wing of this hospital after me."

Delilah had risen to the top of her profession through a combination of towering energy, tireless communication skills and a delightfully creative mind when it came to throwing a bash. I had no doubt her phone call had been to deal with a party scheduled weeks away. Her attention to detail exceeded NASA's planning for a space launch.

"I'm ready down to the last napkin ring. Don't you look smashing in this outfit." She gave me another bear hug, then held me at arm's length and admired my dress. "Ver-ry sexy! Who are you dressing for these days? You got a hot man you're meeting later?"

I laughed. "You could say that." To explain further would have required more time than either of us had. Around us, hotel bellmen bustled, and other journalists were beginning to gather.

Delilah popped her eyes wide. "I want details! Your love life is always interesting. We'll meet for a drink, howzabout that?"

I knew Delilah was always too busy to meet for drinks, but her invitations sounded sincere. "That would be great," I said. "Where do you want me now?"

With a sorrowful shake of her head, she said, "I want you mingling with the crowd when you look this fantastic, but I suppose you should be out here with the rest of the press as guests arrive. We're trying a red carpet theme, see? Make a fuss over the guests as they get out of their cars. Just don't snap any pictures of tacky girls flashing their va-jay-jays, okay? We're gonna keep things classy to-night."

I saluted. "Yes, ma'am."

She rushed off to check on matters inside the hotel, and I joined the jostling pack of reporters assembled to greet the guests. I recognized a couple of real journalists, but the rest were actors hired to look like paparazzi. One local television reporter was doing a sound check with her microphone.

Her cameraman gave me a wave, which I took to be a greeting until he called, "You're in my shot, honey!"

Chastened, I found a spot near the velvet rope and readied my phone camera. Behind me, a pair of gigantic lights projected twin spinning beacons up into the night sky. The lights generated a lot of heat, and the cooling fans created a low roar of background noise that made even the slightest conversation with my fellow journalists—real or pretend—very difficult.

What transpired after that was a long, exhausting half hour of making party guests feel like celebrities. Most of the men eschewed traditional evening clothes in favor of what was currently called "creative black tie." Personally, I thought it was hard to top a good Armani tuxedo with a perfectly knotted bow tie, but I didn't see a single one. Plenty of open collars with satin lapels, though, and even a T-shirt under a tux jacket here and there. A few heavy necklaces, too.

I took a number of photos of women in excellent dresses, and I silently composed a few good lines I could use in my column. Ruffles and sequins seemed to have given way to svelte gowns with minimal decoration, just jaw-dropping jewelry.

Shoes seemed to be of the hobbling variety. I could appreciate a great pair of shoes, of course, but I was ready for the super-high, straps-up-the-ankle fashion to go the way of the dodo. One young woman took a tumble off her shoes on the red carpet. Someone called an ambulance for her.

When I estimated that three-quarters of the guests had arrived, I packed up my camera and went into the hotel to rub elbows and gather some quotes.

The hospital fund-raising drive had been going on for three years, and the gala marked the successful end of the project. I guessed the drive chairpersons planned to announce a triumph, so I cornered one of them before the cocktail hour was over.

"Nora! Darling, what a pleasure to see you. And what a fantastic dress! How have you been?"

My husband, Todd, had gone to medical school with Darcy Hickam's husband, so we'd done a fair bit of socializing before Todd's behavior turned. Darcy was kind but distant to me during Todd's worst years—perhaps recognizing that there-but-for-the-Grace-of-God-go-I—but tonight she turned on the charm. Her day job was managing partner in a big PR firm that had recently landed a national account for a car rental company, so Darcy was no stranger to hard work under big pressure or to saying the right sound bite when needed. Tonight she looked very lean and fit in a purple dress cut down to her wow, and her hair was swept up and teased into an extravagant whoosh with what surely were extensions cascading down her back.

She gave me two air kisses.

"I'm great, Darcy. You look fantastic. And the fund-raising drive is a huge success."

"We worked our buns off," she said. "But it's the most worthy cause I know. My grandfather donated the whole second floor of the hospital back in the day—but you knew that, right? So I took it as my personal responsibility to make exactly the same kind of contribution. Listen, could you do me a favor?"

"Just ask."

"Will you find Jack Lantana and his trophy wife? Maybe take their picture for the paper? He's the guy who won a big defense contract two years ago, and now he's a gazillionaire. We're hoping to talk him into donating a million dollars, and it'd really help, I think, if they got some publicity tonight."

"Already done," I said.

She squealed and gave me an exuberant hug. "You're the best. A step ahead of me. Thanks, Nora."

As I talked to her for a more few minutes about the hospital project, I jotted down the best of her remarks.

"What will you do now that the drive is over?" I asked finally.

She smiled. "Jake and I are having a baby—just as soon as I can get pregnant, that is. We almost put off having kids too long. Now I can't wait."

"Wonderful," I said, trying to put some enthusiasm into the word.

"What's going on with you? I'm sorry to hear your aunt Madeleine died. She was quite the lady."

"Yes, she was."

"My mother used to be very close with Madeleine."

My ears perked up. "Was she? I didn't know that."

Darcy's mother, a principal ballerina with a big New York company, had come to Philadelphia to marry Dwight Hickam, an investment genius who took his millions and retired early to become a full-time ballet aficionado. Natasha and Dwight were still very big in the arts community, long after Natasha left the barre.

"Yes," Darcy said. "Madeleine helped Mom defect. Didn't you know that?"

"You're kidding!"

Darcy nodded. "Mom was started at the Kirov, but was allowed to dance on tour in Europe. She met Madeleine somewhere—I forget—and told her she wanted asylum. So Madeleine orchestrated everything. I guess I have her to thank. Otherwise, I'd still be a gleam in Daddy's eye!"

"That's fascinating," I said. "Madeleine didn't talk about those days. I'd love to chat with your mom sometime."

"She'd enjoy that. On the other end of the spectrum, how's Lexie?"

I didn't like Darcy's change of tone, but I said, "I hope to hear from her very soon."

Darcy eyed me. "You're loyal. That's nice."

I wanted to like Darcy. I respected what she'd done for the hospital, and I was happy for her plan to complete her marriage with children. But her dismissal of Lexie when Lex most needed her friends—it felt as if a sharp foil had pierced my social armor.

"Write her a note," I suggested.

"Oh," Darcy said, "I wouldn't know what to say. And we were never really close."

"Of course," I said, trying to keep my voice neutral. "Well, congrats on a wonderful party. You should be proud."

I roamed the room after that. I found myself thinking about Lexie, though, and had trouble concentrating on my job. She would have enjoyed such a party. I could almost see her holding court near the bar, keeping a flock of men in thrall as she sliced and diced the current economic scene while wearing a killer dress and diamonds to die for. Afterward, we might have strolled down the street for a drink at a popular bar to dissect the evening's gossip.

With my mind elsewhere, I nearly bumped into a pack of old friends surrounding a Philadelphia actor who'd gone off to Hollywood to play a TV doctor. Tonight he had been invited to simply charm the donors. I shook his hand and took his picture with some well-dressed people—a perfect shot for the newspaper's Web site coverage of the hospital fund-raiser. Attractive people having fun often encouraged more donors to give to worthy causes.

Recorded music made it hard to hear any conversation, as movie themes blared from speakers around the ballroom. I almost had to plug my ears when the James Bond theme suddenly blasted from behind me.

Deafened, I moseyed off to circulate among the older party-goers. The gray-haired crowd was just as beautifully dressed and appeared to be having a delightful evening, too, although more low-key. Everyone seemed pleased to be a part of a good cause. I took a few more casual shots without really thinking about whom I was photographing.

Suddenly I realized I had framed two people who surprised me.

Simon Groatley and Shirley van Vincent were standing aside, talking intently.

Arguing. Groatley's face was as red as brick, and Shirley seemed to be lecturing him. Considering he was a womanizing old goat, I was surprised to see him taking her scolding like a chastised husband.

I took another picture quickly, then turned away before they caught me staring. I hadn't realized they knew each other.

The lights flickered, indicating the dinner hour, so the crowd moved toward the tables in the ballroom. I found my seat between two couples who had been friends of my parents, and they regaled me with hilarious tales of Mama and Daddy dancing at parties.

I was glad to sit with people from whom my parents had not stolen. Maybe I had Delilah to thank for that. I didn't often get to hear from people who loved Mama and Daddy for what they really were—fun-loving, upbeat people without a negative bone between them. Sure, my parents were foolish and profligate. They were imperfect parents, but I loved them. Maybe that was a lesson to remember.

A sumptuous dinner of lobster tails and tender steak came next. Long ago, I had learned that people who have given very large sums of money expect a quality meal for their tens of thousands, so smart event organizers didn't skimp on the food.

After the meal, we heard twenty short minutes of speeches

thanking dozens of people for their generosity. Darcy was given a cut-glass bowl for her devotion to the cause. Then the orchestra burst into toe-tapping tunes, and the crowd mobbed the dance floor.

I made my way through a knot of people waiting for drinks at the bar and eventually found Shirley van Vincent sitting by herself at a large round table in an alcove. I had spotted her from across the room and waited until she was alone.

I slipped into a chair beside her, surprising Shirley as she took a sip of coffee.

"Hello, Mrs. van Vincent. I want to thank you again for giving my sisters and me a ride into town in your coach the other day."

She carefully swallowed her coffee—maybe she was composing herself—and then she set the cup down firmly in its saucer. "It was the least I could do, considering Emma's shameful condition."

I refused to take offense. "Emma looks well, though, doesn't she?"

"She's never had a problem with her looks."

Shirley van Vincent looked pretty good, too. I hadn't expected her to clean up so well, but I reminded myself she had been an ambassador's wife. She had changed her horsey garb for a satin ball gown that was probably as old as the one I was wearing. Its color had faded to a dusty rose that was becoming with her white hair and pale skin tone. There was nothing dusty about her demeanor, though. A gold and ruby necklace gleamed on her neck. The hard stone matched the glitter in her eye. She had placed her evening bag on the table, and I could see a silver cigarette case poking out. As soon as she got the chance, I figured she planned on sneaking a smoke.

I said, "I hear the police discovered another body. This time on your property."

"Bunch of old bones, that's all. But they've got yellow tape stretched all over my woods. I told them I want it cleaned up before my horse show. They stopped us from finishing setting up while they sniff around my land. I'll have to get up before dawn tomorrow to show the electricians where to place the loudspeakers."

Everyone had their priorities, I thought.

She pulled her cigarettes out of her evening bag and snapped the bag shut. "I hear your aunt Madeleine didn't die in a volcano, after all."

"How did you hear that?"

She toyed with her cigarette case. "News gets around in the neighborhood. So it's true? It was Madeleine in the elevator?"

I sidestepped the question. "You must be as distressed about her death as I am, considering you were friends."

"We were friends once." With her own brand of diplomacy, she said, "Must have been bad, the way she died."

"Yes. And worse yet, I have a feeling it wasn't an accident."

Shirley fumbled the cigarette case, and it clattered to the floor.

I reached down and retrieved it. Returning it to the table, I saw that Shirley had turned very pale. I said, "I wonder if you have any thoughts about who might have disliked Madeleine enough to want her dead. People in international circles, that is."

"Not my husband, if that's what you're insinuating."

"Heavens, why would I think that?"

With a shrewd glare, she said, "Don't pussyfoot with me, young lady. Surely you already know Madeleine worked closely with my husband. But he had a clear mandate to act only within international law. I started out as his secretary, so I saw firsthand what he put up with when it came to her. What Madeleine did, she did without my husband's participation."

"She helped a lot of people," I said. "Russian defectors—"

"She made life very difficult for my husband. She was reckless and didn't care whose reputation she sullied."

"Did Madeleine sully Mr. van Vincent's?"

"Certainly not. He retired with his integrity intact."

I sensed there was more to her side of the story. "But—?"

"He didn't have an affair with that woman," Shirley spat out. "I'll go to my grave denying that rumor."

I was about to protest when she said that. It had never entered my head that Madeleine and Vincente van Vincent had been intimate. But I saw her jealousy then, and realized that Shirley—a lowly secretary before she married the boss—was still touchy where the smart, beautiful and dynamic Madeleine Blackbird was concerned.

Quietly I said, "I only want to learn more about Madeleine."

Shirley's demeanor finally cracked. "Young lady, your aunt was no paragon decent young women should be looking to. The faster you bury that woman, the better for all of us."

"I can't help wondering who killed her."

"I think you'll discover Madeleine burned a lot of bridges wherever she went. You won't have any shortage of suspects in her murder."

"Simon Groatley?" I asked.

"Who?"

"Madeleine's lawyer. Simon Groatley. You were speaking with him earlier this evening."

"You must be mistaken," she said shortly. "I don't know any Groatley. Now, if you'll excuse me, Eleanor, I'm going to powder my nose."

She rose from the table, snatched up her bag and left. She didn't head for the restrooms, though. She went straight for the door to the hotel terrace, where she probably intended to smoke a cigarette.

She had lied to me, bald-faced. Why deny she knew Groatley?

I wished I'd had time to ask her if she'd seen Madeleine and Pippi the day they made their good-byes to friends in the neighborhood. Shirley might have been one of the last people to see either one of them alive.

I was thinking I could slip out and go home to ruminate a little more on the possibilities when someone tapped my shoulder and asked, "May I have this dance, Miss Blackbird?"

I turned to find Simon Groatley himself looming over me. He extended his hand for mine.

I could hardly say no.

CHAPTER NINETEEN

quickly discovered Groatley was the kind of man who insisted on holding his dance partner as if she might wriggle free and run away like a frightened deer. Clamped to his chest, I could barely breathe as he whirled me into the crowd of dancers. He had a commanding ballroom style, too, moving me purposefully around the floor in time to the music, taking long strides. I suppose he thought he was sweeping me off my feet.

When we reached the opposite side of the dance floor from the orchestra, he eased back a few inches—making enough space to force conversation. And to get a gander down the front of my dress.

He said, "I hear you've been asking questions about Madeleine Blackbird."

"Can you blame me?"

He laughed. "What do you expect to learn? Some deep, dark secret about her?"

"She had a lot of secrets, I think."

"None of them very interesting," Groatley assured me. "What matters now is that we clean up her estate and let the past go."

"So you're going to handle the estate quickly? Save the family a few billable hours?"

Another deep laugh. "These things take time."

"Is that what you discussed with Mrs. van Vincent just now? The estate?"

"I thought she might be interested in buying the land once the rest of the details were settled."

"You weren't discussing Madeleine?"

"Why should we?"

Truly curious, I asked, "Aren't you interested in how she died?"

"My job usually begins when my client dies."

"Oh? I thought your job began when you first start to help a client plan her estate."

His face flushed dark red, and he gave me a cold look down his nose. "You've grown up a lot since I first saw you drawing in a coloring book at your grandfather's feet, Nora. May I call you Nora now? I did back when you wore pigtails."

I had never worn pigtails in my life, but I let that detail pass. "I'm very upset to learn that my aunt died a horrible death. I think she was deliberately murdered, but you seem to have a cavalier attitude about it, Simon. May I call you Simon?"

"I'm not the least bit cavalier. But determining how she passed away is something that should be left to the professionals. Let the police handle the investigation. Right now, our job is to work together to settle her estate and move on. Surely a lovely young woman like yourself has more important things to do with her time."

"I care about how she died."

"How can I encourage you to care a little less?"

I missed a step and stumbled. I didn't fall, of course, because of the grip he maintained on my body. "What are you suggesting?"

"There will be plenty of loopholes in Madeleine's estate," Groatley said. "I'm sure we can find a little something extra for you, Nora."

I could feel the pressure in my chest start to tighten, and it wasn't because of the lawyer's embrace. "You mean, if I stop asking questions?"

"I think you could redirect your energy, that's all," he said. "Wouldn't you like a little extra cash? You have problems with your house, I hear. Maybe you'd like me to arrange to have a few things fixed."

"I can fix my own house."

He guided me off the floor and behind a pillar that provided us a small amount of seclusion from the rest of the ballroom crowd. The next thing I knew, we were spinning down a corridor reserved for the hotel staff. I bumped into a cart loaded with dirty dishes, and Groatley released me so abruptly that I had to catch my balance with a hand on the wall.

Pinning me against the wall by leaning over me, he said, "Let me give you a word of warning, Nora. You're in over your head."

I held my ground, although my heart thumped an erratic beat. "What does that mean?"

"Madeleine did have many secrets. I think she wanted to keep them deeply buried—even after her death. She wouldn't want to cause any pain to her friends or family."

"Are you referring to all the money Madeleine was taking in?"

"What money?"

"I think you know, Simon. Madeleine was earning tens of thousands of dollars every month before she left town. How, exactly? Do you know?"

"I know nothing about any criminal activities, if that's what you're insinuating."

"Then why are you so anxious for me to stop digging into Madeleine's past?"

"I merely believe you'll cause yourself more distress by asking questions. Distress not only for yourself, but also for your family."

"Is that a threat?" I demanded.

"Certainly not," he shot back, putting a hand next to mine on the wall and pressing even closer. "I merely think it's time for you to stop asking a lot of silly questions about things that might stir up trouble. And I'm willing to make it worth your while. Think of how you can most benefit from all this."

"The thing I want most right now is the truth."

Wrong answer. He dropped his hand onto my bare shoulder, fingers biting into my skin. I tried to shake off his grip, but he tightened it. A second later, he pulled me close again—as if we were dancing. Except there was no music in the back hallway.

"Stop it," I said. Before he could try to kiss me—I saw it coming—I stepped hard on his foot, digging my heel into the top of his shoe.

He grunted in pain, but instead of releasing me, he suddenly gripped my shoulders with both hands. The mood changed in a heartbeat. I saw the anger flash across his face. I tried kneeing him in the groin, but he used my instant of being off balance to whirl me around and push my face into the wall. He pinned me there with his full weight so hard he drove all the air out of my lungs. I felt his knee jam between my thighs, forcing them apart. Breathing hard on my neck, he used one hand to gather up the bulk of my long skirt.

I gave up trying to wrestle free and instead flattened both of my hands against the wall. I pushed with all my strength and almost succeeded in shoving him back. I couldn't—but I finally had enough air to let out a yell. To shut me up, he slammed my head against the wall. Pinning me there again, he said crude things in my ear. Called me names.

I had always thought I could fight off a cruel grope. I'd taken classes, and I wasn't weak. But he was very strong. And practiced. He had his bruising moves down to a science—he knew exactly how to overpower me.

Except he picked the wrong place.

A waiter suddenly appeared from a doorway, summoned by my shout.

"Hey," he said. "You can't do that here."

He must have thought what Groatley was doing was consensual, because he didn't sound very firm. But I let out a gasping cry for help, and suddenly the waiter figured out what was happening. He grabbed Groatley by the arm.

The lawyer broke off immediately. He stepped back, and I felt my skirt slip down to cover my legs again. I was trembling so hard I could barely manage to turn myself around. I leaned against the wall, shaken. And humiliated.

Groatley had a disgusted expression on his face—as if I were the one who deserved loathing. "You slut," he said.

He turned on his heel and walked back toward the ballroom, smoothing his hair and the front of his tuxedo.

"You okay?" the waiter asked me, half embarrassed by what he'd seen. He was a youngish man—younger than me—with a ponytail neatly tied back. He glanced down at the neckline of my dress. Groatley had managed to drag it down too low, and I used both trembling hands to pull it up again.

"Thank you," I managed to say. "Thank you very much."

"No problem," he said. "But you shouldn't do that stuff back here. Get a room, lady."

He headed toward the ballroom, too. Even my rescuer assumed I'd been at least partly responsible for what had just happened.

I stayed there, flustered and steadying myself while the meaning of what Groatley had said to me sank in. Had I misunderstood?

No, I was sure he'd threatened me. He wanted me to stop asking questions about Madeleine. He had offered me a bribe first. And when I hadn't responded, he'd attacked me.

Still shaken, I headed back to the ballroom and took a drink from the tray of the first waiter who happened past me. I drank it down without tasting the liquor and felt slightly less nauseated.

Madeleine's own lawyer was a crook and a horrible person, I knew now.

But the question that was searing my brain? Could he have killed Madeleine?

I'd experienced his lightning-fast metamorphosis from anger to punishing rage. Had Madeleine been his target, too? Only she hadn't been as lucky as I had been?

I found my handbag and phone. I rescued my wrap from the hotel coat check and slipped away from the ball before anyone could remark upon the change in my mood. I even heard Delilah laughing uproariously in the hallway, so I took a detour to avoid seeing her again. I telephoned Reed, and he picked me up in front of the hotel.

If Reed noticed anything different about me, he didn't say so. The evening must have still seemed routine to him, while I felt as weak as a child from the shock of what had happened upstairs.

After Reed helped me into the backseat of the SUV and walked around to get behind the wheel, I saw Shirley van Vincent exit the hotel.

A chauffeured car awaited her, and she walked toward it. I couldn't help noticing that Shirley looked ill—weak and pale. Much the way I imagined I looked.

"Anywhere else tonight?" Reed asked.

"No, thank you," I said. "Home, please."

At Blackbird Farm, finally feeling more outraged than feeble, I let myself in the back door and found Michael sprawled on the kitchen floor, cursing.

"What on earth is wrong?" I asked.

He peered out from under the sink and glowered up at me from his prone position. He had a wrench in one hand and a dark expression on his face. "It was either get roaring drunk or take out my frustrations on the plumbing."

I knew Michael didn't get roaring drunk, not ever. If he had more than three glasses of wine with dinner, that was a big night. I felt my own problems evaporate. "I gather your evening with Carrie went badly?"

He sat up and threw the wrench onto the floor with a noisy clang. An adorable smear of grease streaked down one cheek.

He said, "That doesn't begin to describe what a crapfest we had around here tonight. After Carrie left, both your sisters stopped by, not to mention the man in Emma's life. What's his name? Heart Stopper?"

"Emma and Hart Jones came back?"

"Yeah, they came to pick up some clothes for her. That guy wants her bad, Nora, and she's hot for him, too. Trouble is, any minute he's getting married to the rich girl who can do his career the most good, and believe me, I know all the wedding details, because while I made dinner for the whole crazy bunch of them, he stormed around here yelling about his wedding and why Emma should go to some island with him this weekend. And what the hell are shrimp shooters?"

"They're an appetizer. It's a cocktail shrimp with sauce, in a shot glass. It's very pretty, actually, but—why an island?"

Michael's glare intensified. "Because his mother has a beach house there, and Heart Stopper thinks it's a dandy place for Emma to hang out while she waits for the baby to come. He thinks his fiancée won't look for a girlfriend in the Caribbean, I guess. If I'm any judge of character, that guy plans on having both women at his beck and call."

"Did they talk about the baby?"

"Yeah. He wants the kid, which I guess is a point in his favor. Or maybe he just wants everything." Barely holding back his temper, Michael said, "The son of a bitch has had his life handed to him on a silver platter from the get-go."

After my manhandling by Simon Groately, I found Michael's

disapproval of Hart very endearing. "Hart wants to marry Penny and keep Emma on the side?"

"And he's completely up front about that. He's such an asshole he doesn't see what it does to Emma. He wants her available for the booty call, nothing else. His wife, though, plans on being the perfect mother to the baby. They've got lots of plans, all the way to the kid's first year at Harvard."

"Emma's not the kept-woman type," I said, half to myself.

"She's thinking with her hormones right now." Michael seemed to realize he was upset. "Sorry. It's been a bad night."

"Where are they now?"

"They have a suite at a hotel." With a pained expression, he added, "There was a lot of talk about pregnant sex from your sister Libby that I'd like to wash out of my brain with a fire hose, but it gave Emma and Heart Stopper some great ideas they couldn't wait to try."

"I should probably make an effort to talk some sense into Emma. And make sure she's safe."

"If you can talk some sense into her, you deserve a medal. As for her being safe? I sent the crew to watch the hotel. And I gave her a number to call if she wanted them to bust down a door."

Until that moment, I hadn't realized the checkpoint at the end of my driveway wasn't in place. After the evening I'd had, it suddenly felt good to have the house to ourselves.

I put my bag on the kitchen table and stripped off my wrap. I extended my hand to him and helped Michael to his feet. I gave him a kiss on his clean cheek. "What went wrong with Carrie?"

He shook his head as if to dispel a tornado of woes. "What didn't go wrong with Carrie?" He sighed. "You think I should maybe get a pipe and one of those Mr. Rogers sweaters with the buttons up the front, and I'd magically turn into some kind of television dad? I'd like to know all the answers and say the right things. I just don't see another way of getting the father gig right as long as things are going the way they're going right now."

"I'm sorry you're upset."

"I am," he admitted. More seriously, he said, "She's not going to get the promotion she wants, you know. Not after the army figures out who the hell her father is."

"I know. I'm sorry." It broke my heart to say so.

"I was as honest as I could be with her without risking an indictment. She doesn't see the whole picture yet, but she will. If I had a couple more years to clean things up, I might come across looking okay. But right now? Just out of jail? With all the family stuff going down, I make your average terrorist look like a clown at a birthday party."

"That's not true," I said gently. "You're exaggerating."

He turned the water on in the sink and set about washing grease off his hands. But I knew he was mostly right. If Carrie's promotion depended on her having an upstanding citizen at the top of her family tree, she was headed for disappointment. The kind of disappointment that would jeopardize any future between father and daughter.

Michael reached for a towel. "Most people start with a puppy, you know? Work up to the parent thing gradually. Me, I'm barely housebroken myself."

He tossed the towel onto the counter, and I eased myself into his arms. I stroked a ragged tuft of his hair off his forehead. "Did you eat any dinner? I could make you some peanut butter toast."

He shook his head. "Not hungry."

"Or I could pour you a beer?"

"I had a beer. It didn't help."

"Well, then," I murmured, "how about if we go upstairs—all by ourselves for once—and you can help me off with my dress?"

His smile flickered at last. "What about the new underwear you promised me?"

At that moment, I almost told him about what Simon Groatley had done.

But I knew how Michael would react. At best, he'd go into a rage. At worst, he'd order a hit on Groatley's life.

Neither option appealed to me just then. All I wanted was to feel cherished and valued and desired.

So I said, "I think we can skip the underwear and go straight to something else."

I coaxed him with a soft kiss, then a few more.

A minute later Michael chased me up the staircase.

It was after midnight when we heard a noise downstairs.

I lifted my head from Michael's shoulder where I'd been comfortably listening to him talk in circles about Carrie. A world away from a ballroom filled with people whose minds I understood but whose hearts were a mystery to me, here I had listened and heard the truth in the heart of a man both gentle and lawlessly passionate. I felt my love for him as an ache inside myself. More important was knowing I was the one to whom he could say the things he would never speak to anyone else.

But at the rattle and clunk from downstairs, I stilled him with my hand on his chest.

"Did you hear that?"

He lay quiet, listening. "Yeah. You think Emma's come back?"

"If she really went to a hotel with Hart, she won't be back for days."

"Then who—?"

Again, something bumped far away in the great house, and we both sat up in the dark. I clutched the bedclothes around me.

Michael rolled easily out of his side of the bed and made a grab for his jeans. "Oh, boy," he said. "I hope it's some idiot breaking in. I've been looking for a way to burn off some frustration since I got out."

"I thought that's what we just did."

He leaned across the bed and kissed me hard. "Sweetheart, sometimes a man just needs to pop somebody in the teeth."

I scrambled out of the bed. "Let me find my bathrobe. I'll call 911. I don't want you to risk—Michael?"

He was already out on the landing and heading downstairs—a hungry animal hunting prey. I might try to tame the beast, I thought fleetingly, but there was something in Michael that nobody was ever going to control.

Hurtling barefoot down the stairs after him, I called his name again. But by the time I made it down to the first floor, I heard a tremendous crash and somebody yelped like a kicked puppy.

I skidded into the dining room and flicked the light on in time to see Michael jamming someone up against the door to the butler's pantry. It was a man, dressed entirely in black, but limp as a rag doll. His head snapped back and bounced hard off the door.

The man in black wore a ski mask over his face. Gasping for air, he squirmed against Michael's grip. One of the dining chairs lay in splinters on the rug.

Michael kicked a heavy object, and it skittered across the floor in my direction. A gun. I recoiled as if it might go off at my feet.

Then Michael ripped the mask off, and the threatening man turned into my cousin.

"Sutherland!" I cried. "Michael, stop! Don't hurt him!"

"Help," Sutherland squeaked at me, his eyes bugging out.

Cursing, Michael didn't release him. Not until I tugged on his arm.

My cousin slithered to the floor, his legs turned to jelly. He sprawled on the carpet. For an instant, I thought he had fainted.

I knelt down and tapped his cheek with my fingertips. "Sutherland, darling? Are you okay?"

Above me, Michael said, "He just broke into your house with a gun, and now he's *darling*?"

"He's harmless," I said. "He's my cousin, the one I told you about."

Sutherland's eyes flickered to life, and he blinked at me, then up at Michael. Scrambling on his back like a turtle, he tried to make an escape, but ended up huddled against the wall. Hoarsely, he said, "What happened to the skinny kid?"

"What skinny kid?"

"The one who was here this afternoon. I thought he was your boyfriend." He glanced past me up at Michael again and gave an involuntary flinch of terror. "Who's *he*?"

"The kid was a friend of Emma's," I explained. "This is Michael Abruzzo. Michael, this is Sutherland Blackbird."

"If it's all the same, I'll skip shaking his hand." Michael loomed over us. "What the hell are you doing here in the middle of the night, moron? With a gun?"

Sutherland cleared his throat. "Would you believe me if I said I was merely dropping by to—to—"

"To steal the silver?" I asked tartly. I sat back on my heels.

Sutherland looked embarrassed and tried mightily to hide it. "May I get off the floor? It's a little uncomfortable."

Michael growled, "I can show you uncomfortable, pal. Give me thirty seconds, Nora."

"Don't be silly. Help me get him up."

With a grunt of displeasure, Michael hauled Sutherland to his feet. My cousin tottered over to a chair and sat down heavily, gently massaging his neck where Michael had pinned him like a bug to the door.

I tightened the belt on my bathrobe and stood before him. "You have some explaining to do, mister."

"I—I—"

"If you want the truth out of him," Michael said, "there's a thing I can do to his knuckles, no problem. There's a hammer in the kitchen."

Sutherland took him seriously, and said hastily, "I came to pick up something that's rightfully mine."

"Yours?"

"Yes, my stepmother's address book."

"Her—? You mean the black leather book Madeleine kept in her office?"

"It's mine to begin with—or, it will be after we settle the estate. I came back to retrieve it. What the book was doing here, I have no idea." He attempted to muster some indignation. "I suppose you took it from Quintain yourself, Nora."

"No matter how it got here," I said, "it's gone now. We thought you stole it."

"Stole it! It's really gone?" He blinked up at me, confused. "You're not kidding."

"No, I'm not. We thought you took her book while we were busy with the ponies."

"Who did take it? If not me?" Sutherland frowned. "Libby?"

"Of course not!"

From behind me, Michael said, "I can make this go a whole lot faster."

"Why don't you make us some coffee?" I suggested.

"Yes, I could use a drink." Sutherland continued to massage his throat. "Not coffee, though. It keeps me awake. Whiskey and soda? No ice."

Michael scooped up the gun from the floor and checked the clip. He emptied the bullets into the palm of his hand. "While I tend the bar, I'll think about which landfill we can use."

He slid the bullets into his pocket and went off in the direction of the kitchen.

When we were alone together, Sutherland began trembling so hard he had to trap both hands between his knees. "Good Lord, Nora. What are you doing with that—that person in your house? Is he some kind of night watchman?"

"The night watchman is going to beat you senseless," I said, "unless you start talking. Why on earth did you think you had to break into my house? You couldn't just knock? Ask in a civilized way?"

He peered more closely at the picture I made in my vintage satin robe—a Victorian-style masterpiece of lace and light boning that made me look like the BBC's idea of a woman of ill repute. In my haste to get downstairs, I hadn't quite managed to tie the belt properly, and he gave my bare leg a long glance before adding up the astonishing facts. "Good heavens, you're not sleeping with that thug, are you?"

"Sutherland," I said, barely containing my wrath, "in a minute I'm going to clobber you myself! You brought a gun into my house! What were you thinking?"

"Okay, okay. I came for Madeleine's book. Groatley thinks it's vitally important, but he couldn't find it. He believes you took it the morning we were all at Quintain."

"What does Simon Groatley know about the book? Why does he want it?"

"He's covering his ass, Nora. He thinks the book contains all of Madeleine's financial records. He knows you're going to sue him for the way he neglected Madeleine's estate."

"*I'm* the one who's going to sue him? What about you? I thought you wanted Quintain for yourself."

"I do," he insisted. "But—well, it seems simpler if—if—"

I remembered my conversation with the lawyer as we danced around the ballroom. "You cut a deal with Simon Groatley, didn't you?"

My cousin had enough conscience to blush.

I said, "In exchange for you getting Quintain instead of my sisters and me?"

"Groatley's right, Nora. If we all agree right away, there won't be a drawn-out settlement of Madeleine's estate." He implored, "We'll all get our money much sooner if we just cooperate and—"

"We?" I said. "You're including me, after all? Or did you come here to gather evidence against me? Admit it, Sutherland. You teamed up with Groatley so you could shut out the rest of us."

"That's not entirely— I mean— See here, there's no need to talk to me like a common criminal!"

"No? Because I think that's exactly what you are."

"But—"

"And I took a look at the marina manager's paperwork when I went to visit you on your yacht. Except the yacht isn't yours at all, is it, Sutherland? It's registered in somebody else's name."

"I—I—"

"You lied, Cuz. First you tried to make me believe you're a hot-shot yacht racer, but you're actually just a hitchhiker, aren't you? Hitching a ride on a boat owned by somebody who probably has no clue you're aboard. But more important—"

"They do, too," he shot back defensively. "Oh, hell, if you must know the truth, I'm a broker. A yacht broker, and I brought the boat here for the new owner. Except they're spending an extra week hiking mountains in some godforsaken Third World country, so they're not ready to accept delivery. I might as well skip paying for a hotel room, right? So I'm staying on the yacht."

"You're a used-boat dealer! No wonder you're looking to inherit Madeleine's money. You're probably as broke as I am. I can't believe how low you've sunk." To stop myself from clanging him over the head with the nearest silver teapot, I sat down on the opposite side of the dining room table. "It was you who sent all the postcards from Madeleine, wasn't it? Don't lie this time. It had to be you. There's nobody else who traveled that part of the world."

"All right," he said. "Yes, it was me."

"Why?" I cried.

"Because—well, Madeleine was dead, wasn't she? And, okay, I went back to Quintain once or twice. When I needed extra cash."

"You stole more things from the house?"

"Once or twice, that's all," he assured me. "She was already dead, right? What was the harm in letting everyone keep thinking she was having a wonderful time?"

"You wanted us to stay away from the house," I guessed, "so you could help yourself whenever your piggy bank ran low. I can't believe you're such a snake."

Sutherland gave a pretty good impression of looking repentant. But his voice turned sulky. "It wasn't just me. The last time I went to Quintain, somebody else had cleaned the place out."

"Who?"

"I don't know."

"So you figured the party was over, and you might as well declare Madeleine dead and start collecting whatever you could get from the sale of the property. You took advantage of the volcano, didn't you? You figured that was the perfect way to end Madeleine's life." Fed up, I snapped, "Honestly, Sutherland, I'm calling the police this minute."

He seized my hand to keep me from leaping to my feet. "Please don't. It will be too embarrassing. For all of us, Nora."

I glared at him. "Did you kill her?"

"Kill Madeleine?" He shuddered with revulsion. "Of course not! What an appalling idea."

"All the evidence points to you." I wrenched my hand from his grasp and stood up. "You're due more than a little embarrassment, I think."

Michael returned with a glass of water and set it on the table in front of Sutherland. With his other hand, Michael handed me the phone. "Call 911. The cops will love this."

"No!" Sutherland cried. And this time he truly looked pathetic. His thinning hair, his wrinkled neck, his fake wristwatch. He was an aging gigolo, all right. Too old to get by on his charm anymore.

He was desperate to find a way to finance his lifestyle. From the way he had surveyed the decay of Blackbird Farm, I knew he feared he'd end up equally impoverished.

I blew a sigh of exasperation and turned to Michael. "If I call the police, they're going to assume that stupid gun is yours. They'll cross-examine all of us, then drag you off just for the fun of it, and I just don't have the energy for that tonight."

"Me neither." He looked hopeful again. "So I get to beat the crap out of this guy, after all?"

"We need to find you a hobby. Stamp collecting, maybe." I eyed my cousin with distaste. "Do we have to let Sutherland go?"

"We could tie him up in the barn for the rest of the night. Give him time to think about his transgressions."

"That won't help solve the problem."

"Which problem?" Sutherland asked.

I sat down again and glared at him. "Who killed Madeleine!"

Michael sat down at the table, too. "To figure that out, it's time to follow the money, sweetheart."

Confused, I said, "Her estate, you mean?"

"You need to find out where all her stuff went."

"Sutherland took it."

My cousin managed some outrage. "Not everything! Honestly, Nora, I only made a few small trips to the well."

"I thought you said you went to Quintain once or twice, but now it's a few small trips?" In disgust, I demanded, "Did you steal the Fabergé egg?"

"Heavens, no! That would have been too traceable."

Michael grinned coldly. "So you're a cut above the usual stupid felon?"

At something he saw in Michael's eye, Sutherland subsided into his chair.

"All right," I said to Michael, "what should I do?"

He considered the situation for a moment, letting his own felonious side comb through the possibilities. "In the morning," he said finally, "you should go see a guy I know. If he's not inside, that is."

Inside meant jail. I gave Michael a long look. "Is this going to be another Foxy Galore excursion?"

"A different part of the social spectrum," Michael said with a smile. "But Libby's going to love him."

CHAPTER TWENTY

The following morning, I found myself in a disreputable part of South Philly.

Beside me, behind the wheel of her minivan, Libby nibbled on her second orange scone of the day. "So you let Sutherland go?"

"If I hadn't sent him on his way, Michael might have hurt him."

"Do you think our cousin was telling the truth?"

"About much of anything? Not really. He helped himself from Madeleine's house whenever he needed money, and he pretended to send the postcards from her so he could have continued access to Quintain. He says he discovered somebody else was stealing from the house, so that's when he announced her death to the newspapers. But maybe he took everything himself. I wouldn't put it past him. He's hardly got the right constitution for murder, however. He looked positively sick when I accused him."

Libby took another bite of her scone and looked out the windshield. "This neighborhood looks like it belongs in an episode of *The Wire*. Do you see that man on the corner? I think he's selling drugs."

"Look again. He's selling bunches of flowers, Lib."

The two of us peered at the suspicious-looking character on the litter-strewn corner. His flowers did look a little wilted, I had to admit. Up the street was a famous cheesesteak eatery, but in the other direction stretched a warren of alleys that I had never explored.

"Just the same, I'm going to take his picture and send it to my PitterPat followers." Libby handed me her scone on a wadded-up napkin and rolled down her window. She snapped a photo with her cell phone's camera. "My followers will have an opinion about what's really going on here."

"So, your PitterPat followers are definitely—uh—incarcerated?"

"Yes, they're all coming out to me now." Libby used her thumbs to type a speedy message on her phone's tiny keyboard. "I'm a sympathetic ear. You'd be amazed by how many men are unjustly imprisoned, Nora. Our justice system is a disgrace. Once Maximus is enrolled in sports camp, I might start volunteering. Prisoners Aid is a very worthwhile cause, and they need my help."

"Uh-uh." I gave her back her scone and brushed crumbs from my lap. "Libby, you know it's possible your followers might be scamming you."

"How crazy do you think I am? I'll screen anyone before I get really serious. That Man of Yours said he'd help identify the undesirable ones." Before I could object to her plan, she pointed out the window. "Is that the address we're looking for?"

She had parked along the curb across from a busy Italian deli and a Japanese grocery. Both businesses were booming with customers. The bagel shop down the street looked even busier. But in the other direction sat a squat building that took up a full city block.

The neon sign over the door read: UNCLE SAM'S PAWNSHOP and alternately blinked red, white and blue. Dozens of American flags fluttered along the roof. The shop's dirty windows had been papered over with signs so it was impossible to see inside. The signs read: WE PAY BIG CASH FOR GOLD!

"Without a doubt," I said. "That's the place."

"It's very patriotic."

"It is. We have to go around the back. Sam is officially closed on Sundays."

"And That Man of Yours made an appointment for us?" Libby wrapped her napkin around the remains of her breakfast to save it for later.

"Yes. Let's go."

We climbed out of the minivan and buttoned up our coats against the brisk November wind. Libby had chosen a vibrant purple ensemble. Only the top of her T-shirt showed beneath her coat. This morning, it read: SUNDAY IS FOR LOVERS. I suspected she had a similar shirt for every day of the week.

The street was lined with vehicles and bustled with shoppers picking up whatever delicacies they preferred for Sunday dinner. But around the corner, the traffic dwindled to nothing, and it was with trepidation that Libby and I approached the back alley.

We peeked around the back of Uncle Sam's building. The alley was crowded with a Dumpster, a heap of mashed cardboard boxes and a couple of late-model vehicles coated with rust. One had a front tire encased by a parking authority boot.

Libby snapped another photo for her followers.

The back door was unmarked except for a hand-painted *No Parking* sign and a rusted lock.

I knocked tentatively.

We waited.

Libby said, "Either nobody's home, or they didn't hear you."

She used her fist to bang on the door as if leading the vice squad on a raid.

The door swung open almost immediately, and a large, broad-shouldered man stuck his head out. He had a used-car-salesman grin and wore a red bandanna around his unruly dark hair. Otherwise, he was attractive in a South Philly way—all expansive bonhomie with a twinkle in his eyes and a missing eyetooth. He gave us a delighted once-over. "You must be Mick's girls—am I right? I'm Uncle Sam."

"Girl." Libby pointed at me. "I," she said with a distinct flutter of her lashes, "am available."

He pushed the door wide and boomed, "Come in, ladies! Can I offer you a morning beverage? Coffee? Beer? Maybe a mimosa?"

"I'd love a mimosa!" Libby cried. "So festive."

He gave her a more appreciative glance, his large nose hovering over her cleavage with the air of a connoisseur. "Are you feeling festive, pretty lady?"

"We don't need mimosas," I said firmly. "We're on a bit of a tight schedule today."

"That's too bad," he said, his grin undimmed. "On a weekend, I'm allergic to tight schedules. Weekends are for taking your time, smelling the flowers, enjoying the view, am I right?"

"So right," Libby breathed.

"I especially love Sundays. I used to be a preacher, you know. Had my own church and my own flock. There was a little misunderstanding about the collection plate, or I'd still be standing at the pulpit."

"I'm a freethinker when it comes to organized religion," Libby said. "I want to explore as many spiritual experiences as I possibly can."

"Why," he said with pleasure, "we're practically soul mates!"

He ushered us past what must have been the pawnshop showroom. I caught a glimpse of lighted cases full of wristwatches and other merchandise. The walls were hung with musical instruments, several sets of golf clubs and at least one lawn mower. Along another wall sat the big stuff—a pinball machine, a jukebox and two tanning beds.

"Come into my inner sanctum," Uncle Sam said, leading us along a narrow hallway with fluorescent lights buzzing overhead and well-worn vinyl flooring underfoot. "We'll have a little sit-down, just the three of us. Mick said you were looking to find out about some stolen goods. Damn shame. Who'd want to steal stuff from a coupla nice girls like you two?"

If I had to guess Uncle Sam's age, I'd have put it somewhere between forty and fifty, but for a former man of the cloth he had a youthful swagger. He had pushed the sleeves of his Eagles sweat-shirt up to his elbows, and we could see the twin tattoos on his forearms—George Washington sitting astride his horse on one arm, Abraham Lincoln delivering the Gettysburg Address on the other. Both men seemed to have facial features suspiciously similar to Uncle Sam's.

"Actually," I said, "it's our aunt who was the victim. Her art collection has disappeared, as have many other valuable items from her home."

"Damn shame," Uncle Sam said again. "Good that you're making a move, though. Doesn't pay to play the victim. Take action, that's always the best way. Keep your enemies on their toes. I'm paraphrasing here, but that's Sun Tzu, the Chinese general. Smart guy. Have a seat. I'll whip us up those mimosas. Only takes a second."

His inner sanctum was half office, half seraglio. Metal desk, metal filing cabinets, overhead lighting. A thick Persian rug lay on the floor, though, and twin fainting couches sat in front of the desk. Both couches were upholstered in pink velvet and featured multiple pillows with tassels—as if a harem might suddenly need extra seat-ing. Swagged lanterns hung from the ceiling and cast romantic lighting on the luxurious cushions.

"How beautiful!" Libby sang out.

"You have good taste, pretty lady."

"I love my comforts." Libby sighed and flung herself down on the nearest couch. "Wonderful! Nora, you must try one of these!"

There was no other place to sit, so I took the other fainting couch, while Uncle Sam bustled behind his desk. He opened a small dorm-sized fridge and extracted a plastic jug of orange juice and a bottle of cheap champagne. Before I could decline again, he had popped the cork and was sloshing champagne and juice into disposable cups.

"Mick would have my head if I didn't take good care of you two. How is he doing, by the way? Happy to be sprung?"

"Very happy." I accepted a cup. "But if we could talk about—"

"I bet he couldn't wait to get home to you." Uncle Sam gave me an appreciative leer. "I heard he'd found himself a real classy girl-friend, but I didn't believe it. You're a knockout. Mick's had a checkered history with the ladies, you know."

"No," I said, suddenly intrigued. "I didn't know. What kind of history?"

But Libby was unfolding a sheaf of papers from her handbag. "I've made some drawings of the things I best remember from our aunt's collection. There are paintings, of course, but I don't suppose that's your kind of merchandise? So let's look at some of the smaller items."

"Hey, you're a darn good artist." Uncle Sam shuffled approvingly through the first few papers. "Darn good."

"Why, thank you." A modest blush appeared on Libby's cheeks. "These are just rough sketches."

"Very impressive."

"About Michael," I said. "And his history—?"

Uncle Sam took all of Libby's sketches and flipped through them, nodding. "Yeah, I can see this is real expensive stuff. Is this one of them Nanette Fabray eggs? I used to love her. Great dancer. The egg's not my thing, but I have resources. Let's take a look, okay?"

He spun his computer monitor around so Libby could see the screen. He used two large fingers to type on his keyboard and brought up some photographs. Libby leaned closer, and the two of them began to talk Greek statuary.

"This one's probably inspired by Pompeii." Libby pointed at one of her sketches. "My theory is that if it was stolen twenty years ago, it might have turned up in a museum by now. I love carnal subjects for art, don't you?"

"What's not to love? It coulda gone to a collector in the Middle East, though, or maybe China. Those guys are already snapping up a lot of good stuff. Then they hide it for a decade or two before they sell it in the open market. I betcha that's where your egg ended up, too. Let's do a little snooping."

"Good heavens." Libby planted her forefinger on the computer screen. "That's my cousin Sutherland!"

"Oh, yeah? You know that guy? Well, this here's a surveillance tape from a pawn—I mean, a place of business that maybe sometimes overlooks the provenance of their inventory. Looks like your cousin is selling stuff that maybe don't belong to him."

"That's a Russian icon!" Libby cried. "It used to hang in Madeleine's library!"

Uncle Sam leaned closer to watch the action on the screen. "Looks like he's getting about two thousand bucks for it."

"It's worth a hundred times that amount! Nora, do you see this?"

"Why am I not surprised?" I said. Sutherland had lied to me nearly from the first moment he'd blown into town. Now it was clear he'd been stealing from Quintain for years.

"Well, I'm surprised!" Libby said, affronted. "Where is this pawnshop?"

Sam said, "It's belongs to a guy I know in Rome. Good place to unload stuff you don't want seen by the authorities."

"Let's keep looking," Libby said, reaching for the computer mouse. Uncle Sam's hand was already there, but hers stayed on top of his.

I sat back and let the experts take over. But even the confirmation that Sutherland was passing off Madeleine's art collection couldn't keep me from letting my attention roam around Uncle Sam's office. I speculated about the role he played in the Abruzzo crime empire, but Michael hadn't mentioned anything about fencing stolen goods—unless cars came under that heading.

Even though Michael had broken his code of silence and told me a little about his business, I still didn't know him. I had decided to sail into the future with him, but there were still secrets to learn. Or I could turn a blind eye.

My life had started out so simply, I thought. I had been expected to take the path of least resistance—marry a nice doctor, raise a family, maybe get myself elected president of the Junior League before devoting myself to weeding a garden and making sure the next generation of blue bloods did exactly what was expected of them, too. With a little extra effort, I might have gotten a hospital wing named after myself.

Michael, on the other hand, had been born into a different world entirely. Maybe he could be forgiven some of his choices. They came with his birthright. At least now he was trying to make the changes he thought possible.

What had Madeleine said about choices? I couldn't remember just then.

Ironic that Sutherland was the one selling off family valuables in a faraway pawnshops.

"Libby?" I interrupted her intense conversation with Uncle Sam. "Would you mind taking care of this yourself? I just thought of somebody I could ask a few questions."

The two spots of color glowed brighter than ever on my sister's cheekbones, and she barely looked in my direction. "Of course, Nora. Sam and I can handle this."

The two of them bent their heads close to the computer screen as I slipped out.

I hiked a few blocks north toward Society Hill, a quaint Philadelphia neighborhood of old houses that had been beautifully preserved. The cobblestone streets, the brick homes with glossy black shutters and the handsome streetlamps that punctuated each picturesque block added up to a charming part of town that teemed with some of the city's most influential citizens.

I passed a retired senator walking a pair of Labrador retrievers, and he gave me a friendly nod. A block later, two teenage girls—daughters of a former colleague of my late husband—were giggling too intently over a cell phone to notice me.

At last I reached the address of an old friend. Two burly gentlemen stood on the corner beside a large black vehicle containing a police dog. Two more men had taken positions on Marcella's front porch, pretending to look nonchalant. Hard to do with earpieces and little wires going down the backs of their muscled necks. I wasn't surprised to see them. I had prayed I might find someone at the house who could help me now.

I approached them as nonthreateningly as I could manage. "Hello. I wonder if I could see Marcella this morning?"

The two Secret Service agents gave me a brief inspection before one put a finger to his earpiece and turned away to speak. The second came down the stone steps.

When we were eye to eye, he said pleasantly, "Are you expected, miss?"

"No, just dropping in. I'm a friend of Marcella's. My name is Nora Blackbird."

He patted me down while his colleague relayed my name into the house, and a couple of minutes later I was ushered through the front door.

In the entry hall, I paused beside a grandfather clock that tolled as if announcing my arrival.

Marcella Jaffe came down the staircase, slim and elegant in jeans and a deceptively simple pullover sweater, no jewelry but diamond stud earrings. Her long, mahogany brown hair was expertly cut to emphasize her dark eyes and lush mouth. "Nora! What a nice surprise! Just in time for brunch."

I gave her a kiss. "You're so sweet to make me feel welcome when I'm barging in on Sunday morning."

"Nonsense. You never barge."

Marcella—who had graduated with me from Barnard and had been my travel buddy the semester I went to China—was the second wife of Paul Jaffe, the renowned foreign policy wonk who often appeared on Sunday-morning television programs to make in-depth pronouncements about current world affairs. Paul had retired from teaching many years ago, but was frequently called upon by various presidents to help shape White House opinions on foreign policy subjects. Marcella kept his house beautifully and had given him a second family of children—two of whom could be heard banging on a piano and singing in a distant room.

Marcella had other talents, of course. She had written a book about Chinese culture, and was doing research for a second. And Paul needed a savvy, cultured woman to keep his complicated life organized. They made a good team.

Affectionately, Marcella hooked her arm through mine and pulled me toward the back of the house, where I knew the kitchen lay. The house was small, but grand with antiques and good paintings on the walls. A jumble of children's shoes cluttered the floor, though, dispelling any pretense of formality, and I saw finger-painted pictures stuck to the refrigerator with funny magnets. Most of all, books were everywhere—on shelves, on tables, even piled on the floor beside a dog's pillow. Just looking at Marcella's imperfect but cozy home, I realized how far my sister Emma was from this level of parenting. For Marcella, mothering came naturally. I doubted Em's instincts were anywhere close.

Marcella said, "I heard about your aunt. What a tragedy, Nora. Paul says she was a gallant old girl."

"I'm so glad to hear he knew her. Actually, I was hoping I might talk to Paul about Madeleine."

"Oh, I'm so sorry, Nora." Marcella gave me a squeeze. "He's doing *Meet the Press* this morning. He took the train bright and early, and I think he's planning on having lunch after the show with some of those shouty people he enjoys so much. He won't be back until late tonight."

"There was only a fifty-fifty chance he'd be home. But I'd have called ahead if he was the only person I wanted to see." I smiled at my friend. "You look great. Life must be good."

Marcella grinned. "It's great, if you don't mind heaps of dirty laundry and the occasional pizza for dinner. We're just back from a week in the Caribbean. Paul has needed a getaway for months, and I finally insisted. My mom came to stay with the kids, and they had a ball." Marcella paused in the cluttered, fragrant kitchen. "Maybe there's somebody else here who can help you, Nora. But you've already guessed that, haven't you? The security detail outside is hard to ignore."

With a secretive smile, she led me to the doorway of a small sunroom, where a fire crackled in the fireplace and the big windows revealed a backyard garden with leafless maple trees and a swingset. The sunroom was crowded with comfy furniture.

On an overstuffed, flowered sofa, with her slippered feet on a hassock and the pages of the *New York Times* scattered around her, sat the former secretary of state. She wore sweats and a zippered velour jacket—the very kind Libby wore when she wanted to be comfortable. No makeup, hair combed but not styled. Her coiffure was grayer than when she'd served her country, but she looked just as vital as when she'd jetted around the world. She looked up with a smile and took off her reading glasses. The Jaffe family beagle snoozed beside her chair.

Marcella introduced me, saying graciously, "This is one of my dearest friends, Nora Blackbird."

"I remember you," she said. "We met at the Arab-American dinner Thursday evening."

"Yes, we did, but I'm amazed you remember me."

She didn't get up when we shook hands, but remained relaxed on the sofa. "We talked about your aunt, Madeleine Blackbird. Did I give you my condolences? Sometimes I get rattled in receiving lines. There's always so much going on. I try to mind my manners, but it's a challenge."

"Yes, you did. Thank you."

Marcella gave me a gentle push toward a green-striped armchair. "Sit down, Nora. Maybe she'll tell you about the project she's working on with Paul. A paper for the UN. Would either of you ladies care for coffee?"

"A refill for me, please." The illustrious houseguest handed her cup to Marcella.

"No, thank you," I said. I wasn't sure I could hold a cup and still talk sensibly to a woman I admired so greatly.

Marcella left us alone, and I found myself with a woman who had been one of the most powerful diplomats in the world.

Recognizing that the conversational ball was in my court, I said, "Actually, I read somewhere that you were working with Paul these days. Since you were in town for the dinner two nights ago, I was hoping I might find you here."

She smiled. "Is this an ambush?"

"Maybe a little one. After the dinner, you said nice things about my aunt."

She leaned back into the cushions of the sofa, but her gaze remained keen on me. I could see why presidents of rogue nations paid attention when she came to call. She had a manner that was both steely and motherly. "I meant what I said, you know. About someone writing a book about Madeleine. But I realized afterward that such a book might compromise national security. Even now, what Madeleine pulled off might not make everybody happy."

"You'll have to excuse my ignorance," I said. "You see, Madeleine didn't talk about her travels. We're left piecing together her life."

"What kind of pieces did she leave behind?"

"Not much," I admitted. "She collected art and objects from all over the world, so we can see where she went. But as far as I know, she didn't leave any letters or diaries."

"That's a shame. But probably wise. In my career, I had to leave a paper trail big enough to fill a library. Madeleine's work was different, though. What she accomplished was behind the scenes, sometimes above the law."

Surprised, I said, "Above the law?"

"I can't confirm or deny," she said with a wry smile. "Let me assure you that the Madcap Maddy name was a smokescreen. Madeleine accomplished a lot. But not always with the approval of governments or authorities."

"I know she helped a ballerina defect from the Soviet Union."

"Yes, I remember that. Did you know about the time she spent time in Kenya? She found a village where the women had to walk for miles to carry water for drinking and bathing. Along the route, they risked injury from wild animals, but also sexual assault and worse. So Madeleine raised the money and had a well dug right in the center of the village. That's the sort of thing that changes lives in a big way. But she had to fight the local government, bullying officials—the works."

"That doesn't sound like a matter of national security though."

"Not that, no. There were other incidents earlier—long before I accepted my job." She rested her head on the sofa, then looked up at the ceiling and sighed. "Things were so much easier during the Cold War. We knew our enemies, and we built walls to keep them contained. But . . . Madeleine was the kind of woman who traveled in sophisticated social circles. Her calling card got her into places my counterpart could never have gone. Parties with powerful people, country weekends with world leaders who would never have agreed to official meetings with our government. She used her social position to get things done. The Berlin Wall didn't fall in a day, you know. It took a lot of people like Madeleine chipping away at it for years."

"Pippi," I said, half to myself.

"What's that?"

"Aunt Madeleine helped a woman out of Russia—the daughter of a scientist who'd come here to the States."

"Oh, yes, I remember reading something about that when I was first briefed at State." She made a steeple with her fingers. "As I recall, Madeleine went to a swanky party in St. Petersburg—Leningrad then—and sneaked the girl out while the vodka was passed around. While sailing the Gulf of Finland they were detected by Soviet submarines and barely reached Stockholm alive. At least, that's what dispatches said. It would make a great movie. Think Meryl Streep would want to play Madeleine?"

I smiled at the twinkle in her eyes. "You make my aunt sound captivating."

"She was definitely captivating. Pippi was one of many people Madeleine helped."

"But now Madeleine is dead," I said, sobering. "And we'd like to understand why."

"I thought she was trapped in an elevator and died."

I couldn't contain my surprise. "How did you know that? The police haven't announced—"

She winked. "Even an old broad like me is kept in the loop. I hear a lot of things I'm probably not supposed to."

I had just been thinking she exuded the vitality of a much younger woman. She was a broad, all right—in the best sense of the term. But old? Hardly. Perhaps it was her engagement with important international matters that kept her going.

Suddenly I was swamped by the thought that Madeleine was going to miss equally exciting golden years.

My companion's self-deprecating smile faded. "You're thinking Madeleine was murdered, aren't you?"

I took a deep breath to steady my emotions. "There's a chance she could have been accidentally trapped in the elevator, but we don't think so. You see, someone tried to cover up her death. To make us believe she was still alive."

"The police are investigating?"

"Yes." Briefly, I told her about the discussion I'd had with the state police who'd come to my kitchen. "They're not publicly divulging information yet."

She nodded pensively. "It's probably wise to keep things hushed up for a while."

Deciding to take a chance, I said, "Madeleine may have been taken advantage of by someone she trusted. A lawyer. And maybe he killed her. But—well, do you think there might be someone else from her past—her past work in foreign countries, that is—who might have wished her dead?"

"Her most controversial work was a long time ago, Nora. Let me think." The secretary pursed her mouth and looked into the distance for a long moment. "I'll have to mull over what people she might have come in contact with. Do you know of anyone from the diplomatic corps? Someone who continued to stay in contact with her?"

"I'm ashamed to admit how clueless I am about Madeleine's life. For certain, I only know about Vincente van Vincent. He retired to an estate adjacent to Madeleine's home."

"Vinnie? Didn't he have an affair with her, way back when?"

"His wife denies it."

"Why would he choose to live adjacent to Madeleine's home if there wasn't something else going on? Anyway, he's probably no help. He's dead by now, surely."

"No, but he lives in a nursing home. Alzheimer's."

She shook her head in sympathy. "How was his health at the time Madeleine died?"

"I'll have to find out."

"I'll see what I can learn, too."

I sat forward in my chair. "There's another thing I can't figure out, and it seems important. Aunt Madeleine kept a ledger—a book that listed a series of transactions. It looks as if she was taking money from people. Increments of ten thousand dollars, usually. Sometimes more, sometimes a little less. And she wanted the ledger to be destroyed after her death. Can you guess why she accepted money?"

"Transactions?" The secretary frowned and lightly tapped her fingertips against her upper lip as she considered the question. "It could be that she was accepting monetary help from friends to do her work. Moving people around the world—especially people whose countries want them back—can be an expensive proposition. Keeping them safe, keeping them out of sight—that's not easy. It means using extraordinary modes of travel, secure hotels, sometimes private homes, too, of course, but keeping people quiet also comes at a price. In some countries, she'd have spent a lot of money in—well, bribes. That can get cost-prohibitive very fast."

I could barely hide my relief at hearing Madeleine hadn't been doing something sordid. I remembered how it felt to be slapped by Mrs. Banks. If her husband had given money to Madeleine without her approval, she could still be harboring resentment. But I said, "Madeleine was using her husband's yacht some of the time."

"Well, that was probably only an occasional transportation choice. I remember the case of a gymnast from Eastern Europe. When I saw the money our government spent to help her defect, I was appalled. We can't ask the taxpayers to foot that kind of bill on a regular basis. And Madeleine would have gone broke financing it herself. She probably rightly assumed it was easier for private citizens to kick in—and more expedient." With a slight frown, she tugged her earlobe as if to jog her memory. "Wasn't her husband murdered? The one with the yacht?"

"No, he died by drowning. In a hot tub somewhere."

"I don't think that was an accident, Nora."

I must have stared.

She smiled grimly. "Don't be surprised. Considering the work they did, he was probably considered an enemy of many corrupt governments. But he wasn't a professional and probably took few precautions for his own safety. I'm pretty sure his death was mentioned in cables."

"What about Madeleine? Might she have been murdered by the same people?"

"No, if she had been, I'd have heard about it. Our enemies would have crowed about her death, but I don't remember hearing anything about that. I can check to be sure." She gave me a kind smile. "Do you have a card? A way I can reach you?"

I reached for my bag, sensing my interview was reaching its final moments. "You're very generous to offer. Thank you. I wonder if I might ask for one more bit of advice?"

"Fire away."

As succinctly as I could, I told the secretary about Zareen, the young Syrian woman I'd met on the street corner after the Arab-American dinner. The plight of her sister, stuck in Syria when her mother needed her, had taken root in my heart. I wished I could have helped her when I met her, but at the time I hadn't been able to think of a way to do so. I explained the problem and held my breath.

Madame Secretary shook her head. "I'm sorry. We could try diplomatic channels, but that's going to take time. Maybe years." Then, "I wonder if you should use your aunt Madeleine as a role model, Nora."

"What do you mean?"

"Madeleine would have found an unconventional way of helping that family."

"But Madeleine had connections and resources—"

"You're a Blackbird. You have connections and resources, too."

"But . . ."

"Be creative. Take a risk, if you must. Maybe Madeleine didn't always play by the rules, but she got results." She reached over and patted my knee. "Think about it. I will, too. We'll talk in a few days."

Our meeting was over. I stood and shook her hand. At that moment, Marcella arrived with the secretary's coffee cup. I knew she'd been half listening from the next room and had taken her cue from the tones of our voices.

I thanked Marcella for her hospitality, then invented an excuse to slip away. Marcella knew I was fibbing, but she played along. We both understood the unspoken social rules when it came to powerful people who were forced to cope with many demands on their time. I gave my friend a grateful hug and we promised to see each other soon.

At the door, Marcella said, "I'm going to the Lupus Foundation fund-raiser in two weeks. Will you be there?"

"Of course. I'll look for you."

"I'm going stag. Let's sit together."

"It's a date."

Within a minute, I was out on the street waving good-bye to the Secret Service. Walking the cobblestones, I contemplated the advice I'd been given. Think unconventionally. Use my connections.

Aunt Madeleine didn't always play by the rules.

I knew somebody else like that.

CHAPTER TWENTY-ONE

M ichael's cell phone line was busy.

"Libby," I said when we reunited in the minivan, "can you reach Syria by using PitterPat?"

"I haven't tried yet. Why?"

I passed her the card from Zareen Aboudi. "Think there's a way to track down this woman?"

"Let's give it a whirl." She began thumbing the keyboard on her cell phone.

"Meanwhile, I can tell you absolutely that it wasn't just our dear cousin Sutherland who stripped most of the good stuff out of Quintain and sold it on the black market. You'll never guess who else we saw on many store videos!"

"Who?"

"Simon Groatley! He was stealing from Aunt Madeleine!"

"Why am I not surprised?" I muttered.

"You should let That Man of Yours break his legs. Of course, Sutherland has been financing his jet-setting lifestyle the same way, but Groatley was her lawyer! He was supposed to protect her interests! But he was dumping Aunt Madeleine's magnificent collection at bargain-basement prices. The Fabergé egg disappeared into China twelve years ago—probably for less money than it takes to take a date out for dinner and a movie. Well, maybe a movie premiere, but the price was far, far below market value."

I noticed my sister's hair had become slightly disheveled. And if I wasn't mistaken, her T-shirt was now inside out. But she looked wonderfully refreshed and happy.

"Did you get patriotic with the Reverend Uncle Sam?" I said. "Should I be asking if you plan on seeing him again?"

"I think we achieved everything in one visit," she said cheerfully. "A little foreplay is sometimes just enough to assuage hormonal longings, right? There!" She hit a button on her cell phone and used the rearview mirror to tame her hair into submission. "Let's let my followers see what they can do for us in Syria. What's next?"

"I think we should pay Sutherland a call, don't you?"

Libby tossed her phone into her handbag and drove us over to the harbor. Even before she pulled into a parking space, I saw that Sutherland's yacht had disappeared. Assuming he must have sailed off as soon as he escaped Blackbird Farm in the middle of the night, I ran down to the marina manager to ask. I wanted to kick myself for preventing Michael from inflicting some real damage on my rat fink of a cousin.

The marina manager reported that the yacht's owner had claimed the boat and taken it on the morning tide. As for Sutherland, he had no idea where my cousin had gone.

I climbed back into the minivan and told Libby that Sutherland was on the lam. "Maybe we should figure out how to have an international arrest warrant issued."

Libby was intent on her cell phone again. "Check with That Man of Yours. I'll bet he knows. Look, I've got twelve Syrian followers already!"

"In ten minutes?"

"Amazing, isn't it? I'm spreading the Libby brand internationally now!"

"The Libby brand?"

"Yes, I'm a freedom fighter in the war against sensual repression. That's totally me, right? With nice pedicures. I am practically a recipe for humanitarian peacekeeping. I could be the Big Bang of peace in the Mid East regions. Anyway"—she tapped the screen on her phone—"at this rate, we should be able to contact your Aboudi girl in no time. What do you want to tell her?"

"I'll have to check with Michael first. But I have a plan."

"I love international intrigue!" Libby cried. "Now what?"

I checked my watch. "I have just enough time to go home and change clothes. The carriage-driving show starts tomorrow. The van Vincent Classic. But the opening ceremonies are this afternoon. Want to come?"

"Will there be handsome men in attractive horsey clothes? Of course."

We stopped at Libby's house first so she could gather up something to wear, then we headed to Blackbird Farm. Ralphie stood on my back porch, his snout pointed at the door. He tried to muscle past me to look for more cheesecake when I got the door open.

"Never again," I said. "If you come into my house, I'm sending you to the butcher. That's my line in the sand."

Ralphie grunted his disappointment.

By the look of things, Michael had gone to mass with his parole officer. They had come home and were sitting in the kitchen with Bruno, companionably lunching on take-out sandwiches from Gas N Grub and talking football. Libby and I blew through and headed upstairs.

For fox hunt breakfasts, polo matches and horse shows, I liked breaking with wardrobe tradition. No tweed. No flat-heeled boots. I pulled out a metallic Thierry Mugler jacket with a cinched waist, futuristic shoulder pads and lapels cut down to show a purple demi bra underneath. A black mini, lace-covered thigh-high boots—I prayed for no rain—and a pair of gloves to match the bra. I brushed my hair loose and thrust a clip through one side to keep it pinned back behind my ear.

Libby took one look when I came out of the closet and cried, "I'm a *matron* compared to you! Help!"

We peeled off her sweater and slacks and stuffed her into a too-small Guy Laroche dress from Grandmama's collection. The hunter green color worked for the season, and the square bodice gave her an eye-popping cleavage, which clinched the outfit as far as Libby was concerned. The seams strained to contain her. But they held.

Libby critically admired herself in the mirror, rumpled her hair and ran her hands down her ample hips. With her own jacket thrown around her shoulders and a pair of my Fendi platform pumps with a provocative peep toe, she nodded and said, "Thank heaven I brought my Spanx."

We went downstairs and silenced the crew at the kitchen table by simply walking in. Kuzik choked so hard on his sandwich that Bruno had to pound him on the back.

I leaned down and kissed Michael good-bye. "See you later."

"Ugh," was the only word he could manage.

In two minutes, we were back in the minivan and headed for the van Vincent estate. The sun burst through the clouds just as we reached the line of traffic backed up to enter the grounds where the van Vincent Classic was to take place. But my sister and I had spent the drive discussing funeral possibilities.

"I like the idea of a memorial ceremony for Madeleine," Libby said after we listed the choices. "Do you have a plan?"

"I'm thinking after the holidays," I said. "Something tasteful. But not boring. With cocktails afterward."

"Who presides? A minister?"

"No. There's a poet I know—Jeff Fabian. Maybe he'd provide the right tone? And the right language?"

"And he's so attractive," Libby said, clearly planning ahead. "Yes, perfect. I wonder if Sutherland will show up."

"Only if the will is settled by then, I'm sure."

I handed my invitation to the parking attendant and paid ten dollars for Libby to leave her minivan in a freshly mowed field. Otherwise, there was no formal check-in point for the van Vincent Classic. With other arriving guests, we hiked up the same road I'd traveled on foot the night I stole Madeleine's ledger out of Quintain. On the road, a young man in a golf cart slowed down to ask if we'd like a lift. Libby, already panting with the pain of wearing high-heeled shoes, jumped onto the backseat. I climbed in beside the driver, and we toodled up the road, past the van Vincent house to the tents.

I couldn't help noticing how simple a golf cart looked to drive. There was no complicated gearshift to contend with. Just one pedal that said, "Go," and a second pedal that said, "Stop."

"Why can't cars be as easy to drive?" I asked our young chauffeur.

"Cars *are* easy to drive," he said, surprised.

I decided not to disagree with him, but I wondered if driving a golf cart required a license.

All the preparations for the show were complete. Shirley had obviously managed to get the electricians working to her satisfaction, because we heard a steady squawk from the loudspeakers. The whole property looked festive, and Vincente van Vincent's photograph— one taken during his younger days, and with Shirley smiling proudly at his side—appeared on all the posters. On the upper lawn, beautifully dressed guests mingled among the spit-polished carriages on display under the crisp sunlight that streamed through the leafless branches of tall trees. An array of sparkling trophies sat on tables that fluttered with bunting.

No Way to Kill a Lady

A teenage girl drove past us—her pretty white pony pulling a two-wheeled gig at a dainty trot through the admiring crowd. A few people burst into applause. The teenager beamed with pleasure.

A few groomsmen had brought horses out to be admired by the guests. The shining coats of the animals were as smooth as those of otters. Their tails were braided and combed to perfection. We could see that the rest of the horses had been stabled in a series of long, temporary enclosures along the fences of a lower pasture— closer to where I'd found the bones. Down among the trees I could see the flutter of yellow police tape, stretched around to prevent everyone from trampling the crime scene.

We heard passersby remark upon the tape.

"I heard they found the body of a homeless man," one elderly lady clucked. "That's what Shirley told me. Poor fellow must have frozen to death."

"Maybe it's one of Shirley's grooms," responded her equally ancient companion in a less charitable tone. "No matter how cold it gets, she'd kick out anyone who didn't pamper her darlings to perfection."

Also below the lawn, a wide field had been mowed and mani-cured for the week's competition. We could see a coach-and-four taking a test drive around the course. The team of matched chest-nut horses high-stepped precisely as the driver, wearing traditional livery, sat apparently motionless beside his identically dressed navi-gator on the box of the handsome replica coach. They might have been delivering Jane Austen characters to a country ball or a prince and princess away from their wedding at a cathedral.

The marathon course began on the field, but orange cones had been set up to indicate the long competition course, which would run beyond our vista, no doubt through the gamut of challenging water obstacles, steep inclines and sharp turns. I knew spectators would gather at various exciting spots along the route to catch the action. Already we could see small groups of competitors setting off to walk the course on foot to check the hazards up close.

The first person I recognized in the crowd was Simon Groatley. Just seeing him gave me the sensation of a punch to the stomach. He wore a ridiculous tweed riding jacket that had probably never seen a hunting field. On his arm walked a pretty middle-aged woman I didn't know—his latest girlfriend, I supposed. When I caught his eye, he flushed and turned away. I was glad to see he was embarrassed. But I knew how quickly his rage could flare up. He dragged his companion rapidly in the opposite direction, and I felt sorry for her.

Outside the refreshment tent, we bumped into Emma. She stood beside a trash barrel, wolfing down a drippy sandwich and mopping her chin with a paper napkin. She wore her riding breeches pulled low, topped by a man's polo shirt that covered her pregnant belly, but only just. If anything, she looked rounder than two days ago.

She took one look at Libby in her tight green dress and said, "My God, you look like a busted can of biscuits."

"Up yours," Libby said, out of breath. "Are you all right?"

"I've been better."

Her eyes were hollow, and I didn't like her pallor.

I gave Emma a hug to bolster her spirits. "It's good to see you. Where's Hart?"

Emma swallowed her mouthful of sandwich and wiped her lips. For a second, I thought her food was going to come right back up, but she controlled herself. "He dropped me off an hour ago." She tried to sound tough. "He went home to his soon-to-be wife. Tomorrow's her birthday, I hear. They're very big on birthdays. A little adultery is fine, but you don't dare miss a birthday party with the whole family."

I wanted to hold her close. "Oh, Em."

Libby was giving Emma a calculating examination. "Did you sleep with him?"

"Of course I slept with him," Emma snapped. She pushed away

from me. "Why spend time with Hart if not for the sex? We did it three times, once on the floor. You want more details than that?"

"Emma," I said.

Libby gave me a stern look and said, "I'll go get us some drinks." And she left me alone with our little sister to talk.

Emma was full of turmoil, I could see. Her night with Hart hadn't eased her conflict in the slightest. She was more wrought up than ever. She threw her napkin into the trash barrel and turned on me, fierce and angry. "Okay, it's do or die time, Nora. Do you want this baby? You and Mick?"

Of course I did. So did Michael. I wanted to shriek *yes, yes, yes!* A child of Emma's was an answer to my prayers, a solution for Michael and me, a miracle I wanted more than anything.

But I had forced myself to think calmly over the last twenty-four hours. Michael and I had reviewed the many arguments, wrestled with our consciences. And come to a hard conclusion.

The whirl of people around us turned into a miasma of color and noise, but I said quietly, "We want what's best for the baby. And for you, Em."

"What the hell does that mean?"

I summoned the hardest words I'd ever spoken. "It means we believe it would be hard for you to come to the farm and see us with your child and wonder what might have been."

Emma turned away toward the horses and fell silent.

She didn't want me to see her expression, because she couldn't make her face obey any longer. I fought down the same kind of agony that undoubtedly welled up in her, too. We'd had hard conversations before, Emma and I. Back when her husband, Jake, was killed. When Todd was shot. But neither of those events compared to the terrible tearing sensation in my chest as I reached to touch her shoulder.

If Libby had wanted me to make the hard decision, now was the time to do it.

I gathered my breath and my courage. "I know what you've already lost, Em. And this baby must remind you of the life you could have had if Jake hadn't died. I don't want you to go through the pain again. And I don't want to lose you, either. Because that's what would happen, I think. If Michael and I adopted your baby, you'd start to avoid us. You'd stay away and pretty soon you'd be gone from our lives altogether. I couldn't bear to trade you—not even for a child to raise."

In a ghastly voice, she said, "I have to go help Shirley harness her team for the parade."

"Okay," I said, my heart cracking for her. For all of us.

Emma turned away. But she stopped and without looking at me blurted out, "Hart wants the kid."

"He does? For real? That's—that's good, isn't it?" My heart lifted. But Emma was silent. I said, "It's best for the baby, right? Hart may have his faults, but he'll be a good parent. And what about you?"

She shook her head. "He doesn't want me. He says he and his wife will take the kid, raise it. He says she'll be a good mother. That she comes from a big, stupid family—lots of birthday parties, you know? She's actually happy about the situation because it means she doesn't have to get fat." She shot me a cold smile, her eyes glassy with tears. "But I wanted you and Mick to have first dibs."

I reached for her hand. She let me take it, let me squeeze it.

I said, "Oh, Em. Surely if Hart wants your child, it's like having a part of you, too."

She laughed, but it was a bitter sound. "Thanks for that," she said. "I'll take what I can get."

She looked away again and blew a long, unsteady sigh. "I can't wait for this to be over. As soon as I push Zygote out, I'm gonna pour myself a long drink. Maybe stay drunk until he hits kindergarten."

We'd cross that bridge when it came, I knew. For now, I said, "Will Hart and Penny let you see him? Or—?"

"Oh, I imagine I'll see plenty of him when I'm sneaking up the stairs to Hart's bed when his wife's out of town. That's what Hart has in mind, anyway."

"Em, I'm so sorry."

She pulled her hand away. "Don't be. I get what I want, too, right? A good home for the kid, and my freedom. Let the good times keep rolling. That's all I want out of this deal."

I didn't argue with her just then, but I knew she was wrong.

She said, "I think I'll go find one of Shirley's grooms and see if he wants a little nooky with a pregnant lady. But first there's just one favor I'd like from you."

I could barely speak above a whisper. "Anything."

"Ask Mick if he'd beat the shit out of Hart? Maybe the night before his stupid wedding. No permanent damage. Just mess up his face for me, you know?"

"I'm sure he'd be happy to take care of that."

"Thanks."

Emma steeled herself and walked away toward the stable area. From the back, she didn't look pregnant at all.

Libby returned in a while, with two cups of something steamy. She said, "My God, what's wrong?"

I wanted to cry. Maybe I already was. I wanted to run after Emma and take it all back. I wanted to tell her we could fix everything. I wanted so much for my little sister just then.

"I'm okay," I said. "It's Em. Hart and his fiancée want to raise Emma's baby."

Libby said a disgusting word.

"No, it's probably for the best." I made a monumental effort to pull myself together. "Hart may not be perfect, but he knows about family. I just—I hate seeing Em so broken."

"She'll pull out of this," Libby said swiftly. "Nora, some people aren't cut out to be parents, and Emma's one. We both know that, and there's nothing wrong with it. She has her own strengths.

Superhuman, in fact. But—but Hart is being a perfect bastard. Can't he see what she keeps hidden? Why couldn't she show him a little of what's inside, just once? We're such fools about men sometimes. We all are. Here. Drink this. It's a toddy. There's brandy in it."

With unsteady hands, I accepted the cup—with a slice of lemon on the rim and a cinnamon stick, too. I took a sip and then another. I felt the heat of the liquor burn through the lump in my throat. I wanted to think the best of Hart, but hearing Libby dump on him felt liberating. Why couldn't he see Emma's love for him? Was he such an idiot? Or was the pull of marrying into Penny's powerful family more important to him than the truth that surely lurked in his heart?

"Come on," I said, as a new emotion grew inside me like a match struck to tinder. "While I'm angry, I need to talk to Shirley van Vincent."

"Why?"

"She has some explaining to do."

Libby and I walked the length of the exhibits. With every step I felt stronger. I had made the hard choice. And survived. We walked past antique carriages and pony carts, a painted gypsy cart and even an oxcart with two long-horned oxen placidly swishing their tails. Libby put her arm through mine to steady me. Beside an enormous replica of a Wells Fargo stagecoach, a man in jeans and a cowboy hat passed out plastic ten-gallon hats to the children. Beside him, a gentleman in a top hat and tails distributed flyers for his hearse—a six-wheeled vehicle with black feather plumes and a satin-lined interior visible through glass windows. A white carriage at the end of the line contained a young couple in wedding clothes, toasting passersby with champagne glasses.

Farther along, we came upon the various vendors—a farrier with his smoking forge, an Amish harness-maker and his counterpart from Belgium, suppliers of horse feed and diet supplements. Plastic buckets and travel trailers and representatives from companies that shipped horses by air to Europe and back. Everything that experienced horsemen needed and more.

Eventually, I found I could make the effort to be pleasant to the people we encountered along the way. With Libby sticking supportively beside me, I saw many acquaintances from various circles of the horse society and snapped a few pictures with my phone camera. The slim young members of a nearby dressage school were roaming around together—still dressed in their riding clothes and cheerfully slugging drinks. Other guests had come ready to see and be seen. The women wore their autumn fashions with large hats and a few cleverly horsey handbags. I saw many men wearing hunting jackets with patches on the arms and shoulders.

"Nora," a man called to me. I recognized Jamison Beech, his camera around his neck. He wore a suit today with a narrow tie—like me, making the opposite fashion statement than what was expected. With him was a younger man I knew as a neighbor who raised gundogs on a small farm near my property. Smiling, Jamison pulled him over to me. "Meet my nephew."

I gave Jamison a kiss and shook his nephew's hand. I introduced Libby, and they all traded pleasantries. Libby gushed about Jamison's newspaper fashion collage, and he did the gallant thing by taking her picture. Libby beamed with pleasure.

"Say," the nephew said to me, "do you ever let hunters on your farm? My friends and I have been hunting pheasants on Quintain for years, but the birds have flown. We're looking for new hunting grounds."

"Just keep your guns pointed away from the house," I told him. "I don't mind a bit. I'm surprised, though. I'd have thought there would be lots of pheasants on Quintain."

"Yes, but our spaniel club has been hunting there for—oh, twenty years or more. It's time we gave the birds a chance to flourish again."

"Twenty years," I said.

"Yes. I hope you don't mind. I was sorry to hear about Madeleine's death."

Jamison said, "She was a grand old girl." He waxed poetic about Aunt Madeleine for a while, but my mind had wandered.

Finally, I said to the nephew, "Madeleine gave you permission to hunt on Quintain?"

"No, actually, older members say the club used to hunt right here, on the van Vincent farm." He gestured to indicate the busy estate around us. "But Shirley and Vincente were worried about stray shots hitting their Dalmatians or their horses. It was Shirley who told the club president we should hunt on Quintain. She said Madeleine wouldn't mind, so the club went ahead. All the neglected underbrush made good cover for birds. Ideal for bird-dog training."

"I see. Well, you're welcome on Blackbird Farm this year."

"Thanks. We'll stay on the other side of the hill from the house."

Jamison and his nephew waved jauntily and strolled off to enjoy the festivities.

But I found myself brought up short by a thought. Had Shirley really been concerned that hunters might shoot her dogs? Or had she been preventing hunters from discovering the body on her property? Which meant she'd known about it from the beginning.

"Do you have pheasants?" Libby asked, breaking through my racing thoughts. "Maybe we should shoot a couple for Thanksgiving. I could send the twins. They're always looking for something they're allowed to kill. And for Christmas, too. Somehow I get the feeling we're not going to be eating ham for the holidays."

"Uh-huh," I said, hardly paying attention.

We walked on through the displays, but I didn't really see any of the details. I was thinking about Shirley and what she knew. At last came the horses, and that's where the crowd got thick. The pageantry included fearsomely large Clydesdales flashing their white tasseled hooves and elegant Friesians peeking out from behind their thick black forelocks at lanky Standardbreds.

Beside me, Libby suddenly went on alert, exactly like a spaniel on the scent of a fat pheasant. "Nora! Isn't that Sheriff Foley?"

"Deputy," I said, following the direction of her quivering point. "Deputy Foley."

"He deserves a promotion in my book," Libby said. "I think I'll go talk to him. Do you mind? I'll find out if there's any news on Aunt Madeleine's murder."

"Ask him if he knows who stole the ledger. That ought to be a good conversation starter. I think he stole it for Simon Groatley."

"Count on me to twist the truth out of him." Libby hitched up her bosom and set off toward her unsuspecting prey.

As Libby left me to my thoughts, a lot of facts began to fall into place like cards dealt from a stacked deck. Abruptly, I cut up the hillside toward the van Vincent barn, where Emma had gone to help harness Shirley's team. If Shirley was there, too—Shirley who must have guessed by now what I was thinking—Emma could be in danger. I tried to hurry, but my high-heeled shoes hobbled me.

That was when I saw the golf cart parked beside one of the portable toilets. The driver had left the vehicle, so I jumped behind the wheel. I jammed my foot down on the "Go" pedal, and the little cart leaped forward. It roared up the hillside, bumping over holes, wheels spinning.

I steered it around a tree, but ran right over a bush. I forgot about the "Stop" pedal and ended up ramming the cart into a fence. The impact tossed me onto the ground, and I landed on my knees. Scrambling up, I headed for the stable where Emma had gone.

The barn was a long, low building designed by an architect who wanted to make an artistic statement while providing shelter for valuable horses. The building was a cross between an American prairie-style cabin and a Tudor folly. Double doors opened at either end of it.

As I reached the top of the slope, one of the groomsmen bolted out of the side doors and rushed past me, knocking over a rake that had been propping the door open.

I heard Emma's voice rise sharply. "Don't be crazy, Shirley. We were just talking! We weren't doing any harm to your horses."

Automatically, I bent to pick up the rake. I heard an awful whip crack and Emma let out a curse.

"I won't have that kind of behavior in my barn," Shirley snapped.

As I came through the door, I saw Emma standing on the straw-strewn floor beside a huge black horse that was tied by his halter to a ring in the stable wall. She had one hand on the animal's neck to calm him, but as Shirley raised her whip again, the horse snorted and threw his weight against the ring. His eyes rolled white with fear. Then Shirley brought the stout driving whip down hard across Emma's shoulders and Emma went down.

"You Blackbird girls are all alike," Shirley said. "Always stealing men you have no business with."

"Take it easy, you nutty old bitch. What are you talking about?"

Shirley raised the whip again, and Emma quickly rolled under the horse—to escape the whip or to avoid the animal's hooves, I couldn't see. The horse plunged sideways, though, and Emma tried to scramble crablike out from under him, but her belly made her clumsy.

The horse's hooves looked both gigantic and lethal. And he was frightened—half a ton of deadly animal that could break bones or crush a baby with one kick. Emma gave a yell.

Beside the horse, Shirley van Vincent struck at Emma over and over with the whip's heavy handle. My sister threw up her hands to protect herself. The horse snorted and danced around Emma. Any second he was going to hurt her, maybe kill her.

"Shirley," I said.

She turned, and I clobbered her with the rake.

It was probably an unkind thing to do to an elderly woman.

But just then all I could see was my little sister in peril. As I hit Shirley, she fell back and glanced off the side wall. The black horse swerved away from her, making a deep, terrified squeal in his throat.

With Aunt Madeleine in my heart, I whomped Shirley again and knocked her flat onto the straw.

"You killed her," I said, hardly able to believe my own words as I stood over Shirley with the rake in my hands. "It was you! You thought Madeleine was having an affair with your husband, so you trapped her in the elevator and killed her."

"She deserved it." Shirley glared up at me.

"And Pippi," I cried. "You killed Pippi, too?"

"She was going to tell," Shirley said stubbornly. "She saw me turn off the electricity, and she was running for the police."

"So you chased her," I said. "You chased her and killed her! And left her body in the woods?"

"I gave her a decent burial."

"Hardly."

I thought I'd hit her hard enough, but Shirley was tough. She launched herself at me with the whip raised, but I met her halfway. I had to drop the rake to seize her wrist. We grappled. I had a sense of Emma crawling free, but I wasn't sure. The horse swung his hindquarters at us, and I barely avoided a kick. Shirley thrust at the horse, trying to push him toward me, but I had the snapping end of the whip in my hand, and I used my leverage to yank her forward. She collided with the animal, and he knocked her down. This time she stayed there.

I'm not sure how long it took for me to regain my wits, but eventually Emma pried the whip out of my hands and pushed me to sit on a bale of hay. Libby showed up, dragging Deputy Foley. Emma sat with me, our arms tight around each other. There was a lot of shouting, including some from Shirley, who was more angry than hurt.

In a while, only slightly hampered by Libby's interference, Foley put handcuffs on Shirley.

Emma had one hand on her belly, as if holding her baby steady after a trauma, comforting and suddenly motherly.

"You okay?" I asked, fearing something was wrong. "Are you hurt?"

"We're okay. Wow," she said with wonder in her voice. "You were like an avenging angel, Sis. Aunt Madeleine would be proud of you."

CHAPTER TWENTY-TWO

At Thanksgiving, Emma burned the cranberry sauce, and she ended up popping a can-shaped slab of cranberry-flavored goo onto one of Aunt Madeleine's Meissen serving dishes and plunking it onto the table. "There." She stood back to admire her handiwork. "I like the canned stuff better anyway."

Above us on the fireplace mantel hung the portrait of Aunt Madeleine. It hadn't been restored yet, but I had wanted the painting to be with us for the holiday. I thought Madeleine's smile looked a little less secretive these days. Or maybe I simply understood her better now. I gave her a wink.

Libby fluttered into the dining room wearing a ruffled apron with the words EAT DESSERT FIRST embroidered on the front. "Didn't we have Thanksgiving dinner at Quintain one year? With a Lady Baltimore cake at the end?"

I got busy putting candles into Grandmama's last remaining set of silver candelabra. "I can't imagine Aunt Madeleine actually cooking anything. Did Pippi bake the cake?"

"Probably." Libby began laying silverware at each place setting.

"Pippi did all the hard work while Madeleine went to parties and had affairs and got all the glory."

Emma sat heavily on one of the chairs at the big table and rubbed her back as if it ached. She was due to deliver her baby in just a few more weeks and had finally started to slow down. "I don't know. In the end, Pippi died fast, while Madeleine lingered a long time in that elevator. I might have picked Pippi's final moment."

"Maybe we could save this discussion until after dinner," I suggested. I pointed at Libby's daughter, Lucy, who was carefully folding napkins into fans. "When there aren't so many big ears around."

"My children have heard everything," Libby said. "Let me warn you now, Nora. There are going to be lots of uncomfortable questions during dinner. Like why you clobbered Shirley van Vincent. And how come their cousin Sutherland has his picture on CNN. And they're dying to know if we're all going to be millionaires."

We hadn't received anything yet, except that my sisters and I were each wearing one of Madeleine's beautiful diamond rings. After several heated discussions, Libby and Emma had decided to sell theirs. Libby wanted to invest in gym sessions for her baby son, and Emma—although she'd agreed to have her coming medical expenses paid by Hart Jones and his soon-to-be wife—wanted to sock away some money for future rainy days.

I wasn't sure I wanted to part with a final keepsake from Aunt Madeleine. Of course, I'd packed up some of the dishes and photographs and brought them to Blackbird Farm to remember her by. In one of her desk drawers, I had been delighted to find her set of Russian nesting dolls. For our Thanksgiving table, I had managed to incorporate them into a centerpiece that brought back memories. I found myself smiling at them.

But I said, "I doubt we'll be millionaires. Yesterday I met with the partners at Simon Groatley's law firm. Although he embezzled most of her investments over the last twenty years, he made it appear to his partners as if he was acting under Madeleine's orders.

It'll take a while to sort that out. But there's very little cash left. We'll have to sue the firm, I suppose, but just thinking about that makes me weary. And there's not much left but Quintain itself."

"That's all we need in this family," Emma groaned. "Another old house to keep standing."

I sighed at the seemingly insurmountable trouble of maintaining Quintain. "The only people who might have been interested in buying the old place were the van Vincents. But with Vincente so ill and Shirley going to stand trial for Madeleine's murder—once they figure out the statute of limitations, that is—we don't have many other buyers lining up."

"What about the dog club?" Libby suggested. "All those fellows who train spaniels. Wouldn't they like to own a piece of property like Quintain?"

"I'm sure they'd like the land," Emma said. "But who'd want that horrible ruin of a house?"

"Who indeed?" I said, unable to hide my dismay.

Libby gave me a pat as she brushed past me to continue setting the table.

"Why did Simon Groatley want Aunt Madeleine's ledger?" Emma idly picked up a soup spoon and looked at her upside-down reflection in it. "I must have missed that detail."

"Groatley thought the book had something to do with Madeleine's investments. Since he was stealing those, he didn't want any evidence around that might incriminate him."

"How did he know you had it, Nora?"

"At the hospital gala, he asked Shirley if she'd seen anyone try to break into Quintain. She told him she'd seen police lights the night I went into the house, and since Emma was found on the property, he put two and two together."

"And he asked Foley to get it for him?"

"Yes. Deputy Foley thought he was acting on some kind of court order, so he complied with Groatley's request and took the ledger out of my kitchen. He was shocked and very apologetic to learn he'd contributed to a crime."

Libby said, "He's so sweet! Isn't he sweet? He'd like to make it up to us, did I tell you that? Repaying us for any inconvenience he might have caused. I think that's really sweet."

"Yeah," Emma said. "How's he going to repay us? By bringing you ice cream sundaes for the next few months? Until you get enough of his sweetness?"

"Em," I said, still conscious of Lucy sitting nearby. Even though she frowned with concentration as she folded the napkins, I feared she was absorbing every detail. "Let Libby enjoy her fling."

At that moment, my teenage nephew Rawlins bounded into the dining room, flushed and breathless but smiling. "Aunt Nora! Mick says the pheasant is almost fried!"

Libby groaned. "When did we stoop to deep-frying our Thanksgiving dinner? That's what I want to know. What becomes of long-standing family traditions if we let this kind of thing slip past us? It's as if we suddenly moved to a trailer park."

"A trailer park might be a nice upgrade," I said. "Besides, I have two other pheasants in the oven, and Michael's doing something with a duck, too. It's a fun change of pace, that's all. Something new to try. Go check your green bean casserole. Emma, you're in charge of mashing the potatoes, so get started. Come on, Rawlins. Show me to the fryer."

Rawlins wrapped one long arm around my neck and led me through the deliciously fragrant kitchen to the back door. We stepped out into the crisp, chilly air together. On the driveway, Michael had set up his dubious culinary experiment, and the deep fryer was cheerfully burbling a richly scented steam all over the backyard. Nearby, vigilant Ralphie sat hopefully sniffing the air. Once again, he had escaped his new quarters.

"Michael," I called, "did you let your pig out again?"

Michael turned from the basketball hoop where he'd been trying to outmaneuver Carrie. While he was distracted, she stole the ball from him, whirled gracefully and sank a two-pointer. Libby's twins cheered and high-fived Carrie. Since the twins had discovered she was actually trained to carry firearms and knew about all kinds of weaponry, she had become the new object of their morbid fascination.

"Way to go, Carrie!" the twins shouted.

Michael grinned and shook his head, then said something over his shoulder to his daughter before ambling in my direction. "Ralphie's not doing any harm, is he?"

"What if he knocks over that fryer?" I asked. "He'll get burned. Or maybe that's one way to get some bacon for breakfast?"

Michael wound his arm around my waist and pulled me close. "You don't really want anything bad to happen to Ralphie. Admit it. You're getting fond of him, too, aren't you?"

"I have a thing for bad boys."

Laughing, Michael swooped in to kiss me. In a moment, I was kissing him back, feeling very happy to have his full concentration again. Over the last couple of weeks, he'd made progress with Abruzzo family business, and he'd reached an uneasy but satisfying understanding with Carrie, too.

The noise of an arriving car pulled us apart, and together we looked around to see Deputy Foley pull up in front of the deep fryer. He climbed out of his cruiser and met us halfway across the lawn.

"Hello," I said. "You're just in time for dinner. The whole family's here, and we certainly have room for one more."

Deputy Foley shot a frightened glance at the house, which I interpreted to mean he hadn't expected to encounter my sister Libby while making this call. He took off his hat. "Actually, I'm on duty. And I'm sorry to bother you on a holiday. I'm especially sorry to have bad news."

"Bad news?" I reached for Michael's hand, and he took it.

With a pained expression, Foley said, "Yes, Miss Blackbird, we've had a bad fire this afternoon. Your aunt's house—the big castle? It burned up. Down to the ground."

I gave a cry of dismay. "No! I can't believe it! What happened?"

Foley shook his head. "We can't explain it yet. But the fire chief has called the arson squad. He said it looked to him as if somebody set a sophisticated kind of fuse. The interior rooms burned for a long time before anyone saw any smoke. I'm afraid the place is a total loss."

"Wow," Michael said. "Good thing you got out all the things you really wanted. And the insurance bill got paid."

Foley shot him a look. "Good timing."

"Arson!" I said. "Who on earth would want to burn down Quintain?"

Foley said, "Somebody who wanted to do you a favor, I guess. The place was only going to be a headache for you, right?"

"Well, it wasn't going to be easy to take care of the old place, but— Look, you're not suggesting we had anything to do with the fire?"

"No, no. Chief said it had to have been set by a real expert. Somebody who really knew what he was doing."

At that moment, I realized I hadn't seen Michael's bodyguard Bruno in a long time.

But Michael was saying in a friendly voice, "Thanks for bringing us the news, Deputy. Sure we can't convince you to stick around? Dinner's about ready."

Foley looked torn. The fragrance of pheasant had tantalized his nose. "Well . . ."

Libby chose that moment to come out onto the porch in all her glory. "Deputy Foley!" she sang merrily. "How nice to see you!"

Emma stepped out on the porch, too. Her huge belly looked like a cautionary tale.

Foley put his hat back on. "Gotta go."

He bolted for the cruiser, and I could feel Michael holding back laughter.

"I don't want to know," I said to him. "Do I?"

"No," he said. His phone rang in his pocket at that moment, and he pulled it out. He glanced at the ID, then gave me a knowing look before he answered. "Yeah?"

The call was a long-distance one, I guessed, because he plugged his other ear to hear better. To his caller, he said in his most authoritative voice, "She's safe? In Turkey?"

I clasped Michael's arm, my hopes lifting. For days, he had been talking to one of his conspirators in the car transportation business, and I knew there had been a shipment of American SUVs going into Syria.

"Okay," Michael said, sounding very much like the boss of all bosses. "Put her on a plane."

He didn't say thank you, but clicked the phone shut.

"Oh, Michael. You did it? Got Zareen Aboudi's sister out of Syria?"

"I cashed in a few favors. Maybe made a deal I'll regret later," Michael admitted. "Looks like we might have to ship some Mustangs to Eastern Europe in January. But, yeah. She's on her way."

I threw my arms around his neck. "You're wonderful! Thank you!"

"I never thought you'd actually be happy about stuff like this," he said, taking full advantage of my exuberant reaction.

I hugged him with delight. I'd decided to take a lesson from Aunt Madeleine's life and break a few rules to get important things done. "I'm overjoyed. And maybe your contacts will be satisfied that they've done a good deed. I should send them a nice note."

He laughed. "You don't know those guys. Even a nice thank-you card from you isn't going to cut it. But I'll think of something."

"Michael, this feels wonderful." I looked up into his face. "I'm so glad we were able to do this. I love you."

"I love you. And I'm happy you're happy," he said, and kissed me.

Rawlins had gone to the fryer and was tentatively poking the bird. Carrie and the twins stood nearby, making gagging noises—an indication that it was time for Michael to quit with the mushy stuff and get back to his culinary duties.

He took my hand, and we started to walk across the lawn together. He said, "I had a chance to read the letter Lexie sent to you. She sounds pretty good, don't you think?"

"No, but it could be worse." I had been thrilled to finally receive a communication from my friend. My daily notes to her had broken the dam, and she had responded with a short but heartfelt letter to me. "At least she has agreed I can come visit on Wednesdays. I'll be glad to see her face-to-face."

"It's good to hear she fired her lawyers and hired mine for her appeal. Things are looking up for her, Nora."

"I hope so," I said. "I miss her."

"I know," Michael said. He stopped on the driveway, and Ralphie trotted up to his side. As Michael pulled on his heavy oven mitts in preparation for taking our Thanksgiving dinner out of the fryer, he said, "Y'know, we've got a lot to be thankful for."

And maybe more to come.

Ralphie looked up and gave me a wink.